WHY
MU
DOESN'T
GIVE A
*****!

Why Mummy Drinks
Why Mummy Swears
Why Mummy Drinks: The Journal

Gill Sims

WHY MUMMY DOESN'T GIVE A *****!

HarperCollins*Publishers*

HarperCollins*Publishers*
1 London Bridge Street
London SE1 9GF

www.harpercollins.co.uk

First published by HarperCollins*Publishers* 2019
This paperback edition published 2020

3 5 7 9 10 8 6 4 2

A catalogue record of this book is
available from the British Library

ISBN 978-0-00-834048-3

Printed and bound in Great Britain by
CPI Group (UK) Ltd, Croydon

MIX
Paper from
responsible sources
FSC™ C007454

This book is produced from independently certified FSC™ paper
to ensure responsible forest management.

For more information visit: www.harpercollins.co.uk/green

For Rona ... the avalanche

CONTENTS

JANUARY

Wednesday, 3 January

The first day back at work after Christmas and New Year is always a bit of a slog. The sudden realisation that foodstuffs exist other than Toblerone and Quality Street and cheese, and that it's now frowned upon to start on the white wine at 2 pm, is always a shock to the system, let alone remembering that you're a functioning adult with a responsible job and clothes with non-elasticated waists. When your first day back is followed by your first relationship counselling session after what could be described as a 'difficult' Christmas, it's even less fun.

Christina, our counsellor, came highly recommended. Well, Debbie in HR at work said that Christina had saved her sister's marriage after it turned out her sister's husband had been having it off with their twins' first teacher since they started primary school, and said twins were in Year 10 when this all came out, and he also had a thing for being spanked while covered in PVA glue and glitter (hence his attraction to a primary school teacher and their easy access to such things), so I thought that if Christina could wave her magic wand and sort out *that* little peccadillo, then surely Simon and I would be an easy fix – a walk in the park, practically!

After all, no peculiar kinks had come to light. He hadn't betrayed me with a woman I'd bought several 'World's Best

Teacher' mugs and bottles of wine for, someone I'd sat across from while she outlined the importance of reading every night with my precious moppets, all the while having a life-size model of my husband's penis on her bedside table, made from the scraps of clay left over from making Mother's Day presents with her class and decorated with his favourite glitter, had he? I mean, when you put it into context like that, the fact that he *had* had a one-night stand with some sexy *señorita* that he met while on a business trip to Madrid really wasn't *that* bad, was it? Or at least, it could have been so much worse.

That is what I keep telling myself. 'Chin up! It could have been worse!' He could have had a predilection for dressing up as Ann Widdecombe. He could have had a thing about bonking someone dressed as Ann Widdecombe (I'm really not sure which would be more disturbing). He could have followed in the footsteps of Perfect Lucy Atkinson's Perfect Daddy who left Lucy's Perfect Mummy high and dry when he ran off with Lucy's Mummy's sidekick and wannabe, Fiona Montague, leaving Lucy's Mummy to face Fiona (whom I never liked, very smug and always just a bit too try-hard – though clearly Lucy's Perfect Daddy liked how hard Fiona tried, even though he's got very fat since moving in with her and is obviously overindulging in Fiona's bloody endless cupcakes that she was forever posting on Instagram) at the school gate every morning. Of course, the kids are now too old for the school gate as they're at Big School, so I suppose I wouldn't have had to do that anyway. And Simon doesn't like cupcakes.

But on the other hand, it was really quite bad enough. When Simon told me a couple of months ago, I felt like I'd been punched in the stomach. Literally winded. I still don't know what possessed him to tell me. Guilt, he said.

I'd heard people talk about a 'maelstrom of emotions' before, but I didn't honestly know what that meant until then, as I veered wildly between rage and despair and a really quite strong desire to kill him, and periods of calm during which I convinced myself we were mature adults with two children and we'd been together for twenty-five years, give or take, we loved each other and we could get through this – only to have the whole cycle start again. I felt so sick I couldn't eat for three days, which has never ever happened to me before; periods of high emotion normally lead to relentless comfort eating for me. I did lose ten pounds, so one must look on the bright side when one can.

After a couple of weeks of Simon looking hangdog and saying he was sorry, and me finding the rage wasn't really abating at all, and all our attempts to discuss it like mature adults generally ending in me shouting something about ripping his bollocks off if he told me one more fucking time that it didn't mean anything, because if it didn't *mean* anything, then why the fuck had he done it in the first place, and yes, yes, I realised it was 'just sex' but didn't he think that was quite e-bloody-nough, it was clear we weren't really getting anywhere and perhaps we needed some sort of professional help.

I heard Debbie in HR holding forth on the wonders of Christina (she was describing the clay-modelled knob ornament at the same time) and discreetly asked for Christina's number – 'for a friend', obviously, as one does not tell Debbie anything one does not want the entire office to know. In some ways this trait of hers is useful if you want word of something circulated quickly – you can guarantee that if you tell Debbie something and stress it's in 'the *strictest* confidence', every single person in the building will know about it by close of business.

Simon was reluctant to go at first, making British noises about 'airing dirty laundry in public' and 'it all being a bit New Age wank', but he agreed to give it a shot if it would help me stop shouting so much. So off we went.

After the initial session, Simon was surprisingly into the counselling. I think he liked the fact that the first thing Christina said was that she wasn't there to apportion blame or opine on who was wrong or right, but only to mediate and give a safe space for us both to talk without judgement. Simon also very much enjoyed the fact that Christina would not allow raised voices in her office, and so I wasn't allowed to shout at him, which gave him an hour's peace a week.

I thought all that was pretty rubbish, actually. I'd 100 per cent been hoping she'd totally judge, apportion blame, tell Simon how shit he was and take my side, before pronouncing some suitable punishment upon Simon, so he could atone for his sins and thus we could all move on with our lives, once Simon had done some marital form of Community Service – like, oh, I don't know: doing all the ironing for the entirety of the rest of our lives, and changing all the loo rolls for ever more, and being put in the stocks and flogged. Or something like that.

Instead of agreeing Simon was a total shit and must do penance before we were able to move forward, Christina said things like, 'Mmmm. And how did that make you feel?'

Today's session followed the same pattern as usual – Simon was surprisingly good at talking about how things made him feel, especially how his Spanish *señorita* had made him feel ('Alive. Wanted. Like I mattered to someone!'). I was slightly less good at it …

'Mmmmm. How do you feel about Simon feeling like that, Ellen?'

'Fine! I feel *fine* about it! Absolutely fine!' I hissed through gritted teeth, because Christina would not allow shouting or insults and so I couldn't scream, 'You *mattered* to *me*, you insensitive bastard. You wanted to feel wanted, well, how do you think *I* felt? But I managed not to fall into bed with anyone else, *didn't* I? *I* stuck to my marriage vows, even though I could have had sex with plenty of other people if I'd *wanted* to, but I *didn't* because I'm NOT A TWAT, but now you expect me to feel *sorry* for you? And also, for something that "didn't mean anything", it seemed to make you feel quite fucking special. And also – BAAAAASSSSSSTAAAAAARD!'

Then Christina said, 'I feel like I'm getting a lot of anger from you, Ellen.'

'Nope,' I beamed. 'No anger here!'

'I think you've brought a lot of anger today, Ellen. Would you like to talk about it?' Christina mused, while Simon nodded wisely, and I seethed to myself that *of course* I had brought a lot of sodding anger to the session. If I wasn't angry and broken and wretched, would we even bloody well be here, and surely the whole point of all this is that Christina is supposed to make me feel *less* angry, not more so? £70 an hour to be told I'm angry? After our first session I briefly flirted with the idea of retraining as a counsellor, only a good one, one that instead of saying, 'How did that make you feel?' and claiming it wasn't her job to apportion blame, would say, 'Well, that's a bit shit, isn't it?' and 'Your husband is clearly an arsehole!' I'd be excellent at that. Simon told me that that wasn't the point of counselling, actually, and if people wanted opinions like that they could go to Mumsnet for free.

Something finally snapped inside me. Maybe it was the thought of all the shoes I could have bought if I didn't have to pay Christina £70 to tell me I seemed a bit cross.

'Are you surprised I'm angry?' I snarled. 'It's always about Simon. What *Simon* wants. What *Simon* feels. What *Simon* needs. Who cares about what I want? Who cares about what I feel? Who cares about what I need? Nobody. All we do is talk about how *Simon* feels.'

'Well, I do keep asking you how you feel, and you always say "Fine", Christina pointed out mildly.

'Well, of course I'm not fine!' I wailed. 'My husband has had it off with someone else and my marriage is in tatters. Why would you think I was *fine*?'

'But I don't,' said Christina. 'That's why I keep asking you how you feel. *You're* the one who tells me you're "fine" and denies any anger or grief. Go on.'

'Simon says he felt unwanted and neglected. Well, does he not think maybe I felt the same? That I still feel the same, only a million times more now? He got someone to make him feel "wanted", he got a bit of excitement, he got the thrills and the validation and some Spanish sex, and what did I get? Nothing. He's had all his fun and I'm supposed to just get over it and move on like nothing has happened. And I'm still stuck with a man who doesn't even notice me, let alone make me feel *wanted*.'

'I do notice you,' said Simon indignantly.

'No, you don't,' I said in despair. 'You don't even see me anymore. I'm just *there*, like a piece of old furniture. You don't notice how I look, you don't notice what I do, you certainly don't notice how I feel.'

'I *do* notice how you look,' insisted Simon.

'You don't. No matter how dressed up I am, you never notice, you never say anything, you never compliment me. When I ask you how I look, you don't even look up from your iPad, you just grunt, "You look fine" – and that's it.'

'Well, you do. You always look fine. What do you want me to say?'

'Simon, "You look fine" means "Yes, you're respectable, your skirt isn't tucked into your knickers, you haven't got spinach in your teeth and you're fit to leave the house." You don't notice if I have my hair done or I'm wearing a new dress or I've gone to a bit of extra effort. You make me beg even for that grudging "You look fine!"'

'I didn't realise it was a big deal. I'm sorry. I'll not say you look fine again.'

'Pay me a compliment now. Go on. Say one nice thing about me.'

'This is very good,' breathed Christina.

'Ummm.' Simon thought hard. 'I know. You make the best lasagne I've ever tasted.'

I stared at him in disbelief.

'Lasagne? Really? LASAGNE? That's the most noticeable, memorable, NICEST thing about me you could think of? Fucking LASAGNE?'

'Well, you put me on the spot, and the other things I could think of I couldn't say here.'

'So lasagne. That's what I'm reduced to. Twenty-five years together, and you're only here for my lasagne?' I howled.

'Ellen, I'm going to have to ask you not to raise your voice,' said Christina in her irritatingly calm way.

'Oh sorry. Sorry. I wouldn't want to make a *scene* or anything. But seriously, Christina, you tell me I'm angry, and are you surprised I'm angry when that is the sort of thing he says?'

'Ellen, you know I'm not here to take sides. This isn't about me – it's about you and Simon. Simon, how do you feel about Ellen saying you don't notice her anymore?'

'I think that's pretty hypocritical because she doesn't notice me either,' said Simon crossly. 'She doesn't know who I am, she doesn't know what I want in life, she doesn't know what interests or excites me –'

'Tapas, apparently, rather than lasagne,' I muttered.

'Ellen, I'm going to have to ask you not to interrupt Simon again. Just let him speak,' said Christina. Christina's sessions are rather like being counselled by the bloody Supernanny. I really wouldn't be at all surprised if she put me on the naughty step one day.

Simon carried on: 'You want to keep the family together. You don't want the children shuttled back and forth between different homes at the weekend, introduced to step-parents, used as pawns in their parents' games, like you were. And I think most of the reason you're still here is because of the kids, in an attempt to spare them that, rather than an active desire to be with *me*. You say I don't see you. Well, you don't see me either. I could be anyone. An anonymous father and husband figure in your life who you need to keep things together.'

'That's better than the housekeeper, cook and nanny you see me as,' I objected.

'Ellen, this is the last time I'm going to ask you to stop interrupting,' said Christina. 'If you do it again, I'll be forced to give you a yellow card.'

I glared at her. She glared back. It was blatantly obvious the 'yellow card' was no more than an adult version of the naughty step. She never threatened *Simon* with yellow cards. She clearly liked him better than me, and it wasn't *fair*. I half expected her to get down on my level, look me sternly in the eye and tell me I had to the count of three to start behaving myself.

'I don't even know if you love me anymore, Ellen,' announced Simon with a dramatic sigh. 'And that makes me question whether I still love you. I just don't know.'

I opened my mouth to respond to this – fuck your yellow card, Christina – but she suddenly announced, 'Oh dear, this has been very useful, but I'm afraid our time is up!'

So it's OK for *you* to interrupt then, Christina!

I put my coat on in a daze, and we left Christina's office. In the street, the cold air hit me in the face like a slap from a wet kipper and brought me back to my senses.

'You don't love me anymore?' I snarled. 'What has all this been for, if you don't love me anymore? Why have you put me through this?'

'Don't make a scene, Ellen, not in the street!' said Simon briskly. 'Come on,' he added, steering me into the bar next to Christina's office, 'let's go for a drink.'

'Is that really all you're worried about? A *scene* in the *street*? Anyway, we need to get back for the kids,' I objected.

'They can hang on for another half-hour. We need to talk.'

'We've just *been* talking. You've made everything very clear. What's there left to talk about?'

'OK, *I* need to talk to *you*.'

It was a very nice bar. It had cosy booths and ambient lighting, and under any other circumstances I'd have been thinking how totally Instagrammable it was. Simon got me a glass of wine and sat down beside me.

'We can't go on like this,' he said. 'You're tearing yourself into pieces. I can't do this anymore.'

'You can't do this? So even though the person who is supposed to always be there for me, who is supposed to never hurt me, even though this person has basically ripped my heart out and left me in pieces, I need to get over it, because you've had enough of me hurting? You've cheated on me, compared me to lasagne and then told me you don't love me, and what? Am I supposed to be *happy* about that? Yippee! My husband and the father of my children doesn't love me anymore! Hurrah, my life is *fucking complete*, at last!'

'Please keep your voice down,' he hissed. 'I didn't *say* I didn't love you.'

'You did.'

'No, I said I wasn't sure. And that I wasn't sure if you loved me. Of course I *love* you, I'm just not sure if I still love you like *that*. I mean, I don't even know if you want to be married to me anymore,' he said sadly.

'Of course I do,' I protested. 'I wouldn't be going through all this if I didn't, would I? Don't *you* want our marriage anymore?'

'I don't know. I don't know what I want. I know I'm unhappy, and I have been for a long time, long before all this. I know I can't say sorry any more than I have, but it doesn't make any difference. I know I can't keep trying to change the past, I can only change the future, but as things are, you won't let me, because you can't move on from the past. So, I think we need some time apart.'

'What, like you going away for the weekend or something? *Another* jolly?'

'No, some proper time apart. Geoff at work is moving to New York for three months and doesn't want to leave his flat empty all that time. I've said I'll move in and look after it. Gives us both some space, some time to think, some time for us to consider what we really want. I'm going to move in there tonight. I had one final hope that this evening with Christina might have helped you start healing, but it didn't, so something has to change.'

'You're leaving me?' I whispered. 'After all that, after everything you put me through, you're leaving me? And you're doing it using all those old clichés of "I love you but I'm not *in* love with you" and "I just need some space"? Could you not even have come up with an original line? Christ, all that's missing is "My wife doesn't understand me."'

'Well, I *do* need some space, OK, and some time. And you *don't* understand what it's like for me. I can't stay with you if I'm always going to be the bad guy, living with your constant anger. It's destroying us both.'

'And there we go. Well done, you've hit the hat-trick of how to leave your wife. So you're just walking away, moving into Geoff's nice little bachelor pad and living the life of Riley, leaving me to pick up all the pieces – again? Because you're *not happy* that I'm a tiny bit pissed off about how you've behaved and you, what? Want to *find* yourself?'

'Ellen, please, it's not like that.'

I drained my wine. 'It's *exactly* like that.'

'I just want to find out who I am again, that's all. Apart from a father and a husband!'

'I'll tell you what you want. You've had a taste of freedom and fun, and you want a bit more of it, because suddenly the wife and kids feel a bit millstoney round your neck. Especially as the ball and chain won't shut up like a good girl and turn a blind eye and let you have your cake and eat it. So you're going for the easy option and giving up. You get the single life, and I get to keep being a drudge and bring up your children. Well, fine. It's fine. If that's what you want, go ahead, no one's going to stop you. If you thought I was going to sit here and *beg* you to stay, you were wrong. Have a nice life, Simon. Actually, I don't mean that. I hope your knob falls off. Goodbye.'

'I'm not *leaving* you, I just need –'

'Do kindly go fuck yourself. Or whoever else it is that you "need".'

'Ellen, please –'

I walked out of the bar with my head held high, and made it as far as the little play park round the corner before I collapsed on a bench, sobbing. Thank God it was evening and there were no tots bouncing merrily on the seesaw to be alarmed by the mad woman wailing all on her own. All the hours I've spent sitting on benches like these, watching Peter and Jane play (and fight), freezing my arse off, wishing it was time to go home, and never once did I think I'd end up sitting on one crying because Simon had left me. I thought we'd grow old together. I'd never considered a future that didn't involve him.

I dried my eyes on an extremely dubious tissue I found in my coat pocket (at least back when the children were small there would have been several half-eaten jelly babies stuck to it that I could have consoled myself with), and resolved that that was it.

I wasn't relying on anyone else for anything, ever again. Well, apart from getting the number of a bloody good divorce lawyer from Perfect Lucy Atkinson's Perfect Mummy.

It was a shame, I thought pathetically to myself, that I could never go back to that very nice bar and take photos for Instagram, as it would now be forever known as The Bar Where Simon Left Me. If he was going to leave me, he could at least have done it in a dive, and not spoiled somewhere nice for me. Selfish bastard.

APRIL

Friday, 6 April

I woke up in a panic, dry-mouthed and heart racing, convinced I'd slept through the alarm and that the removal men were here already. They weren't, of course, because it was only 3.43 am, but as it was the sixth time I'd woken up like that, the chances of me actually sleeping through the alarm increased every time, and thus so did the panic. It didn't help that in the brief snatches of sleep I'd managed in between waking up I'd dreamt that the removal men turned up but nothing was packed and so we couldn't move, and then in another much, much worse dream, that they turned up, that everything I owned was neatly boxed up, that I was smoothly and seamlessly directing operations as they loaded their lorry, only to make the hideous discovery, while I was standing in the front garden watching two burly sorts lug out the sofa, that I was stark bollock naked, and everyone had been too polite to say anything, but there was every chance the removal men were traumatised for life by the sight of a forty-five-year-old woman standing in the street, tits jiggling, reminding them to be careful with the sideboard as it was a family heirloom.

Actually, I don't even know why the sideboard was in my dream. I don't have it anymore. It was Simon's granny's, so he's got it. Admittedly, he didn't really want it and had harboured an unreasonable hatred for it ever since I'd attempted to 'shabby chic' it up and painted it a lovely *eau de nil*, but I was determined to be fair, and so I insisted he took the sideboard. It was definitely fairness that made me let him have the sideboard and not a malicious amusement at thinking how pissed off he'd be every time he looked at it, nor a sadistic pleasure in thinking how it would ruin the minimalist effect he could finally achieve in his new flat but, because it was his grandmother's, he'd be stuck with it.

After Simon's announcement that he was moving out to 'give us some space', I didn't hang around. I've seen too many friends and colleagues put in the same position, with their partner buggering off, assuring them it was 'only temporary' to give them 'time to think'. They went off to 'think', and then a month down the line the joint accounts were emptied, there was a lawyer's letter on the doormat and an estate agent at the door announcing they were there to do a valuation, because the 'temporary thinking time' was just a ruse to allow them to move out with minimal hassle while sorting out their financial affairs to their own benefit.

I wasn't going to be caught on the hop like that. The next day, when I checked our bank accounts and found that Simon had withdrawn a considerable sum – apparently to cover the rent on Geoff's flat, as it had turned out that Geoff wasn't letting him house sit rent free, as Simon had implied – and after listening to Simon's excuses that the joint account was 'living expenses' and me pointing out that it was his choice to move out into an expensive flat and why the fuck should I be part-funding that, I called the estate agents and the lawyers, removed my share from the remains of the joint accounts and got the ball rolling. Unfortunately, our house turned out to have gone up in value since we bought it, and neither of us could afford to buy the other out, so it had to be sold, all while Simon bleated on that I was being too hasty and he hadn't meant this to be permanent.

Competitively priced family homes in catchment areas for decent schools tend to sell fast, though – rather faster than I'd expected, leaving me without much time to find somewhere for me and the children to go. And so, I find myself lying awake, staring at the ceiling, contemplating a future where I'll not be growing old with Simon in a little stone cottage with roses round the door. However, on the plus side, *I* will be growing old in a little stone cottage with roses round the door. That is what I need to focus on – the positives, not the negatives. The fact is that Simon had always baulked at my visions of quaint and rustic cottages, and muttered darkly about energy efficiency, and lack of double glazing, and low ceilings (surely the low ceilings would make it *easier* to heat, as I used to point out). He'd tut and point out all the flaws in the survey reports of the Dream Houses I showed him, sighing over wet rot and dry rot and rising damp and crumbling pointing, crying, 'Money pit! Money pit!' as I cried, 'Character and soul! IT HAS CHARACTER AND SOUL! What's a little mildew compared with THAT?'

As an architect, Simon was always able to trump me (a mere 'computer person', as he used to refer to my job) on all things house by hurling technical words around and citing the terrible costs of a new roof (according to him, every house I fell in love with would need a new roof, despite the clearly functional and vintagely slated roof having done perfectly well for over a hundred years), and so, one by one, my dreams were crushed under the weight of tedious practicalities.

But now, Simonless, with no unfaithful naysayer crushing my visions of stone-flagged kitchens and mullioned windows anymore, I've found the cottage of my dreams, and we're moving in today. Well, it's possibly not *quite* the Cottage of My Dreams. My finances didn't entirely stretch to that, despite a small stroke of luck in my batshit-mental ex-sister-in-law Louisa deciding her latest blow struck against the patriarchy would be to become a lesbian and move to a women's commune with her new lover Isabel, thus *finally* vacating the house I'd been emotionally blackmailed into buying for her several years earlier. My lingering resentment at being forced to bankroll Louisa's feckless lifestyle with the profits of the one financially successful thing I've ever achieved, my lovely app called *Why Mummy Drinks*, obviously in no way contributed to the breakdown of things with Simon *at all*. But she's gone, her (my) house is sold, and the resulting cash injection added to my share of the Marital Home meant I was able to afford to buy a Vaguely Dreamish Cottage, with not too crippling a mortgage. Hurrah! It will be magical. If you overlook the damp. Which is probably nothing that can't be painted over. And the fact that I didn't have much time to wait around for the perfect house to come on the market so, to afford a house with a garden for Judgy Dog and three bedrooms for the children and me, I've had to move miles out of town.

But anyway. I shall have a vegetable garden, and look adorable in wellies and an unfeasible amount of Cath Kidston prints (well, probably not real Cath Kidston, as it's very bloody expensive and I'm a Single Mother now, but I can probably find some affordable knock-offs on eBay). I'm going to keep chickens – Speckled Sussexes, I've decided, because I liked the name and when I googled them they were described as very chatty chickens. Who even needs a man when you have chatty chickens? I just have to hope that Judgy Dog does not attempt to eat my chatty chickens. I've had stern words with him to this effect, but he just gave me one of his 'I'm paying no attention to your foolish witterings, woman, and I shall do as I please' looks. Luckily, Judgy being *my* dog, having got him somewhat against Simon's will, despite Simon coming to love him almost as much as I do, there was no question of who got Judgy in the divorce. I'd probably have let him have Peter and Jane if he'd really wanted, but I'd have fought tooth and nail for sole custody of Judgy …

Peter and Jane are not entirely enamoured of my Splendid Plan to move to the country. Although in actual fact we're not moving that far into the country, we're still (just) within the catchment area for their school, so they'll not be further traumatised by changing schools, as well as being from a Broken Home (do people even still say that? I just remember, in *Coronation Street*, Tracy Barlow shouting about coming from a Broken Home at Ken and Deirdre when they had one of their frequent divorces – not that it really mattered with Ken and Deirdre, of course, as they'd be back together again by the Omnibus).

Despite this, the children were still horrified at living 'out in the sticks' and the lack of late buses to transport them home from parties and bouts of underage drinking. Well, at fifteen, I suspect Jane at least has been dabbling somewhat with the Bacardi Breezers, or whatever over-sugared shit the Youth of Today drink. Peter is only thirteen, so hopefully I've a year or so's grace before he too starts on the path of depravity. I live in hope, however, that they might both yet declare themselves to be teetotallers, as I've been a Terrible Warning rather than a Good Example when it comes to the Evils of Drink. I attempted to placate them with rash promises of providing plenty of lifts home, and brightly reminded them that every second weekend they'd be staying over at their dad's flat in town, and so it would be a) his problem and b) nice and easy to get home from parties and the dubious pubs that serve underage teenagers. Simon was there when I announced this, and I must say he did not look entirely thrilled at the prospect.

He has meanwhile found his Dream Flat, the minimalist White Box he's hankered after for years. He'd practically drool while watching *Grand Designs* whenever anyone built one of those spare, modern cubes as a house, as he looked round our cluttered sitting room and sighed in despair. There were some rows about his flat too, because, as I pointed out, he could not buy an open-plan loft, because he needed somewhere for his CHILDREN to sleep when they came to stay – something that did not seem to have occurred to him. He finally grudgingly compromised on somewhere that had one decent-sized bedroom, one small room he announced he'd use as a study and put a futon in for Jane (I didn't know you even still got futons – I thought they had vanished after the Nineties, along with my youth and the perkiness of my tits), and what he optimistically called a 'boxroom' for Peter, which Peter and I called a 'cupboard'. Apart from having to shut his only son and heir in a cupboard every second weekend, from the photos it looks like an annoyingly nice flat, although the sideboard will look bloody awful there, so ha!

Anyway, I might as well get up and have a cup of tea in peace, before starting the lengthy and painful process of trying to prise two teenagers from their pits. There's a part of me that wonders if it would be easier to just leave them in their beds and let the removal men load them onto the lorry and install them still slumbering in their new rooms at the other end. And also, how long would it actually take them to notice they were in a different house? In fairness, Peter would notice almost straight away when he walked towards the fridge on autopilot, ready to inhale the entire contents in the name of a 'snack', and found it in a different location, thus delaying his 'snack' by an essential and life-threatening thirty seconds.

It's a strange feeling to think that this is the last time I'll wake up in this house. There have been a lot of 'last times' over the previous few days. Some of them have been quite sad, like the last time I'd say goodnight to the children in the rooms they've slept in since they were tiny. Peter and Jane were less moved by my tearful attempts to tuck them in last night, saying that I was being weird and telling me to go away. Other last times were less sad. The last time I had to adjust the rug to hide the mark on the floor where Judgy puked and his stomach acid stripped the varnish from the floorboards. The last time I'll ever bang my hip on the stupidly placed cupboard in the kitchen. The last time I'll have to wipe the countertops and ignore the large chunk out of the surface where Jane threw a knife at Peter in a fit of rage, probably because of some heinous transgression such as looking at her.

But this isn't the time to dwell on last times. It's a time for FIRST times, for new beginnings and fresh starts! I hope Judgy Dog isn't too outraged by the upheaval and settles into his new home all right.

Saturday, 7 April

Well. We're here. And I'm slowly getting to grips with the chaos and trying to tackle the mountains of boxes!

Yesterday was … interesting. As predicted, Peter and Jane were almost impossible to shift from their beds. Once they were up, they wandered around aimlessly, getting under everyone's feet, as Peter attempted to unpack bowls and cereal so he could have another breakfast and Jane screamed that I'd ruined her life by having the Wi-Fi disconnected in the old house, and what did I MEAN, it might not be connected in the new house until Monday, and how did I not know about the strength of the 4G signal at the new house, and WHY WOULD I EVEN DO THAT TO HER, and Peter drank all the milk so I couldn't even give the removal men a cup of tea, so I had to send him to the shop to get more, while he looked at me pityingly and explained that we were meant to be *moving* and getting *rid* of stuff, Mum, not *buying more*, and I howled that if he didn't get on his bike and get to the shop and return with a pint of milk in the next three minutes, I was taking all his carefully boxed-up possessions, including all his games consoles, and giving them to a charity shop, and if he answered me back one more fucking time I might give him away too, in the unlikely event of anyone actually wanting him. The removal men meanwhile observed all this, expressionless, until Peter muttered something about 'Don't mind her, it's probably her age, and the Change of Life' as he huffed out the door in search of milk and the removal men all sniggered. Bastards.

Finally – finally – everything was loaded onto the lorry, despite my helpful suggestions about the order in which they might want to put it on, and that maybe if they put the sofa on the other side they could pile more boxes around it. The Chief Removal Man finally said, 'Look, love, we do know what we're doing. We do it every day,' and I quietly seethed about being called 'love' because it's one of my pet hates, especially from an unfamiliar man who is talking down to me (although I suppose he might have had a point about knowing how to pack his lorry better than me), but I didn't dare say anything in case they decided that they wouldn't move all my worldly possessions after all on account of me being a snowflake feminist bitch and then I'd be left sitting in the middle of the road with a big pile of boxes and two angry teenagers.

We set off, me chirping, 'Isn't this FUN, darlings! A splendid new adventure! We're going to be SO HAPPY in the new house, I just KNOW it!' while the children slumped in the back seat and complained it was SO UNFAIR that I hadn't let one of them sit in the front because Judgy had already called shotgun (it's his favourite seat – he likes to look out of the window for cats), and I pointed out that I might have let one of them sit there if World War Fucking Three didn't break out over whose turn it is to sit there every single bastarding time we get in the car, and would

they please just CHEER UP ALREADY, because this was a
LOVELY FRESH START and we were going to be VERY
FUCKING HAPPY.

As we turned out of the street for the last time ever (well, in
reality it probably wasn't the last time ever, because my friend
Katie still lives across the road, and so I'll probably be back to
visit her, but it was still a Symbolic Last Time Ever), the new
people who had bought the house turned into it. I accelerated
slightly, lest they spotted me in the distance and tried to come
after me to enquire about the Smell in Peter's room. I'd cleaned
the house, I really had, and in truth it was probably the cleanest
it had ever been since we'd moved in, but nothing I did, not
shampooing the carpets, not liberal quantities of Febreeze, not
all the TKMaxx scented candles in the world could entirely shift
that musty, fusty, Teenage Boy Pong from Peter's room.

When people were viewing the house I had to open his
windows as wide as they would go, empty half a can of air fresh-
ener into the room and hope the stench would be masked for
long enough to dupe any potential buyers, but within half an
hour the smell would start seeping back – an unpleasant combination of sweaty socks, BO, a hint of stale jizz and something
undefinable that can only be described as Boy, all pulled together
with a generous helping of Lynx. It just seems to be something
teenage boys emit, however clean they are, however often you
boil-wash their towels and bedding, however many hours they
spend in the shower, however many cans of deodorant they
empty under each pit ('Darling, seriously, you just need a quick
squirt under each arm, you don't need to spray clouds and
clouds of the damn stuff till we're all choking on a chemical
cloud that whiffs of broken teenage dreams and sexual frustration') and however often you surreptitiously check under the
bed to see if the source of the stench is a crusty wank sock
stashed under there. So far I've been spared this horror, I

presume because I discreetly provide a never-ending supply of Mansize tissues – I was so shocked when I finally realised what Mansize tissues were for (I'd thought it was just because Kleenex assumed men were snottier than ladies).

I remember (many, MANY years ago) when I was in halls of residence at university, and you could immediately tell when you'd turned the corner from the (pleasantly scented with hints of Impulse and Ex'clamation and Wella Mousse) girls' corridor and had entered the boys' corridor, due to the Smell. After we left halls, the university renovated the building (it was planned, we hadn't trashed the place. Much), and I mean they gutted the whole thing and stripped it down to the bare bones. I went in to drop something off to someone after the renovation, when the whole building was spanking fresh and full of new paint and plaster, and the entire concept of boys' and girls' corridors had been done away with and it was all mixed sex, but you could STILL smell the Smell on what had once been the old boys' corridors. So I think the new owners might be stuck with it. Hopefully they'll also have a teenage boy who can just slot into the stinky room and they'll assume it's only his own Smell, and not a lingering whiff of the previous occupant …

Anyway, new owners successfully avoided, off we trundled to our New Start, 'I Will Survive' (OBVS, what else? Though Jane has repeatedly asked me NOT to say 'obvs', or 'totes amazeballs', or 'down with the kids', even in an ironic way) blasting out of the car stereo. The sun was shining, the birds were singing – it was all Most Auspicious.

Unfortunately, about a mile down the road, the sun stopped shining, the birds stopped singing, the sky suddenly turned black and it began to piss down royally. This, needless to say, was Less Auspicious.

The removal men were distinctly unjovial at having to unload in the tipping rain, as if it was somehow my fault and I was some kind of misguided witch who had conjured up the storm on my way here, because mysteriously I actually wanted every single thing I owned in the world to get soaking wet, and they muttered darkly as they lugged everything in. Worse, in all my excitement about my quaint and adorable cottage, I'd neglected to actually measure or work out if any of my furniture would fit in, and there were some ugly scenes manoeuvring my super-king-size bed up the most un-super-king-size cottage stairs, and trying to get my sofa through the door into the sitting room. At one point the Chief Removal Man announced, 'You'll have to saw it in half, love!' and I frostily reminded him how only that very morning he'd informed me that he was a removal EXPERT, and thus I had faith in his expertise and would not be sawing my sofa in half, because he could jolly well work out how to get it in, thank you very much (after all, he's a man, he should have had YEARS of practice at trying to get it in). The sofa was eventually manhandled in, although the dark muttering had turned into open and loud swearing by that point.

Unfortunately, now that the previous owners' artfully placed furniture had been removed and the sun was no longer streaming merrily through the windows like it had been when I'd viewed the property, it began to dawn on me that all the 'quirks' of the house I'd convinced myself were 'rustic' might possibly also be construed as being a 'bit shit', even 'problematic'. The house was also a lot darker and somewhat damper than I remembered, and there were some suspicious marks on the ceiling I hadn't noticed before, which suggested the roof wasn't in perhaps as quite as good order as I'd blithely assumed when I'd dismissed the survey report's queries about it as mere naysaying.

Simon had offered to come with me to view houses, which I'd tartly informed him was quite unnecessary as I was perfectly capable of finding a house without him – after all, there was a *reason* he was now my *ex*-husband. He'd mildly replied that he was only trying to help, and had thought that in his professional capacity he might have been able to offer some useful advice, nothing more. I, meanwhile, declined his offer once again on the basis that I wasn't going to all the trouble, effort and expense of divorcing him only to have him continue to piss on my chips when it came to finding my Dream House. Or even my Vaguely Dreamish House. Looking around the Not Quite Even Vaguely Dreamish House now, I reflected that I'd possibly been a little hasty in rejecting his offer of help.

But never mind, I thought. It'll be FINE! We just have to be positive, as I pointed out to Jane as she wailed in horror at the realisation that she no longer had fitted wardrobes to not put her New Look hauls in, but instead had an alcove with a rail across it in front of which I was planning on hanging an adorable floral curtain.

'HOW am I supposed to cope with that to keep my clothes in?' she shrieked. 'It's fucking *Soviet*, Mother. It's probably one of the things that define you as living in poverty. This is inhumane. I could report you!'

'To who?' I said. 'I don't think fitted wardrobes and constant access to Snapchat *are* actually included the UN's Rights of a Child. I think it's more things like clean water and not being sent down the mines. And anyway, you've never in your entire life put anything away in your wardrobe. You just chuck it all on the floor, so I fail to see how this will actually make any difference to you whatsoever.'

'Do we even *have* clean water?' moaned Jane. 'Are you going to announce next that we have to fetch it from a well? Maybe a river? Or are we lucky enough to have some sort of *pump* in the *yard* that we can fill buckets from so we can crouch in a tin bath once a week in front of the fire and try and scrub the rural dirt from our calloused palms? By the light of an oil lamp?' she added dolefully.

'Don't be SILLY, Jane,' I said as brightly as possible. 'We've a lovely bathroom, with a *proper* vintage claw-footed bath. And hot running water and electricity. You're overreacting, as usual.'

'Don't tell me I'm overreacting!' shouted Jane, 'I'm not overreacting. You're the one who drove Dad away because you were always nagging him and who's ruined our family and made us move to a hovel without indoor plumbing, but you say I'm the one who's overreacting! Maybe YOU'RE overreacting by dragging us out here for no reason rather than just being nicer to Dad instead of BEING HORRIBLE ALL THE TIME!'

I was protesting that we DID have indoor plumbing and wishing I could tell the children there was so much more to Simon and me separating than me just not being that happy, when I was distracted by Peter wandering upstairs and collapsing dramatically on the landing because he was STARVING.

'You're not starving,' I said automatically. 'You're just slightly hungry.'

'I can't find any food,' said Peter gloomily. 'Like, there's literally NO FOOD, Mum.'

'Have you looked?' I asked. 'Because there are boxes and boxes of food in the kitchen.'

'Which room is the kitchen?' said Peter hopelessly. 'I can't tell. There's boxes everywhere, so how am I supposed to know where the kitchen is?'

'Do you think it might be the one with the sink?' I suggested. 'And the fridge? Were they not any sort of a hint to you?'

Peter looked at me blankly. 'Oh,' he said. 'I never thought of that.'

Peter wandered off back downstairs, in search of sustenance, and Jane burst furiously from the bathroom.

'Is there a shower in the other bathroom?' she demanded.

'What other bathroom?' I said.

'There must be another bathroom,' she insisted.

'No, darling, there's only one bathroom, I'm afraid. That's sort of the thing about downsizing. You have a slightly smaller house. The clue is somewhat in the name, you know.'

'But there must be another bathroom. An en suite or something. That can't be the only one.'

'It is,' I informed her, as her face fell.

'But there's no shower,' she wailed. 'How am I supposed to wash my hair?'

'Well, in the bath, sweetheart. Like people did for hundreds of years before the Americans invented showers.'

In truth, I'm not 100 per cent sure whether Americans invented showers or not, but it sounded plausible as they invented most mod cons. Luckily Jane was too distraught to challenge this statement, which made a nice change, as she usually likes to query every single thing that I say.

'I can't,' she whimpered. 'It's not possible. I'm not THREE, to have plastic cups of water sluiced over my head, Mother! This is awful. Are you SURE you don't have an en suite you're hiding from me?'

'Why would I hide an en suite from you?' I said in surprise (though in truth, as I looked around the dimensions of the cottage, which could at best be described as 'bijou and compact', there was a small part of me also hoping for some extra rooms to materialise from somewhere, like the splendid room full of food the Railway Children found the morning after moving into their own slightly less than dreamy cottage).

'I don't know. I don't know why you do anything anymore, Mother. You've abandoned Dad, you've made us come and live in this dump, and all you offer us in return is wittering on about how we're going to get chatty chickens. So I wouldn't put it past you to hide an en suite from me,' she said bitterly.

'That's so unfair,' I said. 'I haven't abandoned anyone.' I bit back my words as I was about to snap, 'Your father was the one who moved out, if you recall, not me. *He* was the one needing his "space to think", not me. I'm the one who's *always* here for you.' But I managed to stop myself in time, as my mother's voice rang in my ears, saying those exact things to me, reminding me how *she* was the victim and encouraging me to take *her* side. I would not have my daughter see me as a victim, and I would not, even if it killed me, say anything to make her feel she had to choose between Simon and me. The only reason I'd managed to stop myself telling the children about Miss Madrid was to avoid making them pick sides. Tears pricked in my eyes at the sheer injustice of it, though, that the more I tried to be fair and not make them take sides, the more Jane raged and hated me and blamed me for everything. Luckily she'd stormed off to find something else to complain about before she saw the treacherous tears. I wiped my eyes and sniffed 'Strong Independent Woman' to myself, as Peter bellowed up the stairs, 'MUM! There's TWO rooms with sinks down here, so how do I know which one is the kitchen?'

I trudged downstairs to explain to Peter in words of ideally less than one syllable that the BIG room with the fridge, cupboards and table was the KITCHEN, and the very small room beside the back door with nothing more than a sink in it was the SCULLERY. There then ensued a lengthy discussion about what exactly a scullery was, culminating in Peter saying, 'Well, if it's just a utility room from the olden days, why don't you just CALL it a utility room?' and me insisting, 'Because this is a lovely, quirky, quaint old cottage, darling, with oodles of character and they have sculleries, not utility rooms. It's all about the soul, you see,' while Peter shovelled Doritos into his mouth and look at me in confusion.

'OK, Mum,' he said kindly. 'We can call it a scullery if it makes you happy.'

I was so nonplussed at winning the scullery battle so easily, and fretting that it was because Peter felt sorry for me (in the old house, everyone but me had persisted in calling the larder 'the big cupboard' despite my frequent exhortations to call it 'the larder' because we were more middle class than a 'big cupboard'), that I forgot to take the Doritos off him before he inhaled the entire bag.

He was still cramming fistfuls of Doritos into his mouth when Jane marched downstairs and announced that she supposed she'd just have to make do with having a bath, and where were the towels? I suggested that perhaps she could help with the unpacking for a little longer before buggering off to bathe herself, but was frostily informed that this wasn't an option and her life had been ruined quite enough. I replied that maybe, just maybe, if she'd shown the TINIEST bit of interest in her new home, the lack of bathrooms and showers would not have come as such a shock to her, but this was met with an eye roll and a snort. I counted myself lucky to have avoided a 'FFS, Mother!'

I'm still trying to pinpoint when the 'Mothers' began. When she started talking, Jane would call me Mama, which was too bloody adorable for words, then when she was about three and a half, a horrible older child at nursery made fun of her for saying Mama, and she switched to Mummy. Then it became Mum, but it happened gradually, so I don't really remember when exactly she gave up on Mummy, although it didn't really matter, because Mum was OK, and anyway, only screamingly posh people with ponies called Tarquin (both the people and the ponies) still call their mothers Mummy past the age of about twelve. But I was quite unprepared for the day when I stopped even being Mum and simply became Mother – a word only uttered when dripping with sarcasm, disgust, condescension or all three. To my shame, I think I vaguely recall a time in my teens when I also only referred to my dearest Mama as Mother in similarly scathing tones, so I can only hope it's just a 'phase' and that she'll grow out of it. Though I'm wondering how many more fucking 'phases' I have to endure before my children become civilised and functioning members of society.

It seems like people have been telling me 'It's just a phase' for the last fifteen bloody years. Not sleeping through the night is 'just a phase'. Potty training and the associated accidents are 'just a phase'. The tantrums of the terrible twos – 'just a phase'. The picky eating, the back chat, the obsessions. The toddler refusals to nap, the teenage inability to leave their beds before 1 pm without a rocket being put up their arse, the endless singing of *Frozen* songs, the dabbing, the weeks where apparently making them wear pants was akin to child torture. All 'just phases'. When do the 'phases' end, though? WHEN? I'm surprised, when every man and his dog was sticking their nose in and giving me unsolicited advice about what to do about my marriage ('Leave the bastard,' 'Make it work for the children,' 'You have to try and forgive him,' 'Screw him for every penny he has,' 'You have to understand that it's different for men,' 'Cut his bollocks off'), that no one told me that shagging random women in Madrid was obviously 'just a phase', and I just had to wait for Simon to grow out of it.

'MOTHER,' shouted Jane, bringing me back to earth with a bump. 'You still haven't found me a towel.'

'Jane,' I said as calmly as possible. 'If you want a bath that badly, you'll have to find your own towel. I've other things to do.'

Peter mumbled something unintelligible through a mouthful of Doritos, spraying orange crumbs all over Jane.

'OH MY GOD! HE'S DISGUSTING! MOTHER, *DO* SOMETHING ABOUT HIM!' screamed Jane. 'Can't he, like, live in the shed or something?'

Peter swallowed, and in the brief window before eating something else shouted, 'YOU live in the shed! Live with the CHICKENS! Ha ha ha!'

Jane screamed more and Peter continued to snigger through his mouthful of salty preservatives and flavourings, and I left the room in despair. I decided to unpack my books. That would be a nice, calming activity. And also, once the books were on the bookcase, they'd hide the large and extremely dubious stain on the floral wallpaper that had looked so charmingly faded and vintage a few months ago, and now just looked like something from the 'before' shots on *Changing Rooms*. Maybe, I mused, as I stacked the books, I could strip off all the paper and do something cunning with bits of baton to give the impression of wood panelling, à la Handy Andy …? Then I found *Riders* and decided to cheer myself up with a few pages, for surely there's no situation so dire, especially not when it comes to cheating men and revolting teenagers, that has not been faced up to by one of Jilly Cooper's characters with a large vodka and tonic and an excellent pun. Jake was just shagging Tory in the stable for the first time, and I was wondering if I too looked a lot less fat without my clothes on – I suspected not, though the horrible realisation was dawning on me that if I were ever going to have sex again, I would HAVE to take my clothes off in front of a strange man, although to be honest, the thought of just never having sex again was preferable to doing that – when a drenched and furious Jane shot into the room, making noises like a scalded cat. The problem, it quickly turned out was quite the opposite – she was very far indeed from being scalded, because having run herself a nice deep bath, she'd plunged in to find that it was freezing cold, because there was no hot water.

'Oh, I expect they've maybe just turned it off, in case the pipes freeze or something,' I said vaguely.

'It's APRIL, Mother,' said Jane. 'The pipes won't freeze in *April*! And anyway, they only moved out yesterday, you said. Why would they turn off the hot water for the twenty-four hours before we moved in?'

I'd no idea, but I wasn't giving Jane the satisfaction of saying so. I poked vaguely at the boiler, hindered rather than helped by Peter, who insisted that if I'd just let him look at it, he could probably fix it. I wasn't sure if he was trying to be helpful or just taking after his father, who always claimed he could fix things and refused to call a professional in until after he'd broken it even more.

'What's for dinner?' demanded Jane, as I hopefully pressed all the switches and turned the boiler on and off several times.

'Oh God, I don't *know*, I'm trying to fix the boiler,' I snapped.

'I only asked. Don't we even get fed now?'

'Jane, you're fifteen, you can make yourself something to eat. I'm *trying* to fix the fucking boiler right now.'

'Can I go to Dad's? I hate it here, I want you to drive me to Dad's.'

'I'm not driving you to your father's because I'm trying to fix the boiler and if you want to go there so badly, call him to come and get you.'

'He didn't pick up. So you need to take me.'

'I don't *need* to do anything, except fix the boiler.'

'You NEVER do ANYTHING for me. I bet if Peter wanted to go to Dad's you'd take *him*.'

'I'm not taking anyone anywhere. This is our first night in our new home and it would be nice if we spent it *together*. Now *please* give me peace while I try to fix the fucking boiler. PLEASE!'

'Mum, when will the Wi-Fi be connected? Can you call them and find out?' said Peter.

'I'M TRYING TO FIX THE BOILER!'

'When *can* you call them, then?'

I kicked the scullery door closed and leant my head against the piece of shit broken boiler. I was only one person, trying to do the job of two. At least if Simon had been here, he could have been the one swearing at the boiler while I dealt with the children's incessant demands for food, lifts and internet access. But Simon *wasn't* here, I reminded myself, as those tears threatened again, and I wasn't going to be beaten by a bloody boiler. I *could* do this. I gave the boiler a tentative whack with a wrench. It had not responded to me hitting it with a pair of pliers, but I was working on the basis that boilers came under plumbing and wrenches were plumbing tools and therefore it might work better. I was quite proud of my logic, but the boiler remained stubbornly lifeless. Finally, I had one last idea before I spent the GDP of Luxembourg on an emergency plumber. I stumbled out to the oil tank (too country for gas) and, by the light of my phone torch, found a valve on the tank that looked suspiciously like it was pointing to 'closed'.

'Nothing ventured, nothing gained,' I muttered, as I barked my shin on a stupidly placed piece of wall, and turned it to open. Either the boiler would burst into life, or I'd burn the house down. I went back inside, stubbing my toe on an abandoned plant pot and surveyed the boiler once more. It still sat there lifeless. I went through the process of pressing all the buttons again, and miraculously, on pressing the reset button, it finally roared into life. I'D DONE IT! I'D FIXED THE FUCKING BOILER!

'MUUUUM!' yelled Peter.

'MOTHER!' howled Jane.

I flung open the scullery door in triumph.

'I'VE FIXED THE BOILER!' I announced, expecting at least a fanfare of trumpets and a twelve-gun salute. 'I was right, Jane. They *had* turned it off. Outside!'

Jane snorted. 'I bet Dad would have known that hours ago.'

'I didn't need a man, I fixed it myself.'

'Whatever. Can I go to Millie's?'

'NO! We're going to have a lovely night together. I'll light the fire and we'll have a picnic dinner in front of it.'

'Isn't this fun?' I said brightly later on, sitting with Judgy Dog before the rather smoky fire.

Jane snorted from beside the window, where she'd discovered an intermittent 4G signal.

'It's quite fun, Mum,' said Peter carefully. 'But it would be more fun with Wi-Fi, if you could phone them in the morning and see when we'll get the broadband connected?'

The fire went out.

Judgy made a snorting noise rather akin to Jane's, and something scratched suspiciously behind the skirting boards.

'It's fun,' I said firmly. After all, as the saying goes, sometimes you just have to fake it till you make it.

Saturday, 14 April

My first weekend here without the children. In fairness, Simon *had* offered to take them last weekend so they were out of the way while I moved, but foolishly I'd laboured under the impression that they were old enough and big enough to make themselves useful – I'm nothing if not an eternal optimist …

Last week passed in a blur of desperate attempts to find work clothes from the general jumble of boxes, days at work mainly spent lining everything up on my desk in beautiful straight lines and appreciating the general tidiness and order of the office, before returning home to demand what the children had been doing all day (lounging around, eating and making a mess

– such are the joys of teenagers in the school holidays), stomping round shouting about the mess the children had made, hurling the trail of plates and glasses left around the house in the dishwasher, and bellowing about who had drunk all the milk again, before spending the evenings in a whirl of unpacking boxes, wishing I could go to bed because I was knackered, feeling somewhat overwhelmed by the sheer number of boxes needing to be unpacked and wondering why the fuck I've so much stuff.

When Simon and I first moved in together, every single thing we owned in the entire world BETWEEN US fitted in his rusting Ford Fiesta, with room left over. Over twenty years later, and it took two vast removal lorries to distribute our possessions, not to mention the skip full of crap, the innumerable bags to the charity shops and several runs to the local dump. I'd packed everything up in a tremendous hurry, flinging things into boxes and promising myself I'd sort it all out at the other end (this rushed packing also led to some raised eyebrows from the removal men as they looked askance at my boxes labelled with things like 'kitchen crap', 'general crap' and – this was one of the last boxes I packed – 'more fucking shit'), but this was proving harder than I thought, as I pulled out Jane's first baby-gro – so tiny, and rather faded and yellowing now, but even so, I couldn't possibly get rid of it.

I had rather a lump in my throat, when I found a box of photos of me in hospital holding a newborn Jane in the same baby-gro, Simon beaming proudly beside me. These must have been some of the last actual photos we ever took, before we got a digital camera. Beneath the box of photos were red books filled with their vaccination records. Did I need them? What if at some point they needed to prove they had been vaccinated? Would that ever happen? I set them to one side in the 'maybe keep' pile, and then I found Peter's first shoes. So tiny! I remembered the day we bought them. There should be a photo of that too – I dug through the box, and there it was, a Polaroid taken by Clarks of a small, furious and scowling Peter, clutching his blanky, who had been unimpressed with this momentous day. Did he still have his blanky, I wondered? We'd gone to the park after he got his shoes and he'd been so pleased with himself as he tottered across the playground on his own for the first time, me hovering anxiously by his side, ready to catch him if he fell. The shoes were definitely for the 'keep' pile. And what was this? A box full of tiny human teeth? Well, of course I was keeping that, even if at some point the children's teeth had got jumbled up and I no longer knew whose were whose.

Jane wandered in at that point. She looked at my little box of teeth that I was gazing at fondly and said, 'You do know, Mother, that one day you're going to be dead and we're going to have to clear your house out and it's going to be like *totally* gross if we have to come across things like boxes of human teeth.'

'But they're *your* teeth,' I protested. 'It's not like I'm a serial killer and I've kept the teeth of my victims as a souvenir. They are keepsakes from your childhood.'

Jane gave another one of her snorts. 'It's still *gross*,' she insisted. 'In fact, it would be less weird if you *had* killed people for their teeth. *Why* do you have them?'

Once upon a time, that special moment had been quite magical, when Simon and I first tiptoed into Jane's room, as she lay there, all flushed and rosy-cheeked in her White Company pyjamas, sleeping innocently, dreaming of the Tooth Fairy and the spoils she'd wake up to. We slid a little pearly tooth out from under her pillow and popped a (shiny shiny) pound coin in its place. We stood hand in hand and gazed down at her, still slightly in awe of this perfect little person we'd made together. We put that tiny little tooth into the special box I'd bought for it, and marvelled at how grown up our baby girl was getting. I wondered if Simon and I would ever do anything together again like that for the children?

Of course, the standards slipped in later years – any old pound coin would do – and quite often I'd forget, and when an angry child burst into my bedroom complaining the Tooth Fairy hadn't been I'd have to hastily rustle up a pound coin and pretend to 'look' under their pillow before triumphantly 'finding' it, and accusing them of just not looking properly. Luckily they fell for this every time, and I still constantly complain about them never looking for anything properly. Now though, looking into the box filled with yellowing little teeth, several of them still bearing traces of dried blood where, the sooner to get his hands on the booty, Peter had forcibly yanked them out, it did seem a rather macabre thing to keep. But on the other hand, a) I wasn't actually going to admit that to Jane, and b) I'd really gone to rather a lot of effort to collect those teeth and so I wasn't quite ready to part with them just yet. Anyway, they might come in useful for something.

'Useful for *what*?' said Jane in horror. 'Seriously, Mother, what exactly do you think a box full of human teeth might be useful for? Are you going to become a witch or something? Eye of newt and tooth of child? Is that why you're getting chickens – you claimed it was because they were chatty, but actually you're planning on sacrificing them and reading the portents in their entrails while daubed in their blood? I'm not having any part of that. I'm going to go and live with Dad if you do that. That's just going too far, Mother.'

'What?' I said in confusion. 'How did you get from your baby teeth to me becoming some sort of chicken-murdering devil worshipper? I'm not going to sacrifice the chatty chickens. The chickens aren't even *here* yet and you're accusing me of secretly wanting to kill them!'

Simon chose that moment to arrive and collect his darling children.

'Dad, if Mum becomes a Satanist and kills the chickens, I'm coming to live with you, OK,' Jane informed him by way of a greeting.

'Errr, hello darling,' said Simon. 'Why is your mother becoming a Satanist?'

'I'm NOT,' I said crossly.

'She collects human body parts,' said Jane darkly.

'I BLOODY WELL DON'T!' I shouted.

This wasn't the scene I'd envisioned for Simon seeing me in my new home for the first time. I'd lost track of time, and instead of being elegantly yet casually clad in a cashmere sweater and sexy boots, perhaps with some sort of flirty little mini skirt to remind him that actually my legs really weren't bad still, while reclining on a sofa in my Gracious Drawing Room, I was in my scabbiest jeans, covered in mud from walking Judgy earlier, with no make-up, dirty hair and clutching a box of teeth, with the house looking like a bomb had gone off and boxes everywhere. Simon meanwhile appeared to have finally cast aside his scabby fleeces in favour of tasteful knitwear and seemed to be attempting to cultivate some sort of designer stubble. Or maybe he just hadn't bothered to shave. Either way, it suited him. Bastard. I glared at him.

'Right …,' he said, wisely deciding the best thing to do would be to ignore this whole conversation and pretend it had never happened. 'Jane, are you ready? And where's your brother?'

Jane looked surprised. 'Ready? What, now? Like, NO, I need to pack. How should I know where Peter is? *I'm* not his mother!'

I sighed. 'I suppose you'd better come in then, Simon. Would you like a cup of tea?'

'Could I get some coffee?'

'Fine.'

At least the kitchen was unpacked and relatively tidy. I reached for the jar of Nescafé, as Simon said, 'Don't you have any proper coffee? You know I don't like instant coffee.'

I gritted my teeth. 'No, Simon. I don't have any proper coffee, because I don't have a coffee maker, because I don't drink coffee, and so I only have a jar of instant as a courtesy for guests, and I only offered you a cup of tea in the first place because I'm trying VERY HARD to keep things between us on an amicable footing, at least on the surface, so we don't mentally scar and traumatise our children and condemn them to a lifetime of therapy because we weren't adult enough to be civil to each other, but I must say, you're doing an extraordinarily good job of making it difficult for me to FUCKING WELL DO THIS!'

'You don't drink coffee?' said Simon. 'Since when don't you drink coffee?'

'I haven't drunk coffee in the house since I was pregnant with Jane,' I said. 'I occasionally, VERY occasionally have a latte when I'm out, but other than that, I barely touch the stuff, because it made me puke like something out *The Exorcist* when I was pregnant. How have you never noticed me not drinking coffee over the last FIFTEEN YEARS?'

'But what about the coffee maker I gave you for your birthday a few years ago?'

'Would that be the coffee maker when I said, "Well, this is a lovely present for you, because I DON'T DRINK COFFEE?"'

'I thought you were joking. Is that why you let me keep it?'

'Yes, Simon. Because there's no point in me having a shiny fuck-off coffee machine cluttering up my kitchen when I DON'T DRINK COFFEE! Are you starting to perhaps grasp why we're getting divorced?'

'Because of coffee?'

'No, the coffee is a METAPHOR!'

'Are you sure you mean metaphor?'

'No, no I'm not. Anyway, the fucking COFFEE is symbolic of the vast chasm and divide between us.'

'Oh,' said Simon. 'Should I just have a cup of tea then?'

'Oh FFS! I don't CARE what you have. I'm going to see if your children are ready.'

Upstairs, I knocked tentatively on Peter's door, then left a few seconds and knocked again. I'm too afraid to enter unbidden in case I witness something that means I can no longer look at my baby boy in QUITE the same way again. While I was standing there, I mentally added more Mansize tissues to the shopping list. Eventually I shouted, 'Peter? Peter, Dad is here! Are you ready?'

Peter finally opened his door and looked at me blankly. 'Dad?'

'Yes, Dad is here.'

'Dad? Here? Why?'

'To pick you up. You're going to his house this weekend.'

'THIS weekend?'

'Yes.'

'What, like TODAY?'

'YES.'

'But I can't go yet.'

'Why not?'

'Because I'm at a really good part in my game and I haven't got a proper computer at Dad's.'

'I don't care, you're going to his house. Now.'

'Can I take my computer?'

'NO! Just pack some pants or something.'

'Pants? Why?'

'SO YOU CAN CHANGE THEM. OMG. JUST PACK SOME CLOTHES.'

'OK.'

I banged on Jane's door.

'Are you ready?' I demanded.

'I'm doing my make-up,' Jane shouted. 'My eyebrows aren't done.'

Eventually, after an HOUR of toing and froing and shouting and bellowing (during which Simon sat placidly at MY kitchen table, eating MY chocolate HobNobs and playing no part whatsoever in getting HIS children ready to spend the weekend with HIM), I finally waved them all off.

Two days. Two whole days. All to myself. What to do? I could go for a run (ha ha, NO!). Read an Improving Book? Or, first things first, I could finally finish the unpacking and get the house straight.

It was very quiet. I unpacked another box, and found the DVD of Jane's nursery graduation. So then I had to find a laptop with a DVD drive so I could watch it. And then I cried all over again like I had on the day she left nursery and I thought my baby was all grown up now she was ready to start school. She was so *little*. In those dark days when they were babies and toddlers, I never thought they'd grow up. I thought they'd be little forever, and God knows, some of those long, long days certainly felt like forever. But all of a sudden, they went and grew up when I wasn't looking.

I checked my watch. 2.41 pm. Gosh. Was that all? Doesn't time ... drag when you're not running round like a blue-arsed fly. I've spent years longing for this moment – to not be constantly chasing my tail, to have some time to myself, to have some SPACE to myself, to have a room of one's own, or at least an hour with the house to myself with nobody fighting or complaining they were hungry or demanding I magically increase the broadband speed or provide my credit card to buy something on the internet that they'd definitely pay me back for but hardly ever do. And now I had it – I wasn't quite sure what to do with myself.

A nap, I decided. A lovely nap. When was the last time I had time for a nap? Probably ... pre-children. I know, I know, we're all told that you're supposed to nap when the baby naps, but then when are you supposed to have a shower, make the dinner, put the laundry on, pay the bills, stare hopelessly into a mirror wondering who this hollow-eyed stranger is staring back at you that bears a vague resemblance to your mother? Exactly. When the baby naps. So, FINALLY, after fifteen years of feeling permanently sleep-deprived, I could start catching up. A nap!

I arranged Judgy Dog and myself on the sofa with a snuggly blanky (Jesus, will I ever be able to say 'blanket' again, or are certain words condemned to be forever ingrained in my mind in baby talk – the same way I seem unable to shake off the urge to shout 'LOOK! COW! HORSEY! WHAT DO COWS SAY? DO COWS SAY "MOOOOOO"? WHAT DO HORSEYS SAY? HORSEYS SAY "NEEEEEIIIIGHHHH!"' every time I pass a field with animals in?) and we cosied down for a lovely nap.

The more I tried to sleep, the more wide awake I became. I stared at the ceiling, wondering what would happen if I died right now. Who would find me? Would Judgy have started eating me by the time the children came home on Sunday night? Would they then be so appalled and disgusted by his cannibalistic ways that they got rid of him and then *he* died alone in a shelter, even though it's not actually cannibalism for a dog to eat a human? The thought of Judgy's lonely death, all by himself in a cold concrete pen, was almost too much for me to bear.

I gave up hope of sleep and scrolled through Instagram instead. Maybe the children were having a horrible time at Simon's and their feed would reflect this and I could feel smug. Except Jane had blocked me and Peter had not posted anything in months apart from photos of gaming scores. WHY HAD MY OWN DAUGHTER BLOCKED ME ON INSTAGRAM? I looked at Perfect Lucy Atkinson's Perfect Mummy's page instead. She was on a girly spa weekend. Why was I not on a girly spa weekend, drinking champagne in a hot tub? Even though champagne makes me belch and I haven't been in a hot tub since I read an article that said they're basically just heaving cauldrons of bacteria soup. But even so!

What about Fiona Montague? Oh, look, she was training for a triathlon and posting lots of photos of her looking great in skin-tight Lycra with 'inspirational' captions. Fuck off, Fiona, you husband-stealing slut. But despite her wanton ways, even Fiona was out and about having fun, and oooh, she'd just posted a new photo – her toes in the bath with a glass of wine because apparently she was about to head out on a 'date night'. Bitch.

Who else to stalk? What about Debbie from HR? Debbie had been out for 'brunch with good friends' and finished her caption with #lovelaughlive. I might have to have Debbie killed. Christina, my erstwhile relationship counsellor, only posted wanky quotes about being true to yourself. That made me feel a little bit better, and I had a bijou judge of Christina.

I searched for Simon's name again, although he'd always been staunchly anti-Instagram, and lo and behold, there he was! @SimonRussell30 (imaginative, Simon – I assume the '30' refers to a random number, and you weren't hoping people would think you were actually thirty). Why did he have an account now, after being so scathing about it for all these years? Not many photos yet, obviously, but there was one last night of two beers clinking, just titled '#Friyay!' FFS. Firstly, who even still says 'Friyay'? Even *I* know that is totally lame. Secondly, why does he get to go out for beers on Friday night when I spent *my* Friday night cooking dinner for his children, doing all his children's laundry so they had clean clothes to take to his house for the weekend and then just as I was about to finally have a glass of wine, having to go and pick Jane up from the cinema because apparently the 'bus hadn't come' – the same bus I assume that passed me heading out of town as I was heading in, as Jane seems to think if she misses the bus that is clearly the bus's fault and it must have just not come and so I need to solve the problem. All while *Simon* was quaffing his 'Friyay' beer. And thirdly, who did the other beer belong to? Who? It could have been a work colleague, of course, but it was a wanky little bottle of foreign lager, not a Manly Pint, so equally could have been a girl's. I realised I'd gnawed off what remained of my nails while scrolling through Simon's photos. #SweetNewPad was another, with an arty shot of what must be his new sitting room (I couldn't see the sideboard. Where was it? After all the fuss he made about me painting it, had he just got rid of it? RUDE). It looked very nice, and considerably more elegant than my own scruffy sitting room. But '#Sweet New Pad'? What was *wrong* with him? And he did realise you don't have to hashtag every caption, didn't he? Twat.

I went to my own page to see what Simon might think if he looked at it. It was less than inspiring. The last photo I'd posted was a pile of boxes, simply captioned 'Moving Day!' I must try harder. I wanted Simon to seethe with jealousy at my sheer *fabulousness* every time he looked at it. Assuming he looked at it. Why wouldn't he look at it? Apart from because he was too busy having mindblowing #Friyay sex with a wanky, beer-drinking twenty-three-year-old with gravity-defying tits and no stretch marks in his #SweetNewPad, of course. Oh God! That was obviously what he was doing, while I lay slumped on a sagging sofa, trying not to cry because me and my cannibalistic dog were both going to die alone and unloved.

In the end, in case Simon did find a minute out of his filthy shag timetable to look at my page and gloat he'd escaped the nagging witch of an ex-wife and remind himself of how much he was #lovinglife with his lithe sex bomb (who could probably contort herself into improbable positions without shrieking, 'Wait, stop, I've done something to my hip'), I went and had a bath and posted a Fiona Montague-style shot with a glass of wine and about a million filters so it looked quite sexy, and put

'The weekend starts here!' It wasn't much, but it was the best I could manage.

Duly bathed (it turns out a bath isn't quite so decadent when there isn't much else you're supposed to be doing), I was bored out of my mind and quite alarmed at the prospect of the many empty hours stretching ahead of me. I'd been so sure I had Inner Resources at my disposal and would be happy with my own company, but it seems it has been so long since I've had the chance to experience my own company that my Inner Resources appear to have buggered off, along with the perkiness of my tits and my natural hair colour.

'Bollocks!' I thought, as I failed to log in to Netflix, Jane having ignored my pleading texts for the password – Peter claims not to know it as he only watches YouTube. I wished I'd had the wit to have arranged to go out or meet friends or do SOMETHING tonight, but I'd been so sure of those Inner Resources I'd not bothered. I vaguely wondered about being an Independent Modern Woman and going to the cinema by myself, but I wasn't sure I could eat a whole tub of popcorn on my own, and obviously the popcorn is the only reason to go to the pictures. And also, I'd have to put my bra back on. I gave up and returned to reading *Riders*. Since I was clearly never going to have sex again, I might as well read about other people doing it.

But then – oh hallelujah – the doorbell rang. Who could it be? I positively skipped to the door, filled with excitement. I was pretty sure it was probably some passing hunky farmer, who had popped by to tell me off for some Terrible Countryside Transgression I'd unwittingly made, and although initially he'd be very cross with me and I'd think him arrogant and overbearing, I'd still notice his Cambridge blue eyes and rugged physique as he sprang onto his tractor, and he in turn would in fact have fallen hopelessly in love with me at first sight, and would only fall deeper over the coming weeks as he berated me further for my charmingly hopeless country *faux pas*, until he could contain himself no longer and declared his undying love for me, just as I was feeling gloomy over a misunderstanding that had led me to think he was marrying the icily beautiful Lady of the Manor, but it was OK, it was me all along. It didn't even really matter that I was in my jammies with toast crumbs in my cleavage, because *everyone* knows in these scenarios that the more grubby, dishevelled and deranged you look, the MORE likely the hero is to fall in love with you …

It was a pair of Jehovah's Witnesses. Judgy, who could at least have earned his keep by seeing them off, refused to move from the sofa.

I shuffled back, gloomy once more, to consider whether I could be arsed starting a seven-season American sitcom. The doorbell rang again. The Jehovah's Witnesses were at least persistent in their desire to save my soul from eternal damnation, I reflected, but I still wasn't really interested in hearing more about it. I flung open the door, ready to explain that it was all very well, but actually I was an atheist, and would THEY like to hear about MY beliefs about how there's no God, THERE'S ONLY SCIENCE?

On the doorstep stood a very welcome sight in the form of my lovely friends Colin and Sam, and Hannah and Charlie. Not quite a rugged farmer to fall in love with me, but probably much, much better, because, really, who could arsed with all the emotional upheaval of falling in love again?

'What are you doing here?' I said.

'Well, that is a nice way to greet your oldest and bestest friend,' said Hannah.

'We thought you might like some company,' said Sam, 'what with it being your first night on your own in the new house. It's always a tough one, that first night without the kids.'

'But how did you know?' I said.

'Oh, Jane told Sophie she was at Simon's tonight,' said Sam. 'So we thought what better way to spend our Saturday night than by getting pissed with you and shouting "Bastard" about Simon in a supportive way.'

'That does sound quite good fun,' I admitted.

'I'll definitely shout "Bastard" the loudest,' said Hannah.

'And also,' put in Colin, 'we haven't even seen your new house yet, so I'm obviously dying to conform to the gay stereotype by coming round and criticising your décor. But also what Sam said.'

I do love Colin. Sam spent several years as a single father, following the departure of his dastardly former partner Robin, and after years of lurking around supermarkets (he read an article about it being a good place to meet men, but felt his trolley full of fish fingers and Petits Filous was off-putting to the single-tons on the prowl in the produce aisle), a flirtation with Tinder (I don't think Hannah and I helped there, we just kept shouting 'No! SWIPE!' every time he showed us a potential date/shag), a period of announcing he was Never Going to Find Love and thus was giving up looking and Focusing on His Inner Self (he pulled a muscle his first week at yoga and was thrown out of the class for shouting 'Fucking hell, I think I've broken my arse!', after which he accepted that his inner self preferred tequila slammers to Downward Dogs), he met Colin at the gym – 'I'm almost afraid to tell people that's how we met,' he admitted. 'It's such a *cliché*.'

'And Hannah told me I was to come and make myself useful, which I suspect will involve being sent for a takeaway and then driving everyone home. Which I think will actually be quite useful of me,' said Charlie.

Oh lovely, lovely Charlie. Hannah's divine second husband is so much nicer than her horrible first husband Dan, who was nothing more than a rancid streak of weasel piss. To my utter horror, I found myself for the first time ever thinking that maybe *I* should have made better choices in my life and married Charlie and not Simon, because once upon a time, at university, about a million years ago, when we were all young and foolish and irresponsible, Charlie had been in love with me, but with the callousness of youth I'd rejected good old dependable Charlie Carrhill for the dashingly gorgeous, romantic and slightly dangerous Simon Russell. Simon *was* so gorgeous back then. I think the very fact he noticed my existence was enough to turn my head and make me fall in love with him, breaking poor Charlie's heart in the process.

And now look at us. All that hope and promise and *love* Simon and I once had, reduced to trying to make him jealous through my Instagram feed. What if I hadn't let Simon seduce me with his wicked smile and come-to-bed eyes and had made a more sensible and considered choice, like Charlie? I gave myself a shake. No one deserved lovely Charlie more than Hannah (my bestest and oldest friend indeed, I reminded myself), and to even begin thinking like that … Well, that would make me a terrible person, and if I was determined one thing was going to come out of this sodding divorce, it was that I was going to be a Better Person. Do Good Works and things like that, and become universally beloved so I don't die alone and unwanted, and small children would call out, 'God bless you, Ma'am' when I walked down the street. I probably wasn't doing very well so far after my Instagramming earlier, though. Maybe I could make up for it by retweeting something worthy later. And actually, divine though Charlie was with Hannah, he hadn't actually been any better than Simon when he was with his first wife, so he wasn't really Mr Perfect either.

'Ellen, are you going to stand there gawping and staring into space or are you going to open that nice champagne I brought?

Go and get some glasses while I decide why all your paintings are in the wrong place,' chided Colin.

'It doesn't matter what you think about my painting placement,' I informed him. 'They're positioned like they are for a reason, to hide a multitude of sins. Likewise, why the sofa is where it is. So it's all staying put, because otherwise it all looks a bit shit.'

Colin sighed. 'You're spoiling all my fun,' he said. 'How am I supposed to be a Proper Gay with you thwarting me at every turn when I try to express myself?'

'Colin, darling, you're a corporate lawyer, you express yourself by making obscene amounts of money for evil corporations, not by prancing around rearranging Ellen's furniture. If you want to unleash your Proper Gay, just stick some Madonna on and leave the sofa where it is,' said Sam.

Colin looked sulky. 'You know I don't like Madonna,' he complained. 'I'm not a total cliché, you know. Anyway, Ellen, cheers! New house, new life, new you, new start! How are you feeling?'

'A bit lost …' I confessed.

'Oh Ellen,' said Hannah. 'Of course you are, that's totally natural. But this is an amazing opportunity for a fresh start. Imagine if Dan had never left me, and I was still stuck with him.'

'But Simon wasn't Dan, was he?' I said sadly. 'I mean, he could be a bit of a lazy arsehole at times, but he wasn't a *bad* person. There were a lot of good bits too. I really do love him. Loved him. I *did* love him, I mean.'

'This is the hardest part,' said Hannah. 'The bit where you think you're going to be on the shelf for evermore, and die alone and unloved in a damp basement flat surrounded by seventeen cats. Remember when I was at that stage?'

'Vaguely. Instead I shall die alone and unloved in a damp hovel of cottage with weirdly placed paintings to hide the mildew, surrounded by terriers who will fight over my dead body. I don't even think the roses round the door are roses, I think they're just brambles.'

'Well, maybe it's time to think about getting back in the game then?' suggested Colin.

'Back in the saddle, so to speak,' added Sam with a lascivious wink.

'Saddle? Game?' I said in confusion. 'What on earth are you talking about? You think I should take up tennis? And riding? Or cycling? Do a triathlon like Fiona Montague?'

'Well, riding of a sort,' snorted Sam with another leery wink. 'Crikey, is Fiona doing a triathlon? I'd have thought she'd be too worried about her make-up running!'

'Sam,' snapped Colin. 'Your *double entendres* are not helping, nor is your winking, which frankly is just disturbing. Please never do that at me. And we're not here to talk about Fiona Montague.'

Sam muttered something mutinous.

'No, Ellen,' Colin went on. 'We're talking about you getting back in the dating game. Finding yourself a man. Getting a bit of cock. You're a beautiful woman in her *prime*, who deserves to have a bit of fun, and we thought you maybe just need a nudge.'

I looked at them both in horror. 'No. Just … no. I can't. It's not possible. And please don't describe me as a woman in her prime, because that just reminds me of Miss Jean Brodie, who was a mad, sex-obsessed fascist who came to no good in the end. I'm not a nympho Nazi, thank you very much!'

'But Ellen, don't you miss sex?' asked Colin gently.

'No,' I said bluntly. 'I don't. I miss Simon. I miss the man I thought he was. I miss having someone to come home to and tell about my day, even if he doesn't listen, and someone to make me a cup of tea in bed on Sunday morning, and having someone I've

spent my whole life with so that sometimes when I see something funny and I know they'd be the only other person in the
world who would find that funny too I can just tell them or text
them a photo and know they'll get my joke without having to
explain it. I miss having someone who remembers our children's
firsts – their first steps, their first words, their first days at school.
I miss having someone who knows me in the way you can only
know someone after twenty-five years together. And he wasn't
annoying all the time. There was a lot of good stuff too, when he
took off his ratty fleeces and wore the nice jumpers I bought
him. We had a lot of laughs together, and now I've no one to
think about going on Nile cruises with when we're old, or to
share my indignation when the first SAGA catalogue drops
through the door, and I miss the thought of all the things we
should have done together when we finally had time and money
and were free from the children. But I don't miss fucking SEX, if
you'll pardon the pun!'

And then I burst into tears. Hideous, wracking tears, the
tears I'd been holding in for months, ever since the furious,
scalding, angry tears the night that he told me he needed some
'space', and I decided after those tears that I could either get on
with my life or I could give in to the tears, but I couldn't do both
because if I gave in to the tears I'd drown in them. But it seems
they were still there and had sneakily found a way to escape,
which after all is what water always does. I sobbed and I sobbed,
while Sam did the awkward man thing of patting my back
gingerly and mumbling 'There, there', until Colin dispatched
him in search of tissues and 'a PROPER drink, darling, something stronger than bloody champagne, but for Christ's sake not
gin, she's in enough of a state as it is!' and I attempted to howl
something about there being twelve packs of Mansize tissues in
the cupboard under the stairs, and Colin took over and pulled
me into a huge bear hug and just held me while I cried and

cried, until the storm started to pass and I became uncomfortably aware that I'd drenched the front of his shirt in tears and, much worse, snot.

As the howling subsided into that awkward sniffling hiccupping that comes at the end of a really bad crying jag, and I attempted to gain some sort of control over myself, Colin handed me a large wad of tissues, and an eye-wateringly strong vodka and tonic.

'Better?' he enquired.

'Uh huh,' I gulped.

'I think you needed that, didn't you?' he said gently.

I *had* needed it. I felt oddly cleansed, and calmer than I'd been for months.

'Ellen,' said Hannah. 'Do you really still love Simon? Do you regret divorcing him?'

'I don't know,' I admitted. 'It's all so confusing. We'd been together so long, and I was so hurt and angry by what he did, but I thought we'd get through it in the end, we'd find a way, but then he started all that shit about "needing space" and not knowing if he loved me, so that was that, really … But it's strange, life without him, because there *were* good bits too, you know. I know you thought he was an arse, but I do, did, I don't know, love him, and despite everything, deep down I always thought he loved me too. I just always thought we'd grow old together. I've thought that since the very first night we got together. And now we won't. And that takes a bit of getting used to, the idea that I'll be on my own now for the rest of my life, with no one to accompany me on that Nile cruise.'

'In fairness, you'd been trying to persuade Simon to go on a Nile cruise for years and he always refused on the basis that you'd only be disappointed when no one was murdered on board so you could don a shady hat and solve the mystery, gin and tonic in hand. Same as he wouldn't go on the Orient Express with you either, because the murder-free reality would just shatter all your Agatha Christie fantasies,' pointed out Colin.

'And anyway, things like that are exactly what we were talking about,' said Sam. 'You seem to think that that's it, that you're now condemned to some lonely nun-like existence for evermore, but it's the twenty-first century, people split up, move on, find new partners all the fucking time, babe. Look at me. Look at Colin. Look at Hannah and Charlie. We've all had failed marriages or long-term relationships, and we've all found someone else. Why do you think you won't?'

'I didn't say I thought I won't,' I pointed out. 'I said I *can't*. There's a difference.'

'But why not?' said Colin, looking baffled. 'Unless you *are* still in love with Simon and feel you've made a terrible mistake, in which case it's probably not too late to tell him, don't be like Scarlett O'Hara and Rhett Butler, both too proud to admit how they feel. If you want Simon, do something about it. You're not actually divorced yet – you could just put all this behind you and move on and we'll say no more about it.'

'I'm *not* pining for Simon,' I said, remembering the very annoying coffee conversation we'd had that morning and his utter uselessness in attempting to galvanise his children into action even when it was officially his time to be responsible for them, and also reminding myself he was probably even now having red-hot contortionist sex to put on Instagram while his children were shut in their cupboards. 'I just miss the companionship and the shorthand of an established relationship. Anyway, I can't tell you why I can't find someone else. You will just have to take my word for it,' and I took a large slug of my drink.

Two more enormous vodka and tonics later, while Charlie was out getting a curry, I thought maybe, after all, I *could* tell the rest of them why I was now destined for a life of celibacy and loneliness.

'I can't have sex with another man,' I announced.

'Why not?' said Colin.

'Of course you can!' said Hannah. 'It's hardly like you were some virgin bride when you married Simon, you'd been round the block a few times by the time you hooked up with our Mr Russell! I mean, you've even shagged Charlie!'

'What, *your* Charlie?' said Colin in surprise. 'When did she shag him?'

'*She* is here, you know!' I said frostily. 'Thank you, Hannah. I thought we'd agreed never to speak of the unfortunate fact that I'd shagged him, not once you two were an item. And it was years and *years* ago, Colin, before Simon, before any such thing as a hint of Hannah and him.'

Colin, who had obviously been hoping for something a little juicier, looked disappointed. 'So if you've not been averse to a bit of the old casual sex in the past,' he said, 'why can't you go back to your wicked and wanton ways?'

'Because I can't be naked!' I burst out. 'I cannot take my clothes off in front of a man! Not *now*!'

'I know it's daunting, babe,' said Sam. 'Men feel like that too, you know. The fear someone might laugh at the size of our dick (not that that has *ever* happened to me. I've never had *any* complaints in that department, thank you).' Colin snorted. 'Or they might think, I dunno, our balls are weird.' Colin snorted again.

'Would you please stop that, *darling*?' said Sam. '*You* are the one not helping now. But you know what I mean, Ellen. It's scary taking your clothes off in front of a new person. But just remember, they'll probably be feeling exactly the same.'

'NO!' I shouted. 'NO, THEY WON'T! Because it's DIFFERENT for men!'

'Of course it's not,' said Colin kindly. 'We might be better at seeming OK about it, but really we *do* get nervous too.'

'NO! Seriously, men can never understand what I'm talking about. Your bodies have not been ravaged by child bearing. My stomach looks like an uncooked focaccia –'

'At least you manage to stay middle class with your metaphors,' interrupted Colin approvingly.

'Well, it DOES. All saggy and dimpled and with stretch marks all over it. It's not a case of just going to the gym, either. No crunches in the world are going to sort the ravages of pregnancy. And my tits. My tits were once perky and firm, but not anymore. Now, I hardly dare take my bra off in winter, lest the floor is too cold, so far south are they migrating.'

'But it can't be that bad,' said Sam. 'You look all right with your clothes on.'

'That is rather the whole point of why I can't take them OFF,' I shouted. 'Just because I can cover the ravages in Zara's finest doesn't change the horror that lurks beneath.'

'I'm sure you're just being self-conscious,' said Colin kindly. 'It really can't be that bad. You're overthinking this.'

In answer, I pulled up my top and showed them my stretch-marked stomach. They recoiled, and then remembered themselves.

'It's fine, really,' said Sam.

'It *does* look a bit like an uncooked focaccia, doesn't it?' said Colin, with interest. 'The stretch marks are like the little holes in the top of the focaccia. Maybe you should just put on some fake tan? After all, a nice baked loaf always looks more appealing than a lump of dough.'

'COLIN!' said Sam.

'I'm trying to help,' said Colin.

'But I felt just the same with Charlie,' said Hannah. 'And it was fine.'

'But you already knew Charlie. You'd known him for years. He wasn't someone *new*.'

'Yes, but he'd never seen me naked.'

'No, but he was Charlie. Lovely, lovely Charlie. You knew he was wonderful and adored you and was a very good person. If I were to have sex again, it would be with a stranger. I mean, not an actual stranger, but in relative terms, when you've spent twenty-five years shagging the same person, really, anyone else counts as a stranger. What if I do sex wrong? What if it's all different now and I didn't get the memo? I can't even remember what any other penises look like apart from Simon's.'

'Not even Charlie's?' said Hannah curiously.

'*Especially* not Charlie's. I have put that right out of my mind. I don't want to think about what Charlie's penis looks like.'

'Why is Ellen thinking about my penis?' enquired Charlie, coming back at exactly the wrong moment.

'I'm *not* thinking about your penis!' I insisted. 'Or any penises. No penises. I mean, as far as I recall, I don't remember being shocked or surprised by Simon's, so I assume that most penises look like his, but even so, to look at someone else's? To *touch* another man's willy, let alone, well, you know! It would be too … strange. Too intimate. It would feel wrong.'

'Or it might feel very right?' suggested Colin. 'You won't know until you try.'

'Anyway,' I said darkly. 'My stomach and my willy worries aren't even the worst of it.'

'Please don't show us your tits,' begged Colin.

'I'm not going to show you my tits,' I assured him. 'The tits are not what I'm talking about anyway. The horror I'm referring to can never be seen by any man. Except perhaps a gynaecologist.'

Sam and Colin looked at me fearfully. Charlie retreated to the kitchen muttering something about heating up the naan bread.

I nodded. 'Yep. I mean my fanny is the issue. Two human heads have squeezed through it. It has been sewn up twice. Basically, I've a fanny that looks like a patchwork quilt and I fear it's not as … embracing … as it once was, so I can't ever be naked or Do Sex with another man again. It was OK with Simon, he saw it all happening gradually, the stretch marks and the sagging, and even the baggy tapestry fanny didn't all happen at once, and also it was mostly his fault. Have you noticed that he has quite a big head that he probably passed on to his children? So that was different. But I could no more inflict my Flaps of Doom on a new man than, well, than I could show them to you. It Just Is Not Going to Happen!'

'Well, anyway, we're not advocating you pick up randoms on Tinder and booty-call them,' said Colin sternly. 'If you meet someone that you find you connect with enough to want to go to bed with him, then he'll probably be a nice enough person to not care that you have a few flaws and imperfections. He'll probably be too busy worrying about his own imperfections anyway. But you can get to know someone first, and then think about bed. There's no obligation to shag anyone you don't want to.'

'But what about dick pics?' I whimpered.

'Well, they're quite useful. Look at it like this, if they send you a dick pic, you can instantly discount them, and not waste any more time on them. Unless, of course, you like what you see …'

'OK, OK,' I sighed. 'I'll think about it. I'm trying very hard to be a strong independent woman and not need a man, though, but it's bloody lonely being a single mother and coping with everything on your own.'

'You *are* a strong independent woman,' said Hannah firmly. 'You've always been a strong independent woman, and really, you've been coping on your own for years as Simon was always working or away so much.'

'I know, I know, but I'm starting to realise he *did* do stuff. It's the little things, you know – like having someone open a bottle of wine for me after a bad day. Someone to warm my feet on in bed. Judgy won't let me, in fact he growls at me when I try.

I don't need a knight in shining armour to rescue me, but occasionally I'd so like someone to bring me a glass of wine after a long day.'

'Well,' said Sam, 'in the meantime, remember you've always got us. You're not on your own.'

Monday, 16 April

And at last the children have returned to school after the Easter holidays or the Spring Break or whatever the fuck they call it these days. I thought things would be easier when they were in secondary school. I thought as they got older they'd get more self-sufficient, they'd be able to get themselves up and out the door in the mornings, they'd not need me to find all their stuff (though why I thought that age would bring them the magical ability to locate lost items, I don't know, given that it had never bestowed that gift upon their father), they'd be able to make their own lunches and breakfasts and possibly even their own dinners sometimes too. Oh, what a poor, sweet fool I was! Trying to get teenagers out the door is possibly even more stressful – more reminiscent of banging your head endlessly against a brick wall – than trying to get bloody toddlers out the door.

The happy fun joy started with trying to get them TO bed last night. I'd duly packed them off at a decent hour, reminding them that they needed their sleep, that they had to concentrate at school today and also that they were still growing, for which I was rewarded with the same whinges about how *everyone else* gets to stay up as *late as they like* that I'd been hearing for the last ten years, and which fell upon deaf and unsympathetic ears. Then there had been the arguments from Jane that it was *not fair* that she had to go to bed at 10 pm, just like Peter, when she was a whole *two years older* and so should be allowed to stay up *much later*, to which my only counter-argument was that she bloody well had to go to bed because I was going to bed, followed by me having to sit in the kitchen and guard the fridge until I was sure Peter was safely in bed to stop him downing three pints of milk before retiring for the night and then complaining when there was nothing to put on his vat of Weetabix in the morning. Then there had always been Simon's role – after I'd shouted in vain at them to go to bed, he'd finally wade in to the argument and bellow that they were to go to bed NOW and they'd be so surprised by *him* shouting at them, that they'd go. Now that it's just me shouting, I think they simply tune out.

THEN, when their lights were still on at 11 pm, despite increasingly furious bellows from me, I had to go downstairs and switch the router off, which resulted in further furious bellows from *them* because Peter had been number one on *Fortnite* and about to win the battle and Jane had been having a like, really, like, important chat with Millie and Sophie on Snapchat and now *her life was ruined*. Neither of them seemed the slightest bit concerned that these things had been happening when they were supposed to be sleeping – it was still *all my fault* according to Jane because Simon apparently let her stay up as late as she wanted over the weekend.

So, after all that, it was no bastarding surprise when the little fuckers showed no signs of wanting to arise from their fetid pits this morning. I banged on the doors, I shouted and I shrieked, all while trying to get myself ready for work. I eventually threatened to go in and dump a bucket of water on them. But all to no avail. Someone needs to invent a special bed for teenagers, so that when their alarm goes off, if they're still in bed after five minutes they get a mild electric shock. If they STILL don't get up, the shock increases in intensity, and so on and so on until they finally deign to arise. Some might say this is harsh, and probably contravenes the Geneva Convention, etc, etc, but those people clearly have never had to get a bloody teenager out of bed in the morning …

Jane finally emerged from her room half an hour before we had to leave, and locked herself in the bathroom. This immediately set alarm bells ringing, because Jane is incapable of spending less than an hour in the bathroom at the best of times.

I banged on the door and shouted, 'What are you doing?'

'I need to wash my hair,' she screamed back.

'But you washed it last night before bed,' I pointed out.

'Well, I need to wash it AGAIN, don't I, Mother,' she snarled.

'But we need to go in half an hour at the most if you want a lift to the bus stop,' I wailed. 'And if I don't give you a lift to the bus stop you'll miss the bus and be late for school and then you'll get another detention and I'll probably be summonsed to see your head of year and made to feel like a shit mother because you were late again, when actually it's *not my fault*, but Mrs Simmons won't see it like that, she'll judge me for being an incompetent single mother and probably have you taken into care because when she starts giving me her judgy look I'll revert to being a sulky teenager too and huffing and rolling my eyes, and last time I had to go and see her she actually asked me if I was *chewing* and Jane, *please*, just be ready in time.'

There was no answer, probably because Jane had her head under the rubber shower attachment I'd purchased as the solution to her hair-washing woes. Jane had looked at it in disgust. 'WTF is that, Mother?' she'd enquired in scathing tones. I'd explained that it attached to the taps, to wash your hair with, and that everyone had them in their bathrooms when I was her age. She gave me the same look of blank incomprehension as when I tried to explain to her about telephone boxes. In fairness, I'd forgotten how rubbish those shower attachments were, and despite brightly telling Jane that it was *just the same* as a real shower, it really wasn't, not least on account of its ability to choose the most inconvenient time to detach one side from the tap and spray water all over you.

Meanwhile, Peter finally emerged from his room and shuffled downstairs. I abandoned trying to prise Jane out of the bathroom and ran downstairs, as he slouched over the kitchen counter shovelling Weetabix into his mouth.

'Peter, how many Weetabix have you got in there?'

Peter considered my question as he crammed another shovelful into his mouth.

'Six?' he finally offered.

'And is there any milk left for your sister's breakfast?'

'Oh yes,' Peter assured me virtuously. 'I put two bananas in as well, so I wouldn't need as much milk.'

I was unconvinced by his logic, especially when I looked in the fridge and found the milk carton had been put back in empty.

'PETER! You've finished all the milk again!'

'No, Mum, I haven't,' he insisted, 'Look.' He took the carton and tilted it, so a tiny dribble ran into one corner. 'There's still some left.'

'No. No, there isn't. That was a full two-litre carton last night.'

'Was it?'

'Well, maybe Jane can just make do with orange juice and toast then.'

'Oh yeah. I meant to say, Mum, we're out of OJ.'

'HOW? That was another full carton last night.'

Peter shrugged. 'I dunno. I only had a couple of glasses. And now there's none left.'

I sighed in despair. I'd been fretting for years about how I was going to feed Peter as a teenager, and now the reality was upon me, I was genuinely fearful I might have to remortgage the house. When we were working out how much maintenance Simon should pay for the children, apparently you can't have 'feeding giant teenage child with a possible tapeworm and hollow legs who can eat like a plague of locusts' taken into account to have the amount increased – according to the law, which has never seen how much a teenage boy can eat, he'll cost no more to feed than Jane. With only one income, the days of blithely flinging anything I fancied in my trolley at Waitrose are long gone, and budget German supermarkets are now my best friends.

Peter turned his bowl upside down and drained the last drops.

'Mum, I think I've left my PE kit at Dad's,' he said.

'What? Why?'

'You said we'd be at Dad's for the weekends, so I put it in the box of stuff to go to his, because I thought that would be best. I didn't know we'd be coming home on Sunday nights. Sorry, Mum. It's confusing, trying to live in two places.'

I wanted to be angry at him for having no PE kit, but I remembered all too well the confusion of the early days after your parents' divorce, when something essential always seemed to be at the other parent's house.

'I'm sorry, Peter,' I said. 'I'm sorry about all this. I really am.'

Peter gave me a very brief hug. 'It's OK, Mum. It's just a bit hard sometimes, you know?'

'I know. You can talk to me about it, if you want?'

'Yeah, no, maybe you can just give me a note off PE?'

Under the circumstances, that seemed the least I could do, although I gave him strict instructions not to tell Jane, as all hell would break loose if she found out I'd given Peter a note just because he didn't have any PE kit.

I went and banged on the bathroom door again to no avail. 'JANE! JANE, HURRY UP! OTHER PEOPLE NEED THE BATHROOM AND YOU NEED TO HAVE BREAKFAST!'

Peter was still in the kitchen playing on his phone and a thought occurred to me.

'Peter, do you follow your sister on Instagram?'

'Yeah.'

'Can I borrow your phone to check something?'

'Why?'

'I just want to look at something quickly, please?'

'OK.'

I clicked on Instagram and went to Jane's page. The first six photos were of Jane with a boy, looking very cosy. He was tagged as @harryx9876. I clicked on his page. More photos of him and Jane looking equally cosy. No wonder she'd blocked me!

'Who's Harryx?' I asked Peter.

He peered at his phone. 'You mean Harry, Mum. That's just his Insta handle. He's a boy at school.'

'In Jane's class?'

'Year above. I think he's like her boyfriend or something?'

Well, that at least explained the incessant hair-washing. What should I do? Should I say something? But then she'd know I'd basically been stalking her. I resolved to say nothing for the time being anyway, and just cajole Peter into letting me stalk her from time to time. Finally, after more hammering on Jane's door to try to make her come and have breakfast and being loftily informed that straightening her hair was far more important than food (I had hoped that what I save on Jane's vanity not giving her time to eat might make up for Peter's tapeworm, except her energy consumption cancels that out too – apparently you don't have the hours of hot water and hairdryers and hair straighteners running taken into consideration when the final maintenance amount is calculated either) and Peter was semi-ready and looking for a pre-school snack, Jane eventually came strolling downstairs, all glammed up for Harryx, just as I was howling that I was going *now*, *NOW* and anyone who wasn't ready would just have to take their chances themselves.

'GET IN THE CAR, IN THE CAR!' I bellowed. 'JANE! What are you wearing? Where's the rest of your skirt? OMG, the school's new uniform policy. You will be sent home!'

'Chill, Mother,' said Jane. '*EVERYBODY* wears their skirts like this, don't be so old-fashioned.'

'Go and change. No, don't go and change, we haven't got time, we'll just have to hope no one notices.'

'Make up your mind, Mother,' huffed Jane. 'You know that memory lapses and a lack of concentration are symptoms of the menopause, don't you?'

'JUST GET IN THE FUCKING CAAAAARRRRR!'

'Mood swings too,' she added helpfully. 'And bloating …'

'I'm not fucking menopausal, I just need you to get in the car!' I begged, as Jane sauntered out the door, before screaming in outrage because Peter had beaten her there and was smugly ensconced in the front seat. I wondered if I went to the GP and just whimpered 'Teenagers' they'd prescribe me valium? And also gin?

I finally got them to the bus stop, and was just kicking them out of the car when Peter stopped halfway out ('Darling, please, there's traffic, what are you doing?') to say, 'Oh yeah, Mum, by the way, I need some money on my thumb for lunch.'

'What?'

'Y'know! My thumb money. You need to put some on it. So I can get lunch?'

'Your thumb. Do you perchance mean your ParentPay account?'

'Yeah. My thumb!'

'Oh, I need mine topped up too, Mum,' said Jane, suddenly sweetness and light and dropping the sarky 'Mother' now cold hard cash was involved.

'Right! You didn't think to remind me of this before?' I said, thinking, 'Wave them off with a smile, don't let them leave on a sour note, be nice, so their last memory of you isn't as a shriek-ing harridan,' and also thinking, 'Why couldn't they ask Simon about things like this, just once? Why do I *always* have to do *everything*?'

'We're reminding you now!' they said in surprise.

'I'll have to do it when I get to work. I'm late. Now please just GO!' I hissed, before brightly adding, 'Bye darlings, love you. Have a wonderful day!'

Arrgh! Fucking ParentPay. Or his 'thumb money', as Peter confusingly insists on referring to it. In theory, a useful and effi-cient website that allows you to top up your children's dinner money accounts (which they then use to pay for their lunches using their thumb print, hence the 'thumb money'. I do have concerns about this and fear the government might steal their data and keep files on them, although in my children's case the files would mainly record the fact that they spend inordinate amounts of money on chips and traybakes while at school, because you can also check what they've bought with their thumbs. I quickly found it was too depressing to look, and I still marvel they've not got scurvy – they must have very sound constitutions, which I expect they got from me), pay for school trips and other extras, all online using your card, instead of scrabbling around to find change/chequebooks/cash to pay for these things. In reality, it's a constant drain of money. No sooner have you topped up their accounts than they're unaccountably empty again. It's very depressing!

Sunday, 22 April

The chatty chickens are here! I'd pondered keeping them in the shed but decided against it (sometimes I wonder how Simon copes without a shed now he's living in a flat, but I suppose he doesn't have me to avoid and only has the children one weekend a fortnight. I bet he wishes he had a shed, though. How has it not occurred to me till now that I should really make the most of my shed-bragging rights against poor shedless Simon? I could really rub salt in the wound by laughing that actually, I use it so little that sometimes I even *forget* that I *have* a shed! That would go some way to making up for all the times he asked me if I'd had a 'nice day off' when I worked part-time when the children were little, when in reality I'd spent the entirety of my 'day off' trying to tackle the shit heap of our house, wrangle his feral fuck trophies and cling on to my sanity while trying to have a wee for the last two hours since inevitably someone needed me for something crucial every time I tried to head to the loo, and so now I thought my bladder was going to burst and I probably had a UTI … Hmm, on second thoughts, taunting him with my shed doesn't even come close. Maybe I'll burn it down in front of him while laughing maniacally and telling him I don't need it. No, better to mock him with a functioning but unused shed …).

The chicken house arrived yesterday, a rather lovely little wood affair with a built-in run, and roosts and nesting boxes and all sorts including special fox-proof wire apparently. I was a little alarmed at the 'easy clean' features, as I hadn't really taken cleaning out chickens into account (I sort of assumed they'd just poop outside and it would be good for the grass or something, but it seems not). Anyway, never mind, I decided that maybe the children could clean out the chickens for me – such a wholesome outdoor activity. After all, the whole point of the chickens (apart from their Instagrammability) was because I'd read somewhere that looking after animals was very therapeutic for children after suffering a trauma such as their parents' divorce. Having paid out so much to bloody Christina to no avail as well, I also reckoned chickens would be much cheaper than getting the children counselling, and I'd get some free eggs out of it too. In a fit of chicken enthusiasm I spent most of yesterday painting the chicken house an adorable duck egg blue so that it would be a worthy home for my Speckled Sussexes to chat to me in. I'd attempted to persuade Peter and Jane that this might be a lovely bonding activity for us to do together, but Jane curtly told me she was 'busy' and after ten minutes of Peter enthusiastically sloshing my beautiful duck egg blue paint all over the lawn, the garden bench, the apple tree and himself – everywhere in fact but on the chicken house, I suggested that maybe I'd just finish it myself.

When I went in to get a cup of tea there were giant duck egg blue footprints all through the house, which was particularly baffling as Peter had taken his shoes off at the back door. How had he got paint INSIDE his shoes? I told myself it didn't matter, it would wash off, and anyway, I was very partial to a bit of duck egg blue (perhaps I shall also keep ducks, as part of my whole-some Country Image? I can see my Instagram feed now, all hens and ducks and trugs of beautiful vegetables, and me skipping about in a pair of fetching dungarees looking like Felicity Kendal in *The Good Life*. I just need to find a way to stop myself looking like a Soviet era mechanic when I put on dungarees).

When the chickens arrived, the children did shuffle outside to admire them. They were very beautiful chickens, and even Jane seemed enamoured of them. I'd told the children they could each name a chicken, and I would name the third. I'd harboured hopes of names of Shakespearean grandeur, or perhaps some classics from Greek mythology (when I suggested they could look to the Greek myths for inspiration, Jane sniggered and said, 'What about Jason? Was that the sort of thing you had in mind, Mother?' to which I pointed out that the chickens were girls and so Jason wasn't appropriate – and also definitely not what I'd had in mind).

'So, darlings,' I said cheerily. 'Have you decided what you're going to call your chickens?'

'Oh yes, Mum,' they said, exchanging knowing looks. I should have anticipated that no good would come of the children colluding on anything.

'I'm calling mine Oxo,' announced Jane.

'And mine's Bisto,' giggled Peter.

'What? No! You can't call them after stock cubes and gravy. How will that make them feel? They'll constantly be worried we're going to eat them.'

'Mum, they're chickens,' said Peter. 'I don't think they really know about things like that.'

'They're *chatty* chickens,' I insisted. 'You don't know what they know about. You'll upset them.'

'Well, you said we could call them whatever we wanted, and that's what we've chosen,' said Jane firmly. 'What are you going to call yours, Mum?'

'Oh fuck it,' I said wearily. 'I suppose if I can't beat you, I'll have to join you. I don't want my chicken feeling different, so she'd better be Paxo.'

At least, I reflected, Jane had called me 'Mum' for once and not a sarcasm-laden 'Mother'. Perhaps the chickens were already weaving their therapeutic magic and soon we'd all be sitting together playing board games and doing jigsaws in the evening and having a good old sing-song round the piano, and being a wholesome, normal and functional family.

From Judgy Dog's reaction when I tentatively introduced him to the chickens, he wholeheartedly approved of the names and couldn't wait to see the chickens live up to them. Fuck. My. Life.

Wednesday, 25 April

I was feeling like a perfect, clever domestic goddess, totally and utterly *nailing* juggling teenage parenting, single motherhood and a demanding career (it's very good being important enough to be given your own office, because it makes timewasting on non-work-related things – like topping up ParentPay accounts – much easier. I'd feel bad about this, if I didn't know for a fact that my old boss, Ed, whose job and office I was promoted into last year, as he's gone to be Busy and Important at the head office in California, had always had a two-hour nap under his desk every afternoon, having insisted that he must not be disturbed, as that was when he made Important Calls. Therefore I feel that since I'm actually rather good at my job and efficient enough to get everything done with time left over, snatching the odd half-hour for life admin is perfectly OK. We'll gloss over the time I spend browsing the *Daily Mail* website, though).

In a fit of said efficiency, I'd ordered a Sainsbury's shop online as there's less temptation to spend money on unnecessary items that catch my eye and look useful or delicious – the budget German supermarkets are all very well until you hit the middle aisles and their tempting arrays of randomness – and arranged to have it delivered after the children got in from school, leaving strict instructions that they were to have put it away by the time I got home. I felt slightly guilty about making my poor latch-key children also put the shopping away after a tough day at school, but then I reminded myself that a) the fridge stuff would all be warm by the time I finally got home and there was no one else to do it, and b) agonising over making your children put away the Arborio risotto rice and Parmesan was surely a first world problem if ever there was one.

I got in the door to be greeted by Judgy's usual performance of 'Hello, I love you, you are the centre of my world, come and sit down so I can sit on your knee and tell you how much I love you!' for two minutes, before he remembered that I had in fact dared to leave him, and so he hated me and I must be punished, even though I knew he'd had a perfectly lovely day with the fabulous dog sitter, who picks him up in the morning and returns him in the evening and who had sent me a photo at lunchtime of Judgy lolling on her sofa, having thrown all the cushions on the floor (he does this at home as well). He does this every day, though, so I'm no longer distressed by it, as he forgives me as soon as there's a sniff of food.

The house, which had been tidy when I left this morning, looked like a bomb had hit it. A trail of shoes, school bags and coats littered the hall. In the sitting room, plates and glasses festooned every surface, while Jane sprawled on the sofa, staring intently at her phone.

'Hello, darling,' I said loudly.

Jane slowly dragged her eyes up from her phone and grunted something.

'Did the shopping come?'

'Uh huh.'

'And did you put it away?'

'No, that's not my job. That's your job.'

'I can't do everything, Jane. I just … can't. Please help me out here. Meet me halfway?'

'If you didn't want to do everything yourself, you should have stayed with Dad then, shouldn't you?' snapped Jane. '*Then* you'd have had someone to help!'

I gave up and went through to the kitchen. The shopping was all over the floor. Jane followed me through.

'*And* you had it delivered in bags!' she said accusingly. 'I mean, don't worry about *us*, Mother! It's not like we *want* a planet to live on in the future or anything.'

'Oh shit,' I said. 'I must've ticked the wrong box. I'll reuse them or take them to be recycled, it'll be fine.'

Jane snorted again.

Peter meanwhile was standing there disconsolately, surrounded by the shopping.

'When's dinner?' he said. 'I'm SO hungry, Mum, and there's *no food*.'

'Dinner will be about half an hour,' I said. 'Peter, there's literally food *all around* you, because neither of you have bothered your arse to put the shopping away.'

'I *did* put it away,' protested Peter. 'I put the fridge stuff away, and then I didn't know where anything else went.'

I opened the fridge. He had indeed 'put the fridge stuff away', if you could call cramming everything in randomly 'putting it away'. There was a block of Cheddar at the front with teeth marks in it.

'Who did this?' I demanded.

Peter shrugged. 'I *told* you I was hungry,' he said.

'Right,' I said furiously. 'There will be no dinner until all this shopping is put away. ALL of it. Work out where it goes, it's not rocket science. I, meanwhile, am going to have a glass of wine and FIVE MINUTES' PEACE, while you BOTH put it away – do not even think about bleating about gender stereotypes or the FUCKING PATRIARCHY at me, Jane, and Peter, PUT IT AWAY AND DO NOT EAT IT. You *can* go fifteen minutes without eating something.'

I poured myself a large glass of wine and stomped out to talk to my chatty chickens, followed by Judgy Dog, who wasn't going to let a little thing like being in a sulk with me mean I could be let out of his sight, especially not to betray him with the chickens. I also suspected him of harbouring hopes of getting into the chicken house and being a winner, winner with a chicken dinner. I've already had stern words with him about how I'd struggle to love him so much if he ate the Speckled Sussexes, even though so far they've not laid a single egg. I expect they're still settling in.

The chickens looked at me balefully in response to my cheery greeting. So far they've proved distinctly unchatty. I can't help but wonder if they've taken against me because of their names? They also refuse to look Instagrammable every time I try to take a picture of them. Instead, as soon as I get my phone out, they hunch into themselves and huddle pathetically and do an excellent impression of an RSPCA advert, despite their extremely pampered life. Luckily Jane does seem to like them, and even deigns to feed them, so there's that. I'm starting to wonder if buying expensive chickens was a mistake, and I should have got some rescue battery hens, who might at least have been grateful for their new home and not looked at me quite so nastily. Maybe I should get some rescue hens too? I fear the Speckled Sussexes might bully them, though.

'What do you think? Would you like some friends?' I asked the chickens. They glared at me. Oxo gave a disgusted squawk. I assumed that was a no.

I gave up trying to converse with them and drank my wine, while reflecting that at least Peter *tries* to help, even if his attempts are more of a hindrance, while I fretted that perhaps his efforts are due to some misplaced idea that he has to be the man of the house, which will go down badly with Jane and her views on the patriarchy if he tries to tell her what to do. Jane has recently become very vocal on the subject of the Oppression of the Patriarchy, although as far as I can see, rather than trying to overthrow it and bring about an equal and fair society, she mostly uses it as an excuse not to lift a finger, and to tell me why I'm wrong about everything, because obviously I've no idea whatsoever what it's like to live in a patriarchal society like she does.

My wine finished, I gave up trying to work out the tangled thought processes of my teenage children, shut the chickens in their house for the night (Judgy would never forgive me if I allowed a dastardly fox to enjoy *his* chicken dinner) and went back inside. Somehow, there seemed to be even more groceries scattered about the kitchen, and the children were opening and closing cupboards in a hopeless fashion, as if the shopping would somehow magically transport itself into its rightful homes.

I sighed again and went through to the sitting room. I removed a banana skin and an apple core from the sofa (at least they're eating fruit, I tried to console myself) and flumped down to enjoy five minutes' peace before trying to do something creative with pasta. Again. I do wonder what our grandmothers and their forebears fed their children on before pasta came to this country. Potatoes? But really, is there anything as useful and versatile as pasta? Another wonderful thing about getting divorced is that we can eat pasta almost every night. Simon did not consider pasta a 'proper dinner'. Simon thought a 'proper dinner' had to contain potatoes. Apart from lasagne. He'd allow lasagne to be a 'proper dinner', even though there were no potatoes. Sometimes I think I must've been a paragon of patience to have put up with Simon's foibles for so long …

Jane burst into the room to demand I tell her where the pesto went. I suggested maybe the cupboard with all the other jars and tins. She asked which cupboard that was. I told her to go and look. Peter came in and asked if the bread went in the fridge. I suggested that perhaps the bread bin might be a better idea. Peter then asked if the rice should also go in the bread bin. I forced myself to take deep breaths and let them get on with it, rather than giving in and going to do it for them, which I suspected was what they were hoping would happen if they could prove themselves sufficiently useless. 'They have to learn some time,' I reminded myself.

My phone binged with a text. Simon. What did he want? Maybe he was going to admit my Felicity Kendal photos on Instagram had made him realise he'd made a terrible mistake, at which point I could loftily inform him that he was Too Late and I had Moved On, and he'd be crushed and miserable and live his life pining for me and my sexy dungarees, perhaps sitting alone in the dark in his flat like Miss Havisham.

Or maybe not …

How do you make lasagne? Sx

WTF?

I'm trying to make lasagne. Sx

Why?

I fancied it for dinner. I didn't want anything too elaborate, just something easy and tasty, so I thought lasagne! How do I make it? Sx

Google a recipe.

I did, they're all really complicated. You have to make two sauces and then bake it and it will take ages, I cba with that, I just want something simple, so how do you make it? x

Like the recipes. A bolognaise and a béchamel and then you layer it all with cheese and bake it. It DOES take ages, and it's NOT simple. I've been telling you that for years!

I thought you had a really easy way of doing it though, and the recipes online were just being too difficult?

No. Lasagne is a fucking bitch to make, why do you think I ALWAYS BLOODY MOANED EVERY TIME YOU WANTED IT?

I thought you were just overreacting.

Fuck off Simon.

But what am I going to have for dinner then?

Not my problem.

Can't you suggest something easy?

Pesto pasta.

But I don't fancy that. I want something nice.

Order a takeaway, go to a restaurant, buy a ready meal.

But I've been away for a week, I'm sick of processed crap and hotel meals, I just want something nice and homecooked.

Then cook yourself something.

But what?

Not my circus, not my monkey!

Why are you being like this?

Because I DON'T CARE WHAT YOU HAVE FOR BLOODY DINNER! BECAUSE WE'RE GETTING DIVORCED! WHAT PART OF THAT DO YOU NOT GRASP?

I was just asking for a bit of help, there's no need to be like that!

Fuck off Simon.

You're so unreasonable.

You're a twat.

See what I mean?

I'm not discussing this anymore, I need to go and make your children's dinner.

What are you having?

Lasagne.

Really?

Yep. There's loads too, I'll probably have to put some in the freezer.

Can I come round?

No.

Peter and Jane reappeared looking virtuous.

'We've put everything away!' they said.

'Thank you,' I said sarcastically. 'I guess I'll go and make dinner now.'

As I searched hopelessly round the kitchen, trying to make pesto pasta, unable to find *anything* after the children's attempts at putting the shopping away, I could hear my phone binging in the sitting room, no doubt with more plaintive texts from Simon.

I'd been pleased with my lasagne taunt (not pleased enough to actually make actual lasagne, obviously, but still – one must take satisfaction in such small victories where one can). And Simon, like his children, has to learn. Though if he learns to make lasagne, I'll be most impressed!

Friday, 27 April

I was minding my own business this evening and rearranging the paintings yet again to try to hide the damp patches, which seem to be spreading, or at least moving around. I did google how to get rid of damp, but the results all looked very messy and expensive, so I'm sticking to my cunning plan of shifting the furniture when necessary. I'd just finished, and was about to sit down, when a little mouse ran out from under the sofa.

It was only a very little mouse, but my reaction was similar to the lady in *Tom and Jerry* cartoons when Jerry would hove into sight and she'd leap on a chair and start screaming 'THOOOOOOMAAAAAS!', only in my case I leapt on the sofa and starting screaming 'JUUUUDGY!', naively assuming that the Proud and Noble Border Terrier might want to earn his keep for once by disposing of the mouse for me.

Judgy, who is normally possessed of deeply murderous tendencies towards all living things, opened one eye, stretched languorously and informed me that he clocks off from murdering once the fire is lit in the evenings, and so no, he wouldn't be getting off the sofa and going to deal with the mouse.

'You bloody useless dog!' I shouted, and dragged him off the sofa, hissing, 'Rats, boy, RATS' at him. He perked up slightly, but then I made the mistake of moving the sofa to try to find the mouse, which had scuttled back under it when I started leaping about and screeching.

Judgy, who frankly is all mouth and no trousers, is scared of furniture being moved, and so he turned tail and fled as I chased him, yelling at him to come back.

Peter, astonishingly, heard the commotion and came downstairs to see what was going on.

'A mouse! Under there, under there! Judgy is no use!' I gibbered.

Peter sighed.

'Traps,' I cried. 'We need traps. And cheese. Maybe there are traps in the shed. I'll go and look. Maybe I can get them with Amazon Prime.'

'You don't need traps, Mum, that's cruel,' said Peter.

'I don't need mice in my house either.'

'It's one little field mouse,' said Peter, who had pulled the sofa out and was looking at the mouse. 'It's sweet, Mum. Can I keep it?'

'No! You can't keep the bloody mouse. Anyway, it probably has a family waiting for it to come home.'

'You didn't care about that when you were shouting about traps,' said Peter reproachfully, as he picked it up and took it outside.

I went to find Judgy, and found him sitting in Peter's bed, as all the other bedroom doors were closed.

'You know, Mum, a psychologist would probably have a field day with the way your dog thinks he's a person and your children end up doing the dog's job,' said Peter.

'Shhh,' I said. 'Don't let Judgy hear you saying he only *thinks* he's a person. He will be upset.'

Oh God. I'm sure Felicity Kendal never had these problems. But then again, she never actually went Proper Country, did she? She just stayed in Surbiton and annoyed Margot.

MAY

Friday, 4 May

Peter spent most of the day intoning 'May the Fourth be with you,' and laughing hysterically at his own wit, before then trying to engage me in long and tedious conversations about how he thought the CGI effects in *The Last Jedi* were not, in his opinion, up to scratch. But never mind that, because I went Out Out with Hannah and Sam and Colin. I feel like these days being Out Out shouldn't be such a big deal, as we no longer need to organise childcare, or tuck precious moppets into bed before we go or be wracked with guilt because we refused a plaintive request for 'Just *one* more story, Mummy, *please!*' because we were already late, but I still get very over-excited by going out. Partly it's because the weekends actually seem very long when the children aren't here, and partly it's because of all those years when it would take weeks to actually marshal everyone together and be able to go out at the same time. Maybe the novelty will never wear off, even though I'm now simply able to announce, 'Darlings, I'm popping out for a drink tonight. Try not to kill each other, and there's pizza in the fridge, so also please try not to burn the house down when you cook it.'

Well, I *say* I can just announce I'm going out, but in reality, either the children have to be at Simon's or I have to embark on a lengthy negotiation with Jane about her requirements for my taxi services. After all the years of ferrying the children to middle-class extracurricular activities, I rather naively thought that by this stage my taxi duties would be over. Little did I know that they were only just beginning! Tonight, however, they were at Simon's, although Jane had smugly informed me that he was letting her stay out at a party until 2.30 am. I wonder if he knows about her boyfriend, the mysterious Harryx (yes, I know it's just straightforward Harry, but I can't stop thinking of him as Harryx). Obviously I can't ask Simon if she's blocked him too, because then I'll have to admit that she's blocked me and I can only nosy at what she's doing by stalking her through Peter's account.

We spent the first hour grumbling about our respective offspring – the Smells, the attitude, the back-chat, the general useless ineptitude of them all.

'Emily's make-up!' spluttered Hannah. 'The *price* of it! Remember when we were her age, Ellen. We were lucky if we had a bit of No 17 – and some Rimmel, if we were feeling flush. The entire contents of my make-up bag can't have cost more than about a tenner. Having said that, the entire contents of my make-up bag *now* probably don't cost much more than a tenner. But not Emily. Oh no. FML! It's all MAC and Benefit and Urban fecking Decay. I had ONE make-up brush. She has about fifty! And, oh my God, the eyebrows. Pencils and powders and brushing things on, and dabbing other things and afterwards, *they still just look like ordinary fucking eyebrows*!'

'And what about the contouring?' I chimed in. 'The time they spend on that, and all the muck they're smothering their lovely skin with, no wonder they have spots, and to what end? They look *exactly* the same afterwards, only slightly more orangey. They're far too young to need to cover their faces with all that crap.'

'Oh God,' said Hannah.

'What?' I said.

'You do realise what's happened, don't you?' she whimpered. 'Just listen to us. We're turning *into our mothers*!'

'Oh no!' I wailed. 'How? How has this happened? As if it isn't bad enough that sometimes I have my phone on selfie mode and glance down and wonder why my mother is staring out at me. But I swore I'd not turn into her, and I *have*. I'm a bitter, grumbling divorcee with two teenage children, just like she was, and now I'll have to get re-married to someone like Geoffrey and become the Queen of the Tennis Club, and take over the Parish Council and torment the vicar about the church flowers and join the Conservative Party.'

'Nooooo!' moaned Hannah. 'How? How? We're supposed to be hip and cool and with it, our generation isn't *supposed* to get old and turn into our parents. I eat *tofu*, for fuck's sake.'

'I'm not sure tofu is a guarantee of eternal youth, you know,' put in Colin.

'It's all right for you, Hannah,' I groaned. 'At least your mother is a nice person to turn into. Mine is a stone-cold bitch, though I suppose you'd probably have to be to put up with my stepfather Geoffrey!'

'Even so,' wailed Hannah. 'I look at Emily and Jane and Sophie, and I think *how* am I not fifteen anymore? How have I become this middle-aged woman?'

'No! We're not middle aged,' I insisted. 'It's not possible. We're still friends. We're still irresponsible and irreverent – we don't sit about discussing politics and the economy. And yet apparently we're grown-ups and are turning into our mothers, when I feel like inside we should still be snogging boys with curtain haircuts!'

'Well, you *could*, Ellen,' Colin pointed out.

'No,' I said gloomily. 'You can't just snog randoms when you're in your forties. I mean, where would you even find someone to snog? We don't go to the sort of parties where you drink too much cider and just snog the face off the first passer-by!'

'Oh God, bloody cider,' Hannah chipped in. 'Every week I have the same moral argument with myself – am I a liberal and open-minded mother by letting Emily take some cider to the parties, showing that there's no great mystery to booze and stopping it being a taboo subject so she doesn't get herself rat-arsed on vodka instead, to see what all the fuss is about, or am I in fact a terrible mother for enabling underage substance abuse and when she's on *Jeremy Kyle* hitting the other guests with the chairs, it will all be my fault?'

'I know!' said Sam. 'I don't want Sophie to be the odd one out, if all the others are drinking, and I try to tell myself that a couple of cans of Kopparberg are not going to set her on a direct path to the Priory, and actually I was doing far worse at her age. But I still worry I'm doing the wrong thing.'

'I think that's part of the problem,' I agreed. 'We were doing SO much worse at their age, that we know exactly how badly behaved teenagers can be if they put their minds to it. I miss my misspent youth, though. It's so dullsville being a grown-up.'

'We all feel like that,' said Colin. 'We all feel like we should still be going to raves and dancing all night, only we fall asleep at 10.30 pm and have twinges from our lumbago.'

'No,' sighed Hannah. 'It's different for men. You don't age like women. You just go a bit grey and saggy and even then people say things like, "Ooh, he's a bit of a silver fox" instead of "She's let herself go, hasn't she?" And that's about it! Whereas *we* have the joys of the menopause to endure, as if periods hadn't been enough fun for thirty odd fucking years! Not to mention child-birth …'

'Oh God,' I mumbled. 'Maybe I *should* take Colin and Sam's advice, and get back in the dating game. Maybe I should do it *now*, before I totally turn into my mother and the only hope of companionship in my dotage is a Geoffrey Mk II, and I'm a dried-up hag for whom love and passion are merely a forgotten passing whim.'

'OOOOH, REALLY?' said Colin and Sam in unison.

'Oh, why not!' I groaned. 'I suspect Simon already has. He's now posted several photos on Instagram of two drinks, so he's *clearly* having wild unrestrained sex with a perky bombshell who probably knows positions that weren't even *invented* when we were reading about the Position of the Fortnight in *More*.'

'Simon's *dating*?' said Hannah. 'Has he no shame?'

'I'm not sure a photo of two drinks is conclusive evidence that he's shagging anything that moves,' said Sam.

'There was more than one, and in one of the photos, one of the drinks is a Cosmo. What more evidence do you need?' I said.

'How many photos altogether?' said Colin.

'Well, two,' I admitted. 'I might have had a bijou stalk again last night. How many do you want? I'd rather hoped he might at least have the decency to pine over me a bit, but apparently not. So sod it! I might as well have one last hurrah before everything sags and crumbles even more than it already has. As it is, the children keep making pointed references to memory loss and confusion being menopausal symptoms. I don't mind that so much, but their little barbs about "bloating" really sting.'

'Mine do too,' said Hannah. 'I think I'm teetering on the brink though – I've *stopped*.'

'OMG, have you really? That is one benefit, I suppose.'

'Stopped what?' said Colin in confusion.

'Smoking? Doing magic mushrooms? Hammer time?' suggested Sam.

'No, *periods*!' I said scathingly. 'Stopping is the one trade-off for the night sweats, hot flushes and other general miseries of menopause, though you're lucky, Hannah. I read somewhere that quite often you don't *just* stop, first you have months or years of total bloodbaths until they finally fuck off for good! How do you feel about it?'

'Fine, actually,' said Hannah. 'It's only been a couple of months, so I suppose they might not definitely be over, but I can't say I miss them.'

'You don't feel like you're drying up and withering then?' I enquired.

'God no! And apart from the children's remarks about bloating, I haven't had any other horrors yet,' said Hannah smugly.

'Of course, maybe you're not going through the change at all. Maybe you're knocked up,' said Colin idly.

Hannah choked on her mouthful of Sauv Blanc. 'Don't be ridiculous. Of course I'm not pregnant. Why would you think that?'

'Periods stopped, people saying you look a bit bloated … Darling, I know *very* little about the female anatomy, but even I can put two and two together and realise it might be a possibility. Apparently it's very common. Loads of women think they're menopausal, but actually they're up the duff.'

'But I'm forty-five,' whispered Hannah in horror. 'I'm too old.'

'Cherie Blair was forty-five when she had her last baby,' put in Sam helpfully.

'Yes, but she had *staff*. I *can't be pregnant*. I just can't. Emily is fifteen – if I have a baby now, everyone will spend its whole life assuming Emily is really its mum and I'm just bringing it up for her.'

'I don't think people do that anymore,' I said.

'They *do*,' insisted Hannah. 'Remember on *EastEnders* when Kat Slater turned out to be Zoe's mum, not her sister?'

'Yes, but even that storyline was *years* ago,' said Colin. 'I really don't think people will assume Emily is a Fallen Woman if you have a baby now.'

'Has Charlie ever said anything about babies?' I asked.

'We decided we were too OLD to start all that nonsense again,' said Hannah in a panicky voice. 'We *are* too old. You're all being ridiculous. Of course I'm not pregnant. The very idea!'

To confirm that our suggestion was beyond the realms of possibility, Hannah defiantly downed the rest of her glass of wine.

'Do you have any fags?' she demanded.

'Hannah, you've only tried to smoke once in your life. When *you* were fifteen. And you were sick. If you say you aren't pregnant, that's fine, we believe you. You don't have to prove it,' I reasoned.

'Of course, you could always make sure,' said Sam.

'How?' said Hannah.

'Well, just go and do a test.'

'What, now?'

'Yes!'

'HOW?' said Hannah. 'Pregnancy tests aren't the sort of thing we carry around with us, just in case, you know, like tampons.'

'Oh!' said Sam in disappointment. 'I sort of thought they were.'

'WHY?' I said.

'I dunno?' he shrugged.

'There's a late-night chemist down the street, though …' suggested Colin.

'NO!' said Hannah. 'I don't need a pregnancy test, because I'm *not pregnant*!'

'Just to put your mind at rest?' soothed Colin.

'I don't need my mind put at rest, because I'm not pregnant,' insisted Hannah, pouring another glass of wine and taking a hefty slug. 'But if it will stop you all going on about me being pregnant, then fine. I'll piss on a stick and prove it to you. But you can bloody well go and buy it,' she added to Colin, 'since it was your idea and they're jolly expensive and I'm quite happy sitting here drinking wine and *not being pregnant*!'

Colin was out of his seat and off down the street before you could say 'unplanned pregnancy', racing back a couple of minutes later proudly brandishing his booty.

'I got a two-pack,' he announced. 'So you can really make sure.'

'Put it away,' hissed Hannah.

'Go and do it,' said Colin.

'I don't need a wee yet,' said Hannah.

'I'll get you a glass of water,' said Sam.

'I don't *want* a glass of water. I'm quite happy with my wine,' snapped Hannah.

'But wine isn't good for the baby,' said Colin.

'For the last time, there's no baby, I'm not preggers, I'm only even doing this damn test to shut the pair of you up. Women *know* when they're pregnant, don't they Ellen?'

'Err, well, sometimes?' I ventured.

'I *would* know,' insisted Hannah. 'I've been pregnant twice before, you know. There are *signs* and *symptoms* long before you need to confirm things with a test. You get tired, your boobs get sore, you just feel different. I go off booze. Can't even stomach the smell of wine. So *clearly* you are all just a bunch of drama queens, because I think I know my own body, thank you very much! Mmmm, lovely wine.'

'I got the one that detects from the earliest opportunity,' said Colin.

'Oh FFS! Right, I'll go and squeeze out a piss, just to get some peace. Come on, Ellen. You can be my witness, because God knows, I'm not dragging my pissy stick through the pub to prove to everyone that I'm not in the family way!'

Hannah chuntered off to the loos, with me trailing in her wake. I nipped in for a wee while I was there too, because two children and not getting any younger. Hannah huffed and puffed in the cubicle next to me. Words like 'Ridiculous!' and 'Obsessed' and 'The very idea!' floated over the dividing wall as she did the necessaries. Then a resounding silence. Followed by a horrified howl.

'FML!'

'Oh no!'

'It's the two lines. That's the preggers one, isn't it?'

'Yep. Do the other one. Maybe it's wrong.'

'Oh fuck, oh fuck, oh fuck. I don't think I've any wee left.'

'Try, Hannah! Just try! Just squeeze a few drops out, that's all you need.'

'I AM TRYING! Oh Jesus, all those pelvic floor exercises and trying not to piss myself and now when I really need to I CAN'T FUCKING PISS! Hang on … I think something's coming. Oh God, I hope that's enough …'

We sat for the next three minutes, holding our breath, biting our nails. I wondered if I should be in the cubicle with Hannah, but they don't really build them for multiple occupancy.

The next wail, when it came, was even more anguished. 'Two lines again!' sobbed Hannah, flinging open the door and collapsing into my arms. 'What am I going to do? All that wine. What if I've pickled it? What's Charlie going to say? What am I going to do, Ellen? I don't *want* another baby. I don't want to go back to those days. But it's Emily and Lucas's brother or sister. I can't imagine life without them. But how can I go back to the beginning yet again?'

All I could really do was keep hugging her and assuring her that it would be OK, that I'd be there for her *whatever* happened and *whatever* she decided, that I'd always be her best friend and I'd always have her back, but that she needed to talk to Charlie too. I rubbed her back and made soothing noises, just like when New Kids on the Block split up, and reminded her to breathe, please, and that there had so far been nothing so bad in our lives that we hadn't got through it together, that men had come and gone, our children had tormented us, PND had tried to suck us under, but we'd always have each other and so we could deal with anything that life threw at us. Even as I reassured her, though, there was a little part of me that was hugely relieved that it wasn't me.

Hannah finally managed to take a deep breath, sniffed a few more times and gulped, 'I think I need to go home now.'

'Come on. I'll get us an Uber and take you home.'

'No. Thank you. I think I could do with ten minutes on my own to get a grip of myself, and then I think I should probably tell Charlie by myself. It's going to be weird enough crashing in half cut from the pub and explaining how the fuck I found out I was pregnant tonight without having you there too.'

'Let alone Colin and Sam!'

'Oh shit. Colin and Sam. I can't face them. I can't actually imagine saying the words out loud yet, even to Charlie, let alone anyone else. Anyway, Charlie should really be the first to know, before I tell anyone else. I mean, you don't count. You're my oldest friend and I told you about the other two babies before I told anyone else too, including Dan, or my mum. Oh Christ. What will my mother say?'

'She'll be fine,' I assured her. 'She'll support you whatever you decide. Do you want me to come with you to get a taxi or something?'

'No, it's fine, I'll get an Uber myself. I need time to think first anyway, on my own. I've got my bag here and I didn't have a coat. I'm just going to go. Say goodbye to the boys for me, yeah?'

'I think they might guess what has happened, you know?' I warned her. 'The length of time we've been in here and your sudden disappearance might give the game away.'

'You're probably right,' she agreed. 'But I still can't face seeing anyone or saying the words yet. Not till I've told Charlie and seen how he reacts.'

'Charlie loves you,' I reminded her. 'Charlie isn't Dan the Shitty Streak of Weasel Piss. You'll be OK.'

'Will I? Oh Jesus. This was *not* how I was expecting tonight to finish, you know. OK, I'm going to go now. I'll call you tomorrow.'

'Call me tonight if you need me. Anytime. Seriously. Love you.'

'I love you too. Thank fuck I've got you.'

'You've got loads of people who love you,' I reminded her. 'Don't forget that.'

I waved Hannah off and made my way back to Sam and Colin, suddenly feeling very sober.

'Shit!' they said, when they saw my face and that I was alone.

'Shit indeed!' I said. 'She's gone home to tell Charlie. All the magazines tell us how our forties are meant to be these amazing years, but actually, we've still got all the teenage problems to deal with via our own kids, and we're still of child-bearing age, if only just and –'

A horrible thought suddenly occurred to me.

'Oh my God, what if Simon impregnates Cosmo Girl and starts another family, and I have to buy them Christmas presents and all that? That would be so *weird*! I *knew* I should have made him have the snip, but he was always too selfish, whinging that he wasn't having anyone cutting *his* bits open. And now he shall go forth and sow his seed and neglect his existing children, and I shall be left to wither, and deal with the fallout *yet again*!'

'I think you're jumping a bit ahead of things there?' said Sam.

I shook my head sadly 'No. We're all doomed. I'm *so* over middle age, I almost just want to fast forward to being so old that you can be as rude as you like to people and drink sherry in the mornings.'

'You don't like sherry,' said Colin.

'I'll learn to like it,' I said with dignity.

Wednesday, 16 May

Well, the main news is that Hannah is definitely having the baby. Charlie is thrilled and delighted to be about to become a daddy and has wrapped her in cotton wool, which is a very different experience to her first marriage, when Dan (TSSOWP) liked to frequently remind her that pregnancy wasn't an illness and millions of women had been having babies every single day for millions of years, so there was no reason why she couldn't just get on with things as normal. Charlie meanwhile wants Hannah to give up work, spend her time 'resting' and get a cleaner.

'He keeps trying to make me drink milk,' she grumbled. 'I'm not six. It's lovely that he's so excited and caring and wants to look after me, but FML, Ellen, it's also quite annoying. I've got seven more months of this to go.'

Charlie's reaction to the baby gave me the courage to give Colin the go-ahead to set me up an internet dating account, because maybe I'd meet someone lovely like Charlie. Only without the baby bit, obviously, and I'd prefer to find someone who encouraged me to drink wine rather than milk.

Colin texted his description of me, claiming I was into art galleries, theatre, country walks and fine wines. I suggested that this was stretching it a bit, but he texted back to loftily inform me that dating profiles were like CVs and everyone lied.

So how do you know who's worth dating, if they all lie?

You find someone whose hobbies you like the sound of and assume that's the sort of thing they'd like to be doing if they weren't glued to their sofa watching box sets on Netflix. Now send me some photos.

These ones are nice?

WTF, Ellen. What are you wearing?

Dungarees. I was trying to look like Felicity Kendal in *The Good Life*. Didn't you see them on Instagram?

No. I would have told you to take them down. Take some more.

Don't you look at my Instagram? What about this one?

You look constipated. Also, try taking it from slightly above.

How about this?

Not that far above, you look like you're peering out of a hole!

After much toing and froing, I managed to take a selfie that Colin approved of. He wouldn't let me have Judgy in the photo.

Unfortunately, Peter and Jane came in while I was trying to take a photo and were appalled by the entire idea.

'Oh. My. God. Mother, have you learnt nothing from Hannah?' demanded Jane. 'It's bad enough for poor Emily, that her mum might as well be walking round with a big sign saying "Still Shagging!", but imagine if *you* got pregnant? The SHAME for me! You're not even married! How would I live down my mother getting herself impregnated on a one-night stand?'

'Jane, you call yourself a feminist, so I thought you'd be all for women's sexual liberation. Shouldn't you be pleased that if I so desired I could simply use a man for sex and if I got pregnant (which I WON'T. In the event of anything like that happening, I'd take ALL the precautions), you should be glad we live in a society in which a woman can raise a baby without needing a man?'

'I AM in favour of women owning their sexuality,' said Jane. 'Just not you! You're my mother. It's different. And actually, I can't even talk about this anymore; it's too disgusting for words.'

Peter's reaction was slightly different. 'If you want a man, Mum, couldn't you just get back with Dad?' he said sadly. 'I'm sure he misses you, Mum. And I miss him living with us. Why go to all that trouble, when you've already got a perfectly good man who loves you? I don't want a new dad, I just want us to be a family again.'

I doubt Simon misses me. He seems to be hiding it well if he does (margaritas last weekend), but more important than Simon's Instagram were my feelings of oh shit, oh shit, oh shit, oh shit at Peter's other comments.

'Peter, sweetheart, no one is ever going to take your dad's place. He will always be your dad, and I'll always love him because he's your dad. But we can't live together any more, we don't love each other like that. You know that, darling. But it doesn't mean we don't love you more than anything in the world.'

'Yeah, I know. Just … it'd be nice, that's all.'

'I know. But, darling, it's not going to happen. I'm sorry. Would … would you like a hug?'

To my astonishment, Peter said, 'Actually, yeah. Mum?'

'Yes, sweetie?'

'If you get a new man, and he's a complete tosser and we hate him, can we tell you and will you promise to dump him?'

'Of course. You're the most important thing.'

'OK. Is there anything to eat?'

I was so grateful to have been granted physical contact with one of my children that I happily turned Peter loose to inhale the contents of the kitchen – but I rather regretted this later when I looked at the ravaged fridge and tried to find enough food to construct a meal from out of the crumbs he'd left behind.

This is the tightrope we walk with divorce, though. Are we putting our own happiness above that of our children? Should we put up, shut up, live in misery, so they can have a 'proper' family? What even *is* a proper family anymore? Does such a thing exist? There are so many blended families, step-siblings and parents, families like Sam's with two daddies or two mummies, single-parent families, children being raised by grandparents, so is there even still a 'normal' to really adhere to? Even by the time the children left primary school, at least half the parents in the class had divorced – some more dramatically than others, obviously. And if you do stay together 'for the sake of the children', when can you deem them old enough to separate? When do you put yourself first? Do you end up like the couple in the old joke aged ninety-eight who went to a divorce lawyer, and when asked why they were getting divorced at their age, replied, 'We were waiting for the children to die first.'

At what point does your own unhappiness with a miserable marriage, with a partner you at best do not love and at worst is abusive, spill over into affecting your children, so that in fact they're better off if you split up? I could make the argument that *my* parents were divorced and it never did me any harm, and certainly my mother's rage and bitterness over my father's infidelities were such that she might well have actually murdered him if they had stayed together, but I don't think she was any happier for throwing him out. But then again, my mother is a strange woman and I'm still not entirely sure what *does* make her happy, apart from looking down her nose at other people, so she's probably not the best example.

Am *I* happier? I don't know. It's strange, of course, this new single life. Certainly, I'm happier than I was at the end of my marriage, when I howled on that park bench, although that wouldn't really be hard. But is that enough? Can I live with myself, if my happiness has been bought at the expense of my children's? All I've ever tried to do is do what was best for them, yet maybe I should have done more? Simon and I are having a very civil and amicable divorce (by the standards of divorce), we try to put the children first, we didn't have petty fights about who got the *Best of Blondie* CD (I did, obviously), and we do our best to be polite to each other in front of the children. I know lots of people have far worse experiences, ex-husbands withholding maintenance, ex-wives withholding access to the children (and vice versa on both counts), locks changed, accusations and counter-accusations, and lengthy court battles. I was even slightly smug we'd managed to avoid all that, but in the end maybe our children will still be damaged and traumatised.

If we can manage a civilised divorce, maybe we *could* have saved our marriage. Maybe that is what's giving Peter hope; maybe we're not doing better than the people who have hideous, acrimonious divorces; maybe their children see that there's no way their parents could live together, but because we've insisted on drawing a polite British curtain over the more sordid aspects of our split, our children think that there's still a chance of a reconciliation. Maybe we should have told them about Miss Madrid, instead of the usual line about Mummy and Daddy not loving each other anymore? But what would have been gained from that? Oh FML. I hate being a grown-up!

Saturday, 26 May

I've been dabbling in the world of online dating for less than two weeks and have come to the conclusion that all the men on these websites are pigs. Actually, that is unkind to pigs. Pigs are actually very intelligent, emotionally aware animals, which is something I try not to think about too much when I'm eating bacon …

Anyway, the men on dating sites! They seem, by and large, to be chauvinistic, sexist, Neanderthal liars who are only interested in a quick shag. I was very excited to get lots of 'waves' on my first day. Several of the men looked really rather interesting, so I accepted their messages. Three of them wanted me to send a photo of my tits. One of them sent a dick pic. And another sent me a 'friendly' message suggesting I leave the section for 'political views' blank (I'd ticked the 'liberal' box) as he just thought he should make me aware that no man was going to be interested in a woman with opinions on politics. And block and block and block and block … One man's profile photo on closer inspection had been taken at the 2004 Olympics (as a spectator, not a competitor, alas), which meant he probably did not look quite the same as back then – also, if you're going to use an old photo of yourself, I'm going to judge you for being stupid enough to use one that clearly has a banner in the background for Athens 2004!

There was one man who seemed fairly nice and normal. His photo appeared to match the age he claimed and his hobbies did not suggest he might be a serial killer, so we exchanged a series of messages and he didn't say anything along the lines of 'Say what you like, but I don't think Hitler was all bad,' which is always reassuring. We were just starting to get slightly flirty, when he stopped messaging me. Just … stopped. I thought maybe his internet was down or he was busy. I sent him another message the next day saying, 'Hope you're OK, you're very quiet!' (well, he was, given we'd been exchanging about twenty messages a day), but still nothing. He definitely must have lost his phone, I decided, or had to make an emergency trip to Outer Mongolia and couldn't get 4G, until I saw the little 'online now' dot next to his name. I thought maybe he hadn't seen my last messages, so I sent him one just saying, 'Hi, what are you up to?' but still nothing. The bastard had simply cut me off and was ignoring me.

Why? He hadn't even *met* me! I was being flirty and charming and witty, and he'd just fucked off and abandoned me. I didn't even have to *meet* a man to put him off me, it seemed.

I've been assured that this is all fairly standard practice for internet dating, and your prince does not just materialise from the pixels. There are a lot of toads to be waded through first, before you find anyone who looks like they might be even a potential frog, but it's very disheartening. So disheartening, in fact, that I think it's probably not for me.

However, I do have a new male in my life! It's not a rooster. I looked into roosters, and they're noisy and nasty and also quite rapey. Filled with gloom at the prospect of my lonely future, with only the Judgy Gaze of Judgy Dog, the mysterious scrabblings behind the skirting boards and the unchatty chickens (who have given up even their disgruntled squawks and now regard me in sullen silence) to keep me company on long winter nights, I took myself off on a whim to the council cat and dog home to find myself and Judgy a new pal. I had a vague idea about a Staffie, as there are so many of them in shelters, but when I got there, in the very first pen, was the ugliest dog I'd ever seen. His legs were too long, his nose was too short, his ears were too big, his tail was quite bald, and his body was completely the wrong shape for the rest of him. He looked like he'd been made out of the sweepings from the factory floor when all the other dogs were finished.

I stopped and looked at him. He looked back at me. The bald tail gave a tentative twitch, and a glimmer of hope seemed to spark in his eyes, which were the only beautiful thing about him.

'What about this one?' I asked the lady.

'Barry?' she said in surprise. 'He's been here a few weeks. No one ever stops and looks at Barry.'

'Why not? Is there something wrong with him?'

'Well, no, but look at him. He's not going to win any beauty competitions.'

'How old is he?'

'We're not sure, but quite young.'

'And is he fully grown?'

'Oh yes. Definitely. Are you interested? He does have a lovely nature. Really, he's a wonderful dog, I'd recommend him to anyone, but most people are put off by his looks. He hasn't got mange, by the way. That's just his coat.'

I looked at Barry again. He really was the most repulsive-looking dog I'd ever seen in my life.

'What will happen if he isn't rehomed?'

'We try to get another shelter to take them. Assuming they have room and assess the dog as being fit to be rehomed.'

'And if you can't find anywhere?'

'Then eventually we have to destroy them. We have new dogs coming in all the time, and we just can't keep them indefinitely.'

'And how do you rate Barry's chances?'

'Not great.'

'And the Staffies you have?'

'A bit better. More people are hearing what nice dogs they really are, and if no one adopts them from here, they've a chance of being taken by one of the specialist Staffie rescue charities. But poor old Barry is a proper old Heinz 57, so the breed charities won't take him. We'll just have to hope that one of the other shelters can, because I don't think anyone is going to fall for his matinee idol looks.'

'I'll have him,' I announced. 'He's not that ugly. And he looks like he has a kind heart.'

'Oh he does, he does,' the rescue lady assured me, as she opened the cage and led Barry out. 'Come and get to know him a bit, and we'll see how we get on.'

The council shelter, under pressure to take in too many stray dogs, were not as stringent in their checks as some of the charity dog rescues, and were just glad of someone willing to take a dog off their hands, and so it was that today I went and picked up Barry and brought him home.

Judgy was unimpressed. He did his best indignant snorting at Barry, who cringed behind me, making 'Please love me' faces while Judgy glared at me, as if to say 'I AM YOUR BABY, WHO IS THIS INTERLOPER?' before stomping off to take up residence on the sofa to make it clear who the soft furnishings in the house belonged to.

Jane looked at him and said, '*What* have you done now, Mother?'

'I've got another dog, obviously.'

'Are you *sure* he's a dog?' said Jane doubtfully. 'I've never seen a dog that looks like that.'

'He's really weird looking,' said Peter.

'You shouldn't judge on looks,' I said sternly.

'What will Dad say?' said Peter. 'He always said you weren't allowed to get another dog.'

'It's nothing to do with him. This is my house, and I'll have as many bloody dogs as I like!'

Peter mumbled something about cheese and sloped off in the direction of the kitchen.

Barry did his tail twitch at Jane, who continued to look at him with suspicion.

Barry twitched his tail again and looked up imploringly at Jane. Jane recoiled.

'Are you sure he's even a dog?' she said in disgust.

'Well, I'm *fairly* sure … although the evidence is dubious,' I admitted.

Barry edged closer to Jane and made a strange noise in the back of his throat, somewhere between a whimper and a grunt.

'Why's he making that noise?' she demanded.

'I think he's saying, "Please won't you like me, just a little bit? I mean very well,"' I suggested hopefully.

Jane peered at him again.

'He does have nice eyes,' she admitted.

Barry, sensing weakness, shuffled closer still to Jane and made his little imploring noise again. Jane reluctantly patted him, and Barry shuddered in ecstasy.

'He's never been loved,' I said sadly, 'never had cuddles on a sofa or known what it is to be warm and safe.'

'Oh all right, Mum,' said Jane. 'You can stop with the emotional blackmail now. I suppose he's not that ugly.' She bent down and scratched Barry's ears, and he collapsed to the floor with joy at the sensation and rolled over. Jane rubbed his tummy. 'Ooo's a good boy, den?' she crooned. Barry grinned up at her in bliss. 'Oh Mum, look, he's smiling. Doesn't he have a lovely smile?'

He did have a lovely smile. 'Is best boy?' beamed Jane. 'Is MY best boy? Oo IS, isn't oo? Is I silly for thinking you wasn't the most beautifullest boy? Is I? I IS! Does I wuv oo? Does I? I DOES!'

I relaxed. Barry had at least one ally in the house apart from me. It turned out it was just as well Jane had fallen in love with him, because Judgy made it clear he was going to bully Barry mercilessly, even though Barry was considerably larger than him, and the chickens, when I tentatively introduced him to them, were disapproving and squawked at him, which made him belt back inside with his tail between his legs. Later on, I couldn't find Barry anywhere, and was slightly afraid that between Judgy and the chickens he'd been made to feel so unwelcome that he'd run away, until I tracked him down to Jane's room, where he was sprawled on her bed, all four paws in the air, beaming away.

'I've blocked Milly Armstrong,' Jane informed me indignantly.

'Really?' I said, unsure I had the strength to deal with another round of teenage girl angst.

'Yes! I Snapchatted her a photo of Barry and she said he was the ugliest dog she'd ever seen – can you imagine? I'll not have anyone insulting Barry, and so she had to go. By the way, Mum, Barry's sleeping in here tonight, OK?'

So it seems I've not got myself another dog. I've got Jane a dog. On the other hand, seeing how happy she and Barry are together, I can hardly begrudge them it. I'm just waiting to see what Peter fleeces me for, since I'll undoubtedly be accused any minute now of loving Jane more because I got her a dog, and so what am I going to get him?

Wednesday, 30 May

At best, today could be described as a … mixed day. On the plus side, there's a new man at work. A HOT man. A hot, straight man, who is of an age that you don't feel like you should be on a register for thinking impure thoughts about him, like I sometimes feel when I'm watching Jack Whitehall on TV … Anyway, least said about my cougar pervings the better. So, his name is Tom, he's the new head of finance (so probably good with money, with actual investments and stuff, not that that is important, I'm just *sayin'*) and he's forty-seven, a Libra, divorced, no kids, hobbies include skiing, watersports (I'm always dubious about people who list their hobbies as watersports, because I fear that they're referring to the *other* sort of watersports, not windsurfing and kayaking, etc. This suspicion has only been confirmed by the number of sleazy-looking men on dating sites who list 'watersports' under their hobbies – I'm 99.9 per cent sure they aren't talking about canoeing!) and hillwalking. I'd be more put off by these numerous outdoorsy hobbies if I hadn't obtained all this information from Debbie in HR. Debbie had gleaned all this from Tom's CV (data protection and GDPR are as nothing to Debbie), and so quite possibly had also told him that according to *my* CV, my hobbies consisted of going to the theatre (last thing I saw was the pantomime. When Jane was ten), swimming (I've my 200m badge, *and* I've been known to enjoy a dip from time to time. On holiday. In one of those pools with a bar you can swim up to and have a cocktail) and hillwalking (I've walked up hills. Usually in towns with pubs at the top, but it still counts), so it's entirely possibly he's as terrifyingly outdoorsy and sporty as me. Debbie, whose dedication to the ancient art of gossip is truly admirable, also breathlessly informed me that he rides a motorbike. Once, this news would have given me a frisson of excitement at the thought of a James Dean-esque bad boy with the spice of danger about him, but now all I could think was that my hips might not be up to getting on a motorbike, and it really probably wasn't very safe. Debbie was quick to assure me that he also drove an Audi (she processes the parking permits), which possibly meant that he was a complete knob, as most Audi drivers of my acquaintance are (Colin takes umbrage whenever I say this and points out that he's an Audi driver, and I have to assure him that he's the exception that proves the rule).

Show-offy wanker or not, he was quite attractive. I might have been a bit OTT in describing him as HOT, but after the horrors of LoveMeDo.com and FindTheOne.com and ShagFest.co.uk (all right, I exaggerated the name of the last one, but it seems to be the worst for guys who are 'looking for fun, but no LTR', which apparently stands for 'Long-Term Relationships' and is a warning sign they're probably married sleazes looking for a bit on the side), anyone with their own teeth who isn't waving their unsolicited cock in my face is going to come across as a bit of a hunk. So maybe he wasn't *hot* hot, but he was nice-looking enough in an average sort of a way. And as a kind gentleman reminded me on my first night browsing LoveMeDo.com – at my age, I can't afford to be picky.

Anyway, we had a brief chat, and he seems a reasonable person – i.e. he managed to conduct an entire conversation without saying anything like 'Of course, I'm not a racist, but …', which is a good start, so assuming Debbie is right about his singleton status, I might start taking a little more care over my appearance in the mornings – nothing too much, of course, just maybe a bit more mascara, and not covering a stain on a (clean!) T-shirt with an artfully draped cardigan that I then can't remove so I spend the day sweating my arse off and wondering if I'm starting the menopause, while Alan and James, my team leaders, ask me if I'm feeling all right because I'm a bit of a funny colour. Of course, perhaps it's all pointless anyway, as Debbie sadly pointed out that I'm a Virgo (it's quite worrying how much Debbie knows about everyone in the building) and apparently they're not compatible with Libras since earth signs and air signs don't get on. But even so, I could definitely envisage a *frisson* with him. And many good Instagram opportunities. Take *that* Simon, with your two beers and your bloody Cosmos!

So that was the good bit of the mixed day. The less good bit was when I got home, to find the usual detritus up the hall, and crumbs smeared over the kitchen, no sign of my children, and a reproachful-looking Judgy, who still hasn't forgiven me for the arrival of Barry, despite the fact that Barry spends all his time glued to Jane when she's at home, and therefore hasn't really impacted much on Judgy's life at all, as he's still *my* Most Precious Baby. I tracked my children down to their fetid lairs and established they were both still alive, and that their days had been 'fine' and that 'nothing' had happened, and that yes, they were hungry (silly question), and went downstairs to pour myself a glass of wine while I made dinner. There wasn't a single glass in the cupboard. Not a wine glass, not a tumbler, not the random pint glasses that everyone has in their cupboards even when they're long past the age of stealing glassware from pubs. Nada. There were also no mugs, and no bowls or plates. Even the children's special Royal Doulton Peter Rabbit and Bunnikins porringers that they were given as babies and had never been used lest they got broken had vanished. There were two possibilities. Either we'd been broken into by a thief with a strange fetish for mismatched crockery or the foul sewer rats who shared my home under the guise of being my children had struck again.

I stormed back up the stairs, ranting about listeria and filth and mould and general rancidness, and flung open their doors in fury. Sure enough, ALL my dishes EVER were strewn around the pits of hell that a few short weeks ago were clean, fresh slates for them to put their own stamp on. Well, they had done that all right. Unfortunately the stamp I'd envisaged had not contained quite so much of their sweat and saliva and worse in the form of the dirty clothes and CRUSTED FUCKING PLATES AND MOULDERING GLASSES!

I berated them at length. I had to tone down the berating to an icy whisper, as raised voices upset Barry and make him quiver with fear, and while I could happily have strung both my precious moppets up by their own grubby underpants, I drew the line at upsetting the dog. Eventually, they staggered downstairs under the weight of EVERY BASTARDING DISH I OWNED (Peter had gone so far as to eat cereal out of a mug in lieu of washing up a bowl, and had tried to make porridge in a jam jar) and dumped them in the kitchen.

'NOOOOO!' I howled, as they attempted to turn tail and slink off again. 'You can bloody well wash them and THEN put them in the dishwasher, on a hotter than Hades cycle to sterilise them and attempt to stop us all getting fucking cholera!'

'Actually, Mum, that's not how you get cholera,' put in Peter. 'It spreads through contaminated water –'

'Well, what the fuck do you call that then?' I demanded, pointing at a slimy glass on the counter.

'No, Mum,' said Peter patiently. 'Someone with cholera needs to contaminate the water with their infected faeces; I didn't shit in the glass.'

'Well, thank God for small mercies,' I snapped. 'Typhoid then. And stop swearing.'

'That spreads the same way,' chimed in Jane helpfully. 'That's why Typhoid Mary killed so many people.'

'Because she shat in the glasses?' I said weakly.

'NO, Mum, because she was a cook, and a typhoid carrier, so she infected the food. And you can't tell us to stop swearing when you're just as bad.'

'Well, anyway, just wash them and then put them in the dish-washer, and you'll have to wait for dinner because we've nothing to eat off, because you're both filthy pig trolls.'

Peter was suggesting just soaking the dishes in the bath and then putting them away would be enough, arguing that the mouldy, sticky, smeary dishes didn't need to be sanitised in the dishwasher at all, and Jane was explaining that we couldn't get Legionnaires' from them either, and even E. coli was unlikely, when my mother rang. It's a rare occasion when taking a phone call from my mother is the lesser of the evils on offer, but this was one of them.

'Ellen, is everything all right?' demanded my mother.

I looked at the chaos surrounding me. 'Yes, Mum, of course, why wouldn't it be?'

'Well, I thought I should ring and check, because usually Jessica rings me on a Tuesday night and she didn't ring last night, and so I wanted to know if everything was all right. Why didn't your sister ring me?'

'I don't know …?' I ventured. 'Maybe you'd be better calling Jessica and asking her?'

'Yes, but I know how busy Jessica is. I don't want to disturb her if she's got a lot on her plate, so I thought I'd phone *you* instead and check. Is everything all right?'

I had by now gathered that by 'everything', my dear mother did not mean everything in *my* life, but rather in the perfectly colour co-ordinated, organised down to a micro-second, 100 per cent Instagrammable world of my sister (except that despite the totally Insta-perfection of her life, Jessica Doesn't Do Social Media, as it's Just a Waste of Time, and she's Far Too Busy and Important).

'I *don't know*,' I protested. 'I haven't heard Jessica *isn't* all right. I'm sure we'd have been told if some disaster had befallen her.'

'Maybe it's something with the children ...' mused Mum. 'She did say last time that Persephone was struggling with taking her A level maths so young. Well, she wasn't struggling with the work, of course, but for some reason none of the other people in her maths class want to talk to her, even when she offered to explain how to find the discriminant of a quadratic polynomial to them, which is ridiculous. You'd think they'd be glad of Persephone's help. And obviously, Gulliver was very upset that he didn't win the Young Poet Laureate competition, and of course, he was robbed really. I think the winner was only chosen because he was from a state school, as part of all this positive-discrimination nonsense. Gulliver's entry was by far the best, so *he* was the one discriminated against.'

'Mum,' I protested, 'you can't say things like that,' while think-ing, 'I mean, don't ask about *me*, Mum, obviously, or *my* chil-dren. It's Jessica and her perfect life that *matters*, after all. It's not like there's anything happened to me recently that you might want to concern yourself with ...'

'Of course I can. I read a very interesting article about that sort of carry on just the other day.'

'Was it by any chance in the *Daily Mail*?' I said weakly.

'Actually, it *was*, darling. It might have been by that lovely Toby Young, I can't remember, but *such* a lot of sense he talks. Did you see it too?' said Mum brightly.

'No, Mum. Just a lucky guess.'

'Anyway, I need you to ring Jessica and make sure she's all right.'

'Why can't you just ring her?' I asked.

'Because I don't want to *bother* her,' Mum said.

'So how will me ringing her not be bothering her?' I said, perplexed as ever by my mother's logic.

'It just will,' said Mum briskly.

'Maybe I could just email her?'

'NO, Ellen, I need you to ring her.'

'But no one rings each other anymore,' I said. 'We text and we email and we WhatsApp and we Messenger and some of us have even mastered the dark arts of Snapchat, but no one actually calls anyone up on the electric telephone anymore just for a chat. The only people anyone I know *actually* phones these days is their parents. By the time Peter and Jane have left home, they probably won't even do that. I'll get a monthly text from their Fitbit or something confirming that they're still alive. They're fine, by the way, thanks for asking.'

'I assumed as much,' said Mum blithely. 'I can hear them shouting at each other in the background and screaming at someone called … is it … Barry? Have you got a handyman in? At this time of night? Oh, *Ellen*! You haven't picked up a *man*, have you, and brought him home to be a replacement baby daddy?'

'I don't think you're supposed to say baby daddy either,' I insisted. 'And also, I'm pretty sure there's no such thing as a *replacement* baby daddy. You either are or you aren't, unless you're on *Jeremy Kyle* getting your DNA or lie detector results.'

'OH ELLEN!' wailed Mum. 'TELL me you're not going on *Jeremy Kyle*. Bad enough you've picked up a man, and one called Barry at that, but darling, no. I forbid it!'

'I haven't picked up a man. And what's wrong with being called Barry?' I said, utterly confused as to how the conversation had ended up here. 'Barry is my new dog.'

'Oh, thank God for that,' gasped Mum in relief. 'Why would you call a dog Barry, though? That's not a dog name, it's very confusing. What sort of dog? A proper one this time, like a nice black Lab, instead of that vicious little rat dog of yours?'

'Judgy is a Proud and Noble Border Terrier,' I snapped. 'He's not vicious, and he's certainly not a rat dog! And Barry isn't exactly a black Lab, no … Anyway, I've joined some internet dating sites, isn't that exciting?' I added, in an attempt to deflect the conversation away from Barry's dubious parentage.

There was a chill silence. 'Why would you do that?'

'To meet someone!'

'But's it's so *common*,' wailed Mum. 'It's like placing an advert in a Lonely Hearts column.'

'Not quite.'

'It's desperate, Ellen, is what it is. How many times have I told you that boys don't like desperate girls?'

I took a deep breath. 'Well, you also told me that I shouldn't trust a man in patent shoes because he'll try to use them to look up my skirt, and that I shouldn't marry a very blond man because my hair was too dark and the children would be born ginger. You also inferred that ginger grandchildren would bring shame upon you. And you told me that drinking whisky would make people think I was a slut and then recently you told me not to divorce Simon, because having a divorced daughter might reflect badly on you when it came to the elections for the tennis club chair, even though you yourself *divorced my father for also being a cheating scumbag*. So you'll forgive me if I take your advice with a large pinch of salt. Millions of men and women meet like this, Mum. It's perfectly normal.'

'No,' said Mum darkly. 'No good will come of this, you mark

my words. They're all murderers and perverts on those websites, so excuse me if I try to pass on the benefit of my life experience to my daughter. I'm only trying to help. If you want to meet a man so badly, why don't you join a bridge club? After all, that's how I met Geoffrey. Or better yet, just patch things up with Simon. He's an *architect*, darling. They don't grow on trees, you know! It's quite ridiculous you getting divorced. I don't know *why* you've let things come to this.'

I most nobly refrained from pointing out that Geoffrey, although well off and in possession of his own teeth, as well as a charming Georgian rectory in Yorkshire, was also a boorish, racist homophobe, and I agreed to consider joining a bridge club, even though I can't play bridge and don't even know if bridge clubs exist anymore. My mother has that effect on people, which was why her iron rule over the tennis club was never really in any danger of a coup from Marjorie Lonsdale, despite my shameful single-mother status. I didn't respond to the comments about Simon and his architectural suitability and the inference that the divorce was clearly all my fault. As far as Mum is concerned, everything is my fault anyway, so I don't know why this would be any different. But nonetheless, it stung.

'Now go and ring your sister and let me know if she's all right.'

'Yes, Mum,' I said again. Agreeing with everything seemed like the quickest way to get off the phone.

I hung up and sank down at the kitchen table, with my head in my hands.

I heard a sloshing noise and something was plonked unceremoniously on the table in front of me.

'Mum?' said Jane. I looked up. There was a brimming jam jar filled with red wine on the table before me.

'It was the only thing we could find clean. Since the dishwasher hasn't finished yet and we didn't want you to get cholera or typhoid,' said Peter.

'We thought you might need it. Was that Granny?' asked Jane. I nodded, too drained by the conversation with my mother to speak.

'Well, anyway, I need to go and message Sophie,' announced Jane, sidling out of the room, clearly taking advantage of distracting me with wine and my momentary weakness after dealing with my own mother to get out of washing the rest of the dishes.

'Granny's a bit of an evil bitch, isn't she?' said Peter conversationally.

'Don't call your grandmother a bitch,' I said automatically.

'But she is,' insisted Peter.

'Yeah, OK, fair point,' I agreed.

'You shouldn't let her get to you,' said Peter. 'You know she only calls to wind you up when she's bored. *We* don't let her get to us anymore, not once we realised that we'd never be as good as Persephone and Gulliver, and so she'd never like us as much.'

'Darlings, of course Granny loves all her grandchildren equally,' I said without much conviction.

'Nah,' said Peter. 'She loves them better, and she loves Auntie Jessica better than you. It's actually a thing, you know, Mum. It's called Golden Child Syndrome. Anyway, we don't give a shit, because she gives us the same amount of money for Christmas and birthdays as the Golden Ones, and we don't have to put up with her bollocks. So it's win–win. You just need to stop caring what she thinks.'

'Darling, your *language*!' I remonstrated, in a feeble attempt to reclaim the adult's position in the conversation, since all of a sudden my son seemed to have become much wiser and more grown up than me – and also far more aware of what went on around him than I'd given him credit for.

'Anyway, Mum,' said Peter. 'Would you like us to make dinner? You look tired.'

I was quite choked up by the unexpected kindnesses shown by both my children for once (all right, it was only a glass of wine from Jane, but it was a start), as well as Peter's insights into my relationship with my mother, but I wasn't so overwhelmed by these flashes of maturity to overlook the fact that although he meant well with his offer of making dinner, the resulting carnage would probably see me cleaning pasta sauce off the ceiling, the dogs and possibly even the chickens.

You never know whether you're coming or going with teenagers. One minute they're screaming at you about how much they hate you, the next they're offering you a cup of tea like nothing has happened, then five minutes later they're back to hating you again because of some perceived slight that has ruined their life for the eleventy billionth time that day. It's nothing if not a rollercoaster, although thank God for the odd slivers of hope amid their bile and rage to keep you going and give you a glimpse of the person they might turn out to be one day. Perhaps it's some sort of self-preservation thing. If they were constantly and unremittingly vile for the four or five years it seems to take them to work the fury out of their system then we'd probably just drown them or something. In the meantime, there was still Peter's kind offer of dinner to deal with.

'Thank you, darling,' I said, taking a swig out of my jam jar of wine, and feeling like a ridiculous hipster. 'I think we all deserve a little treat, though, don't you? Why don't we get a takeaway?'

Obviously World War Three then broke out about whether to get Indian, Chinese or Thai, but it was worth it, if for no other reason than to stick a tiny two fingers up to my mother, who considers takeaways too common to mention, unless you're at the seaside, where fish and chips is permitted as long as you eat it on the beach. The thought of us getting a takeaway on a week night for no reason whatsoever would have given her a fit of the vapours. Ha!

JUNE

Saturday, 2 June

Well, I rang Jessica the other night as Mum instructed me to, and she was mildly hysterical as apparently Persephone and Gulliver have gone COMPLETELY off the rails and turned into teenage tearaways. According to Jessica, Persephone has developed an interest in self-mutilation and is determined to throw her future away, and Gulliver has joined a thrash metal band. A little further questioning revealed that in fact Persephone had not had a facial tattoo and a tongue split, and nor had Gulliver run away to tour with Megadeth, but in fact Persephone had got a nose piercing and was refusing to sit the Oxbridge Entrance Exams early, and, horror of horrors as far as Jessica was concerned, was insisting that she didn't know if she wanted to sit them at all, while Gulliver had left the school chamber orchestra in favour of playing keyboards in the lunchtime 'Rock Band' run by Mr Beale, the music teacher.

'Do you think you might be overreacting a bit, Jessica?' I enquired mildly. 'I mean, as teenage rebellions go, these are pretty mild.'

'MILD?' shrieked Jessica. 'Perhaps by *your* children's standards this is mild, but Gulliver's piano teacher said he had a chance of getting into the Juilliard, and how will that happen if he doesn't *focus*?'

'He's only thirteen, Jess,' I pointed out.

'And Persephone? How will she be taken seriously on a PPE course with a face full of metal?'

'Even Samantha Cameron has a tattoo,' I reminded her.

'Oh, I wouldn't expect you to understand,' Jessica said crushingly. 'After all, you let Jane get a belly-button piercing.'

'What? No, I didn't.'

'Persephone saw it on Jane's Instagram. Don't tell me you didn't know?'

FUCKING Instagram. I was limited in how often I could 'casually' borrow Peter's phone to stalk Jane before he objected and/or told her what I was doing.

'Of course I knew,' I said, trying to sound like a responsible mother whose daughter has not blocked her on Instagram so she can get questionable piercings and stick her tongue in spotty youths' ears.

'Are you all right, Ellen? You sound a little odd.'

'Yes, yes, I'm fine!' I said, amazed that Jessica had actually even asked, but not entirely sure where to start, given that to Jessica my divorce, my crumbling hovel, I mean Dream Cottage, and my children's desire to express their emotional trauma at coming from a Broken Home through piercings clearly did not take precedence over the possibility of Gulliver not getting into the Juilliard. 'I have to go,' I said. 'Just call Mum, OK?'

I stomped upstairs to enquire after Jane's belly-button piercing, to be met with indifference and be told that 'Dad said I could.'

I then promptly rang Simon to ask him what he thought he was doing, letting Jane get a piercing without consulting me, especially since she'd nearly fainted when she got her ears pierced.

'But she told me that you said it was OK,' he insisted.

'And you didn't think to check with me?'

'Why? She said you said she could.'

'And you just believed her?'

'Why wouldn't I?'

'Because teenagers *lie*, Simon.'

'Well, how was I to know?'

I couldn't even rage at him that I'd had to find out through Jessica, because that would involve admitting that Jane had blocked me.

I got off the phone and returned to my endless weekend 'To do' list. I swear as soon as I cross something off that list, a dozen new things appear by magic. I was staring at it gloomily, trying to pick the least hateful thing to do first from either the domestic delights of ironing, bog scrubbing, washing machine drawer de-gunking, etc, or the life admin tasks like looking into car insurance quotes (that was one of the things Simon was so good at – partly because he's a tight bastard who feels he's somehow 'getting one over' on the insurance companies if he can find a cheaper price), booking dentist and eye appointments for everyone (Simon was surprised when he sent me a text saying it had been a while since his last dentist check-up and when was his next appointment?, and I reminded him he had to do that for himself from now on. Although maybe there would be some value in trading jobs between us – I could book his dentist's appointments, which let's face it would really be no effort as I'd be booking everyone else's at the same time, and he could trawl the internet for cheap insurance quotes for me, which he enjoys doing anyway. Or is that a bit peculiar?), and ringing Dad and Natalia. After my *tête-à-têtes* with my mother and sister this week, calling Dad and my stepmother seemed quite an attractive proposition, as although my father has spent most of his life as a dreadful philanderer and nothing will convince Jessica that Natalia has only married him in his dotage in order to cheat her, Jessica, out of her rightful inheritance, they're considerably less batshit mental (I must stop saying that. I chastise the children for it, but it's the only phrase that really sums up Mum and Jessica) and definitely much nicer people than the rest of my family.

I'd just picked up the phone when Hannah banged on the back door and staggered in.

'Coffee,' she moaned feebly, flinging herself down in a chair, 'for the love of God, give me coffee.'

'Have you been out on the piss?' I said in confusion. 'Are you allowed to do that these days when you're preggers?'

'Nooooo,' groaned Hannah despairingly. 'You're not allowed to do *anything* now when you're upduffed. ALL Is Forbidden! *Verboten*! *Especially* when you live with a fucking doctor who is taking the whole Becoming a Father and The Miracle of Life VERY seriously indeed. He's joined Mumsnet! He started a parking thread about our neighbours in AIBU, complete with diagrams. But honestly, Ellen, I can't do anything. He won't let me have coffee because it's bad for the baby. He's got me on decaf everything, I've been hiding Nespresso pods round the house like alcoholics hide bottles of vodka, but he's at home this morning so I couldn't get to my stash, and I *need* a fucking coffee!'

'Why come all the way over here, though? Why not go to one of the lovely hipster coffee places round the corner from your house?'

'Because Charlie might see me,' she said darkly. 'And because he barely lets me leave the house alone, in case I feel faint or try to lift something. I'm not even allowed to go to the shops. He's so ridiculously overprotective that it's almost making me feel nostalgic for Weasel Piss Dan, the man who stole my post-birth tea and toast because he didn't think I 'looked like I wanted them', the bastard! I had to tell Charlie I needed to come and see you because you were having some sort of divorce-related meltdown, and even then he wanted to drive me here in case I found negotiating a roundabout stressful, because stress is bad for the baby and my blood pressure. Arrrrghhhhh! Oooh, thank you.' She gulped thirstily at the mug of coffee I thrust upon her.

I contemplated telling Hannah that actually, I *was* having some sort of divorce-related meltdown, on account of my ex-husband constantly undermining me with my children, and my daughter mostly regarding me like something she'd stepped in, and I clearly sounded like I was on the verge of a breakdown because *Jessica* of all people had asked if I was OK, which was slightly worrying, but I decided Hannah had enough problems of her own – I didn't want to burden her with mine – especially when she took a sip of coffee and then squealed, 'Ow, ow, hot, hot!'

I sighed. 'Of course it's hot. You literally just sat there and watched me make it. You're as bad as Peter, who's surprised that food eaten directly out a pot just removed from the stove is hot.'

'I don't care,' sighed Hannah. 'What's a few third-degree burns to my mouth in return for the sweet, sweet kiss of caffeine. Though don't you have anything nicer than Nescafé? I am with child, I think I deserve good coffee.'

'I'll get good coffee for next time,' I promised.

'Honestly, I'd forgotten how much being pregnant just makes you feel like a bloody incubator,' sighed Hannah. 'Your body is no longer your own. Everyone feels entitled to put in their tuppence worth and tell you that you should be doing this, or you should be doing that, or ooooh, you don't want to do that. I'm not even showing yet, and it's going to get worse, with all those fucking weirdos who think it's OK to go up to a pregnant woman and ask to touch her bump. Why do people think that's OK? At no other time would you go up to a stranger and demand to touch them and get shirty if they, quite rightly, tell you to piss off, would you? So where does this thing come from that it's OK to ask to touch up a pregnant woman?'

'I think there's something about it being lucky?' I ventured.

'Well, they can fuck right off! I don't care how unlucky they are, they can fall under a bus for all I care, they're NOT touching me,' yelped Hannah. 'More coffee, please.'

'Are you sure? You did drink that very fast,' I said doubtfully.

'DON'T YOU BLOODY START AT ME!' shouted Hannah. 'I need some voice of sanity amid the madness of freaks wanting to suck the luck out of me, and over-solicitous husbands intent on stripping every last shred of pleasure from my life. Do you know the latest advice, Ellen? They say you should only sleep on your left-hand side. Better for the baby. Better oxygen supply or something. Oh yes, what monster would sleep on their right? Charlie suggested installing some sort of wedge behind me to stop me rolling over in my sleep. I told him exactly where any wedges would be going, and they wouldn't be stopping me rolling over, although they might interfere with his ability to walk.'

'Cake?' I offered, in what I hoped was a soothing voice.

'Cake?' echoed Hannah bitterly. 'Oh no, all that fat and sugar might be bad for the baby, and what about gestational diabetes? Apparently if I'm craving something sweet I should try a nice piece of fruit. YOU GIVE THAT CAKE BACK NOW, ELLEN RUSSELL, DON'T YOU EVEN THINK OF TAKING IT AWAY FROM ME!

'An' you know wha' else?' Hannah mumbled furiously through a large mouthful of cake. I was slightly alarmed by the way she was cramming it in with both hands, pausing only to wash it down with further gulps of scalding coffee, and it was becoming increasingly plain that there was going to be no cake left for me to enjoy as a little afternoon treat later, but I nobly reminded myself that Hannah's need was greater. 'He won' go out to dinner!' she spluttered, spraying crumbs over me. Barry, whose radar for fallen food is far more sensitive than Judgy's (Judgy won't get off the sofa for less than fillet steak – he's very spoilt), materialised hopefully beside Hannah.

'Jesus!' said Hannah in surprise. 'What's *that*?'

'Jane's new dog! He was supposed to be my new dog, but Jane and he bonded. Don't let her hear you saying anything derogatory about him. She's very protective. You might be her godmother, but you'll be dead to her if you insult Barry.'

'Emily did say something about Jane having some sort of weird-looking wolf dog,' said Hannah. 'He's quite big, isn't he? I thought you preferred smaller dogs?'

I looked at Barry again. Hannah was right. He was quite big. I'm sure he hadn't … loomed … over the table quite like that when he first arrived. No, I told myself, I was imagining things. The shelter had assured me he was fully grown, and surely they'd know. Wouldn't they?

'Anyway,' Hannah went on. 'I was saying about how Charlie won't even go out to dinner now. He read something about how pregnant women should only eat in restaurants that have been given a special health rating for their kitchens, clearing them of any risk of listeriosis. So that's basically none.'

'We ate out all the time when we were pregnant with Jane and Emily,' I said. 'We survived. So did they. The only reason we didn't eat out with Lucas and Peter is because we were poor by then, having been bankrupted by the first babies, and we had squawking toddlers in tow. I mean, obviously, avoid dodgy kebab shops and anywhere that uses a K instead of a C in the name, but otherwise, I think he's being a bit OTT.'

'THAT'S WHAT I SAID!' yelled Hannah. 'Is there any more cake? I have to keep eating to keep the morning sickness at bay. I haven't had any yet, but I'm worried that if I go too long without food it might start. I'm SO over being pregnant, Ellen, and I don't even have my twelve-week scan till next week. Do you want to come?'

'Won't Charlie be there? I don't want to step on his toes. And I'm not sure I can get the time off work, but I'll try.'

'Don't take time off, it's fine. You're right, Charlie will be there,' said Hannah gloomily. 'He was a complete pain in the arse at the dating scan. Actually asked them to warm the gel because he was worried the cold shock of it on my tummy might have been Bad for the Baby! And now he's planning how to announce that I Am With Child. He actually wanted to do one of those Facebook posts with Emily and Lucas holding the scan photo and wearing "Big Brother" and "Big Sister" T-shirts. They were horrified. They said they might as well wear "My Mum's Getting Some!" T-shirts and be done with it. I see their point. Those photos are cute with toddlers, but not with hulking great teenagers who couldn't even look me in the eye for a week, so mortified were they by the physical evidence that I'd had sex. And everyone keeps telling me how *lucky* I am, and how I should be so *happy*, and how there are so many women who would give anything to be pregnant, and I *am* happy, and I *do* know I'm lucky, and I *know* there are so many women going through hell struggling to get pregnant, but does that mean I'm not allowed to feel fed up and bloated and cross that every fucking person I encounter now seems to feel they're entitled to comment on everything I eat and everything I wear and everything I do, and I'm probably going to get piles, and I'm going to have to go back to sleepless nights and shitty nappies and never being able to leave the house without a screaming infant attached to me in some way and I think I'm getting morning sickness now, I feel quite sick, and I just want a moan sometimes, but apparently I'm not even allowed that, because I'm just supposed to focus on how *lucky* I am.'

'I think you probably feel sick because you've just inhaled half a Victoria sponge and a pint of coffee,' I pointed out. 'I'm not totally sure you can blame that on pregnancy. Do you feel better for getting that off your chest?'

'I do actually,' said Hannah, perking up. 'Do you have any ginger nuts? Apparently they're good for nausea.'

'No,' I said firmly. 'You've had enough. You may be eating for two, but it's bad enough Peter clearing out my cupboards on a regular basis without you doing the same!'

'You're so mean,' grumbled Hannah. 'It's almost like I'm not your best friend or something. Where are your kids anyway? Dan has actually taken his children for the weekend, so I have blissful peace at home.'

'Where do you think? Lolling in their pits … Jane was at a party last night – I had to pick her and three other giggling teenage girls up at 1.30 am. Cider had clearly been partaken of, but thankfully no one puked in the car, so they're all sparko up there now, and Peter stayed over at Sam and Colin's so he and Toby are no doubt turning Toby's room into a fetid stench zone with their rancid arses, after gaming all night, and then at some point they'll appear and each consume a family-size pack of cereal and three pints of milk. I'll have to brave the tiger's lair shortly and try to wake the girls up, as it's Simon's weekend to have them. I fear a hungover Jane. Actually, I just fear Jane generally. Did you know she's got a belly-button piercing?'

'Has she? That'll be why Emily is banging on about wanting one too,' sighed Hannah. 'Remember those days, though? Remember how we were convinced if we put on enough scented lip gloss right before getting in the car that our parents wouldn't smell the booze off us? How naïve we were! And now we're picking up our own teenagers and pretending not to notice that they're clearly half cut, and checking the levels in the vodka bottles.'

We fell silent in contemplation of our own lost, misspent youth, before we were roused from our reverie by Barry almost tipping the table over as he forced his way under it in search of more cake crumbs. Was he *really* that size last week?

Poor Hannah. Obviously my problems are still nothing compared with Jessica's, but at least I'm not facing three years of wiping another human being's arse!

Thursday, 14 June

OMG! OMFG! Oh My Fucking God! I have a date. A DATE! With Tom the semi-hot, Audi-driving finance director. We were chatting by the lifts and he oh-so-casually said, 'Oh, by the way, I don't suppose you fancy trying that new Italian place in town this weekend, do you?'

I was totes cool and mega-casual with my answer, just said, 'Yeah, that might be good, who else is going?' and he said, 'I thought maybe just you and me. Big crowds in restaurants can be a pain in the arse, don't you think?' and then I twiddled my hair and simpered, 'Oh yes, I totally agree' and may have attempted to bat my eyelashes, and then he said, 'Are you OK? Have you got something in your eye?' and I flicked my hair coquettishly and said, 'No, no!' and then was worried he might think I had dandruff and had got it in my eye, and also feared that my flirting techniques might be several decades out of date, so I considered a winning smile, but I was fretting about whether I might have sesame seeds in my teeth from the sushi I had for lunch, which also made me worry that I had rancid fish breath, so I just said, 'Err, what time then?' and he said, 'Will I pick you up?' and I said, 'No, no, I'll see you there!' just in case a) the children said something unfortunate to him, b) he was a psychopath who decided to murder me on the way there, which would be annoying, as I'd heard that Italian place did an awesome spaghetti alle vongole, and it would be a shame to be murdered before I'd tried it, or c) he picked me up on his motorbike instead of in his Audi, thinking he was being cool and then I either was wearing the wrong stuff, or I couldn't get on it, or I got on it, but the helmet fucked my hair and I'd spend all night resenting him because I'd spent twenty minutes putting heated rollers in and his stupid motorbike had ruined the effect …

'Umm, eight o'clock?' he said, looking slightly surprised his gentlemanly offer had been turned down.

'Lovely!' I trilled and jumped in the first lift that came (always leave them wanting more. I remember the *J17* advice like it was yesterday) before I realised that I'd been on my own floor, but then I had to go somewhere in case he was still there when I got out of the lift again, so I popped into HR to see Debbie.

'OMG! Tom asked you out!' squealed Debbie when I went in her office.

'How do you know?' I said in confusion. He'd *literally* just asked me *three minutes* ago. Does she have a network of spies? Under the guise of reading *Take a Break* beneath her desk when Scary Gabrielle the HR boss lady isn't looking, is she actually running some kind of surveillance mission on the building? Is that how she knew I liked *Take a Break* and started passing copies on to me when she was finished? I always thought her (often inappropriate) levels of knowledge about her co-workers were gleaned from reading through their records when Gabrielle was in meetings, but now I'm starting to fear that Lord Varys's web of espionage in the Red Keep was nothing to Debbie's almost supernatural nose for gossip.

'You look all mysterious and sort of coy,' said Debbie. 'And also your horoscope said that questions would bring you new opportunities, and Tom's horoscope said that it was time to stop thinking and start doing, so it wasn't hard to guess. Though I'm still not convinced there's much long-term compatibility for Virgos and Libras.'

'I'm not looking for long-term compatibility,' I said. 'I'm simply sharing a meal with a colleague. And as long as the issues between Libras and Virgos do not extend to Libras murdering Virgos in dark and deserted lanes, then it doesn't really matter. Why are you reading our horoscopes anyway, Debbie?'

'I read everyone's horoscopes,' said Debbie in surprise, 'so I can plan my week around who might be coming in to see Gabrielle. I wonder how much star-sign compatibility has to do with murders? That would actually make a really good TV series – an astrologist who works with the police to help them discover who might have murdered the victim … that would be brilliant.'

'Except you know astrology isn't real?'

Debbie snorted. 'You can think what you like. But *I* know the truth! Do you want a Quality Street?'

'Can I have a coconut one?'

'Of course! Even though you doubt the stars. Anyway, you're the only one who likes the coconut ones.'

'Do you always have chocolate in your desk?' I asked idly.

'Yes,' said Debbie. 'You have to in my job. Gabrielle's a fucking bitch, so it gets me through the day, and it also cheers people up on the way out if they've been in to see the Tyrant Queen.'

'Fair enough.'

Debbie let me take all the coconut Quality Street back to my office, so, all in all, today I was definitely #winning.

Saturday, 16 June

Tonight was date night. First I had to endure Olympic-level whinging from Jane because she wanted to go to a party and who would pick her up if I was going out?, and I'd *promised* I'd be available to pick her up *whenever she wanted* when I made her move out of the town and it *wasn't fair*, despite me pointing out that she'd been at parties for the last five fucking weekends, including two nights when she should really have been with

Simon, but she'd begged to have all her friends back to our house to sleep over after the party, and Simon, paling at the thought of either a flat full of fifteen-year-old girls or a furious Jane, sulking over how her life had been *ruined* (again), had happily agreed that he didn't mind if she just came home to me instead of going to his.

Jane then suggested that she could still go to the party and just sleep over at someone's house, which ordinarily would have been fine, as several parents did owe me for all those pick-ups and post-party sleepovers I'd done, but I further ruined her life by telling her she could bloody well stay in for one Saturday night, as I wasn't entirely convinced that Peter was old enough to be left by himself for the whole evening, especially not while I was on a date, with an actual man! I could see the *Daily Mail* headline already – '13-Year-Old Boy Trapped in Burning House While His SLUT MOTHER Trawled the Town for COCK Because All Women Are Sinful WHORES!' Or, you know, words to that effect.

Of course, I'm not actually sure who would be more use if the house were to catch fire while I was out. Although Jane is nominally the oldest, and thus the responsible one, she's not good in a crisis, whereas Peter is much more unflappable (I sometimes wonder if that's just because he can't actually divert enough brain power from his contemplation of his next meal or snack and his games to actually panic) but possessed of no more common sense than his sister.

Jane was incandescent with rage about this, and even more furious that I was wilfully ruining her life with my immense selfishness. I hadn't even told her I was going on an actual date, murmuring something vague about 'meeting friends', as I couldn't face the inevitable rants about how disgusting it was that I was going out with a man at my age, and why couldn't I just take up knitting or something – anything more appropriate to my encroaching cronedom rather than *dating*. She was even more unhappy when I told her that she'd have to make dinner for herself and her brother too, triggering a rant about the patriarchy, until I snapped that I'd asked *her* to make dinner rather than her brother because I wanted her to stand some chance of getting some actual food, and if I turned Peter loose in the kitchen he'd just eat everything in sight, quite possibly without bothering to cook it, and then Jane would be left to starve. She ominously muttered something about coming from a Broken Home at me instead.

Of course, I could have asked Simon to have them, and I was quite tempted, as that would serve Simon and his two beers and all his bloody cocktails right (he put a new photo on Instagram last week of his dinner in a nice restaurant, bastard), but although part of me very much wanted him to know that I was On a Date with an Actual Man, part of me also wanted to see where things went with Tom, in case they fizzled out and Simon asked about him and I had to admit that another man also found me repellent. Of course, I might find Tom repellent, but either way, I didn't want Simon to know until there was really something for him to know. Maybe then I could post something on Instagram about a romantic minibreak, with champagne in the bath in a boutique hotel. *That* would show Simon and his wanky overpriced salad photos!

Anyway, I was finally ready to go. I'd changed about fifteen times, trying to strike the right balance between 'quite up for it' and 'tits hanging out'. Getting dressed for a date turned out to be harder than I had anticipated, which didn't help with my pre-date nerves, especially when I'd changed so often I ended up sweaty and frizzy-haired, but with no time to have another bath. So extra deodorant and another go over with the hair straighteners it was. I was quite pleased with the result in the end, if I do say so myself. A hint of cleavage, but in a sturdy top of the sort that one's tits cannot make a break for freedom from. Jeans tight enough to be a little bit sexy, but not so tight that I'd not be able to do justice to my dinner (I was quite determined that if nothing else was going to come of the night, then I'd at least get a decent feed out of it). Heels high enough to walk in without tottering, but spiky enough to whack through his eye if he turned out to be a murderer (*Single White Female* was really quite an instructive film). My hair had even gone sort of right, apart from the frizz, and I'd taken the time to put on two shades of eyeshadow and even rub a brush over them so that they 'blended', although in truth my attempts at blending had only succeeded in smearing both colours together into one slightly sludgy colour, which I told myself firmly was in fact a 'smoky eye'.

I went into the sitting room to say goodbye to the children. Well, Jane. There was no sign of Peter.

'OMG, is that what you're wearing?' said Jane in a horrified tone.

'What's wrong with it?' I said anxiously.

'Nothing,' said Jane. 'I mean, if that's how you want to look, then that's fine.'

'What?' I said in panic. 'What's wrong? Do I look fat? Is it too young for me? Are the shoes sending the wrong message? Has something happened to my hair?'

Jane considered me for some time. 'It's just a bit … basic!' was all she could finally came out with.

'Basic? WTF does that even mean? What's "basic"? This is a Hobbs top. It cost £89. Well, it didn't because I got it in the sale for £23, but it *should* have cost £89. How is that "basic"?'

Oh God, I looked 'basic'. Is 'basic' better or worse than 'mumsy'? I'd tried on literally everything I owned and this was definitely the best combination, but I was still 'basic'. And now Tom would take one look at me and go 'Eughh, basic', and never want to see me again, and when I die alone and unloved the dogs will probably shun my lifeless corpse because of my basicness, and the first thing whoever finds my body will say will be 'Christ, what's she wearing, that's the most basic body I've ever seen.' As if I weren't nervous enough, I now had my essential 'basicness' to worry about. I wondered if I should put on some statement jewellery? What even *is* statement jewellery? Do I have any?

'Jane, would some statement jewellery help?'

Jane shrugged. 'Ha! Nope. Statement jewellery is even more basic.'

What? Statement jewellery is a *thing*. Magazines talk about it all the time. Statement jewellery or statement lipstick. Apparently not for the Youth of Today, though.

'What about different lipstick? Maybe something really bold and striking?'

'Absolutely. If you want your mouth to look like a baboon's arse!'

No. I did not want my mouth to look like a baboon's arse. I'm sure dating was much simpler when all we had to think about was whether to go for Heather Shimmer or Coffee Shimmer lippy, and even then, you didn't really have to worry about it, because it would all be snogged off within the first hour anyway.

'Oh FFS! I'll have to do as I am. Where's your brother?'

'How should I know? I'm not responsible for him.'

'Well, you sort of are tonight?'

I went to the bottom of the stairs and yelled 'PETER?' Eventually, after what felt like shouting his name about eleventy fucking billion times, a faint 'Wha'?' drifted down the stairs.

'I'm going out now.'

'K.'

'Bye then.'

Nothing. I was going to miss my bus if I didn't hurry. I dashed back into the sitting room and grabbed my bag.

'Mother?' said Jane.

'Not now, I'm late for the bus,' I gabbled.

'Why are you getting the bus and not driving? You hate the bus. You always say there's too high a chance of coming into contact with other people's bodily fluids.'

'So I can have a glass of wine with my dinner and relax, sweetheart.'

'You shouldn't need alcohol to have a good time,' said Jane primly.

'You're perfectly right, darling. So you won't be wanting to take any Kopparbergs to your next party then, will you, what with not needing alcohol to have fun?'

'What? No! I didn't say that! Mother –'

'BYE, darling, I'm going now,' I said firmly, and fled out of the door before Jane could lecture me about anything else.

I caught the bus by the skin of my teeth. There was indeed a strange smell that contained more than a hint of bodily fluids. I tried not to touch anything more than I had to, but at least worrying about what the smell was provided a modicum of distraction from fretting about the 'basicness' of my appearance. Jane's other putdown is 'extra', which as far as I can ascertain is the opposite of 'basic' and is the Young People's Way of saying something is 'A Bit Much'. I don't know if they actually have a word for the perfect happy medium that falls bang in the middle between 'basic' and 'extra' – it's entirely possible that they do – but I'm unaware of it because Jane has never had reason to use it in my presence.

I arrived at the restaurant without incident, just as it started to drizzle, and felt very smug at beating the universe's attempt to thwart my evening by frizzing my hair with the damp, as my nervous sweat was doing quite a good enough job of that on its own.

I entered, did that tricky thing with the maître d' where you explain about meeting someone while frantically scanning the room trying to see if they're there yet so you don't look like a saddo who has made up having friends, spotted Tom, waved frantically and squeaked, 'No, no, I can see him, it's fine!' and sashayed over as sexily as I could manage without falling off my heels. We had a slightly difficult moment when we tried to do that hug-and-kiss greeting that Europeans are so good at and British people are so bad at but feel obliged to do now, even though we're shit at it and always end up just bumping our heads together and not knowing how many kisses to go for, but then he asked if I wanted a cocktail to start (OF COURSE I DID), which was much more civilised.

Away from the office and its harsh lighting (I once appealed to Scary Gabrielle to have more ambient lighting put in, saying that we'd all work better if we had more flattering light to work by, and Gabrielle said that wasn't a thing and told me to stop wasting her time, even though no one is quite sure what Gabrielle does all day because Debbie deals with most things, while Gabrielle just hangs upside down from the ceiling of her office), Tom looked even more attractive in the dim light of the restaurant. I could only hope the same was true for me.

'So, what did you do earlier?' Tom asked.

Obviously I couldn't tell him the truth, which was 'eleventy billion loads of laundry, cleaned up cheesy dog sick because one of my precious moppets left the fucking fridge open, argued with my teenage daughter about why she wasn't getting a tattoo, whereupon she declared that it was her human right to "express herself", and I was ruining her life and stifling her creativity, texted my ex to remind him that no matter what said stroppy teenage daughter claimed I'd categorically *not* agreed to a tattoo, forcibly stopped teenage son inhaling the remaining contents of the fridge after the dogs had raided it, ruined teenage daughter's life again by asking her to feed the chickens, and tried on everything in my wardrobe only to be told I looked basic' and just said, 'Oh, you know. Pretty chilled day. I'm reading the Booker Prize winner at the moment. It's really interesting. Have you read it?' (This wasn't a lie, I am *trying* to read it, and not really getting anywhere, so I prayed Tom would either not have read it, or would make very clever comments about it that I could just nod and agree with, but I thought saying I was reading it would make me look highbrow.)

'Yeah, no, I don't really read,' he replied. Oh. That was even worse than him asking me my thoughts on the difficult intellectual book and expecting me to have intelligent opinions about it. I don't really understand people who just 'don't read'. I tried my hardest not to judge, though, and attempted to find some redeeming feature to make up for him not reading.

'What did you do today then?' I said.

'I went for a run this morning, and then this afternoon I went to the gym for a weights session and a swim. I'm training for an Ironman,' he said.

'Gosh! That sounds … interesting. Er, what exactly *is* an Ironman?'

Tom explained. At length. Frankly it sounded hideous. You swim for miles, go on a ridiculously long bike ride – and *then* you run a marathon! I've literally no idea why anyone would want to do this to themselves, but Tom seemed quite excited by it.

Describing his training regime for this Ironman thingamajig took us right through the starters (bruschetta for me, carpaccio for him, but he didn't eat the Parmesan). Over our main courses (delicious creamy pasta for me, grilled salmon, no sauce, with a plain salad for Tom) I enquired whether he was looking forward to the new series of *Game of Thrones*.

'I don't really watch TV,' he said. Fuck me. He didn't read and he didn't watch TV, not even *Game of Thrones*. What's life without a healthy dose of Tits 'n' Dragons?

'Do you like films then?' I tried.

Tom brightened up. 'Yes. I like James Bond films.'

Yay! 'Any other sort of films?'

'No. Just James Bond.'

'So, do you have any hobbies?' What the fuck does he *do* with himself? Is he into woodworking or model railways? Does he just sit at home and interfere with himself in the evenings?

'Training. I love training. I don't really have time for anything else.'

'Wow. But that can't take up that much time, surely?'

'Well, I go to the gym straight from work for two or three hours, then by the time I get home and make myself something to eat I'm pretty knackered, so I just go to bed because I'm up at 5 am to get a decent run in before work. Then at the weekends, that's my chance to really ramp it up. What sort of exercise are you into?'

'Mainly just walking the dogs.'

'Oh. How many dogs do you have?' he asked politely.

'Two. I have three chickens as well. Do you have any pets?' Jesus, this conversation was like writing to your German penpal when you were fourteen.

'No. I don't really like animals in the house. I think it's unhygienic.'

'Right. I think there have been studies that show that people who live with animals are actually healthier.'

'Mmm, I just couldn't be doing with the dirt and hair everywhere. Do you want any pudding?'

'Um. Do you know, I'm actually pretty full. And I'm quite tired. Shall we just get the bill?'

I insisted we split the bill. It only seemed fair, given that we clearly had nothing in common and there wasn't going to be a second date. On the plus side, Tom was a cheap date, as he only had one small glass of red wine, which he described as 'a bit naughty'.

He did insist on walking me to the bus stop (he offered a lift home, but I couldn't face another twenty minutes of stilted conversation about the pros and cons of a paleo diet vs a keto diet, even though to me they sounded like exactly the same thing). Luckily the bus came quickly.

'Thank you for a lovely evening,' said Tom.

'Yes, thank you. See you Monday!' I trilled and leapt on the bus, immensely relieved that he hadn't felt obliged to even make noises about how we must do this again sometime.

So that was my first date in twenty-five years. I tried to remind myself that I couldn't afford to be 'too picky' at 'my age' (how helpful that is when people say things like that), and that Tom seemed to be a fairly decent human being, given he'd not yet asked to see my tits or told me that women really had no need to hold political views or announced he did think that Nigel Farage made some very good points, actually. According to the *Daily Mail* and the dating sites, I should just be grateful that any man had taken an interest in me, and grab him with both hands. Why? Why is a woman in her forties supposed to be grateful for anything she can get, whereas men apparently still can browse happily from a *smorgasbord* of women of any age from about eighteen up? Women are tutted at and judged if they're with a younger man, and somehow deemed embarrassing and inappropriate, whereas a goaty old man parading round with a twenty-two-year-old girl is deemed perfectly natural. All I want is someone to make me laugh, who vaguely shares the same interests as me and likes dogs. Is that so much to ask for?

I got home, still pondering the unfairness of society's judgements and thinking Jane-like thoughts about the patriarchy (according to Jane, the few things she doesn't blame on me are all the fault of the patriarchy, which she's planning to topple singlehandedly).

Jane was in the sitting room, glowering at me.

'Where have you been?' she snapped.

'Out for dinner. You know that.'

'Yes, but who with? I thought you were out with Sam or Colin or Hannah, but Sophie and Emily said they're all at home tonight, so who then?'

'A friend.'

'You don't *have* any other friends apart from them.'

'I do! I have lots of friends.'

'Like who?'

'Katie.'

'Have you even seen Katie since you made us move here? Or is she just someone else you've casually abandoned?'

'I've seen Katie. We had a coffee at lunchtime last week.'

'So you won't have been having dinner with her tonight then, will you? Were you out with a *man*?'

'Well, yes.'

'On a *date*? Have you no shame?'

'I've nothing to be ashamed of. I'm allowed a life. I'm allowed to have dinner with a man.'

'No, you're not. It's disgusting lusting after MEN at *your* age!' shouted Jane. 'It's *embarrassing*! And what do you think Dad would say, if he knew you'd been out with another man?'

'It's none of his business. We're getting *divorced*,' I protested. 'Other people get divorced and move on with new partners. So why am *I* not allowed to have a life?'

'BECAUSE THAT'S DIFFERENT! YOU'RE SUPPOSED TO BE MY MOTHER! You're not meant to be out with other men. It's not fair. And it's not *right*. The only man you need to be with is *Dad*!'

Barry appeared at the top of the stairs, whining in fear at the raised voices. 'And now you've upset Barry!' hissed Jane. 'You're upsetting everyone, and you don't even care. You only think about yourself!'

'*That's* not fair!' I said in shock. 'I went for dinner with a man I work with. I'm allowed to do that. It was just dinner. Nothing was going to come of it romantically anyway, but I'm allowed to make new friends and I'm allowed to have a life and I'm allowed to find a new partner if I want to. Am I supposed to be a nun for the rest of my life, devoting myself to your humble service? You have a boyfriend, why can't I have one?'

'HOW DO YOU KNOW ABOUT THAT? HAVE YOU BEEN STALKING ME? HOW DARE YOU DO THAT TO ME? I CAN'T BELIEVE YOU, THAT IS NONE OF YOUR BUSINESS!'

'So, just to clarify – I'm your mother, I'm supposed to look after you and keep you safe, but *your* boyfriend is none of *my* business, but if *I* get a boyfriend, then that's *totally* your business?'

'Exactly! You're my *mother* and you don't *need* a boyfriend, and Harry is nothing to do with you and you're NEVER to snoop in my life again! You don't UNDERSTAND ME, you don't UNDERSTAND WHAT IT'S LIKE and I HATE you! I'm going to go and live with Dad!'

'You do that!' I yelled.

She flounced up the stairs with Barry and slammed her bedroom door.

I went through to the kitchen and poured myself a glass of wine, with a slightly shaking hand. The threat to go and live with Simon wasn't a serious one. She played that card at least once a week, and had not yet followed through on it – partly because her room at Simon's is very cramped and the futon, which she initially raved about as being very cool, is lumpy and uncomfortable, but mainly because he wouldn't let her bring Barry. Jane is a monster, a raging ball of hormonal fury and perceived injustice. So just a normal fifteen-year-old girl coping with her parents' divorce, in fact.

She was wrong about me not understanding her, though. I understood her only too well, but no parent in the history of the world has ever succeeded in convincing a teenager that a) their parents were once teenagers too, b) that it's the nature of being a teenager to feel misunderstood, angst-ridden and that life is deeply unfair to them, c) that although they might be sure that they're the only one who has ever felt like that, that their anger and distress at the injustice of the world is far more righteous and deeper than everyone else's, they really are not the only ones going through that, d) that one day this fury and sense of unfairness will pass and they'll be slightly embarrassed about what a total tit they once were, and e) that their poetry is really quite bad and not life-changing and soulful, and one day they'll feel an immense sense of relief when they burn it, thus ensuring no one will ever be able to read their embarrassing outpourings.

I sternly told myself that I should try to be more sympathetic to Jane's plight, to concentrate hard on remembering who was the adult and who was the child in our encounters, and to focus on supporting her and not letting her wind me up, to remember that however much it might seem like her behaviour is about me, actually it's not about me, it's not about the divorce, it's just about her being a teenager and finding her own way in the world. God knows being a teenager was wretched enough back in my day, but it must be ten times harder nowadays, with all the social media and constant messaging and having to worry about whether anyone has 'liked' your Instagram post or watched your stories, and of course, apparently all the boys are addicted to porn now and so want to do things that would make the editors of *More* magazine blush, and allegedly they all demand that girls send them topless photos, which wasn't something the problem page in *Just Seventeen* ever had to cover, with its eternal advice of 'Why not tell a trusted adult, like the school nurse, about this?' which always made us howl with laughter at the very idea of confiding any of our worries about snogging or sex or whether one of our boobs was bigger than the other (at least one letter every week was about asymmetric boobs, which was perfectly normal according to *Just Seventeen* but do tell the school nurse anyway), or fears that we might be gay because we'd wondered what it might be like to kiss a girl (again, this seemed to be a weekly dilemma, and again, telling the school nurse was the solution). Our school nurse was a fire-breathing harridan who took a malicious pleasure in stabbing us as viciously as possible with our rubella and BCG vaccinations and spent the rest of the year jealously guarding her precious stock of plasters, paracetamol and tubigrips from our grasping hands, insisting our headaches would be cured with water and our sprains were all in our mind and actually the best thing for that cut would be to get some air around it. Occasionally she'd reluctantly venture forth from her lair, clutching a few bandages and grudgingly hold a first aid class, which only ever taught us how to put someone's arm in a sling and inevitably ended with her shouting because someone (usually Hannah and me) had disrespected her bandages and tried to turn their friend into a mummy. The thought of confiding in her about *anything* was enough to bring us out in hives, not that we'd have got any sympathy about them from her …

I keep thinking it will get easier, this parenting lark. That once they could walk and talk, tell me what they wanted, didn't need their arses wiped and slept through the night, that it would be better. When they were at school all day, that things would be calmer. That once they were more independent, could get the bus, learn to manage their own time, make the odd meal, be treated more as adults than children, that I'd be #nailingit. But it doesn't get easier, it just gets … different. They walk and talk and bang their heads and skin their knees and shout 'FUCKING HELL, MUMMY!' in the supermarket, and you apply ice packs and patch them up and pretend you've no idea where they've learnt such language, and they start school and you worry about bullies and whether they'll have any friends, and are they happy and how have they got nits again, and then they become teenagers and they hate you, but despite this they don't need you any less, and you're still worrying about bullies, but also about them getting their drinks spiked at parties and should you have let them have that cider, and teenage pregnancy, and I'll have to try to persuade Peter not to watch porn, even though he will, and teach him to respect women, and that no means no, and at some point I'll really have to attempt to disconnect him from that bloody computer and get him to interact with real people, because despite all my precautions to keep him safe online, what if he's talking to murderous psychopaths, although on the other hand, he does live with Jane, so he's probably quite adept at dealing with murderous psychopaths, and what if Jane gets pregnant, or they fail all their exams, or they go travelling for a year and I don't know if they're alive or dead or any one of a million other scenarios that I lie awake at night worrying about?

I wonder if I'll ever stop worrying, or fretting about them, even when they have children of their own?

I realised in annoyance I hadn't even taken a photo of my dinner to put on Instagram to intrigue Simon and make him wonder who *I'd* been out with.

Saturday, 23 June

I really, really wish that someone could just invent a way to arrange time better. Most of the time I don't have enough time. I'm rushing and juggling and dashing around like a blue-arsed fly, and then every couple of weeks the children go to Simon's and I don't have to pick them up or drive them around or make them dinner, and I've forty-eight hours to do with as I will (mainly laundry), which then seems to drag on for about million years but I still don't manage to get all the laundry done, or find myself an improving hobby, but it would actually be a lot more helpful if there was some way of taking some of those hours and adding them onto the days when there isn't enough time to do anything properly, because there are endless lists of things needing to be done.

I ticked another thing off the list at least, and saw Dad – I met him for lunch today, on his own for once, as Natalia was in Russia visiting her mother. It's quite unusual for me to ever have any time on my own with Dad, between the kids and Natalia, and so it was actually very nice, being able to have a proper grown-up conversation without interruptions from the children or breaking up arguments between them or having to tell them to put their phones away or realising that we were talking about family jokes and events that Natalia didn't understand, which was really quite rude of us.

'And how are you, darling?' said Dad.

'I'm fine,' I said brightly.

'And how are you really? I think you're very brave, you know.'

'Brave? Me? Why?'

'It's not easy, doing what you're doing. Starting all over again, making a new life of your own. It takes courage, and I'm proud of you.'

'You're the only one then. Mum is ashamed of me, her and Jessica both think I've overreacted and shouldn't have started divorce proceedings and should have just let Simon have his "space", and my children think I've ruined their lives. Well, Jane does. She tells me so at least five times a day. Peter mostly just grunts and eats, but he gives me the odd hug out of the blue, so I don't think he totally hates me. And Simon? Well, I've no idea what Simon thinks. We talk about the children and that's about it. Well, I say "talk". I mostly just tell him not to let Jane get any piercings and tattoos, and make sure her skirt covers her bum before he lets her out the door.'

'Well, I think you're brave. I wasn't. I should have left your mother long before I did. I shouldn't have married her, really. It was one of those things. All our friends were getting married and we somehow just drifted into it ourselves, but I should never have let things get to the stage they did, but I was worried about what people would think. Even after she caught me cheating on her, I probably still would have stayed, if she hadn't thrown me out. Your mother's not a terribly nice person, darling, but she's a bloody strong one. I see a lot of that in you.'

'I'm nothing like Mum,' I protested.

'No, I know, but you have a similar strength. And stubbornness sometimes too. That's probably why you always clashed with each other so much. You're more alike than either of you would ever probably admit.'

'I don't feel very strong, or very brave,' I said gloomily.

'Well, you are, you are both, you just need to believe in yourself more. And you've always got me, you know, and you've some very good friends around you – make sure you let them help you when you need it. Now, tell me, how is Hannah? Expecting another baby, I hear. That's also very brave.'

After lunch, Dad said, 'There's a nice exhibition on at the gallery down the road. Do you fancy it?'

'I can't,' I said. 'I have to go and get Jane and take her for a haircut, and then Peter needs a lift to his friend's house. Maybe another time?'

'Of course, darling. I know how frantic you are. I just want to say again that I'm awfully proud of you. Anyway, enough of my sentimentality. Off you go. Always busy, you young people. Bye now.'

Being called a young person will never get old.

Saturday, 30 June

Peter and Jane are at Simon's this weekend, Jane still sulking about Simon's refusal to allow her to have multiple girls to sleep over with her, Simon still baffled by Jane's need to be constantly surrounded by friends. I tried to explain that this is just a thing teenage girls do, that they're pack animals and must never be alone.

'Is that why girls go to the toilet together?' he asked.

'Partly,' I replied. 'But mostly it's so we can talk about boys, and have someone to borrow a tampon or make-up from in an emergency.'

Simon just shook his head and muttered something about how he didn't think he'd ever understand women. I thought of several excellent cutting retorts to this, but decided to be a grown-up and keep them to myself, just as Simon attempted to persuade his offspring into the car while trying to defuse the usual screaming row about who sat in the front, and I stopped myself asking who the second shadow was in the photo he posted last weekend of himself at the top of a big hill (he's still sticking closely to the Instagram clichés).

Child-free, I fed the dogs and pondered how it was that Barry appeared to now be three times the size he'd been when he arrived, together with an appetite three times the size. I can no longer deny it, even to myself, that despite the assurances of the shelter, Barry was far from fully grown when he came to us, and possibly still has some way to go. I'm slightly alarmed at just what size of wolf–horse hybrid I might finally end up with. I also wonder at what point Jane will admit defeat and agree that Barry is just too physically big to sleep on her bed anymore. Peter has also clocked the fact that Barry is 100 per cent Jane's dog now, so he's demanding a python. On the plus side, apparently you only need to feed pythons once a week, which even Peter might remember to do. On the downside, it's a mother-fucking python and I'm not having one in the house. It might eat Judgy. Or the chickens. Obviously, the children have completely abandoned the chickens and chicken care is now entirely my responsibility, but at least if they do end up needing therapy when they're older, I can point out that that is their own fault for not looking after the therapeutic chickens I got them. I trudged out to feed the chickens, and got the usual disgusted glares in return.

'What?' I said. 'What do you want from me? I feed you, I clean up your poop, I've not reproached you for the utter lack of eggs, I stop Judgy from eating you, and all I ask for in return is a bit of chat. Is that too much to ask for? Is it? Do you not know how to chat? Is that the problem? Do I need to talk to you more, to encourage your chattiness? Only every time I've tried to talk to you, you've either ignored me or tried to peck my toes off. Are you mute because you're now traumatised because I haven't talked to you *enough*? Have I ruined your lives, as well as my children's? Is that it?'

Paxo fluffed out her feathers and turned her back on me.

'Only, I do hear you, you know, muttering among yourselves when I'm not here and then clamming up as soon as I appear, like bitchy girls at school. Mean girls, that's what you are. Nothing but mean girls.'

I suddenly realised that I was a) holding a conversation with three indifferent chickens, and b) accusing the chickens of being deliberately mean to me. I reflected that it was probably just as well that I was going over to Sam and Colin's later to hold actual conversations with real live people instead of chickens.

I was going to be good at Sam and Colin's, I really was. I drove there with excellent intentions about how I was going to stick to fizzy water in solidarity with Hannah, and also to be a clean-living, healthy-eating person, who, as Jane likes to remind me, doesn't need alcohol to have fun. But then it was such a hot night, and the wine looked so nice, the condensation slowly trickling down the bottle, and then Hannah said, 'Oh FFS, Ellen, have a drink and come and get the car tomorrow. *Someone* might as well have fun tonight!'

'Well, thank you very much,' said Colin tartly, and Charlie reminded Hannah for the third time since I'd arrived that she needed to think of her blood pressure, and Hannah rolled her eyes and shoved another ginger nut in her mouth, and Charlie chuntered about sugar and Hannah snarled that she needed the fucking ginger nuts to keep the morning sickness at bay, and Charlie attempted to suggest that Hannah's nausea might be something to do with the constant consumption of ginger nuts, and Hannah snapped that when Charlie had swollen ankles, stretch marks and piles, then he could fucking well tell her how to manage her pregnancy, and suddenly a glass of wine (or two) and coming back for the car tomorrow seemed a jolly good idea.

The doorbell rang again, and Sam dashed off to answer it.

'Is that Katie and Tim?' I asked.

It was indeed Katie and Tim, my old neighbours from across the road at the doomed Marital Home. And another man. On his own.

'This is Jack!' announced Sam. 'Jack, this is Charlie' (Charlie gave a manly handshake) 'and this is Hannah' (Hannah mumbled something through a mouthful of biscuit). 'You met Katie and Tim on the way in, Colin I think you know already, and then this is Ellen,' he finished, sounding distressingly like he'd only just stopped himself from adding a 'TA DAAAAA!' at the end.

Oh no! This was supposed to be just a relaxing dinner with friends. I didn't know it was going to be a set-up. I was wearing my special stretchy jeans so I could eat more because Colin is a bloody fabulous cook. I'd been looking forward to getting mildly pissed (yeah, OK, who was I kidding, telling myself I wasn't going to drink tonight? I know perfectly well that I have very little willpower when it comes to people offering me pink sunshine wine. Or any wine. Or gin) and having a lovely catch-up with all my friends, including Katie and Tim, who I hadn't seen properly in ages.

And now, now I realised that the whole thing was a bloody set-up, and I was going to have to pretend I was a proper person and have serious grown-up conversations and act like I knew who the Foreign Secretary was, and try to remember some cool bands to be 'into' if he asked what sort of music I liked (is that still a chat-up question? How the fuck should I know? No one has properly chatted me up in twenty-five years, unless you count the disastrous night with Tom, who was more interested in telling me how many eggs he ate a day). And all of this under the scrutiny of my nearest and dearest friends, watching to see if Jack and I were managing to perform some sort of mating dance over the olives and overpriced, undersalted nuts. Fuck it, I decided. I wasn't doing it. They couldn't make me. Doubtless they'd claim they meant well, but they had blatantly hoodwinked me, and *I could not be arsed*. I was going to be myself, and if this tosser wanted to know my views on … on … I dunno, the Arctic Monkeys, or the interesting thing that happened on *Question Time* last night, I'd simply inform him that in actual fact I was planning to marry Rick Astley when I grew up, and my preferred evening viewing was *Say Yes to the Dress*, and he could fuck off with his pretentious thoughts on wankdom.

'Jack's a vet!' added Sam. 'Ellen has two dogs and three chickens!'

Jack tried to look interested. In fairness, it must be a pain being a vet at social occasions, much like being a doctor, with everyone wanting you to examine their bunions or something, or me when I say I work for a tech company and then they immediately embark on a tedious anecdote about the problems they're having with Windows 10 and could I tell them how to fix it.

'Gosh!' Jack said. 'Errr, what sort of dogs?'

I thawed towards him slightly. After all, he was taking an interest in my babies. 'A Border terrier and some sort of unknown wolf–horse hybrid dog,' I said.

'I *love* Border terriers,' said Jack. 'Such tough little dogs, and amazingly strong characters.'

What a very clever, knowledgeable man Jack was, I decided. With lovely eyes. Lovely blue eyes, with laughter lines around them. I wondered how soon I could excuse myself to pop to the loo and put some more eyeliner on and maybe some lipstick, and hoick up my bra a bit … ooh, hang on, he was saying something.

'What's the wolf–horse hybrid, though?' he went on. 'I don't think I'm familiar with that.'

'Ha ha ha, nor me,' I said brightly. 'I got him from a rescue. They told me he was fully grown, but I don't think he's ever going to stop growing. He's going to end up like Clifford the Big Red Dog, only sort of a mangey greyish brown colour.

'Do you have any animals of your own? Ha ha ha,' I enquired, tossing my hair coquettishly.

'Two Patterdales,' he said.

'Oh, how lovely, ha ha ha.'

'Not really,' he replied. 'They're mildly psychotic. But I love them, when they're not trying to kill things. Although that's most of the time. One of them bit my daughter last time she was over, because she sat in Baxter's chair.'

'Ha ha ha, that seems fair,' I said. 'Judgy has been known to growl at me if I try to make him move out of my seat!'

We were soon exchanging information about our children (Jack had one daughter, age nineteen, he'd been divorced since she was ten, she'd just started university), and jobs, and how we knew everyone (he met Sam when Sam brought his Staffie in to see him, and then it turned out they were both members of the same tennis club – Sam develops a passion for tennis every year post-Wimbledon, plays obsessively for three or four weeks, then declares he has tennis elbow and gives up again till the following year – they got chatting and Sam invited him to dinner), when Colin suddenly said, 'Ellen! Give me a hand in the kitchen, will you?'

Oh, how rude, when I was getting on so well with Jack.

'What *are* you doing?' he hissed.

'What? I'm just talking to Jack.'

'No, you're not. You're flailing your head around, it looks like a bladder on a stick. And what's with all the "ha ha ha's"?'

'I'm flirting,' I told him with dignity. 'Your dating websites didn't work, so I assume you've invited Jack for me, so I'm making the most of the opportunity.'

'That's not flirting, that's hideous. You look and sound deranged. And you're doing some weird starey thing with your eyes.'

'I'm being coquetteish.'

'Well, don't. It's awful. Just be yourself.'

'But what if he doesn't like myself?'

'Well, that's his loss, isn't it? But the rest of it needs to go, or he'll be so terrified he'll make an excuse to go home before we've even had the starter. Now go back out there and try to be normal.'

I duly went back out and did my best to be normal, though Colin did kick me under the table when I started babbling about otters and their opposable thumbs, and how they sleep holding hands and have a little pocket to keep their favourite rock in, because apparently not everyone loves otters as much as I do, but

I felt that my otter knowledge would definitely have impressed Jack, what with him being a vet. Really, given they had set me up with him, they seemed determined to thwart me at every turn. But the wine flowed, the food was fabulous and, despite pointed questions from my so-called friends about whether I'd partaken in any highbrow cultural activities recently (did they know me at all?), the conversation was funny and interesting, and Jack did not ask me any questions about politics or music or French films.

After pudding, Hannah started yawning and Charlie took her home to bed, Hannah for once not protesting at his overprotectiveness.

'Well, what shall we do now?' said Colin idly, over coffee and brandy.

'Oooh!' said Katie. 'We should play that game again, like last time we were here. My mum has the kids, and we don't have to rush home for a babysitter.'

Jack looked slightly nonplussed at what this 'game' might involve. I was slightly worried too, because I really did quite like Jack and wanted to make a good impression, and although I'd not go so far as to pretend to like Coldplay to have him fancy me, I feared the game Katie was talking about might offer a less than favourable impression of me, even though I am very good at it.

'Do you mean Cards Against Humanity?' said Sam.

'That's the one,' cried Katie. 'The one where you have to give the most awful but funny answer that you can to theoretical questions.'

'Ha ha ha, yes, but we played that last time, Katie!' I said brightly. 'What about Scrabble?'

'BOOOORING!' said Katie. 'Cards Against Humanity!'

'Trivial Pursuit?'

'Honestly, Ellen, you're no fun,' huffed Katie. It was too late anyway. Colin had appeared bearing the box of cards and also a bottle of tequila. Oh fuck a doodle doo. Maybe, I thought hopefully, I could impress Jack with my capacity for tequila. Or at least get him so drunk he didn't remember the rest of the night …

JULY

Sunday, 1 July

I woke up this morning with a screaming hangover and only a very hazy recollection of the rest of last night, apart from a hideous memory of thinking it was hilarious to offer the answer card 'Three dicks at the same time' to the question 'Why am I sticky?' while slamming down another shot of tequila.

I staggered downstairs to let the dogs out, and then once they had accomplished their business I followed the Trail of Shame through the house, making sure I'd not left my shoes in the taxi, that I'd managed to return home with my bag/purse/phone and had locked the doors, watched by Judgy in disgust and by Barry in confusion, as I hoped fervently that my head would not fall off while wondering why the light was *so bright*.

I found all my goods and chattels. There was an anxious moment when I could only find one shoe, leading to me surreptitiously opening the front door to peer down the path to see if it was outside, before recoiling from the hideous, burning light that was so hurty and bad, but the shoe turned up on top of the coat rack – either I'd decided to remove my shoes by high-kicking them off or I'd become confused about how to put away one's outdoor apparel – oh fuck! At the thought of high-kicking, a wave of shame washed over me as I had a flashback to a scene where I insisted on demonstrating a questionable dance move called a 'slutdrop', then got stuck in the 'drop' position and had to be hauled to my feet by Colin. My phone was dead, as I'd managed to plug it into a charger that wasn't connected to the mains, so I put it on to charge. When it finally gasped back into life, it started the doom laden 'bings' that accompany every morning after.

BING – 'And how are we feeling today?' Fuck off, Sam, bloody awful!

BING – 'What time did we leave? How did we get home?' Katie, I required empirical evidence to ascertain I brought my shoes home. What makes you think I'd know how you got home? Also, do you remember the slut drop, and do you think Jack was impressed or appalled?

BING – 'That was fun! What did you think of Jack?' Why did you bring out the tequila, you know what it does to me!

BING – 'Did you all get shitfaced? I'm so jealous!' Never mind, Hannah. We'll have a massive piss-up for you once you've dropped, in lieu of a pastel cupcaked baby shower.

BING – 'Hi, this is Jack, we met last night. I just wanted to say –'

Oh fuckdiddling twatsticks. What have I done? What did I say? What offence have I caused or rash claims have I made?

I tried not to be sick in the sink as I waited for the kettle to boil and pondered the meaning of Jack's incomplete text. Did he think I was so pissed I needed reminding who had been there (a not-unreasonable assumption, I grudgingly admitted, as another hot wave of embarrassment crashed over me at the memory of the slut dropping). And what did he want to say? You're a disgrace and should be ashamed of yourself? I was astonished by your amazing contortions and would like to see more? You should know better at your age? You're witty and charming and flirt beautifully and I love you and want to spend the rest of my life with you? After last night I'm taking out a restraining order against you; if you come within one hundred metres of me you could be arrested? To be honest, given the amount of tequila that was consumed, the possibilities were endless!

I was tentatively sipping a cup of tea and hoping it stayed down, still agonising over what the rest of Jack's text might have said, when my children erupted back into the house.

'What are you doing here?' I said in surprise. 'You're not meant to be home till tonight.'

'ASK DAD,' shouted Jane, storming upstairs, followed by an overjoyed Barry.

'What? Where's your father? Peter, what's going on?'

Peter already had his head buried in the fridge, but managed to remove it to say, 'Jane had a fight with Dad and wanted to come home, so I thought I'd come home too, because Dad never has any good snacks, and also I need you to write me a note saying you know I haven't done my French homework.'

'What? Why haven't you done your French?'

Simon sidled through the door at that moment.

'Christ!' he said. 'What happened to you?'

'I am a tiny bit hungover!' I said with as much dignity as I could muster.

'Oh yeah, the kids said you were going to Colin and Sam's last night! Hope you had fun while I was stuck at home babysitting.'

'I'm going to say this once more, and once more only, Simon,' I said calmly (mainly I was speaking in a calm voice because I was too hungover to stand raised voices, even my own). 'You cannot "babysit" your own kids. They're your children. You're parenting them. Like a parent. Which is what you are!'

'God, it's just an expression,' said Simon sourly. 'You're as touchy as your daughter!'

'Speaking of *your* daughter, what have you done to upset her?'

'I haven't done anything to upset her, but I do need to talk to you about her. I caught her texting a *boy* today!'

'A boy,' I repeated. 'And when you say texting, do you mean texting or sexting?'

'What do you mean?' Simon said blankly.

'Texting or sexting? There's a difference.'

'Yeah, Dad,' sniggered Peter through half the family-sized block of Cheddar he'd managed to cram into his mouth. 'Texting is just, like, chatting, and sexting is dirty stuff.'

'I knew that,' said Simon coldly.

'Did you?' said Peter. 'Are you sure?'

'Stop arguing with me,' snapped Simon.

'I'm not arguing,' argued Peter.

'Peter, could you possibly go upstairs and bring all your dirty laundry down, and let your father and me discuss this in peace?' I suggested, seeing the veins in Simon's forehead beginning to pulse alarmingly.

'Right, so tell me what happened?'

'She kept getting texts all morning.'

'She was out of bed?'

'Well, no, but I could hear her phone binging. And then when I finally went into her room to insist she got up, she was giggling at a text, and I managed to look over her shoulder and it was from a boy. Called Will.'

'Will Anderson?'

'I don't know! It just said Will! And so I said she was far too young to be texting boys, and she said it was none of my business, and I said "I am your father, young lady, and if I say you're too young to be texting boys, you're too young and that is all there is to it." And then she had a complete hissy fit and screamed that I was oppressing her and that she could text who she liked, and something about it not being fair and hating her life and the patriarchy and she demanded to come home, and I thought that best because you're much better at dealing with this sort of thing than me.'

'Great,' I said. 'Thanks very much. Just dump it all on me again, why don't you? For Christ's sake, Simon, she's fifteen! Short of locking her in a nunnery, she's going to encounter boys. And anyway, her boyfriend is called Harry.'

'What! She has a boyfriend? She's too young. I FORBID IT!'

'She's FIFTEEN. FIF-FUCKING-TEEN! Think what you were doing when you were fifteen.'

'EXACTLY!' roared Simon, scarlet with rage. 'That's exactly why I don't want any scummy little hornbags sniffing round my baby girl! I know *precisely* what fifteen-year-old boys are like, because I used to be one, and they can keep well away from Jane, with their filthy thoughts and their sex obsessions. I WILL NOT HAVE IT! Boys that age are only after ONE THING!'

'Yes, I know!' I said. 'I was once a fifteen-year-old girl too, remember? I know teenage boys are sex pests, but you can't wrap her up in cotton wool and protect her from the world. You have to trust her, trust her judgement, trust her common sense, and accept she's growing up.'

'And why didn't you tell me she had a boyfriend? Why did she tell you and not me?'

'She didn't tell me. If you looked at her Instagram, you'd have known anyway.'

'I'm supposed to look at her Instagram?'

'Well, yes, I find it's the best way to find out what's actually going on with them. Are you seriously telling me that you let her get her belly-button pierced and stay out till God knows what time and you don't even stalk her online to see what she's doing? FFS, Simon, that's what Instagram is *for*. Stalking and trying to make your life look better than it is.'

'How was I supposed to know? I don't even know why I've *got* an Instagram account.'

'I assumed to document your new cool single life,' I said tartly.

Simon collapsed in a chair with a groan. 'Hardly. It's tough without you, with the kids. I didn't think it would be like this. I never know what I'm supposed to be doing. And I don't want them to grow up. Especially not Jane. I want her to stay my little girl. I don't want some sleazy yob pawing at her and groping her. And I can't even think about the *sex* thing.'

'Well, I'm sorry you find it hard to cope with the kids on your own. It rather proves my point that you saw me more as a nanny than a woman, though. But this is Jane, Simon. I don't think she's going to let anyone grope her unless she wants to be groped. She's a fairly tough cookie, but it's what kids do. They push boundaries, and eventually, most of them have sex. Also, try to keep your voice down, she'll hear you.'

Simon groaned again and dropped his head into his hands. 'Oh God, I *know*, but I hate it. I wish we *could* just lock her in a nunnery or something.'

'You're being quite hypocritical too,' I said. 'It won't be long before Peter is one of those boys pestering girls for blowjobs and to show him their tits! Hang on a sec.' My phone binged again. It was Jack.

> Sorry, somehow sent too soon! Bit hungover ;-) And then my phone died and I couldn't find a charger. So, I just wanted to say I really enjoyed meeting you last night and I wondered if you maybe would like to have dinner or a drink sometime?

YESSSSSSS! I STILL HAVE IT! I'M NOT GOING TO DIE ALONE AND CONDEMN MY DOGS TO A LONELY DEATH IN A SHELTER AFTER THEY'VE BEEN BRANDED CANNIBAL DOGS! I wonder if it was the slut drop that swung it for him? Or my excellent flirting? Also, take THAT Simon! Soon my Instagram shall be a coupled-up wonderland. In. Your. Face. I smirked smugly.

'What are you grinning about?' demanded Simon.

'Oh, nothing,' I said airily.

Jack seems like a man on my wavelength. Also I'm pleased to see he punctuates his texts properly, and uses full words instead of abbreviations and emojis. However perfect he might be in other ways, I'm not sure I could love a man if he sent a text saying 'do u wanna hav dinner sum time?' But what to do now? What's the etiquette? How soon do I reply? How long do I leave it? Are they the same thing? Will I appear too keen if I text back straight away and he'll think I'm easy? Do I care if he thinks I'm easy? I mean, I never used to bother, but that was in the Nineties and we were all supposed to be ladettes and get shitfaced on bourbon and shag around, and it WAS quite good fun, but I have two children now and am supposed to set a good example. I wondered if I could ask Jane how long to leave it before texting back when a boy asks you out? No, I couldn't possibly ask Jane for dating advice, especially as I do quite like Jack.

'Ellen? Ellen, are you even listening to me? I'm trying to have a serious conversation about your children and you're grinning inanely.'

'*Our* children. They're not just mine.'

'You're not listening to me.'

'Well, what more is there to say? They're going to grow up whether we like it or not, and we just have to make the best of it that we can. Now, if you'll excuse me, I have things to do.'

'What, is that it?'

'What were you expecting?'

'Are you not going to tell Jane she can't see that boy anymore?'

'No. Because what good will that do? You can tell her, if you like.'

'You're being so unsupportive.'

'What, like you were when you let her get her belly-button pierced, or stay out till 3 am, even though you know I don't let her stay out past 1.30 am? You need to deal with this and get over it.'

'This is all very hard for me, you know.'

'Well, it's not exactly a fucking walk in the park for me either, Simon,' I snapped, as I thought, 'But ha ha ha, at least I'm not now a dried-up, unloveable old crone. I PRACTICALLY HAVE A BOYFRIEND!'

Despite my crippling hangover, all in all it wasn't a bad day, as Simon did at least give me a lift to get my car, which saved me getting the bus, even if he was a bit huffy about it, and as long as he's the subject of Jane's ire, she's being much nicer to me, although I suppose I should remonstrate with her for describing Simon as a patronising bastard, although she really does have a point.

Thursday, 12 July

I fear Peter and Jane suspect about Jack. Well, not that there's anything to suspect about Jack. We've been texting (NOT sexting) quite a lot. He sends me photos of his dogs. I like this, because a) I just like photos of dogs, and b) it gives me an excuse to send him photos of Judgy and Barry. Well, in fairness mainly of Judgy. I adore Barry (traitor though he is, what with choosing Jane over me, and I think he's *still* bloody growing. Between him and Peter I will be bankrupted just by buying food), but no one, not even Jane, could call Barry photogenic. Apart from anything else, he's now so bloody enormous it's difficult to get all of him in a photo without standing about half a mile away, but as his looks have not improved at all over time, I feel it best that Jack meets Barry and sees his True and Noble Soul shining out before he's put off by a photo of him. Luckily, Judgy is photogenic enough for them both.

We still haven't managed to actually meet up, but there has been lots of chatting back and forth, as well as dog photos, some of it funny, some of it getting to know each other, some of it, dare I say it, a little flirtatious! The trouble is, every time one of the children are in the room when I get a text from Jack, I immediately start blushing and trying to clear the screen on my phone, even though so far there has been nothing actually blushworthy sent. However, they can obviously tell I'm acting oddly and are starting to demand to know who the message is from, etc. So far I've alternated between blatantly lying and claiming it's work or Hannah, or telling them to mind their own business, and reminding them, especially Jane after the recent scenes with Simon (he bought her affection back last week with a very expensive pair of trainers that she claimed she could not live without, so they're at least getting on again), that they don't like it when I nag them about who is messaging them. Apparently that is different, though, and while I must respect their privacy, as their mother they do not have to extend the same courtesy to me.

I fear they've decided to take matters into their own hands, however, now they suspect me of having a gentleman friend. Despite their initial resistance to the very idea of me meeting a man, any man, anywhere (a Martini Man perhaps), they've started nagging me to go along to the Speed Dating Night at their school, organised by the PTA as their last fundraiser of the term. Apparently so many parents are now divorced or separated that they thought it would be a 'fun' thing to do. I think it sounds like hell, but Peter and Jane keep telling me that I should go, and saying horrifying things like 'Oscar Watson's dad thinks you're hot, you know!'

I can only assume that they've resigned themselves to the fact that I might at some point meet a man I could imagine having a relationship with, or at the very least a shag, and have decided that the best thing to do would be to take matters into their own hands and pair me off with someone they deem vaguely suitable. I'd have thought that the last thing on earth they'd deem suitable was me getting off with one of their schoolfriend's dads, but maybe they're counting on the fact that the embarrassment will be mutual, and therefore the whole thing can be hushed up, rather than the fear of someone spotting me snogging a random at a bus stop (as if I would. Well, I might. It would depend entirely on the man, I suppose. Though I never much liked snogging at bus stops when I was young, the ever-present whiff of wee and the fear of missing one's bus was always somewhat off-putting).

They went on and on about it, however, so I finally capitulated and agreed to go. What's the worst that can happen? Apart from the fact I'll have to pay a tenner for the privilege of a small glass of lukewarm chardonnay so astringent it gives me heartburn, and having to spend the evening making polite small talk, when I hate small talk. Oh well. I can always wow them with my fascinating disquisition about why otters have opposable thumbs. It worked on Jack, after all. Maybe, if nothing else, I'll meet another fellow otter fan. Maybe men are like buses – none come along for ages, then there are loads at once, and I might end up with multiple admirers vying for my hand. That wouldn't be so bad, although it's fairly unlikely, I must admit. I thought I might manage to weasel out of it by reminding them that it was my weekend to have them, and so Jane would have to miss the inevitable party to stay at home with Peter, but they both assured me that that was fine, as actually they have arrangements with Hannah's kids and will be sleeping over there that night.

I've a nasty feeling that somewhere out there, some unfortunate single father is also being mercilessly groomed by his offspring as part of some sort of grand masterplan by the hell fiends to set us up together. I shall think of the otters. I did ask Peter what Oscar Watson's dad's views were on otters and he looked confused. I do hope they haven't picked out Freddie Dawson's dad for me. Two minutes in Mr Dawson's company and it's plain to see where Freddie's … unfortunate manner comes from. And he *says* Mrs Dawson went off with a door-to-door fish salesman called Roger, but as far as I know, no one has ever seen her since, and Mr Dawson had new monoblocking laid shortly after her departure. I mean, I know that doesn't prove anything, but I have my suspicions. Also, he looks at your tits when he's talking to you.

Friday, 20 July

Well, tonight was the infamous Speed Dating Night. I should have suspected something was up. The children were too nice to me. Jane offered to do my make-up for me, and spent ages 'contouring' and doing my eyebrows. The effect was remarkably similar to when I rub on my foundation with my fingers and ignore my eyebrows completely, but still, it was nice of her to make the effort, and so of course I agreed with her that I could totally see the difference between her methods and mine, and yes, her way was much better.

Off I shuffled, thinking how much I'd rather be on the sofa with a glass of Sauv Blanc, texting Jack, who had taken the piss mercilessly when I confessed what the children were forcing me to do, before making me promise not to get off with the geography teacher – I got the Fear slightly at that point, as it hadn't even occurred to me that teachers might be taking part.

To my surprise, the school hall was packed. You could hardly move, due to sex-starved single parents in desperate hope of finding love at last. I spotted Perfect Lucy Atkinson's Perfect Mummy across the room, but it was too busy to go over and talk to her and find out if she was also only there under duress from Lucy, or if she really thought there was a chance of pulling tonight. I fought my way to the front of the queue and dutifully collected my glass of paintstripper and my number, filled in my questionnaire, and the hellish merry-go-round commenced. There were no otter fans among the first few speed dates, though it turned out that Mr Dawson isn't the only father who has a thing about talking to one's tits. And then, down into the seat across from me plonked Simon.

'What are you doing here? I hissed.

'I could ask you the same question,' he replied.

'Don't think I *want* to be here,' I said crossly. 'The children nagged me into it. Went on and on and bloody on at me until I agreed.'

'Me too,' said Simon in outrage. 'They were like demented budgies, wittering incessantly about it. I thought you'd started feeding them Trill.'

We looked at each other, realisation slowly dawning.

'I think,' said Simon, 'that we may have been set up!'

'You mean, they thought if they could get us both along here, we'd realise that compared to everyone else, actually we *are* compatible and it's all meant to be?' I said in horror.

Simon nodded grimly. 'I did wonder why they were so keen to set me up with Perfect Lucy Atkinson's Perfect Mummy,' he said.

'She would eat you alive,' I said. 'They claimed it was Oscar Watson's dad for me. Jesus, just when I think this night can't get any worse, they go and pull this *Parent Trap* shit on us.'

'It's pretty awful, isn't it?' said Simon. 'Look, our time's nearly up. Now we've rumbled why they forced us along here, there's not much point in staying, is there? Shall we just go and get a proper drink somewhere?'

'What, together?' I said. 'Us? In a, like, pub?'

'You spend far too much time with teenagers,' said Simon. 'Yes, in a "like" pub. Or indeed, just "a pub". Why not? We're grown-ups, and just because we're separated doesn't mean we can't have an amicable drink together, does it? Surely the idea of a nice cold vodka martini somewhere that doesn't reek of teen-age BO, ancient cabbage and sexual frustration is appealing?'

'Well, when you put it like that …' I admitted. 'There *is* that strange school whiff, isn't there? It's not exactly conducive to romance. I'm not sure the school hall was the best choice of venue really. You need to be proper teenage horny to be able to still think of sex without the smell putting you off.'

The bell rang for us to move on. 'Come on,' said Simon. 'If you're very nice to me, I'll even buy you a bag of crisps.'

'Salt and vinegar?'

'What else?'

So off we trotted and found a very civilised bar, and Simon did indeed buy me the promised vodka martini, and I tried not to think about how the last time we'd sat at a table in a bar together he'd announced he was moving out.

'You look nice,' he said. 'I like your top.'

'Oh,' I said. 'Thank you. I've had it for ages.' This was true. I wasn't wasting a new top on the school Speed Dating Night.

'So, what've you been up to, anyway? All we ever talk about is the children now.'

'Oh this and that. You know. Work, obviously. I read that new Booker Prize book.'

'Oh God, so did I. What did you think?'

'I don't know, I didn't really understand what was going on.'

'Me neither, but I thought it was just me. Maybe that's the secret to winning something like the Booker Prize – write something completely random that no one can understand but no one wants to be the first to look thick and admit it.'

'Maybe.'

'Maybe I'll give it a go,' sniggered Simon. 'After all, I wrote some pretty unintelligible poetry back in the day.'

'Yes, I remember,' I said dryly.

'What? You used to love my poetry.'

'No, I loved the fact someone had written a poem for me. The actual poem itself was, a bit …'

'Shit,' said Simon. 'Just say it. My poems were shit, believe me, I know. I discovered a box of them when we moved. I had to burn them, just to try to remove the lingering shame that I was ever quite so pretentious.'

'Well, writing poetry was pretty much *de rigueur* to go with the rest of your tortured artiste look back then, though, wasn't it? You were definitely channelling a slightly Byronic vibe.'

'Stop it, you're embarrassing me even more,' said Simon. 'God! What was I *thinking*?'

'I liked your embarrassing Byronic phase,' I protested. 'Better than the ratty fleeces and *Wheeler Dealers* years.'

'Well, at least someone liked it,' sighed Simon.

'Anyway, what about you? What have you been up to?'

'Not a lot. I go for a beer after work with Geoff sometimes – he always makes us go to these poncy bars that don't do proper beer. I decided to try to get fit, and went hillwalking with another guy from the office who's really into it, but it was vile. I'd forgotten how much I hate hillwalking.'

Hmmm. Could the mysteries behind Simon's Instagram photos have just been explained? Poncy Beer Geoff and

Hillwalking Man? What about all the cocktails and the fancy dinners, though?

'Is that all?' I said casually. 'Doesn't sound that exciting.'

'I joined the gym.'

'You hate the gym.'

'Yeah, well, unfortunately I only remembered that when I'd signed up for a year's membership. I had thoughts about doing an Ironman competition –'

I choked on my drink in a most unladylike way.

'– but then I found out what was involved! It's insane! Who would do that?'

'Indeed.'

'Oh, and I still go and see Christina every week.'

'Christina?'

'Yes, the counsellor?'

'*Our* counsellor? But why? We're getting divorced! Why see a relationship counsellor now?'

'She's not *just* a relationship counsellor,' said Simon stiffly. 'She does all sorts. I find her very helpful, actually.'

Ha! I *knew* that bitch liked him better than me. I *knew* she was secretly taking his side.

'And actually, Christina has encouraged me to start dating again.'

'Bitch!'

'What?'

'Nothing!'

'I was saying, Christina said she thought I should try to see how it felt to see some other women, see if I was ready.'

I swallowed down the retort that one would have thought he was more than ready, given his willingness to see all of Miss Madrid, and wondered if I could get Christina struck off for BLATANT FAVOURITISM of her clients. Instead I politely said, 'And how's that going?'

'Not very well, to be honest. I joined some sites … but no one looks like their photo when they turn up, and none of them are interested in Mies van der Rohe, even the ones that say they're into twentieth-century architecture in their profiles,' he squawked indignantly.

'Oh dear,' I said, trying and failing to sound sympathetic. Clearly Simon frequents far more highbrow dating websites than I do. That is probably a good thing, though. Imagine the shame of coming across each other online. Metaphorically speaking, of course.

'And then there was the one who told me straight away that she was looking for someone to have a baby with as soon as possible –'

'Do you want another baby?'

'God almighty, no! But why not put *that* on her profile?'

'Would you have met her if she had?'

'Of course not!'

'Well then.'

'Another one spent all night showing me photos of her cats. I must admit she *was* gorgeous and my hopes did rise when she asked if I wanted to see her pussy, but after an hour of admiring Mr Fluffy Bottom in various poses, most of them flashing said hairy arse at the camera, her charms waned somewhat …'

I laughed, despite myself.

'And it's costing me a bloody fortune,' he went on indignantly. 'They all want to drink expensive cocktails.'

I downed my own expensive cocktail and waved my glass at him. 'Well, there has to be some compensation for an evening in your company, darling. Same again, please!'

While Simon was at the bar, I pondered his revelations. So. No mind-blowing sex with a twenty-three-year-old contortionist? Or is he just being too considerate to mention it? Though if you were swinging from the chandeliers on a regular basis, you'd hardly describe your life as 'pretty boring', would you? Could it be that despite everything, *Simon* might be the one to die alone and unloved, because I pretty much have a boyfriend now (whatever, I'm counting Jack as a boyfriend for the purpose of point-scoring against Simon, if nothing else) and so I'M WINNING?

Even so, it's still unfair that he manages to attract all these different dates online with apparently no effort at all, while I just got either rude messages and dick pics or was ignored. I resolved to casually drop my date with Tom the Ironman into conversation, so he knew he wasn't the only one who could still get some, and mine was way fitter than Simon. I didn't have to mention he was also mind-crushingly boring, did I?

After another drink, Simon suggested we got something to eat, and I *was* very hungry, and so we had dinner and more wine, and maybe some brandy, well, actually three brandies, and then he said we might as well share a taxi and when we got to my house he proposed a nightcap, and I didn't really want to go into a dark, cold, empty house alone (apart from the reproachful dogs) when actually I'd had a good night. So he came in, and we had a whisky, and I mentioned Tom and his Ironman training, and Simon looked all sort of broody and Heathcliffy about that, and then he kissed me. And it felt so very nice to be kissed, properly kissed, after so long, and even nicer when it was someone who felt so familiar and knew exactly how I liked to be kissed. One thing led to another, and well, it ended up being a bit more than kissing. Quite a lot more than kissing. The large packet of condoms I'd bought with the intention of catching Jane in a good mood and presenting her with them, along with a lecture on safe sex, came in handy. Well, not all of them, obviously. Simon is forty-six now. But three of them, anyway.

He's still here, sound asleep, and I'm wide awake, and now the brandy and wine and martinis are seeping out of my bloodstream and my admittedly always questionable judgement is starting to return, I'm wondering exactly what the fuck I thought I was doing, and feeling like a total Jezebel. What sort of fucking IDIOT shags their ex-husband after too many drinks? There's a part of me that is also thinking, Jesus, I hadn't realised how much I needed that though, but also I'm worrying about what if Simon thinks we're now back together, which would be awkward, and then the Whore of Babylon part of me is pondering the chance of maybe making this a regular thing – being fuck buddies until I get a better offer, because damn but it was *good*. But also, what about Jack? Have I cheated on him, even though all we've done is text? Maybe I should wake Simon up and send him home? But on the other hand, maybe we could have a quickie in the morning before we fall out again? Would it even count as cheating on Jack given how many times Simon and I have had sex before? What's another three times in the grand scheme of things? Or four? … Oh dear.

I'm also rather annoyed that to some extent we fell for the children's extremely unsubtle plan. I can't think about all this now. Like Scarlett O'Hara, I'll think about it tomorrow. Yes. Tomorrow. I can't believe I did that. I can't believe I'm thinking about doing that again. Oh God, what a *mess*! This must never happen again. I was feeling so superior to Simon last night, and then I just went and fell into bed with him like nothing had ever happened. Maybe I should just wake him and tell him to go? Would that be rude? I wish I could turn the clock back so this hadn't happened.

I can feel Judgy's furious glare burning through the door. He was always outraged to be banished for sex, this isn't going to have put Simon up in his estimation! Poor Barry didn't even know what was going on, I don't think he's ever been in such a situation before!

Saturday, 21 July

Simon was still here when I woke up. It was strange, waking up next to him again – both completely familiar and at the same time totally awkward. What's the protocol for accidently shagging your ex-husband? Given they've seen two human heads emerge from your fanny, is it OK to still fart in bed like you used to? Or does one have to return to the niceties one observes with a new partner, and pretend one does not fart because one is a lady?

We got up and made breakfast. Simon was delighted to find that he didn't have to chip three-year-old Nescafé out the jar, because in deference to Hannah's secret coffee binges I'd invested in a cafetière and some proper coffee. We sat at the kitchen table and made small talk, which wasn't as awkward as I thought it might be, and it was nice having someone to talk to over breakfast apart from the dogs.

'You know,' said Simon, looking round my kitchen, 'it wouldn't take much to extend this, make it into a big kitchen/family room and put a shower room off the utility room. Give you all a bit more space.'

'Yes, I know,' I said, my good will towards him starting to wane as he immediately began to interfere in my life again. 'That is actually my plan. It's just a matter of finding the time, not to mention the money.'

'Well, I could draw up the plans for you,' he suggested. 'I AM an architect, after all. What's the point in paying someone else to do it, when I could do it for free? And I could probably get you a decent deal with one of the builders we use through work.'

'Why would you do that?' I said in confusion. 'Is this some roundabout way of paying for sex? It's really not necessary.'

'NO!' said Simon. 'I'd do it because it would be a nice thing to do for you, *and* for our children. I still care about you very much you know, Ellen.' He put his hand over mine. I made a non-committal noise, and pulled it away and then went pink as my phone chimed with a text from Jack.

Hope the geography teacher's palms weren't too sweaty ;-) xx

'Who was that?' said Simon. 'Why are you blushing?'

'No one!' I said quickly 'Just, um, one of those companies wanting to claim back PPI for me.'

My phone started buzzing and Natalia's number flashed up. I answered it, relieved at the distraction and change of subject, although the fact I should really have rung Dad and Natalia was yet more guilt, albeit of a different sort than the Scarlet Woman guilt induced by being texted by one man while having breakfast with another one who really shouldn't be here at all.

'Natalia! Hi!' I cried brightly. 'How are you? I've been meaning to call.'

Natalia made a strange noise, and then in a gulping voice, quite unlike her usual brisk tones, said, 'Ellen, is anyone there with you? Apart from the children, I mean?'

Oh shit. How did she know? Was she judging me? Surely not. She was married to a reformed serial shagger who had had more wives than most people have had hot dinners. Oh God, maybe my sluttish ways were genetic?

'Err, Simon has just popped by,' I said carefully.

'Good, that is good, I did not want you to be alone right now. Ellen, I am at the hospital. Your father has collapsed. They think it's a massive stroke, but it does not look good. You should come Ellen, now.'

'Daddy?' I babbled in confusion 'There must be some mistake. He'll be fine, he's never been sick in his life –'

'Ellen, you need to come to say goodbye,' interrupted Natalia gently.

I dropped the phone.

It was all a bit blurry after that. Someone was making a horrid squawking noise, which transpired to be me. Simon picked up my phone and took over, asking Natalia which hospital they were at, ringing the children, and driving me to collect them from Hannah, where luckily for once they were ready and dashed out and got in the car, because I wasn't fit to talk to anyone, not even Hannah, and then we all made the long drive to the hospital.

'Is Grandpa going to die?' whispered Jane, white-faced, from the back of the car.

I opened my mouth to assure her that no, no of course he wasn't, the hospital was doing everything possible, but I just started crying again.

Simon intervened. 'I think from what Natalia said, that yes, he probably is, darling. I'm so sorry. You all need to be brave now, you and Peter and Mummy, and look after each other.'

Peter said nothing at all, just stared out the window and bit his lip.

We got to the hospital, where Simon dropped us off and went to negotiate the fiendish parking systems that all hospitals seem to have these days, because obviously, if you're at a hospital for whatever reason, you don't already have enough problems and want nothing more than to drive round a complex one-way system to find the car park that is actually three miles away and has only one space left.

I hustled the children along the corridors, always so many corridors in old hospitals, all painted that strange beige you don't get anywhere else. I'm not sure what's more dispiriting, the beige corridors of the Victorian bits or the bright white lights of the modern parts.

Natalia was sitting by Dad's bed, on her own. I realised for the first time how much Natalia had given up to be with my father – she was so much younger and had left her friends and family to spend her life with a man old enough to be her father.

She looked round as we came in, then stood up. Her eyes were red and her face was deathly white. 'What a stupid expression,' I thought hysterically, looking between Natalia and my father lying in the bed. He was the one who was dying, and he wasn't deathly white at all, he was a rather horrid shade of bluey grey. Vaguely I wondered if Farrow & Ball had that colour on a paint chart, and what they called it.

'I'll leave you alone with him,' Natalia said hoarsely. She'd obviously done most of her crying already, and was trying to hold herself together for us.

'Natalia, no,' I said. 'Wait. I mean, yes, we'd like some time alone to say goodbye, but you shouldn't be on *your* own. Wait till Simon gets here. He's just parking, but he'll look after you.'

Simon appeared and suggested a cup of tea. Natalia laughed. 'You British. Tea. Always tea. Tea will cure everything. I'd rather have vodka. But sure, we'll have tea.'

'Do you really want vodka?' said Simon.

'My husband is dying. In fact, he's as good as dead. They are keeping him comfortable so his children can say goodbye. Of course I'd rather have a stiff drink than the endless cups of fucking tea people keep trying to give me. I'm drowning in tea, and such *bad* tea! Not like we have in Russia. It is sewage, this tea,' she said fiercely.

'Fair enough,' said Simon gravely. 'However, I might be able to help.'

He produced a hip flask from his pocket and held it out. 'I took the liberty of filling it while you were getting dressed,' he said to me apologetically. 'I thought it might be good for shock and things.'

Natalia grabbed it and they stepped out into the corridor.

'What do we do?' whispered Jane.

'I don't really know, darling,' I whispered back. 'I think we just tell him that we love him, and we'll miss him. They say your hearing is the last sense to go.'

'Do you think he heard Natalia demanding vodka then?' said Peter, which was the first time he'd spoken since we picked him up from Hannah's.

'Quite probably,' I said. 'I think if he did, it would have made him laugh. He always said he couldn't abide weeping women, wailing and howling and dripping tears everywhere. When I was a child he used to give me £5 to stop crying. Do you remember, Daddy?' I said, sitting down beside him.

And suddenly it was easy. What I'd envisaged as a dramatic 'Oh Daddy, MY DADDY' farewell deathbed scene, accompanied by suitable weeping and wailing and gnashing of teeth, became quiet and gentle. The children and I sat by him and held his hands, talking about stories from when I was little and their memories of him from their childhoods. We even managed to laugh. I still couldn't believe I was sitting there, saying goodbye to my father. My vibrant, larger than life, badly behaved dad, who was always utterly unremorseful when caught philandering, who made martinis that would blow your socks off, whose solution to tears was a £5 note and whose mantra had always been that life was just too short not to have fun. I remembered how the last time I saw him he told me how proud he was of how strong I was. I was determined I wasn't going to let him down now. He said my strength came from my mother, but he was the one who made me believe in it.

'Well, Daddy,' I said. 'No one could accuse you now of your regrets being about the things you didn't do, could they?'

'*How* many times was Grandpa married again?' asked Peter.

'Errr, four,' I said. 'I think. Possibly five.'

'Counting Granny and Natalia?'

'Obviously counting Granny and Natalia. He wasn't Henry VIII,' I said indignantly.

I was telling them about the time I got A+s for an entire term for my history essays, because he'd so shamelessly buttered up the repressed spinster history teacher at Parents' Night, when Jessica burst in and the calm was shattered.

'Oh Daddy, MY DADDY!' she howled. 'How are you here first, Ellen? Where are the doctors? I need to talk to them. NOW! No one less than a consultant. I'm not being fobbed off with some junior. Neil. NEIL!'

My long-suffering brother-in-law appeared in the doorway.

'I bet Ellen hasn't even spoken to a doctor, go and find me one at *once*. A proper one. Persephone, Gulliver! Come and say goodbye to your grandfather. Where's that woman he married? Don't tell me. Now she's finally managed to finish him off, she probably thinks she needn't bother being here for the end. I shall be contesting the will. And I want an autopsy. Make sure there's no foul play!'

'Hello Jessica. I see you managed to make it,' said Natalia, who had a little more colour in her cheeks thanks to Simon's hip flask (well, technically it was my hip flask).

'Natalia,' huffed Jessica. 'Where are all the doctors?'

'They check on him regularly, and the machines will go off if there's any change,' said Natalia.

'Hmmm. *NOT* good enough!' said Jessica. 'I shall talk to them and arrange some proper care. Hopefully it won't be too late. If he dies, then it will be on your conscience, Natalia. And yours, Ellen. What have you been doing since you got here?' Jessica sniffed the air suspiciously. 'Do I smell *alcohol*? Has someone been drinking? How disrespectful.'

'I expect it's just the alcohol from the hand sanitiser you can smell, Jess,' I said. Natalia shot me a grateful look.

The doctor arrived with Neil, and explained to a hurrumph-ing Jessica that there was nothing more they could do except keep Dad comfortable until he slipped away.

We left Jessica and her children to have some time alone with Dad, and went down to the canteen with Natalia.

'When did you last eat?' I asked her.

'I could not,' she shuddered. 'I am sorry, Ellen, I could not eat anything right now. I do love him. I know you and your sister did not believe it when I married him, but I do. I fell in love with him the first time I saw him. And now I do not know what I'll do without him,' she sighed. 'I'll get on with things, of course. It's what he'd expect. To wallow in grief and give up would be letting him down.'

'He never loved anyone else like you,' I told her. 'I saw him with plenty of wives and girlfriends over the years, but it wasn't like how he was with you. I wish he'd met you years ago. You made him so happy.'

'We all wish things like that,' said Natalia. 'But if I had met Ralph twenty years ago, he'd not have been the man he was when I *did* meet him, so maybe it would not have worked for us. Everyone has a time, and we had ours. I wish it had been longer. Do you think everyone wishes that? Even people who are married for eighty years? Do you think at the end they still think, "No, you cannot go yet, I need more time with you?"'

'I don't know. I really don't.'

'And if you had more time with Simon? Why was he at your house at that time in the morning?'

I was saved from answering by Simon returning from the counter with the children, carrying many cups of the dubious stewed tea and a selection of cakes and sand-wiches. Natalia refused everything. Peter stared longingly at the food.

'It's OK, Peter,' I said. 'You *are* allowed to eat.'

'Are you sure?' he said. 'I didn't know if it was, you know, unseemly.'

'Even grave matters of life and death are no match for a teenage boy's appetite,' I pointed out, as Peter wired into the sandwiches.

Jane picked at a Belgian bun and said, 'Do you believe in heaven, Natalia?'

'No,' said Natalia calmly, 'I don't. I won't see your grandfather again after today. I do not believe in religion, but we have one life, and we should make the best of it that we can. Remember what he always said, Ellen?'

'Life is short, let's have a good time?' I ventured.

'Yes. Ralph believes life is a gift and we should cram in as much as we can.'

'Well, he did that all right,' I said.

'He did,' said Natalia. 'He wasn't a saint, your father, but he always made the most of life. And he'd hate to think that we did not do the same, after he was gone. He'd want us to get on with our lives.'

'Even Auntie Jessica?' said Jane incredulously. 'After all that upstairs?'

'Jessica is in pain too,' said Natalia. 'She's just showing it in a different way. At least, I'm telling myself that is why she's behaving like that, because it's the only thing stopping me from slapping her very hard in the face.'

Jane perked up. 'If you slap Auntie Jessica, can I slap Persephone?'

'Why?' said Natalia.

'I've just always wanted to.'

'No,' said Natalia. 'There will be no slapping anyone today. If I can restrain myself from slapping Jessica, the rest of you can certainly refrain from violence.'

'Come on,' she said, heaving herself to her feet. 'We should go back. Simon, is there anything left in that flask?'

Simon handed it over and she gave it a shake. 'Do you want some?' she offered. I did, rather. Jessica is always easier to deal with after a shot of Dutch courage, and high emotion always brought out the worst in her, not to mention that it would also possibly calm the whirl of thoughts in my head about the future without Dad, how I was going to get the kids through it, and what I was going to do about Simon, who kept trying to hold my hand when no one was looking. But Natalia's need was greater, so I nobly shook my head.

Back in Dad's room, Jessica was googling American drug trials, while Persephone and Gulliver sat by the bed looking awkward and Neil hovered.

The doctor came in and stared at the charts and the machines, then murmured something to Natalia.

'She says it won't be long now,' said Natalia.

Everyone milled vaguely. The room was really too small for us all.

'Look,' said Simon. 'Why don't the children all say goodbye now, and then they can come with us, Neil, and Jessica and Ellen and Natalia can stay with Ralph until, well, you know.'

'Good plan,' said Neil with relief.

'It should just be Ellen and me,' argued Jessica. I reminded myself that if anyone got to slap Jessica today, it was Natalia, not me.

'Fuck OFF, Jessica!' I said. 'She's his *wife*! We're only here, getting to say goodbye to him, because she had the decency to call us. Just back off and try not to behave like a complete and utter bitch for once in your life.'

Jessica was so unused to me standing up to her that she did in fact shut up, and sit down.

And then we waited.

Sunday, 22 July

I always thought there would be more drama in death, that there would be some tangible sign of life leaving. A midwife once told me that the most astonishing thing about being present at a birth is that all of a sudden there's another person in the room, someone who hadn't been in the world just a few seconds earlier. I always thought being there when someone died would be like the opposite of that – that there would be one person less in the room, that you'd *feel* that they had gone. Some people say they can feel that, of course, but I didn't.

Mostly it was a long, wretched evening, trying not to think about how uncomfortable the hospital chairs were or how much I needed a wee, because I was too afraid Dad would die while I was in the loo and that would somehow be distressingly symbolic, of what I don't quite know. The doctors assured us that he wasn't in any pain, but I couldn't help but wonder how they *know*, though? I mean, it's not like anyone in that condition has ever actually been able to say anything? It didn't seem like the time to ask.

Jessica just sat and looked lost, although whether at the prospect of losing her father or because she was shocked to finally find herself in a situation that she couldn't control by bossing someone around, taking charge and making a fuss until she got her own way, I wasn't sure. I suspected a combination of both, and wondered if Jessica was internally composing a Stern Letter to the Grim Reaper about the shoddy customer service she'd recently experienced.

Natalia just held one of Dad's hands and stared into space, occasionally biting her lip very hard. Dad's breathing became slower and slower. The nurses came in and out, asked if we wanted anything, and then one of them said something quietly to Natalia. Natalia muttered something back and the nurse nodded.

Natalia looked up at us. 'Ellen, Jessica. May I have two minutes alone with him? Please?'

Jessica opened her mouth, but I was quicker. 'Come on,' I said briskly, trying not to feel guilty about how good it felt to stand up and stretch my legs, or consider that this was a perfect opportunity to go for a wee.

'Two minutes,' said Jessica nastily. 'No more.'

'That's all I'm asking for,' said Natalia calmly.

Luckily Neil was sitting outside the room, and I thrust Jessica at him. 'Hang on to her for a couple of minutes,' I instructed him, as I bolted to the nearest bathroom.

When I came out, Jessica looked more like herself again and was arguing with Neil about being allowed back into the room, snapping bossily once more that *she* was the eldest and should be making the decisions, as Neil attempted to remind her that Natalia was our father's next of kin. He looked relieved to see me.

We went back into the room, as Natalia gently kissed Dad. 'Goodbye, you old bugger,' she said, her voice cracking.

Jessica wailed. 'He's gone! You sent us out and he's gone!'

'No, he is not. Not yet,' said Natalia. 'But it will be very soon, and I wanted a moment alone with *my husband*. I do not think that is too much to ask.'

'Of course not,' I said.

'Do you want to do the same?' asked Natalia. I hesitated.

'No!' said Jessica slightly wildly. 'No, I don't want to be left on my own in here!'

'Actually,' I said. 'Maybe just a minute?'

Natalia shoved Jessica out the door, none too gently, and it was just Dad and me. What do you say? A whole lifetime of things left unsaid, left for another time, assumptions made that they knew what you thought, or felt, and all of a sudden, no time left to say them in.

I sat down and squeezed his hand. In the end, there was really only one thing to say. 'I love you, Daddy,' I whispered. 'Bye now.'

'Bye now' had been Dad's standard sign-off for everything. When Mum kicked him out, when he took me to Edinburgh for the first time when I went to university, walking me up the aisle to marry Simon, when he decided to move to Portugal – he'd hop in his car with a cheery 'Bye now' and speed off. 'Long hellos and short goodbyes, darling,' he'd explain. 'Never look back, it upsets everyone.' He was right, of course. Nothing was to be gained by looking back and dwelling on the past – the current situation with Simon was evidence enough of *that*.

I opened the door and beckoned Jessica in. 'I think you should have a moment with him, Jess,' I said softly.

'NO!' insisted Jessica. 'No, I just can't, and anyway, I wouldn't be having to if anyone had made sure he'd been properly treated in the first place!'

Natalia's hand twitched suspiciously. I shared her longing to slap Jessica for managing to make my father's deathbed all about her, but before either of us had the chance, Neil intervened. I had only seen my brother-in-law put his foot down with Jessica once before, and that was when she wanted to send Persephone to a school in Switzerland for gifted children. Persephone was five at the time.

'Jessica!' thundered Neil. 'NOT NOW! If you don't want to be alone with your father, no one will make you, but this isn't the time or the place for this.'

Jessica's anger subsided and the three of us filed back in.

Dad's breathing got slower and slower, the spaces between each breath so long that it seemed impossible that there could be another one. I found myself holding my breath with him. I don't know why. Finally, the next breath didn't come. The doctor came in and put her hand on Natalia's shoulder. Dad was gone.

Simon drove us home in the early hours of the morning, a silent, wretched journey.

I slumped on the sofa when we got in, aware I should be comforting my children, reassuring them, trying to make their pain and confusion go away, but quite unable for the moment to do anything at all. Simon made me a cup of tea. I rather saw Natalia's point. I was heartily sick of fucking tea. Peter came in and sat beside me.

'Mum …?' he said.

'Mmmm?'

'Mum. Mum, I don't want you and Dad to die. Please promise you won't die, Mum, and Dad, you can't die, please!'

He burst into tears.

'Oh Peter.' The only thing worse than your own grief and pain is seeing your children hurting. Peter's tears galvanised me out of my stupor. I wrapped my arms around him, like he was little again, despite the fact he was taller than me and wore size nine shoes. 'Oh darling. I'm not going anywhere, I promise.'

'But you will,' he gulped. 'Everybody dies.'

'Well, yes, but I'm not going to for a very long time, and neither is Daddy, OK? We'll be here for you, for as long as you need us.'

'You can't promise that, though. You could have a car accident, you could get hit by a bus, you could fall over putting your socks on and die – between five and ten people *every year* die in a sock-related accident, and even more people die putting on their trousers. And I wish I wasn't an atheist now. It must be nice to think that you'll see someone again one day.'

'Sweetheart, you can't live your life thinking about "what ifs?". That's a joyless existence. Life is for hoping for the best and enjoying yourself, so that if something does happen you have minimal regrets. I saw those sock statistics too, and I always sit down to put my socks on now, so that's one less thing to stress about. I know it's tough, the thought of someone being gone forever, but they're not, not really.'

'Is this going to be about how as long as you remember them, they're still alive?' he sniffed. 'Because you know that's not the same, Mum. Memories aren't the same as someone still being here.'

'No, sweetheart. It's a thing I saw about physics. You love physics, don't you?'

Peter gulped in agreement.

'Well, it was a talk by someone – I think he was called Aaron Freeman – about how, thanks to the first law of thermodynamics, no energy gets created and none gets destroyed, and so all the energy that makes you has always been here, in this world, and always will be. So everyone is still here, in one form or another. You know how you're always saying to me when I do something stupid that "Physics always wins, Mum"? Well, it really does!'

That seemed to comfort Peter a little, and he calmed down.

'Try to get some sleep, darling,' I said.

'Mum?'

'Yes?'

'Can Dad stay tonight?'

'I don't know if that's a good idea.'

'Please? Just tonight. He can have my bed and I'll sleep on the floor. I just want everyone together tonight, Mum, *please*.'

'Well, if your dad is OK with it, that's fine with me,' I said. To be honest, I'd rather have been alone, but if Peter needed everyone together tonight, that was more important. Simon had come into the sitting room and he nodded. 'Of course I'll stay if that's what Peter wants.'

'I might make up a bed on the sofa for you,' I suggested, thinking of the complex ecosystems doubtless lurking in Peter's room. And God knows what dubious stains were to be found in his bed, despite my weekly boil-washing of his sheets.

I went upstairs to check on Jane. She was sitting on her bed with her arms firmly around Barry's neck, looking red-eyed but calm.

'How are you?' I asked.

'I have Barry,' she said.

'Do you want to talk about it, sweetie?'

'Not really, Mum. I … I talked to Barry. He understands a lot. If it's OK with you, I'd rather just talk to him. I don't really know what I'm feeling or what I want to say, but talking to Barry helps me make sense of it all in a way that talking to a person wouldn't, because then I'd have to start explaining it to *them* instead of to *me*, and also, I just think Barry knows how I'm feeling to start with and I don't have to explain all that too. So I'll just talk to Barry, I think. It's what I usually do about stuff.'

Barry looked up at me and gave his tail twitch. He'd grown no more beautiful as he grew vaster, and maybe I was just over-wrought and overemotional, but there did seem to be an under-standing and a wisdom in his big brown eyes that was lacking from many humans. Jane cuddled him closer.

'All right,' I said. 'As long as you have someone to talk to.'

'Yeah,' said Jane. 'Mum, wait!'

Jane came over and gave me a fierce hug. 'Mum, look after yourself as well, not just everyone else. And, Mum? I … I love you. But *don't* bloody tell anyone I said that. And well, you should probably talk to someone too. About stuff.'

I felt my resolve to not cry in front of the children waver and the tears start to come. I hugged her back and sniffed, 'Thank you, darling.'

'Even if you talk to Judgy about stuff,' she whispered. 'Or the chickens. Maybe not the chickens – they hate you. But someone, as long as you let it out, OK.'

'OK,' I gulped. Jane let go, suddenly realising she'd inadvertently had a moment of physical affection with her mother, and shuffled back to Barry.

'Oh, and Mum,' she added.

'Yes, darling,' I said tenderly, so proud of my mature and empathetic daughter.

'How many days off school do you think Grandpa dying will get us?'

I was quite relieved to see that Jane, when all was said and done, was still Jane.

I went downstairs with spare pillows and blankets for Simon.

'Do you want to talk about it?' he asked.

'No. Not really,' I said after considering his question. 'I'd like to just stop thinking about it for a bit. I think maybe I'll call Hannah tomorrow and talk to her.'

'Would you just like a hug?'

'No, definitely not. I'm hugged out. I've vastly exceeded my daily quota for physical contact with other human beings.'

'OK.'

'Do you know what I'd like?'

Simon looked hopeful.

'Not that! FFS! A fuck-off gin and tonic,' I said.

'I can do that.'

I gulped gin and stared into space for a while. Suddenly a thought occurred to me.

'You've been driving my car all day,' I said accusingly.

'Yes?' said Simon. 'You weren't in any state to be driving?'

'But you're not insured on it anymore.'

'I have third party to drive any car with the owner's permission through my insurance,' said Simon. 'Is that really all you can think about to talk about right now? Car insurance?'

'It's a safe, neutral topic,' I said. 'Jane already wants to know how long she can have off school; I think car insurance is slightly less callous. Can I have another gin and tonic?'

After another long pause I said, 'Simon? What do you remember about my dad?'

'The first time I ever met him, he took me aside for one of those "man to man" chats.'

'Did he? You never told me that.'

'Yes. He said, "Right, if you're serious about my daughter, you need to know that if you mess her about, anything I might do to you would pale in significance compared to what she'll do to you. I've brought my daughter up to not take any shit from anyone; Ellen doesn't need me making threats on her behalf. I will, however, help her dispose of the body if need be, however many parts it may be in."'

Despite everything, I was laughing. 'Why didn't you ever tell me this?'

'I don't know. Scared you'd make good on your father's promises?'

I knew I should go to bed, but it was comfortable and warm on the sofa, and I was somewhat hazy with gin after not eating in hours. We talked some more and had another gin, and eventually I fell asleep on Simon's shoulder. I was dimly aware of someone tucking blankets around me and whispering, 'Let me look after you, darling.' I think I mumbled back something about 'Don't need looking after! Strong independent woman. Fuck the patriarchy!' but I might have been dreaming. Simon was still there, hovering over me with yet another cup of tea, when I woke up a few hours later, dry-mouthed, fuzzy-headed, with a crick in my neck and Judgy's breath in my face.

'Do you want me to stay today?' he asked.

'No, I'm fine,' I said. 'Anyway, it's now, what time, 10.30 am on Sunday morning, and you haven't been home since Friday night, which means you've been wearing the same pants since then, which is gross. I'll be fine.'

'Your obsession with clean underwear never ceases to amaze me,' he said dryly.

'It's the result of thirteen years of living with Peter and reminding him constantly to change his pants,' I protested. 'Though at least now I can assume he does, with the length of time he spends in the bathroom and the amount of Lynx he sprays all over himself. Surely the Lynx isn't to compensate for his pants? Are the kids up?'

'No, they're still asleep. I've put a wash on,' he said virtuously.

'Oh, thank you,' I said in confusion, not entirely sure how I felt about my ex-husband going through my dirty knickers.

I trudged through the utility room to let the dogs out, and glanced at the washing machine. My heart sank. White shirts and Jane's plaid shirt (that apparently one is no longer allowed to call a 'lumberjack' shirt) were all chugging around, along with my much-loved and treasured pale pink cashmere jumper. On a 60° wash. I swallowed my irritation and tried not to say anything – after all, Simon was *trying* to help. Despite the fact I must have explained to him eleventy fucking billion times how to separate laundry and that you don't need to wash anything except sheets and towels higher than 40°, and even then not usually, while cursing his bloody mother, who had treated him like a prince and never expected him to lift a finger at home, thus meaning that he was sent out into the world with rather unrealistic expectations of magic laundry and tidy-up fairies who whisked around and made everything nice when he wasn't looking and refilled his drawer with clean pants. I reminded myself that I was dealing with grave matters of life and death today, and there were more important things to worry about than ruined cashmere jumpers.

'I've cleaned out the fridge for you too,' announced Simon smugly. 'Honestly, your fridge-keeping skills haven't improved since we separated, have they? There was mustard in there that expired two months ago …'

'Was it mouldy?'

'What? I didn't open it, I just threw it away. It was out of date.'

'But if it wasn't actually mouldy, then it was fine.'

'But it was out of date. That's very unhygienic.'

'No it's not, but throwing out perfectly good food is just wasteful. *How* many times have we had this argument?'

'Well, if you stopped keeping out-of-date stuff in the fridge, we wouldn't have to.'

'Yes, but it's *my* fridge. I can keep what I like in it, and seriously, the dates on things are just a guide. That's all. If it looks fine and smells fine, it probably *is* fine.'

Simon snorted derisively as I peered into my sadly denuded fridge. Admittedly, there was never much in it, but the few items that escaped the depredations of Peter and his mates – such as the potatoes, carrots, mustard and Thai curry pastes – had been removed in Simon's ridiculous pursuit of 'hygiene'. I chuntered furiously to myself, and then took several deep breaths and suggested it was time for him to go. Frankly, he was irking me now, and I wanted peace and quiet to just *think*. Apart from anything else, there was a very shallow part of me that was wondering if it still would be OK to go on the holiday in a couple of weeks that I'd booked and paid for. I wondered if I could ask Natalia if it would be inappropriate? Maybe not. That in itself would probably be deemed inappropriate.

'Ellen, are you listening to me? You're a million miles away. I don't think you should be on your own,' he objected.

'What? No, I'll be fine. And I'm not on my own. The kids are here, and the dogs. And I'll have to be on my own sooner or later, so it might as well be sooner. Start moving on and all that.'

Simon hovered anxiously and chuntered about being worried about me, before I finally managed to edge him out the door.

After he left I breathed a sigh of relief. The last thing I needed was people *fussing*. Really, I was fine. I just needed to get on with things, and there was no point at all in wallowing in self-pity. Everything suddenly felt a bit flat, though, and I seemed to be lacking the impetus to get on with things. I made a cup of tea and slumped back on the sofa, and Judgy headbutted me as I was trying to take a sip, spilling it all over me.

'FFS, Judgy! What are you doing?' I snapped. Judgy ignored me and clambered onto my knee, making huffing sounds, before sneezing and looking at me pointedly.

'Oh Judgy!' I said. 'What happens now? I don't know what I'm supposed to do. I don't even know how I'm supposed to feel. I think I'm supposed to be rending my garments in grief and feeling like I can't go on for another moment, but I just feel a bit … empty?'

Judgy sneezed again.

'You're right,' I said. 'It probably still needs to sink in.'

We then had a long chat, Judgy and me, about lots of things, not just about all the good stuff about Dad, but also about all the times he'd been a selfish twat, deeply annoying, mildly sexist or just downright unreasonable. I ended up having a Jolly Good Cry, which Judgy was indignant about as he doesn't like getting wet, and then I felt a bit better. Jane is quite right. There's something very therapeutic about talking to dogs.

Friday, 27 July

Today was Dad's funeral. I'm not very good at funerals – I always worry that my shoes are too slutty and is lip gloss inappropriate? I also have a tendency to giggle hysterically at the wrong moment, not that there's a right moment to giggle at funerals, obviously, and it's not even that I find something funny. It's just that I'm trying so hard to be sombre and respectful that I end up cocking it all up.

I'd declined to buy Jane the new dress she'd claimed she needed for the funeral, on the basis that I didn't think her choice of a minute black body con number was really appropriate, despite her argument that it made economic sense because she could also wear it to parties afterwards, so really it was justified as she'd get lots of use out of it. I suspected that it was more the parties that she was thinking of, rather than the funeral. Jane insisted this was unfair, as I'd bought Peter a new shirt and trousers for the occasion, although I pointed out that Peter owned precisely *one* smart outfit, bought for his school Christmas disco last year, and since he'd grown approximately a foot since then his current shirt and trousers were now far too small, making him look like a Victorian urchin bound for the workhouse when he'd tried them on. Jane, on the other hand, had a room bulging at the seams with clothes, and I was quite sure she could find something to wear.

In the event, Jane was quite respectable in a black skirt and jumper.

'You look nice, darling,' I said in surprise.

'What? Why are you sounding so surprised?'

'Sorry, I didn't mean to. Right, let's go, shall we?'

'Can I put on Radio 1?'

'Fine.' Listening to the manic tones of the Radio 1 DJs was at least preferable to having to listen to them both complain about Ken Bruce all the way to Natalia's house, however much more of a mellow DJ he was. And the very fact they had even deigned to take their earphones out was a plus.

It wasn't till we were almost there, and waiting at traffic lights, that I glanced down and realised Jane had teamed her respectable skirt and jumper with her bright purple glittery Doc Martens.

'Jane, your *shoes*!' I wailed.

'What?' she snapped. 'Grandpa was the one who bought me them, when you said they were too expensive.'

'Yes, but they're not very funereal, are they?'

'He liked them. That's good enough, isn't it?'

I gave up. It was too late to do anything about it anyway.

Jessica had spent the week screaming down the phone at me and bombarding me with emails because Natalia was organising the funeral, and in Jessica's opinion she wasn't doing nearly enough about it. She was furious about Natalia's choice of coffin, of cremation, of the length of service, the hymns, the order of service, the flowers – everything was wrong, according to Jessica. Eventually, Natalia sent us both a scan of a letter from Dad.

Darling N,

It occurs to me I might pop my clogs at some point and you'll be left to clear up the mess (not, I hope, literally). I know this is awfully morbid of me, but I thought I'd better let my views be known on what to do with me! I'd like to be cremated. I don't fancy mouldering away being eaten by worms. For God's sake don't feel you need to spend a fortune on the coffin – it's going to be burnt! Get the cheapest one available, I insist, and spend the money on a jolly good piss-up somewhere nice afterwards. Some sort of service will probably be expected, keep it short and sweet, funerals are deathly boring (pun intended). You and my girls need to look after each other now – I'm awfully proud of you all, you know! Oh, and everyone has to say how wonderful I am at the shindig afterwards, obviously, and put my ashes on the delphiniums, I might as well be useful! Love you, sweetheart, hopefully you'll not need these instructions for a very long time,

Bye now,

I cried for quite a long time after reading this, while Jessica filled my voicemail with furious messages.

We arrived at Dad and Natalia's house (I suppose I must get used to calling it Natalia's house now), and were having a cup of tea while being lectured further about funeral etiquette by Jessica (she'd taken exception to both Jane and my shoes. Annoying Jessica was only part of the reason I'd chosen mine, though …), when the doorbell rang.

'It's too early for the cars,' said Natalia, as she went to answer it.

Next thing, bloody Mum breezed into Natalia's kitchen, followed by a stunned Natalia, who was lost for words for possibly the first time ever.

'Hello darlings!' cried Mum.

'Mum!' cried Jessica. 'You made it.'

'Of course, darling! I'm burying my husband today, I have to be here.'

'Cremating,' I said.

'What?'

'He's being cremated.'

'But how common,' complained Mum. 'No one consulted *me* about that.'

'That's because you've been divorced for over thirty years, you hated his guts and you haven't spoken to him since my wedding, when, if I recall correctly, you told him to tell me to stop making the whole day about me, because it was your special day too.'

'I *am* the mother of his children. I should have been consulted,' said Mum coldly.

'Why is Granny here?' said Jane, coming into the kitchen in search of biscuits. 'And what *is* she wearing?'

Mum was dressed in head-to-toe black, with an enormous hat, evidently determined to extract every last ounce of drama and sympathy from the day. Her deep-rooted loathing of Dad was in no way a barrier to her love of being the centre of attention.

'Jane! Darling!' squawked Mum. 'Come and give Granny a kiss. But what are those *shoes*? You can't wear them. I won't have it. Surely that woman' – she glared sourly at Natalia, who was still speechless – 'must have a decent pair of court shoes or something you could borrow? You too, Ellen. You look like a cheap prostitute in those heels.'

'Jane is perfectly nicely dressed, and Ellen's shoes are very elegant,' said Natalia firmly. 'Ralph would not want anyone to feel uncomfortable today. He wanted his life celebrated, not a sad day full of formality.'

Mum ignored Natalia and ploughed on regardless. 'Ellen, do you really think that is the right shade of lipstick for you? I know you're upset, but it's not doing much for your complexion, is it? And you might have done something with your hair.'

'I'm not wearing any lipstick,' I ground out, thinking that if Natalia didn't snap and slap my mother roundly about the head, I might just do so myself.

'Oh. Well, maybe *that's* why you look so washed out, darling. You should put some on.'

'Mum looks fine,' snapped Jane. 'Why are you always picking on her, Granny?'

'Oh Jane,' sniffed Mum. 'I'm just trying to offer my daughter some useful advice. How can you say I'm picking on her?'

'Jesus, Granny, it's her dad's funeral today and all you've done is criticise her shoes and her make-up and her hair. Don't be so mean to her!' exploded Jane.

'Ellen, are you going to allow your daughter to speak to *me* like that?' demanded Mum.

Jane's outburst, unexpectedly standing up for me, had made me want to cry again.

'Can't we all just try to get on for a few hours?' I implored wearily. 'Today isn't going to be fun, so let's just get through it without making things worse.'

'I just won't say *anything* then,' whimpered Mum, 'since apparently my input is unwanted. I was just trying to be *helpful*.'

'Oh good, the cars are here,' said Jessica.

Jessica had insisted on proper funeral cars to take us to the crematorium, and Natalia had caved in, muttering something about 'picking her battles'.

'Oh good,' said Mum brightly. 'Which car am I in? Will I go in the first car with you and Neil and my grandchildren?'

'Natalia should go in the first car,' I pointed out.

'But what about me?' said Mum petulantly. 'Where am I supposed to go?'

'Well, why can't you drive yourself in your car? I presume that's how you got here?' I suggested.

'Oh no,' Mum laughed. 'Don't be silly! Geoffrey dropped me off. We thought we might as well make a weekend of it. He's popped out for a round of golf and will pick me up later. So I *have* to go in one of the cars, darling, don't I? So I'll just go first with Jessica and Neil – where *is* Neil, Jessica?'

'In the study, working. He's so dedicated,' sighed Jessica. I'd once spotted Neil at another family occasion when he'd claimed to be unable to switch off for an hour lest the stock market collapsed without his watchful eye – he was hiding in a corner playing Tetris on his phone. In fairness, I was just jealous that I'd never managed to successfully avoid my bloody family through claiming a pressing need to work …

'But the cars only take four people each,' I reminded Jessica. 'There were only supposed to be eight of us going! Now there's nine.'

'I will just drive myself,' said Natalia. 'If it means that much to Yvonne that she gets a spot in the car, let her fucking have it. I am more interested in saying goodbye to my husband than scoring points about who goes in which fucking *car*!'

'You can't drive yourself, Natalia,' I protested. 'I'll drive you.'

'Can we come too? I don't want to go in the creepy dead people's car,' said Jane.

'Well, then what will we do with all the space in the other car?' complained Jessica.

'FFS! I don't care. Jane, get Peter. Come on, Natalia. The rest of you can sort yourselves out. *We're* going to the funeral!'

We met Simon in the car park at the crematorium. He put his hand on my arm, looked soulfully into my eyes and said, 'How *are* you, darling?'

'Stop it,' I said.

'Stop what?'

'You're being weird. And annoying.'

'Sorry, I was just trying to be supportive.'

'Well, I don't like it.'

'Will you come and sit with us, Dad?' said Peter. 'You can sit between me and Mum.'

'Of course,' said Simon. 'If your mother doesn't mind?'

'I don't mind. Just don't be weird.'

The service, in the end, was really quite jolly. Natalia had done Dad proud. Apart from the sombre death muzak playing when we went in, and the slight Sovietness of the crematorium, complete with dusty plastic flowers, a municipal smell and the fact that halfway through the service it dawned on me that the grey splodges on the carpet were from people spitting their chewing gum out – seriously, what kind of *animal* spits out gum on the floor at a *funeral*?

Jessica had demanded that Persephone (who appeared to have come as Wednesday Addams from *The Addams Family*) and Gulliver be given special roles, so Gulliver read out rather a strange poem he'd written and Persephone played the piano, which was actually very nice. Natalia had asked if Peter and Jane wanted to say anything, but they had looked horrified at the notion of having to stand up in public 'in front of loads of *old* people', as Jane had put it, and had declined. And then Dad's best friend Christopher, whom he'd known since university, stood up and instead of a proper eulogy told a lot of inappropriate stories about Dad, including some rather blue jokes, and everyone pissed themselves laughing, except for Mum, as unfortunately Christopher hadn't realised Mum was there and made a joke about knowing how Dad liked to dice with danger because why else would he have married such a crazy cow as Yvonne? Natalia laughed especially hard at that part. There was a difficult moment on the way back to the car, when Peter said, 'Aren't we doing the grave thing, then?'

'What do you mean, darling?'

'Well, all the funerals on TV, everyone goes to the grave and they chuck dirt in. Or is that only on TV?'

'Peter, where are we?'

'At the crematorium?'

'And what happens at a crematorium?'

'People are cremated, durrrr!'

'Right, so if you're cremated …'

Peter looked at me blankly.

'You don't have a grave …?' I prompted.

I despair somewhat of how Peter is going to fare in the world when he has to actually do joined-up thinking of his own.

Afterwards, at the hotel Natalia had booked for the wake, it was all a bit of a haze, even though I couldn't get pissed because I was driving. Hannah and Charlie were there, and Simon of course (Sam and Colin were in Ibiza, and I'd insisted they mustn't cut their holiday short), and lots of people I'd never met or who said they remembered me from when I was five and how I hadn't changed a bit, which was worrying as I'd had a truly tragic pudding-bowl haircut when I was five and hoped my style had improved somewhat since then …

There was plenty of champagne and canapés though, and Natalia surveyed the room with a certain grim satisfaction.

'Everyone seems to be having fun,' she said. Unfortunately Mum overheard her.

'It's a *funeral*, Natalia,' she said in loud, scandalised tones. 'You aren't supposed to have *fun* at a funeral. It's meant to be a sombre and sacred occasion.'

'Bollocks,' said Natalia stoutly. 'Ralph wanted everyone to have a marvellous party at his expense to remember him by. Whenever we went to a funeral, he always said he did not want his send-off to be some godawful depressing affair. He wanted people to say for years afterwards, "Do you remember Ralph Green's funeral? What a smashing do that was!" We are all going to bloody die, none of us can escape it, so surely the point of a funeral should be to remember the good times, not wallow in misery and anticipate our own forthcoming end?'

Remember the good times. Natalia certainly had plenty of them to look back on with Daddy. And what about Simon and me? We had good times too, of course we did, but the last few years seem mostly to be memories of arguing about childcare and why he could never wipe the counters down after he made himself a sandwich and me slamming in load after load of laundry and stamping around shouting, 'No, DON'T WORRY, I'LL DO IT, I'll just do bloody everything, won't I?' They all seem like little things, but cumulatively it's all those little things that add up to grind a marriage down. The sex was good, of course (I blushed at the thought of how recently I had been reminded of that), but there hadn't been an awful lot of that in the latter part of our marriage either. There hadn't been an awful lot of anything, except bickering and nights on the sofa in front of endless episodes of *Wheeler Dealers*, to the point where I still have some sort of Stockholm Syndrome crush on Edd China, just because I was forced to watch so many reruns.

I was distracted from my reverie about Simon and Edd China (such lovely big hands) by the realisation that Natalia and Mum were now having a full-on barney about who Dad loved best. 'Ellen, tell her!' ordered Mum. 'I was the mother of his children, so clearly I was the love of his life!'

'He had not spoken to you since Ellen's wedding,' hissed Natalia. 'If he had to mention you, he called you that batshit-mental old cow.'

A large lady, who I thought might be called Jean, bore down on me to envelop me in a bosomy hug, which nearly asphyxiated me with the amount of Chanel No. 5 she appeared to have tipped down her cleavage, before putting her hand on my arm and tilting her head and saying, 'How *are* you, dear?'

I opened my mouth to reply, but before I could, Jessica appeared, bristling with indignation. 'Persephone is *drunk*!' she howled. 'Clearly this is Jane's doing, so what are you going to do about it?'

'Mum,' said Peter. 'Mum, I feel a bit sick.'

'Ellen, your Uncle Edward wants to know if there's going to be anything to eat apart from canapés. He doesn't like canapés apparently,' said Simon.

'Mum, I dint get Pershephone pished,' slurred Jane, washing up in Jessica's wake with a rather green Persephone. 'Pershephone jus' wanna try the champagne. S'nice, champagne. But it wasn' me got her pished.'

'Wash your idea to put vodka in it,' mumbled Persephone. 'Oh God. I don' feel ver' well. I think I'm gonna be –'

Persephone didn't finish her sentence, because she leaned over and puked copiously over Jessica's shoes.

The-lady-who-might-be-called-Jean recoiled and edged away.

Jessica and Mum starting screaming.

Natalia started laughing hysterically, then said, 'Oh Jesus, I *wish* Ralph was here to see this, he'd have loved it,' and burst into tears.

'Fuckin'ell!' was Jane's contribution, while she swayed alarmingly.

'I can't do this!' I said. 'I just can't,' and I turned and fled.

I was sitting on the wall outside the hotel when Hannah's mum came out and joined me.

'Hello, sweetheart,' she said. 'I've brought you a large gin. Do you want a ciggie?'

'I thought you'd given up?'

'Don't be silly, darling! At my age, we might as well enjoy our vices! Don't tell Hannah, though. She's very touchy on the subject of vices at the moment, poor thing. Anyway, I wanted to see you on your own, see how you are. *Adore* the shoes by the way.'

'I can't have gin, I'm driving.'

'Hannah will drive you home and Charlie can bring their car. I've organised it all. Just get that down you, and have a little ciggie and everything will seem better, I promise. Now, how are you, and tell me honestly?'

I love Hannah's mum. She's everything a mum should be and everything I *try* so hard to be to my kids. Mrs P, as I've always called her and still do, is endlessly kind, wickedly funny, utterly irreverent about everything, and for most of my life has been there for me with chocolate, gin or cigarettes, depending on my age and the nature of the crisis. She asks no questions if you don't want to talk about it, and she listens sympathetically, without offering advice if you don't ask for it. She didn't bat an eyelid at acquiring virtually another daughter in her life, and it's a sign of what a wonderful person Hannah is that she never for one moment minded sharing her mum with me.

'Honestly?' I said.

'It's me, sweetheart. If you can't be honest with me, who can you be honest with?'

'Honestly, I think if one more person puts their hand on my arm, tilts their head at me and says, "How *are* you?" in a concerned whisper, I might scream.'

'Yes, I remember the hands on the arms when my parents died,' sighed Mrs P. 'It's grim, isn't it? And worst of all is the fact that you know perfectly well they don't actually give a damn how you are. They are just patting themselves on the back for being so *caring* as to ask. If you dared to answer anything other than "Fine" or "Oh, you know. Bearing up," they'd be out of there faster than a ferret up a trouser leg. Anyway, *do* you want to talk about it?'

'Not really,' I admitted. 'I don't know what there is to talk about. I'm not really sure how I feel. Sad, of course, but I think I should feel sadder, and oh, I don't know. How should I feel?'

'Unfortunately, there isn't a standard chart for us to compare our grief to and work out if we're normal,' said Mrs P. 'Some people rend their garments with woe because their cousin's auntie's granny's budgie is dead, others just bottle it all up and pretend it isn't happening. I suspect you're going for the bottling, which I don't recommend, although it's preferable for the rest of us, rather than your mother's current display ...'

'Is she still screaming about Persephone being sick?'

'No, Simon was actually rather masterful and took control of everything. He told your mother to pull herself together, Jessica to get Persephone into the loos and Peter to go to the loo too if he really felt sick, though it turned out he hadn't been on the fizz. He'd just eaten an entire tray of mini beef Wellingtons, followed by a plate of macarons, which is quite something.'

'And Jane?'

'Simon sent her to sit down with a glass of water and asked Natalia to look after her while he got someone to clean up the mess, so the last I saw, she was being taught Russian swear words. Simon was quite impressive, actually. Talking of Simon, what *is* going on with you two?'

I went scarlet again.

'Nothing!'

'Really? Hannah told me you told her that you and he had … had a, what does Emily call it? A hook-up? Hannah didn't approve, but I think she's probably already made that clear. But here he is, sitting with you at the funeral, taking charge inside when it all goes wrong. So are you and he back on then?'

'No!'

'Would you like to be back with him?'

'I don't know … I don't know. It's all so confusing!'

'You're the only one who can decide that. I see how he looks at you, though. If I were a betting woman, I'd put money on him still being in love with you.'

'You *are* a betting woman. You taught Hannah and me how to play poker and cleaned us out of three weeks' pocket money!'

'Oh yes. So I am. Well then. Simon is still in love with you. If you want him back, you could have him. The question is, do you want him?'

'Sometimes. It was … nice … the other night. Having someone there.'

'Someone? Or specifically Simon?'

'*I don't know*! That's the problem. Sometimes things are really good between us, and sometimes there are so many things about him that still annoy me. Natalia was talking about remembering the good times, but there were so many times that weren't good with us too.'

'Well, looking to the past isn't going to make your mind up, is it?' said Mrs P. 'Close your eyes and think about your future, how you imagine your life turning out. Actually, no, don't close your eyes. People will think we're peculiar. Just think about your future. Do you see Simon in it?'

I thought. And then thought some more.

'I don't know,' I said. 'I think – I hope – there's *someone* there, even just someone to go on holiday with, but I don't know if it's Simon.'

'Well, there's your answer then, for now. Keep closing your eyes now and then – as long as you're not in public – if you're having a wobble, or even if you're having a really good day, and ask yourself who you see in the future. Sooner or later, you *will* know. Come on, let's go back inside and get you another gin and see what the latest drama is. Perhaps there'll be a fight,' she said hopefully. 'After all, your father always said the sign of a good party was if there was at least one fight, a divorce and an unplanned pregnancy as a result. Hopefully we won't have either of the last two. Poor Hannah's condition is quite enough for me.'

AUGUST

Friday, 3 August

Another Friday night spent sitting in my car, watching pissed teenagers staggering around while I wait to pick up Jane and co, praying that they'll not be vomitously pissed/have taken drugs/been shagging/got themselves pregnant.

Jane was supposed to be grounded, on account of the whole getting royally pissed at her grandfather's funeral/shouting 'Fucking hell' in front of her grandmother/pouring enough drink down her sheltered cousin's throat to cause her to puke, but while giving her a stern dressing down, when she burst out with the 'THIS IS SO UNFAIR!' rage, it transpired that while it *had* been Jane's idea to mix the vodka with the champagne, it had been Persephone who'd supplied the vodka, nicked from Jessica's drinks cabinet.

'I mean, I feel quite sorry for Persephone, actually,' said Jane. 'Auntie Jessica doesn't let her do anything. She's not even allowed to get the bus in to go to the cinema – Auntie Jessica drives her there, waits and drives her home. She went to a party once, but then Auntie Jessica found out there were boys there and went and dragged her out! It makes you seem not quite as bad.'

My delight at being deemed 'Not quite as bad' a mother as Jessica, and Jane's alternating between saccharine pleas and furious 'YOU'RE RUINING MY LIFE' foot-stomping about Tilly

Wright's birthday party (there are so many Tillys, Millys and Olivias in Jane's class they have to be known by their full names. Ditto the Oscars, Ollies and Reubens in Peter's class) led to me eventually caving in and agreeing that she could go to the party, but she was *not* staying out past 12.30 am. This led to her life being ruined all over again, obviously. Somehow, amid all this, I found myself being persuaded to let her have all her friends to sleep over as well.

There's something vaguely post-apocalyptic about the fallout from teenage parties – I could hear the ghastly music from where I was waiting and could see them shambling around the garden, snogging, lurching, puking in the dahlias – and, my God, the *swearing*! I am, myself, not averse to a jolly good swear. I like to think I can construct entire sentences consisting only of the word 'fuck' with admirable ease, but my language becomes positively nun-like compared with the streams of obscenities uttered by drunken teenage boys. I do hope Peter doesn't swear like that when he's not around me. I mean, he almost certainly does, but I'll adopt the ostrich-like approach of every mother since the dawn of time and pretend it's only *other people's* children who are vulgar and horrid and swear like dockers and nick their parents' vodka and have underage sex, and convince myself that MY children are quite, quite different …

Were we this debauched as teenagers? Surely not? Surely we just had a few ciders and a bit of a giggle? Well, there was the night that Rebecca Philips's mum and dad went away for the weekend, and we all went to her house for a party, and Lizzie Edwards got completely shitfaced on Malibu and starting puking, and Rebecca had hysterics because her mum had just had the hallway re-carpeted and so Hannah, in a noble but ulti-mately misguided drunken gesture, attempted to catch the puke in her hands, which obviously led to Hannah throwing up too, and us all spending the next morning desperately shampooing the carpets to remove any trace of vomit, Malibu or vodka and coke. None of us could face Malibu for years after that. Or the time that I fell out of a window when I thought I'd try to climb along the roof to see who Caroline Roberts was snogging in the spare room, only I didn't really think it through and just fell out – luckily a) I landed on grass, and b) I was so pissed that I didn't break anything. And all the nightclubs and pubs we went to with fake IDs, and the unsuitable boys we snogged, and the tables we danced on, in those awful clingy bodies with the poppers in the crotch that were so problematic when you went for a wee. I keep seeing things in magazines threatening that bodies are making a comeback, which makes me shudder. Normally I'd embrace the return of anything with Nineties' associations, but not them. My bladder is no longer up to faffing around with poppers before I can have a wee!

It was very late and I wondered if I could just have a little nap while I waited for Jane and her friends. Everyone tells you how little sleep you'll get with a newborn, but no one tells you that you'll get nearly as little kip when they're teenagers, because you'll be expected to spend your weekends picking up them up in the small hours of the morning, before lying awake, wondering if you should check on them in case someone needs to be put in the recovery position, because although they had only seemed a bit giggly, what if they had taken some awful 'legal high', whatever that is, apart from something the *Daily Mail* is always banging on about, and had an adverse reaction, before resentfully waking up at 8 am the next day because you've somehow lost the ability to lie in, while your darling teenager and her pals snore the day away until you've had enough and burst into the fetid pit, telling them they've 'missed the best of the day', and suggesting they should think about getting a nice hobby, instead of sleeping all day, and anything else suitably mortifying you can think of to say, so your teenager hates you more than ever.

Sophie finally tottered out and lurched into the car. 'Lo, Ellen!' she said brightly. 'Jane an' Emily an' Milly are *jus'* coming!'

'Oh good,' I said sarcastically. 'Sophie, is that a love bite on your neck?'

'Oh bollocks!' said Sophie, going scarlet. 'Please don't tell my dad.'

'Your dad was once a teenager too,' I reminded her. 'I think he's aware that there are such things as love bites in the world.'

'Yeah!' said Sophie. 'But he's also a *dad*, so he'll just go ballistic and start lecturing me about self-respect and everything again. He's got no idea what it's like to be a teenager.'

'I won't tell him, Sophie, but don't you think he might notice himself?'

'Oh no!' Sophie said airily. 'I'll wear a scarf, or a polo neck or something. He'll *never* know!'

I chuckled to myself somewhat at Sophie's blissful naivety in assuming that Sam would in no way put two and two together and connect her returning from a party with a jaunty scarf around her neck with her sucking faces (though hopefully nothing else) with a spotty youth all night.

Jane and Emily appeared just then, along with Milly, who to my dismay was being propped up between them, more than a little the worse for wear.

'Oh Christ!' I said.

''Lo Mum, Milly's feeling a bit sick,' said Jane. 'Prolly something she ate.'

'No shit, Sherlock!' I muttered, as we piled a pale green Milly into the car.

'Wait!' slurred Milly, then she leaned out the door and projectile vomited something that smelled suspiciously coconutty. Oh no! Please no!

'What has she been drinking?' I enquired, feeling a little queasy myself.

'Jus' a lil bit of Malibu!' Jane insisted. Oh FML. It was Carpetgate all over again! Also, why does teenage vomit still feature so prominently in my life?

And thus began one of the longest drives of my life. Milly seemed to stabilise, and Jane assured me that she couldn't possibly have any sick left in her as she'd been fairly well cleared out before they even brought her out to the car, so I felt safe to turn onto the dual carriageway.

As soon as there was nowhere to pull over, Milly sat up.

''M'gonna be shick 'gain!' she mumbled.

'No!' I shouted. 'No sick! Think of something else, Milly.'

'Shick!' insisted Milly.

'I've got a plastic bag!' I cried triumphantly, rummaging in the glove box, with one hand on the wheel.

'Oooh, Mum, you shouldn't have a bag like that,' complained Jane. 'It's really environmentally unfriendly.'

'Well, darling, I'm more concerned about the immediate environmental effects if Milly pukes all over the inside of my car,' I pointed out, thrusting the bag into the back of the car.

'What am I supposed to do with it?' wailed Jane.

'Catch the sick!' I bellowed. 'Hold it and catch the sick!'

'I can't,' whimpered Jane. 'Emily, you'll have to do it.'

'But you're sitting next to her.'

'Gonna puke!'

'FFS, someone catch the fucking sick!' I shrieked.

In the front, Sophie twisted round, grabbed the bag, leaned back and thrust it under Milly's nose as she heaved.

'Oh God, I'm going to be sick too,' moaned Jane.

'Me three,' groaned Emily.

'Man up!' I snapped, 'Your mother once caught vomit in her bare hands, Emily!'

'Euggh!' retched Emily.

'I feel much better,' announced Milly.

'Oh my God, the bag's leaking. I'm gonna puke too,' groaned Sophie.

And so we drove on into the night, a leaking bag of vomit in the footwell, three teenagers threatening to puke, and one recovered teenager now slurring something about how much she loved all her friends.

Finally we got to Milly's house. Luckily she wasn't staying over at mine like the other girls, on account of her going to Lanzarote with her family on an early flight the next morning, and apparently she'd promised she'd not be drinking at the party. I wasn't sure who I felt more sorry for, as we heaved her out of the car – Milly, who was clearly going to be thoroughly in the doghouse after getting herself shitfaced the night before going on holiday and would now have to travel with a hangover, or poor Milly's mum, who was going to have to deal with a pissed-up fifteen-year-old in addition to trying to get the rest of the family out the door for a lovely family break.

As we attempted to get Milly upright, it became clear that she'd not sobered up as much as I'd hoped. Jane let go of her and Milly immediately developed an alarming list to starboard.

'For Christ's sake, *catch* her,' I hissed, as Milly toppled towards the ground.

'Oh right, yeah,' giggled Jane, grabbing Milly's arm just in time before she hit the deck.

We finally got Milly up to her front door, retrieving her from a lavender bush halfway, as she'd collapsed into it and announced her intention to go nighty bed there. I rang the doorbell, sorely tempted to go for the teenage trick of leaving your pissed mate propped in the porch and doing a runner, although I feared that might be considered irresponsible at my age. So I did the next best thing, which was to wait until Milly's mum opened the door, looking thunderous, and gestured to Milly, who was attempting to climb under the doormat and go to sleep. I simply trilled,

'Here's Milly! I think she's a little tired!' then ran down the path and leapt into my car before anything could be said.

As I got back in the car, Sophie remarked, 'You were so cool about that, Ellen. My dad would have gone mental.'

'Well, it might surprise you to learn that I was a teenager once too, you know,' I chuckled, chuffed to bits at being the 'cool mum'. 'I mean, the things we got up to when we were your age, you'd be surprised … I wasn't always grown up and sensible, and I've had my fair share of snogging unsuitable boys after too much cheap booze. Did I ever tell you about the time I fell out of a window?' Get me. Relating to the Young People. Bonding with them. SUCH a cool mum was I!

'OH MY GOD, MOTHER! Will you just shut up? You're so embarrassing! I think *I'm* going to be sick, hearing you talking about snogging. Why do you always do this? You do it on *purpose* to ruin my life, don't you? Why can't you just be normal? IT'S NOT FAIR!' shrieked Jane.

FFS. Teenagers. I wonder how long this exhausting love/hate rollercoaster lasts?

At least one annoying or hopeful thing, depending on how you look at it, is that Emily and Sophie are never anything less than charming, polite and delightful when they're at my house, yet Hannah and Sam complain that their respective daughters are hideous hell fiends at home, and remark on what a delight Jane is in comparison, so I suppose at least they can all pull it out of the bag and behave in a civilised way with other people. It's just a shame they can't do the same for their parents.

The remaining girls decided they weren't going to be sick now, which was nice, but they wittered like demented budgies all the way home. All the same, I do rather envy the girls. To have your whole life ahead of you, with all of that promise and hope and expectation, to have no one to think about or worry about but yourself. No lying awake at night, worrying if your decisions have ruined the lives of the people you love best or wondering if you've wasted your life, and if you might still have time to do all the things you once planned to do. At one time I too was going to change the world, and I wonder what the Teenage Me would think of me now, given that the most exciting thing that happened for me this week was buying a new clothes horse. Would she despise me as much as Jane does (Jane's parting shot as she got out of the car was to inform me that I wasn't allowed to speak in front of her friends in future)? Would she say, 'What *happened* to you, Ellen?' or would she be too transfixed by how my frizzy, badly behaved teenage hair is now smooth and sleek (GHDs, Teenage Me, the most wondrous invention of the twenty-first century).

It must be wonderful to still have that teenage invincibility, to feel like *anything* is possible, to have so much enthusiasm for life that you stay awake all night talking, just because you have so much excitement for the future and so much to say about it (though, of course, it helps that you have the teenage slothful ability to sleep all day and bugger all to get up for).

Maybe I need to channel fearless teenage Ellen, frizzy hair, Heather Shimmer lippy and all, and start flirting with Jack again. I texted him after Dad died, telling him what had happened, and he said he was terribly sorry, could he do anything etc, and then he sent a few 'How are you, you know where I am' messages, but the whole spark had gone out of it. In fairness, I suppose it's a bit inappropriate to start sending silly jokes and *double entendre* messages to someone who has just suffered what the undertaker kept gloomily referring to as A Significant Bereavement, and it felt equally inappropriate to reply to his polite concern with rude gifs, and so things have fizzled out there slightly. But I shall soon grasp the bull by the horns and suggest an Actual Date. Teenage Ellen would be proud of me, being a Strong Independent Woman, and without even a drop of Mad Dog 20/20 passing my lips!

Hopefully it will work rather better than Teenage Ellen's first attempt at being a Strong Independent Woman, when, on account of being incarcerated in an all-girls' school and not knowing Any Boys at All, apart from sweaty-palmed, dog-breathed 'friends of the family', Hannah and I found ourselves completely without anyone to take us to our first school dance. When I lamented this to Dad, he pooh-poohed the very notion and insisted we didn't *need* boys to go with, it was the 1990s, goddammit, and we could jolly well go by ourselves. So we did. We were the only ones *sans* escort, and we spent a miserable night sitting on the sidelines, being scorned as frigid no marks by the popular girls, who had cool, handsome brothers to set them up with their friends. Hannah and I both still twitch at the rustle of taffeta, conjuring up as it does a breath of Excla'mation perfume on the air, mixed with a hint of illicit vodka cunningly 'hidden' in a Coke can and a whole lot of teen-age mortification. When I complained bitterly about this to Dad afterwards, he airily said, 'Don't be silly, darling. Who wants to be like everyone else anyway?' At the time, I thought 'ME! *I* want to be like everyone else!' but of course he was right.

I could still hear the girls jabbering away as I drifted off to sleep, no doubt to have nightmares about violently coloured, bow-bedecked taffeta and bolero jackets (me, obvs, not them), but for once I didn't have the heart to get up and bang on their door while shouting did they want some fucking Trill if they were going to carry on with their budgie impressions. Maybe I'm going soft in my old age.

Thursday, 9 August

Hurrah, we're off on holiday today. I'd toyed with cancelling it, as it *did* seem a bit callous to go on holiday so soon after Dad's funeral but a) it *was* all paid for, b) Natalia insisted that Dad would want me to go, c) the children were really looking forward to it, d) I was greedily anticipating a week without anyone trying to ransack brimming cupboards and complaining there was no food – let the all-inclusive buffet take the strain instead – and not coming home from work to a shit heap of a house because my children can't use a glass more than once or put a crisp packet in the bin, let alone, heaven forbid, *empty* the bin, and e) hopefully no one would be asking me how I *was*, with that 'caring' expression on their faces – I had thought work might have been a respite from all the 'How Are You's', but it turned out to be even worse – hushed voices and 'understanding' looks from everyone, and Alan asked me if I needed to talk because I bollocked him for not doing something on time.

I suppose at least it makes a change from them assuming it must be PMT when I lose my rag at someone for being a useless fucker. Surprisingly, Debbie, who I was braced for being the worst of all, has been remarkably low key, apart from bringing me a whole tin of Quality Street all for myself – result! So I am very much looking forward to some time away from People. I mean, there will obviously be people there, but hopefully they'll all be more interested in getting their money's worth out of the all-inclusive cocktails and canapés. As, for that matter, will I, while trying to keep Jane off the free drink and stop her getting knocked up by a Spanish waiter, while also reminding Peter that it's really very rude to stare at the ladies sunbathing topless, as his eyes bulge out of his head and he vanishes 'to the toilet' for a suspiciously long time …

The airport was a heaving mass of irritable families and out of control Trunkis, though. I sniggered to myself as I watched a frazzled mother yelling, 'Wait for me, you bastard,' as she struggled along in the wake of her husband, who was Importantly Finding the Gate, as she lugged two toddlers, their Trunkis and various bags, bottles and essential soft toys. I remembered those hideous days all too well. It was counted a holiday success if we actually managed to board the plane before I turned to Simon and demanded a divorce. By the time I'd been rammed in the ankle for the sixth time by a passing be-Trunkied child, Jane had decided she wasn't talking to me because I wouldn't buy her another bikini in the airport Accessorize and Peter had fleeced me for the GDP of Belgium in Pret because he fancied a snack, I was feeling slightly less smug.

My desire to be free of People for the week was thwarted almost the moment we got on the plane – I'd declined to pay extra to choose our seats, and so we were split up. Well, I told the children, it was on principle about the money, but secretly I was hoping this would happen so I'd get peace on the flight without Jane trying to persuade me to buy her a vodka and coke because we were 'on holiday' and Peter claiming he'd die of starvation if I didn't spend £3.99 on a tiny tube of Pringles. Instead, I found myself sitting next to Doris. Doris went to Tenerife every year and always stayed in the same hotel, and last year she thought she hadn't booked in time and would have to stay in the hotel across the road, but it was OK, because in the end there was a cancellation and she got into 'her' hotel, and she could definitely recommend the best place to get a full English breakfast and the best Irish bars, and be careful of the tapas places because they didn't wash the salad and they put garlic in *everything*.

'Right,' I said weakly.

Doris then proceeded to tell me her entire life history (four children, six grandchildren, two husbands both divorced, every Easter she goes to Whitby with her sister, she doesn't like bingo, the school think her youngest grandson might be dyslexic but they don't know yet, she went to Turkey once but she didn't care for it because you can't beat Tenerife, gin gives her the shits but vodka is OK, there's too much football on the telly and she doesn't understand Netflix). 'And what about you, dear?' she asked. 'Pretty girl like you, are you married? Children?'

I mumbled I had two children, but wasn't married.

'Divorced, are you?' she said.

I nodded. 'Well, in the process of. Separated.'

'Bit of a shit, was he?'

I shrugged non-committedly.

'You're better off without him, love,' said Doris firmly. 'We all are. Fuck 'em. We don't need men. I've got my pals and I've got my cats and I've got my kids, and I've never been happier!'

I rather warmed to Doris.

Monday, 13 August

Jane isn't speaking to me again, because having refused to buy her a new bikini at the airport (because she already had eight and we were only going for seven days) I treated myself to one from the Zara down the road from the hotel. Jane told me it was inappropriate and not suitable for a woman of my age.

Peter isn't speaking to me because he decided to sign us both up for water volleyball, because apparently he 'thought it would be fun for us to do something together, Mum', and I wore my new Zara bikini, which it turned out isn't really suitable for doing anything in except lying very still by the pool, and my left tit escaped and nearly took a nice German man called Karl's eye out.

Karl is most definitely speaking to me, and keeps suggesting we meet for a nightcap, but I am heeding Doris's wise words, while Peter glares at us.

The children not speaking to me means that for the first time ever I have read all the books I've lugged on holiday (Peter keeps asking why I don't just get a Kindle, but it's not the *same* as choosing your actual holiday books, though it would free up a lot of space to take shoes for me not to wear) instead of managing one chapter of the first one, reading each line over and over again as I deal with the interruptions from one or other of my precious moppets wanting a drink or an ice cream or someone to play with them in the pool or to blow up their inflatable again or to complain they're too hot or too cold or that there's a bug near them. The poor couple on the sun loungers next to me have sat down for approximately thirty seconds all week, in between wrestling slippery sunscreen-covered toddlers and retrieving lost hats and strapping them back into their floaty vests and stopping them crying because the sun is too sunny. They arrive each morning with a vast buggy, laden with enough supplies to cross the Sahara, but they've had a row by 10.30 am every day because he's forgotten something essential as she spits, 'You had ONE job' at him through clenched teeth. 'Treasure these moments' people tell you. 'You're making precious memories' and 'You'll miss these days when they're gone.'

Looking over at the younger mum, still no further into *Eleanor Oliphant Is Completely Fine* than she was when she arrived, hissing, 'For fuck's sake, Richard, did you not think to *check* that the baby wipes were in the changing bag because now he's shit himself all up his back and there are no wipes? Do I have to remember everything? Honestly, it's like having another child to deal with,' and him snarling back, 'Well, *darling*, all you had to do was *ask* me to check if they were there,' and her clearly wanting to scream at him, but she's trying to conduct this row under her voice, so rage whispering, 'I asked you to check there was everything we needed,' and him replying, 'But you didn't mention we'd need baby wipes. You should have said,' as she snaps, 'I shouldn't *have* to say. You should be able to realise that we'd need them for God's sake,' I don't think they're going to miss these days when they're gone or reflect fondly on these happy memories one day.

To be honest, it's remarkable any couple gets through the early years of parenthood without killing each other. Maybe Simon and I didn't do so badly after all, getting as far as we did. By which I mean maybe *I* didn't do so badly getting this far without trying to drown him in a foreign swimming pool for also being a useless bastard who always forgot we'd need essential things like wipes, sippy cups and sunscreen to take to the pool and who thought nothing of filling the children full of multiple cans of Coke when I wasn't looking and then feigned injured innocence when they turned into demented sugar-crazed hell beasts attempting to twat the ever-living fuck out of each other.

For some reason, Simon has taken to sending me updates on the weather at home, with corresponding emojis (usually sad faces, as apparently it's pissing down). Fucked if I know what that means or why he thinks I care – one of the best things about being separated is being freed from the tyranny of Simon's obsession with the weather and checking his eleventy fucking billion weather apps every three minutes to see if it's going to rain, as he seemed to be under the impression that if he studied enough radar pictures he could somehow control the weather.

Sunday, 19 August

We got back from holiday on Thursday, and I feel like I've done nothing but wash piles of sandy, chlorine-scented, sunscreen-stained laundry ever since. But NOT TODAY! Today was a special day, as I finally had a date arranged with Jack and we were meeting for brunch. Even though I find 'brunch' a deeply annoying concept, I wanted Jack to think I was the sort of sophisticated person who brunches, so I didn't want to say no, sorry, I hate avocado, when he suggested it.

I therefore awoke full of anticipation for a lovely Grown-Up day, even though my awakening wasn't as Instagrammable as I could have hoped – I once had visions of me, post-divorce, sprawled in glorious solo bliss on crisp white sheets in a giant bed. The reality, especially when the children are not here, is that I sleep perched in a small corner of my bed, while Barry and Judgy sprawl in bliss over the rest of it – Barry taking up most of the room, but Judgy also managing to occupy far more space than seems possible for such a small dog. Judgy, moreover, likes to sleep with his head on the pillow and he snores, so between the snorting and grunting and the dog breath and no room to move, really it's like Simon is still here. The only thing missing is being nudged hopefully in the back.

Jack and I did the Awkward Hug Kiss on the Cheek Oops You Kiss Both Cheeks Thing when I arrived (Why? Why do people keep doing this? Who likes this, or is good at it?) and then Jack suggested Bloody Marys, which to be honest are really the best thing about brunch. Well, that and the bacon.

Jack scanned the menu, pulling a face.

'Lots of avocado, isn't there?' he said in a neutral tone.

'Mmmm,' I said, equally neutral.

'So … what do you think you'll have?'

'Um, I think maybe the Eggs Benedict?'

'No avocado?'

'Not for me, thank you, but don't let that stop you.'

'God no! Hate the stuff.'

'Oh thank fuck! Me too. It truly is the snot of Satan. I blame social media. Not just for the avocado, but for brunch too.'

'Really?' said Jack, looking slightly confused.

'Yes! I mean, was brunch even really a thing before Instagram and Facebook? Obviously "brunch" has existed for a while, but once upon a time brunchers were either over-achieving Americans or totally smug media hipster wanker types. And then Facebook happened, shortly followed by Instagram, and before you could say "heirloom tomatoes" we were *all* trying to be totally smug media hipster wanker types and wanging on about our artisan fucking eggs on our heritage bastarding sourdough toast and everywhere, but FUCKING EVERYWHERE you looked, there was "smashed" avocado. "Smashed". Why do they call it "smashed"? Is it to make it sound a bit more edgy, a bit more dangerous than calling it what it is, which is avocado mush? And who thought avocado even needed to be "edgy" in the first place? It's avocado!'

'Wow, you *really* don't like avocado, do you?'

'No! But the thing about brunch and all the fucking avocado was that it was quickly apparent that there was absolutely no point at all in having brunch unless you took a photo of it and posted it on your timeline, because have you even HAD brunch if no one knew you'd had brunch?'

'I don't know? I'm sorry, I wouldn't have suggested brunch if I knew you hated it so much!'

'Oh I don't hate *brunch*! It's really the only socially acceptable way to drink vodka before midday, so how could I hate it? I'm just a bit bitter about it, and about all the *photos* of brunch, because the sudden appearance of all those overhead shots of green slime on undercooked toast adorned with sprigs of unidentifiable herbal matter coincided nicely with me being stuck at home with the sort of recalcitrant toddlers who could not be taken out to chi-chi brunch establishments because of their inevitable desire to run amok leaving carnage in their wake, like tiny Vikings, pillaging at will.

'And so I used to spend Saturday and Sunday mornings *furiously* scrolling through my timeline, cursing the UTTER BRUNCHING BASTARDS who were smugly scoffing down their overpriced eggs before they embarked on some form of culturally stimulating activity like going to see a French film or perhaps some performance art, and then maybe having a mooch around some quirky independent shops and buying themselves something lovely and unique and tasteful to make their home even more FUCKING INSTAGRAMMABLE. While *my* cultural activities consisted of watching *Lazy Town* repeats and thinking impure thoughts about Sportacus and wondering if he'd keep the dastardly moustache on and do backflips into bed and all shopping was done online because of the aforementioned pillaging and running-amokdom, and so for many years I harboured deep hatred and rage against all who brunched. But now *I* am a bruncher, it's different! Hang on till I put a photo of my Bloody Mary on Instagram!'

'So, you have a thing for Sportacus?' Jack said faintly.

I realised perhaps I'd been talking too much, and possibly over-sharing a *tiny* bit.

'Had,' I corrected him. 'I *had* a thing for Sportacus. In my defence, I wasn't getting much sleep, and it could have been worse. Apparently a lot of mums have a real thing for Mr Tumble, which is just *wrong*!'

'The scary clown? Wow! Though I did like that other programme he did with the blonde girl with improbably perky tits.'

'I don't think you're supposed to look at the presenters' tits when you're watching kids' TV with your little darlings,' I reproached him.

'Well, you're not supposed to imagine Sportacus backflipping into bed, either,' Jack pointed out.

So, despite my worries that we'd have nothing to talk about in person, we didn't stop talking – about our children, of course; he was very proud of his daughter, who's about to go into her second year of university, when she told him she spent Friday and Saturday nights in the library, until he found out that 'The Library' is the name of a cheap bar, notorious for riotous student nights. I touched on the travails of Jane, and those alarming *volte-faces* from hatred to love and back to hatred, and he assured me his daughter had been the same and that they do come through it, and I also told him about Peter making me do volley-ball and nearly having Karl the Nice German Man's eye out with my errant nipple, and he choked a bit on his eggs and I confessed that I might as well admit now that I wasn't *nearly* as improbably perky as Sarah-Jane from *Higgledy House*, and he said he wasn't sure *anyone* was naturally that perky and part of the fun of watching was to see if she ever had Justin's eye out with them, and then we went for a walk round some lovely antique shops, though I declined to buy anything because I kept thinking how expensive everything was, when you could get lovely things in charity shops for a fraction of the price, and then I had to go home and let the dogs out.

As we walked back through the park, he said, 'I had a really nice time today.'

'I did too,' I said. 'It was fun.' Fun? FFS, it sounded like we'd been to a bloody Wacky Warehouse or something. Why did I say 'fun'? Maybe Jane is right. WHY DO I SPEAK AT ALL? Perhaps I should try being silent and mysterious?

'Sooooo, shall we do it again? Soon?'

'Oh yes, please!' I said, trying not to sound *too* keen.

'Great! Um, I'll call you?'

'Yes!'

And then, he leaned in and kissed me, before I could witter any more polite inanities at him. I've spent a lot of time in the last year wondering what it would be like to be kissed by a man that wasn't Simon, who was really a very good kisser. I'd worried that some of those teenage boys who had slobbered over my face in my youth might simply never have grown out of the habit (one boy I kissed when I was fifteen *literally* spent the whole time snogging my chin – it was disconcerting and unpleasant and did nothing for my teenage skin whatsoever), and that in the event of anyone ever kissing me again, it would be a similarly moist experience. But actually, Jack was a *fabulous* kisser, even better than Simon, though obviously I wasn't making comparisons at the time. I did wish, however, that I'd thought ahead slightly and not had eggs. I also worried somewhat about how do you know if *you* are a good kisser? I mean, no one has ever complained, but then again I said nothing to the chin-snogger either, so that's no guarantee that I'm any good at it. *Just Seventeen* gave no tips on how to tell if your snogging was up to standard. I tried very hard not to think about the eggy breath and *Just Seventeen*, though, and simply concentrate on the very nice kiss.

Judgy wasn't a bit grateful for me cutting my date short for the sake of his bladder, but Barry gave me a lick to say thank you. From his breath, I think that unfortunately he's been eating chicken shit again. Luckily Jack's breath was much nicer. Also, Simon had liked my Bloody Mary photo, *and* left a comment saying, 'Looks good! Hope you're having fun! Wish I had one of them!' Does that mean he wishes *he* was the one having brunch with me, or that his darling children are driving him to drink? Maybe he's just being polite. At any rate, I'd rather think about that snog with Jack than whether Simon's Instagram motives are honourable or not. God, I really hope I wasn't too eggy!

Friday, 24 August

I'm at a festival. My legs are a strangely lurid shade of orangey green, as I decided my fading holiday tan wasn't sufficient to get away with not-quite-hot-pants-short shorts, and so I panic-slapped on some fake tan on Thursday night, but the tan was rather out of date. I'd convinced myself that the sludgey green shade in which it came out of the bottle was just the 'guide colour' but it wasn't – the tan was distinctly off and, despite scrubbing desperately at myself when I realised my mistake, the strange colour stuck. On the plus side, there are many people here rocking a far more peculiar look, so I'm pretty sure I'm blending in seamlessly.

How did I end up at a festival? Colin's workmate had booked tickets for his family months ago, but then his wife unexpectedly got pregnant (there seems to be a lot of it about. Luckily Jack told me he's had the snip, so if we ever get to the shagging stage that's at least one less thing to think about) and it's her due date this weekend, so he gave them to Colin. There were four tickets, but since Sam declined to go, claiming that camping would play hell with his back, and we were *all* less than keen on Sophie's suggestion that her, Jane, Emily and Millie Watson could go together, Colin suggested that he and I and Jane and Sophie all went.

Jane and Sophie weren't overenthusiastic about this plan and argued vociferously as to why at the age of fifteen they were more than old enough to be turned loose in a large field full of drugs and glitter and unsuitable men (admittedly my ideas of what went on at festivals were largely based on Pulp's excellent song 'Sorted for E's and Wizz'), but they eventually capitulated and agreed to being chaperoned when it became apparent that the only way they were going to go was under the loving care of Colin and myself.

So, after a whirlwind of emergency Amazon Prime and BooHoo purchases and arranging Friday off work, we were away.

Jane was aghast when I bounded out the house, in full-on Festival Chic.

'What *are* you wearing?' she howled. 'Dear God, Mother, what do you think you look like?'

'I'm channelling Kate Moss and Jo Whiley at Glastonbury!' I said proudly, doing a twirl in my cut-off denim shorts and glittery wellies (I drew the line at Hunters. I wasn't paying a hundred quid for a pair of bloody wellies).

'Who? You look *insane*!' said Jane in horror. 'Why can't you just be normal? You're too old to wear stuff like that.'

'Nonsense,' I said briskly. 'Jo Whiley is fifty-something and *she* still pulls it off.'

'Well, whoever she is, you're not Jo Whiley, are you? You're my mum. You can't go like that.'

'I jolly well can,' I said indignantly. 'Anyway, I haven't got time to change. We're late for picking up Colin and Sophie.'

Peter slouched out to say his farewells before Simon collected him, and he recoiled as well. 'Mum, those shorts are *really* short.' he hissed.

'No, they're not,' I insisted.

'They are. It's going to be like water volleyball all over again, only with your arse.'

Simon chose that moment to arrive to get Peter (I'd tried to persuade him to take the dogs too, but he'd declined, so they were staying with the lovely dog walker), and his eyes nearly popped out of his head as he looked me up and down.

'Wow!' he said.

'Don't *you* start,' I said crossly.

'I'm not,' he said. 'You look great. Really great. But will you be warm enough? My weather app says it might rain, you know.'

'Oh do fuck off, Simon. I don't care what your weather app says, I don't care if my arse falls out while I'm dancing and I don't care if I get frostbite on my bum, because I'm throwing caution to the wind and am damn well going to have some *fun* this weekend!'

'I was only trying to help,' said Simon sulkily. 'You go and have *fun* then. Don't mind me and Peter, left behind while you have *fun*. We'll be fine, won't we, Peter? I thought maybe we'd go play Laser Quest and then go out for pizza. That would be *fun* too, won't it?'

'Actually, Dad, I've arranged to go over to Lucas's, and Hannah said I can stay for dinner, if you can drop me off on the way into town? And I'll text you when I'm ready to come home,' said Peter.

'Well, what am *I* supposed to do today?' whimpered Simon.

'No idea,' I said brightly. 'Anyway, we're even later now, so get in the *car*, Jane! Peter, I'll see you on Sunday night, and don't eat Hannah out of house and home. Bye, Simon,' and with that I hopped in the car and sped off.

We arrived and started unloading the car. Colin did give me some strange looks when he was loading the bags into the car, but when we got to the car park he started tutting as he peered in the boot.

'Ellen, what IS all this?'

'It's my stuff.'

'You have a picnic hamper. A wicker picnic hamper?'

'Yes. It has all the plates and glasses and cutlery cunningly strapped into it. It's *adorable* and was only £25 from TKMaxx.'

'Oh dear, you really *haven't* ever been to a festival before, have you?' he sighed.

'Well, no, but what's wrong with my hamper?'

'You don't bring wicker hampers to festivals, sweetie.'

'Why ever not? It will be extremely useful.'

'It really won't. You know we have to carry everything to the campsite?'

'It's wicker. It weighs barely anything. That's the point of wicker.'

But Colin missed this as he'd returned to rooting judgementally in my boot.

'Are these … did you bring … *deckchairs*?' he said incredulously. 'And you've got a whole Sainsbury's Bag for Life full of fairy lights.'

'Battery-powered ones,' I said proudly.

'What the fuck are you planning on doing with them? We're at a sodding festival, darling. You're not guiding the bloody Space Shuttle in to land.'

'I'm going to glamp our tent so it's adorable and quirky,' I insisted.

'I assume that is what the cushions are for as well?'

'Yes. I'm going for a sort of Cath Kidston meets Bedouin look.'

'Oh *God*, Mother!' wailed Jane. 'Why do you *always* have to be so *extra*?'

'Well, it's better than being *basic*,' I retorted, feeling very proud of myself at being so Down with the Kids and mastering the language of the Youth.

'It's really not,' said Jane.

Although the girls grudgingly agreed to camp beside us, they were quite insistent that under no circumstances were we to speak to them, stand closer than six feet near them, acknowledge their existence in any way, shape or form, or generally do anything at all that might cause them to be associated with us.

We agreed to this, not least because I felt that having a sullen fifteen-year-old in tow would do nothing for my street cred either, as well as making me look old.

The tents finally up, with very little help from the girls, who mostly stood around staring at their phones and flicking their hair about, we turned them loose, but not before I issued many pleas about not drinking, or taking *anything* people might give them, reminded them that in the unlikely event of them managing to procure drink, the cider would probably be a lot stronger than the Kopparberg that they were used to, and generally wrung my hands and fretted while the girls rolled their eyes and swished their hair menacingly at me.

The girls roaming at will, Colin made the excellent suggestion of getting a drink and then going to see some bands. Unfortunately, it's quite hard to find a decent glass of chilled Sauv Blanc at a festival, so Colin persuaded me to go native and have a pint of cider, which was actually jolly nice, but very strong, as I'd feared. I had a couple more anyway, and then I was very drunk and a nice lady covered me in glitter – well, it was only meant to be my face, but the fallout resulted in glittery tits too, which was very jolly, and I'm not sure what bands we saw, but I think I sang anyway, and then I had to go nighty bed, but on account of all the cider I did have to stumble to the loos several times in the night, and festival loos are every bit as bad as I'd feared … and then some. I think I'll just burn everything I've worn this weekend when I get home, in case it made contact with a festering Portaloo. Also, it's amazing how far glitter can spread – I found it in my knickers on one of my many pee trips. I dread to think where else it might have wedged itself, and I'm not sure I'll ever feel clean again.

Saturday, 25 August

I don't know why I've never been to a festival before, it's remarkably good fun. We started the day with something called a 'breakfast burrito', before going to see more bands. I'm a bit over music already, to be honest, but if you ignore the wanky music bits, it turns out that festivals are like Christmas and it's perfectly acceptable to start drinking with your breakfast (also, breakfast burritos are surprisingly delicious in a disgusting sort of a way). I was disappointed in a general lack of strategically placed straw bales for me to perch prettily on à la Jo Whiley, but at least it's stayed dry, even if that has meant my legs and feet got very sweaty inside my wellies.

The girls have not gone as AWOL as we feared though, as the iniquitous prices charged by the food stalls has meant that they appear as if by magic at feeding time and hover hopefully until we've forked out for their grub, before vanishing into the amorphous mass of Seething Youth once more.

Most of my glitter had rubbed off in the night, so after a couple more pints of the excellent cider, I went and got re-glittered, and this time got my tits glittered too. Colin did a double-take when he saw me.

'What *have* you done?' he demanded. 'You look like a human glitterball.'

'I'm pretty,' I responded with dignity. 'I *like* being glittery. This is fun. Let's have more cider!'

'It's just as well you like being glittery,' grumbled Colin. 'Because you're going to be glittery for weeks to come. I probably will be too, since I'm sharing a tent with you.'

'I hope so. Glitter is good! What's that horrible noise?'

'That,' said Colin, 'is Jane and Sophie's favourite band. The whole reason, in fact, why we're here.'

'It sounds like someone's murdering a cat.'

'I'm pretty sure my mother said the same to me about Oasis.'

'Fuck … but did your mum wear nearly hot pants to a festival and cover her tits in glitter?' I asked hopefully.

'Thankfully not,' shuddered Colin. 'That wasn't an image I needed.'

'Do you think I'm mentally scarring my children for life?'

'All parents mentally scar their children for life. It's a hazard of the job. I think you're probably scarring yours in a good way, though.'

'Really? Despite the divorce? And the nearly hot pants and the glittery tits and being on my fourth pint of cider at only 4 pm, so I can't really feel my face?'

'Your face is covered in glitter, trust me, you don't want to feel it. You're here, aren't you? At a festival that you didn't really want to come to, for Jane? You're not perfect, but you're not a bad mother either.'

'I hope not,' I sighed. 'Colin?'

'Yes, glitter tits?'

'WHY have I never been to a festival before? I'm having such a lovely time.'

'Because Simon always talked you out of it, remember? He'd grumble that it would be loud and unhygienic and Too Busy and that there would be People.'

'Oh yeah. Simon never wanted to do anything fun because he complained there might be People there. Same as he'd never go to a hotel on holiday, only a villa because he didn't want to be bothered with the People, never mind that that meant I spent all holiday cooking just like at home, because obviously his villas had to be as secluded as possible because People, and he wouldn't drive to restaurants in the evening because he was on holiday and wanted to have a beer. He really is a selfish bastard, actually.'

'He is, sweetie.'

'But now I can do whatever I like. I can go places with People, and to hotels and to FESTIVALS. I'm going to go to lots more festivals. In fact, I can do anything I like now I don't have to worry about Simon grumbling and whining.'

'Yes, you can.'

'I CAN. I can do ANYTHING. I CAN DO ANYTHING!'

I stood up on my chair and roared this, glittery arms in the air, as I wobbled alarming and Colin yelled, 'Steady on now,' and a horrified voice said, 'Get *down*, Mother, people are *looking*. What do you think you're *doing*?'

'I'm having a life-affirming moment of emancipation from the fucking patriarchy, Jane, I thought you'd be proud!' I proclaimed as I climbed down from my chair.

Jane snorted in disgust. 'Whatever. Will you buy us some cider?'

'No, you're underage,' I said sternly.

'Well, you're too old to be covered in glitter, but you are,' said Jane crossly.

'Yes, but it's biodegradable,' I said.

'That's not really the point. Go on, Mum … please, just one pint of cider?'

'Please!' begged Sophie.

'Oh, fuck it,' said Colin, and handed the girls our two pints. 'Don't tell your dad.'

'Colin! That's very bad. Underage drinking,' I objected, attempting to be the Voice of Responsible Parenting, which isn't easy when one is eleventy billion sheets to the wind oneself.

'Well, it's not like they're not already drinking most weekends anyway,' Colin pointed out.

'Yes, but that's only pishy fruity cider, not *proper* booze,' I insisted.

'This is nice, though,' said Jane, taking a slug.

'I'll get some more,' slurred Colin and lurched off.

'Just don't tell *your* father either,' I warned Jane.

The prospect of being supplied with even a modest amount of booze (that they didn't have to pay for) mellowed the girls' stipulations about not being seen with us, especially since their wristbands marked them out as underage, so every time someone from security hove into view we had to hold their cider and look like proper lushes. The cider even cheered Jane up enough to sit beside me and talk.

'Thank you for bringing us, Mum,' she muttered.

'S'OK, sweetheart. S'been fun. Did you enjoy your band?'

'Yeah, yeah it was good. They were smaller than I thought they'd be.'

'They always are. Always. Ed Sheeran is only diddy. Even littler than Justin Bieber!'

'Mum, people my age only listen to Ed Sheeran in our parents' cars. He literally just writes songs by numbers now for people with no imagination to have played for the first dance at their weddings.'

'Very rich, though. For a short ginger man.'

'You know you shouldn't judge him for being short and ginger. Judge him for his music. God knows that's enough to judge anyone for!'

'I *like* a bit of Ed Sheeran.'

'I know, I've been in your car.'

''Course, he's no Rick Astley. Now *there* is a sexy ginger man!'

'Oh. My. God. Mother, we were almost having a bonding moment, and you had to spoil it by talking about how sexy Rick Astley is. What's WRONG with you? You're sick.'

'Do you mean like when young people say something is "sick" to mean it's really good and very cool?' I asked hopefully.

'No! I mean as in there's something *wrong* with you, with this continuing obsession with Rick Astley.'

'But he's cool now! Rickrolling made him cool, and now he goes on tour with the Foo Fighters. And I'm a single lady. "ALL THE SINGLE LAAAAYDEEES", I warbled. 'Maybe I *will* end up marrying Rick Astley.'

'Don't sing, Mother. People are watching.'

'But it's Beyoncé. Beyoncé is hip too.'

'Nothing is "hip" or "cool" anymore, Mother. And Beyoncé and the Foo Fighters are all old people's music.'

'So what do the Youth say then, instead of hip and cool?'

'I'm not telling you, in case you embarrass me by trying to use the words in front of my friends. Can I have another cider?'

'Only if you tell me what the "in" words are.'

'No. And you're not going to marry Rick Astley either.'

'I might,' I said sulkily.

'You're always telling me that a women doesn't *need* a man.'

'I didn't mean Rick Astley, though. He's different. I used to cut his photos out of *Smash Hits* and stick them on my wall.'

'What's *Smash Hits*?'

'More cider!' hiccuped Colin, tottering up with another round of drinks.

'Don't you think the girlies have had enough?' I said doubtfully.

'No!' said Jane, grabbing a pint and gulping thirstily.

'Oooh,' I said excitedly. 'I love this song. Let's dance!'

'Mum!' said Jane in horror. 'That's the sound system from the bar! And it's playing Ed Sheeran. You can't come to a festival and dance to that.'

'Yesh I can,' I chirped merrily.

Later, much later, after the girls had gone to bed (with an unflatteringly distrustful reminder from Jane that I was not to do any drugs), and Colin and I'd been to the rave tent (a mistake; my glow sticks kept inexplicably slipping out of my hand and flying through the air, and I think people got a bit shirty about it

– it wasn't MY fault, the glow sticks were defective), we sat outside and looked at the stars, and I said something very deep and meaningful and profound about the enduring nature of the universe. It was very important and would probably bring about world peace if only I could remember what the fuck it was. It started raining very heavily at that point, though, and we had to run to the tent for shelter.

This morning, though, I woke up with a mouth like a badger's arse and considerable glitter *chaffage* going on. Luckily the girls were also rather fragile, and a unanimous vote was taken to go home due to the continuing rain making everything somewhat less fun, and causing my glitter to streak.

The car is now full of glitter, the house is covered in glitter, I've scrubbed and scrubbed but I still seem to get no less glittery. I just transfer it to other surfaces, and I fear I've become some sort of human glitter version of the Magic Porridge Pot, producing endless glitter, until someone says the magic words …

SEPTEMBER

Sunday, 2 September

Tomorrow, the children are back to school, and it'll be like the summer, the holiday and the festival never happened at all, the only evidence being an abundance of glitter still lightly coating every surface in the house.

I'd suggested several times over the summer that perhaps, for once, Simon could help with the delightful task of equipping the children for school, instead of leaving it all up to me, and indeed, I'd responded to several of his 'caring' texts asking how I was, and if there was anything he could do, by saying that yes, actually, this would be very helpful indeed, but obviously he did sweet fuck all about it, until this weekend, when everything was almost sold out, which meant he returned the children tonight, complaining of exhaustion and acting like he was some kind of sodding superhero for taking his kids uniform shopping for the first time in ten bastarding years.

'I mean, it wasn't easy, you know, Ellen. Apparently Jane has very specific requirements about her school skirt, although some of those skirts were *obscene*. How is it legal to sell them as school skirts? How? And how can they justify charging £27.99 for a tiny scrap of fabric? It's disgusting! Obviously, I told her I wasn't buying her anything of the sort and tried to get her to have a nice pleated skirt from John Lewis, but she wouldn't even go in there.

'Anyway,' he went on virtuously, 'I went to six shops with her, and we found one in the end. And then there were Peter's trousers! The exact sort of skinny, not too tight, not too loose, although one pair were rejected for being the "wrong sort of grey". Grey trousers are grey trousers – how can they be the wrong grey? But, we got there.'

'This is the trouble with shopping with teenagers. They have their own ideas, and they make sure you know about it. At least you didn't have to go into the hell of Hollister.'

'And the expense!' Simon whimpered. 'Do you have *any* idea how expensive it was to kit them out? Sorry, Ellen, am I boring you? You seem more interested in your phone? You don't seem very appreciative of the fact I've spent all day and a vast sum of money on kitting out your children for school.'

I looked up from a text from Jack and said, 'Welcome to my world, Simon. I've been doing it for several years, *and* I buy their other clothes, I buy their food, I put a roof over their head, I take them on holiday. So I'm very aware of how expensive and time-consuming it is to keep *your* children.'

'Yes, but I contribute to all that too,' blustered Simon.

'You do,' I conceded. 'You pay a percentage, quite a small percentage, of your salary towards your children's upkeep, and the rest of your money is yours, to do with as you will. Whereas everything I earn is supposed to go towards keeping them housed and fed, and never mind if there isn't anything left for me at the end of the day. It's *fucking* expensive being a single parent, and the system isn't financially in favour of the parent the children live with most of the time. Not to mention how much time it takes me ferrying them about, cooking for them, doing their laundry. You have them one weekend a fortnight and you think you're some sort of hero.'

'Well, you were the one who involved the lawyers,' shouted Simon. 'Don't complain about it now.'

'Yes, and *why*? Because *you* left *me*? Was I supposed to wait around and let you do everything on your timescale, when *you* were ready? Sorry if this doesn't suit you, but maybe you shouldn't have left in the first place. And maybe you shouldn't have shagged someone else, while we're on the subject of *why* we're getting divorced.'

'Oh God, are you always going to keep bringing that up?'

'Well, if you didn't want to be reminded about fucking someone else, maybe you just shouldn't have fucked someone else, should you? And actually, that was just the straw that broke the camel's back. Don't you think it significant that it's been over TEN YEARS since Jane started school, and this is the first time you've ever taken them uniform shopping? And that even then, despite all your supposedly "caring" offers of help, when I actually asked you to do something of practical help, I STILL HAD TO NAG YOU INTO IT! Because you didn't actually want to do anything to help; you just wanted to look like a nice guy and possibly get another shag out of it.'

'That was NOT what I was thinking, and I AM a nice person,' said Simon in outrage. 'I was *concerned* about you. I just thought you needed emotional support, rather than practical help.'

'Has it never occurred to you that sometimes offering practical help IS providing emotional support?' I pointed out. 'NOT that I need support. I AM FINE!'

'Clearly,' said Simon. 'You seem fine. Perfectly fine. I mean, what's not fine about being a complete bitch after I've spent the day taking your children shopping?'

'I'm not being a bitch, I'm pointing out facts. And THEY'RE YOUR CHILDREN TOO! And because you've waited until now to get the uniform, I take it you haven't washed or labelled any of it, have you? Always half a job, isn't it, Simon, assuming I'll just pick up the slack. Jesus FUCKING Christ, we're getting

DIVORCED! DIVORCED! And yet I'm still doing everything for this family, carrying the whole bastarding load, getting no thanks or recognition for EVERYTHING THAT I DO, while you've always acted like you deserve a bloody medal if you ever actually manage to get off your backside and do something to help. Fuck my life!'

'Oh FFS! What do you want from me? I'm trying to help, I'm trying to be nice – and it's never enough. And now you're probably going to start ranting about the patriarchy like I've been listening to Jane do all afternoon.'

'Yes, well, maybe that's because now I get to spend my Sunday night waiting for uniform to come out the tumble dryer and labelling it, all because you couldn't be arsed going shopping earlier in the summer. You've always wanted everything to be on your terms and it's just not going to be like that anymore, Simon. I have my own life now. And also, why shouldn't Jane rant about the patriarchy if she wants to, if it stops her generation making the mistake mine made of believing the hype when we were told we could "have it all", when all that meant was we'd just end up bloody DOING IT ALL, WHICH ISN'T THE SAME!'

'God, calm down! Why are you being so irrational about this?'

'Irrational? IRRATIONAL? Do you know, in all the years we were married we never once went on a family holiday that *I* chose and in all those years you never once bought butter?'

'What has butter got to do with this?' Simon huffed.

'It's *symbolic*! Of how you used to look in the fridge and tell me there was no butter, and expect me to magic some out of thin air, instead of it occurring to you to go to the shop and buy some.'

'I don't remember doing that?'

'Well, you did. Not just butter. Yoghurt too!'

'So what you're saying is that you think we'd still be together if *I'd* bought more dairy products and let *you* choose the holidays?'

'No,' I sighed. 'Look, it doesn't matter.'

After he went, as I loaded a seemingly endless pile of white shirts into the wash, trying to make sure I'd removed all those tiny little bits of cardboard the manufacturers tuck into random crevices for no apparent reason other than to fuck up your washing machine if you miss one and cover your laundry with tiny flecks of cardboard that set like cement, I did wonder if I'd perhaps been slightly harsh – Simon had at least heeded my instructions enough to buy the non-iron shirts, and the complaints from the children about how many shops they'd been obliged to visit to acquire their sibling's idea of suitable uniform suggested he might indeed have had quite a trying day with them. I toyed with texting a brief thank you to him for sorting the whole thing out, but then I found more glitter in the tumble dryer and remembered my lovely weekend at the festival and all the things I never did for all those years because of him, and thought, 'Fuck it.'

My phone binged with a text from Simon.

Sorry I never bought butter. Do you fancy meeting up sometime without the kids for a catch-up? Maybe brunch somewhere? I'll make sure there's enough butter ...

Maybe we *should* have brunch. After all, sometimes he can be quite funny, when he's not being an arsehole, and ultimately it would be good if we could be friends – good for us, as well as for the children. We might end up like one of those übercivilised ex-couples who all go on holiday together with their new partners. Maybe not. That's a bit weird. Also, Simon hates brunch

(People), so the very act of going for brunch will be quite purgatorial for him ...

Monday, 3 September

My impassioned speech to Jane about how important this year is going to be for her, with her GCSEs in the summer, appeared to fall on deaf ears. As I implored her to concentrate, knuckle down and work hard, etc, because these exams will have an effect on the rest of her life, she just shrugged and told me to 'chill'. Saying that, I think I spent most of my GCSE study leave going clubbing, so what do I know?

The good news at work, though, is that there seems to have been a collective decision made that my period of mourning is officially over and people are treating me normally again without the 'caring' arm pats and head tilts, which means I can actually get on with my job without someone tiptoeing in every two minutes with another cup of tea and a whispered 'You know where I am if you need anything.' Of course, the bad news is that Debbie has therefore withdrawn my special Quality Street privileges and bestowed them instead on Mike from shipping, whose wife has run off with an Elvis impersonator she met in a chip shop. Remarking that this sounded rather like a bizarre real-life mash-up of Jilted John and Kirsty MacColl songs was apparently neither supportive nor sympathetic, but Mike had just eaten Debbie's last blue Quality Street and to be perfectly honest I can see why his wife left him, the selfish bastard, so I wasn't feeling the love for Mike and his need for coconutty chocolate goodness to heal his broken heart.

It's a relief, however, to have my lovely colleagues return to muttering something about PMT under their breath instead of looking at me wide-eyed and asking me if I need a hug when I tear them a new arsehole for being incompetent twatbungles. Obviously I don't *call* them incompetent twatbungles to their faces – well, not since someone made a complaint to Gabrielle (I explained it was simply robust industrial language, but she said I wasn't allowed to say things like that in the office as people's feelings could be hurt). Apparently my suggestion that if they actually did their job properly in the first place I wouldn't need to call them anything because we wouldn't have a problem wasn't the solution either. So now I have to be much more passive–aggressive in my approach, and not question their intelligence, competency or parentage, which really leads me to see why people end up phoning in to Jeremy Vine to complain about 'Political Correctness Gone Mad!'. A small part of me also suspects that a) Gabrielle is the sort of person who thinks it's unladylike to swear, in which case she's very fucking wrong, and b) the people who have a problem with me bollocking people for incompetence have issues with having as their boss a woman who knows more about what they're supposed to be doing than they do, but that's just me being judgemental, obviously …

Tuesday, 11 September

Happy Birthday to me! I'd been quite adamant that I didn't want a fuss, just a quiet night in with my children, the only concession to marking the occasion being a £12 M&S dinner with wine (well, two £12 dinners, as Peter can eat one on his own and they can never agree on a pudding, which also meant two lovely bottles of wine for me, not to be drunk on the same night, obviously, though I am still smarting that they have put the price up. A £12 dinner just isn't the same as a £10 dinner).

I was a bit bloody put out, though, that neither of my precious moppets even *acknowledged* my birthday when they finally lumbered out of bed. I'd insisted I didn't want a fuss, but was it too much to ask for a card? Maybe a box of chocolates? Fuck it, even just a 'Happy Birthday, Mum!' and a cup of tea would have been nice. I finally trilled, 'Have you forgotten something, darlings?' at them brightly, and they looked at me blankly, before Jane said, 'Oh YEAH! I've got PE today. Thanks for reminding me, Mum,' and Peter said, 'I've got cooking, Mum, I need to take in my ingredients. I need panko breadcrumbs and soya milk and strawberries and, I'll just airdrop you the list actually, will I?'

I was duly airdropped a lengthy list of exotic ingredients that we did not have, necessitating a mercy dash via the shop on the way to drop them at the bus. Unfortunately our local village shop also does not run to such exotica, and the chi-chi little deli, which might, doesn't open till 10 am, as its hipster owners like to spend the morning doing yoga first instead of engaging in filthy commerce. Thus it was that a complaining Peter was sent off with a box of orange Paxo breadcrumbs ('It's practically the same thing, darling; Paxo/panko, what's the difference, really?'), a bag of apples, a litre of UHT milk and various other substitutions that he insisted were not suitable, while I hissed, 'Well, darling, maybe if you'd given me some warning, I could have got the actual things you needed, couldn't I?'

Off I went to work, chuntering to myself at my ungrateful offspring. I've never had much sympathy for those people who are all martyred about no one ever remembering their birthday, because in my opinion if you want people to remember your birthday you have to remind them. But I HAD reminded them. Just last night I'd asked them what they fancied from the £12 M&S dinner FOR MY BIRTHDAY DINNER TOMORROW, because it was MY BIRTHDAY tomorrow, and yet, this morning – nothing. Little fuckers. All those years, blowing up balloons, putting up bunting, going out of my way to make their birthdays *special* and *important*, so they felt like they had one day that was All About Them, and how do they repay me? With sweet FA, that's how.

I know, of course, that I did not do all those things in the expectation of reward from them one day – I did it out of love – but even so. Not even a cup of fucking tea! Not even a text from Simon, to wish me Happy Birthday after twenty-six bastarding birthdays with me. He *knows* how much birthdays matter to me … He always says he wants to help and be there for me – well, say Happy Twatting Birthday then, Bollocksface! So far, the only acknowledgement of MY SPECIAL DAY was a card from my bloody mother, containing a voucher for a facial and a note insisting that I had the rejuvenating version, because she thought I wasn't aging very well and it might help.

When I got to the office and checked my phone there was a text from Jessica, wishing me a Happy Birthday and informing me that as we all had too many possessions, instead of a present they had bought a goat for a family in the developing world, in my name, with a link to the Oxfam website to view my new goat. I thought this was quite a nice idea, till it turned out that the link just took you to a generic photo of a goat, not your own special goat, which was a bit shit. I'd been looking forward to seeing my goat grow and mature over the years, perhaps writing to it and sending it goaty Christmas presents – although given the ultimate fate of goats in the developing world, perhaps it was best that there wasn't an opportunity to form a bond with my goat, as it would be somewhat disheartening to have your goaty Christmas present returned on the basis that your goat had formed a large part of the Christmas dinner. Still, it was a nice thought from Jessica, I comforted myself. It would have been nicer if I could at least have *named* the goat, though? What would one call a goat? Well, I decided, surely the only possible option for a goat these days would be Goaty McGoatface. It's possible the poor starving family relying on Goaty McGoatface to save their ailing fortunes might not get the joke, though.

Debbie is in charge of birthdays at work and so spent the morning unsubtly handing around a card to be grudgingly signed by the office, before everyone was summonsed for cake and a ceremonial singing of 'Happy Birthday'. Even Gabrielle deigned to attend, managing to look like she'd rather be anywhere else, with her mouth in its usual cat's bum expression. The one consolation of Gabrielle's face permanently looking like a bull-dog with a smacked arse licking piss off a nettle (it's my birthday, I can mix my similes if I want to), is that she's going to end up with much worse lines round her mouth from that than I ever will as a result of all my illicit cigarettes from the age of fourteen.

Once everyone had eaten the cake and shuffled off back to their desks (it did not escape my notice that Mike had managed to sneak in and nab himself some cake, the greedy bastard. Were all my coconut Quality Street not enough for him? His poor wife was probably only in that chip shop in the first place in desperate search of sustenance because he'd eaten everything else in the house), I retreated to my office, ostensibly for a conference call that took five minutes, and spent the rest of the afternoon taking stock of what I'd achieved in my forty-six years on this earth.

Two children, who may or may not become well-rounded, civilised and useful members of society – there are hopeful signs, but the jury is still out.

Two dogs, one who is definitely not a well-rounded, civilised and useful member of society, but instead displays somewhat psychopathic tendencies, and one who really, really *wants* to be a useful member of society, but due to now being only slightly smaller than a Clydesdale tends to cause carnage wherever he goes. Poor Barry. He does *mean* so extremely well.

Three bastarding evil chickens. They are chatty, you know, those Speckled Sussexes. I see them out there, yabbering away to each other, and as soon as I go out they clam up, turn their backs on me and mutter nasty things under their breath, *exactly* like spiteful, cliquey schoolgirls. I should have called them all Heather. They might yet meet a similar fate – I've more than once considered not shutting them up at night and letting them take their chances with the foxes, but a) I fear this isn't responsible chicken husbandry and b) I'd feel rather bad if directly or indirectly I had a hand in their demise.

One ex-husband. Let's draw a veil over Simon, shall we? I'm not sure he can be counted as an achievement.

Quite a reasonable career, even if it can never match up to my brief moment of glory designing a smash hit app and making lots of lovely money a few years ago. A career is a good thing; that is definitely a tick.

Shoes? Can I consider my shoes? I *do* have a lot of shoes. The children used to be obsessed with one of those bizarre American children's programmes about a pair of twins who used to be Ben from *Friends* who went to a school on a boat. I never worked out *why* they went to a school on a boat – they started out living in a hotel, again for reasons I couldn't fathom, and then were sent to the strange cruise-ship school. One of the other children at the boat school had a whole submarine that used to follow the ship, filled with her shoes. I'm pretty sure I've enough shoes to fill a submarine, so perhaps I should count that as an achievement. I don't have a submarine, though, nor can I think of any reason why I'd fill it with shoes if I did.

Lovely Friends. They're definitely a tick as well. My family less so. They can go in the box with Simon, labelled Things Best Not Discussed. Except Natalia, of course, although I'm not sure if one can count a stepmother as an achievement of one's own. Fuck it, it's my birthday. I shall count Natalia.

What else? House? Yes, I shall count my house. I worked hard for it and bought it with my own money (and some of the bank's). Car? Does that count? I suppose if a submarine's worth of shoes counts, then I should count my car too, but it feels a bit like I'm clutching at straws to fill my list. So to summarise: the sum total of my life amounts to two children, two dogs, three chickens that hate me but that I keep alive anyway because I'm not a monster, five friends (I've counted Colin and Charlie as well as Hannah and Sam, but not Katie's husband Tim, because he's nice, but dull, even though including him would have bumped up my list as well, but I've already cheated slightly with the car) and a stepmother.

It doesn't sound an awful lot when you look at it like that. I've not changed the world, I've not discovered a cure for cancer or created Great Art that will live on through the ages. There will be no blue plaques outside houses where I've lived. I sit in an office and shout at people to make them work faster to design more things to sell that will be obsolete and forgotten in a year or two, my two beautiful children may choose to pass on my DNA to future generations, but then again so do millions of other people – that's not really anything earth-shattering, except in the sense people keep saying the world is overcrowded and unsustainable, and I've contributed to that.

I got home to find the house empty except for the dogs – Barry gave me his usual hysterical greeting of 'OH MY GOD I THOUGHT NO ONE WAS EVER COMING BACK AND I'D BE ALONE FOREVER!', despite it only having been about an hour since the dog walker dropped them off, and Judgy gave me a disgusted look, farted, and went and sat in my favourite seat on the sofa. Well, at least Barry was pleased to see me. There was no sign of the children, as I attempted to remember if they had anything on after school today or had just fucked off to a mate's house without telling me. I texted them both, enquiring whether they'd actually be home for dinner or not, and trudged out to feed the chickens and shut them up for the night. Oxo pecked the tassel off my previously stylish loafer and attempted to swallow it. I half wished that it would choke her, although I managed to retrieve it in the hope of reattaching it. But she had snapped the leather thong off. Denied her tasselly snack, she contented herself with taking a chunk out of my hand instead.

I checked my phone to see if there was any response from my darling children or maybe even a text from Jack, who I was sure I'd dropped hints to about my birthday, but of course there was not. I took the wild and crazy step of attempting to telephone my precious moppets and *speak* to them, but obviously neither of them picked up. I don't understand how it is that they spend literally ALL DAY almost surgically attached to their phones, texting, Snapchatting, taking selfies and doing God only knows what else, but the minute I try to use the phones for the *actual purpose* for which *I* pay their credit – to get in touch with them and check their whereabouts/plans, etc (because clearly they'd never willingly share such details with their aged mother unless they wanted a lift or money from me) – they maintain an impressive radio silence, always claiming when I berate them that they 'hadn't heard' their phone or 'had no signal'.

Finally, after an increasingly furious barrage of texts to them both I got a reply from Jane. It simply said 'K'.

'K'. This 'K' response drives me round the twist. 'K'. I mean, is it so much to ask, after I carried them inside for me for nine months, after ruining my lady bits giving birth to them, wiping their arses and letting them puke down my cleavage, drying their tears, teaching them to ride their bikes, steri-stripping them back together when they fell off their bikes, acting as unpaid chauffeur, cook and bottle washer to their various whims, AFTER ALL THAT, they can't even be bothered to twitch their fucking finger twice to even send me the response 'OK'.

I opened the first bottle of wine and decided to bin off dinner. What was the point in cooking lovely things for one? Well, it wasn't really cooking, as kind Messrs M&S had done all the work; it was just chucking some things in the oven and micro-wave, but even so, that suddenly seemed a lot of effort, especially since I'd practically lost a finger in Oxo's latest attack. I briefly considered having a slap-up meal for three with the dogs, but I feared what sort of wind lemon and herb-marinaded seabass might give them – choking on toxic waves of fishy dog farts would be the final nail in the coffin of the Birthday That Never Was. I opened a packet of Doritos instead and slumped on the sofa with my wine and the dogs and had a little cry to myself. I'm really trying very hard to be a Strong Independent Woman who doesn't need anyone, but it's difficult to remember that when almost everyone has forgotten your birthday. Judgy has grown no more compassionate in his old age and reacted as he always does to crying women by snorting in disgust and taking himself off to a drier seat, and poor Barry of course thought it was all his fault and tried to make amends by bringing me all his toys and then sitting on me to say sorry, which only made me cry harder, and then nearly choke as I inhaled a mouthful of dog hair. I wished it were dark – sitting in the dark is much more conducive to wallowing in self-pity.

I'd managed to work my way down a good half of the bottle before I finally heard anybody's key in the lock. I hastily dried my eyes on the bloody (literally) kitchen roll with which I'd attempted to reattach my severed finger (not something I'd recommend), before I was found sitting alone, sobbing, and was forced to endure the ultimate humiliation of explaining that I was crying because no one had remembered my birthday, like a petulant five-year-old who had been given the wrong sort of Barbie, only slightly more pathetic, because of course at forty-six you aren't supposed to bother about birthdays or presents anymore, and it was difficult to explain that it was just about *someone* taking the time to *bother*, rather than about actual presents (though presents are always nice, obviously).

Jane opened the door to the sitting room. 'Oh *there* you are,' she said. 'What did you do to your hand?'

'Oxo. She pecked my finger off,' I said sulkily.

'I assume you're exaggerating about pecking your finger off. Did you do something to annoy her? She's very highly-strung, you know.'

'She's a bastarding chicken!' I snapped. 'Chickens are not meant to be volatile! And she *would* peck my finger off given the chance, so it's as good as.'

'Whatever. Can you come in the kitchen?'

'No.'

'Why not?'

'Because I'm not making dinner. Because I'm sick of being treated like a dogsbody. Because if you can't even extend me the courtesy of letting me know when you'll be home or if you want dinner, then why should I put myself out for you? Do you know where your brother is, by any chance, or is he still MIA?'

'He's in the kitchen,' said Jane.

'Well, I'm not making him any bloody dinner either,' I huffed. 'He couldn't even be bothered to reply to my messages at all, or come and say hello, so I'm not sharing my Doritos.' I clutched them to my chest protectively with my non-chicken-savaged hand.

'Fine,' said Jane, 'suit yourself.' And she walked off.

'Bugger,' I thought, 'I had a lot more of that rant to go. How annoying that she's thwarted me by pissing off.' I considered following her, but decided to stay put as I didn't want to appear weak, and also after consuming half a bottle of wine at high speed on a few Doritos and a small piece of birthday cake, I feared my tirade of justified anger might sacrifice some of its high moral ground if I was struggling to stay upright. I slumped down further into the sofa and poured another glass of wine, feeling more abandoned than ever, as Barry obviously had followed his beloved Jane through into the kitchen.

'Come and give Mummy a cuddle, Judgy?' I pleaded, but he just looked at me and pushed a cushion onto the floor with disdain.

Jane stuck her head back in. 'Well, if you won't come through, we'll have to come to you,' she said crossly, throwing the door open. To my surprise, and some horror, given I was half pissed and blotchy-faced from self-pitying snivelling, there stood Hannah and Charlie, Sam and Colin, Katie and Tim and all the children.

'HAPPY BIRTHDAY!' they chorused.

'What the fuck!' I wailed.

'You didn't *honestly* think we'd forgotten, did you?' said Peter smugly.

'I did,' I whimpered.

'Ah ha, well that proves it was a *proper* surprise and you really didn't know anything about it,' chortled Peter gleefully.

'No,' I said, attempting to discreetly fish Doritos crumbs out of my cleavage. 'I really didn't.'

And then, despite my best efforts, I became quite overwhelmed and burst into tears. 'I thought no one cared,' I sobbed.

'Oh Ellen,' said Hannah. 'How could you think that?'

'I look dreadful.'

'You look fine,' said Hannah firmly. 'And anyway, it's just us, and even if you didn't, it wouldn't matter. Whether someone has mascara on or not becomes irrelevant after over thirty years of holding their hair out of their face while they're sick because they never learn that sambuca doesn't agree with them.'

That shook me out of my self-pity.

'Thirty years,' I said in horror. 'How can we be old enough to have been friends for thirty years?'

'Thirty-five years, actually,' said Hannah. 'It's only the thirty years of booze-induced puking.'

'That is most unfair,' I said with as much dignity as I could muster, given the subject matter. 'I've not spewed due to booze since *at least* 2005. I'm practically a lady!'

'Of course you are,' put in Sam in a comforting tone. 'Now be a lady and pop upstairs and fish those crumbs out of your bra in private and fix your face, and by the time you come back down we'll have the canapés, or as you like to call them ca-naypes, heated and the cocktails poured.'

'Oh God, I do love you all and I'm sorry I doubted you. I just wasn't expecting anything like this. You've all gone to so much trouble. And cocktails and ca-naypes, my favourite things.'

'I know,' smirked Sam. 'Although I remember the first time you met Colin and realised you'd been calling them "ca-naypes" all night and then had to explain that you *did* know they were pronounced "canapés", it was just your idea of an amusing joke.'

'One I still don't entirely *get*, by the way,' added Colin. 'But you have somehow converted *me* to pronouncing it as "ca-naypes" too, and so now *I* end up having to explain the same thing to people. Anyway, we all thought you deserved a treat for your birthday, after everything that had happened this year. The children organised most of it, though.'

I sobbed some more and my bloody kitchen roll soon disintegrated completely, as I thought of all the times I'd ungraciously thought my children couldn't organise a piss-up in a brewery.

'Come on, Ellen,' chided Katie. 'We don't all have strapping teenagers who stay up all night. I need to get my own precious moppets home to bed at a decent hour, and I intend to manage several cocktails first. And more importantly, the cocktails will get warm and the ca-naypes will get cold.'

I pulled myself together, and shuffled upstairs to de-Dorito and make myself look presentable.

'You could at least have warned me they were all there,' I said sternly to Judgy, who had decided to come with me and take up residence on my bed. He sneezed at me, then lolled on the pillows.

I went back downstairs as the doorbell rang. I opened it, and there was Simon.

'Hi Ellen,' he said awkwardly. 'I hope this is OK, the kids invited me …'

'Of course,' I said, thinking, 'as long as you've brought me a present.'

'It's just … well, I'm sorry, but the thing is, I'm not actually on my own, she's just getting something out the car.'

'Really? You've brought a girlfriend to my birthday party?' I said coldly.

'No, it's worse than that. I'm *really* sorry, but it's –'

'Hello Ellen!' cried an all-too-familiar voice.

'Louisa!' I finished for him. Simon's batshit sister. Super.

Louisa elbowed Simon aside to envelop me in one of her unhygienic hugs.

'I'm so thrilled to be able to be here with you to celebrate, Ellen,' she said, staring deep into my eyes in a very disconcerting way. 'And I can tell I've not come a minute too soon. Look at your chakras. They're a *mess*.'

'Louisa,' I said again weakly. Louisa, with six children and an unbeatable ability to leech off anyone within a hundred-mile radius who pays her the slightest bit of attention, while proclaiming that she can't get a proper job because she's An Artist, and blaming everything she *doesn't* like (working, washing, looking after her children herself) on the oppression of the patriarchy, and claiming everything she *does* like (lazing around doing bugger all squared, talking about her fanny and living off other people) is a result of her brave feminist fight against The Man.

'Errr, where are the children?' I enquired. 'And Isabel?'

'I've left Isabel!' declared Louisa. 'Her ideology was irreconcilable with mine. She expected me to clean the yurt and help with the cooking and childcare when I was trying to write. I'll not be oppressed by domestic drudgery, not by a man *nor* a woman. So it's over, I've left the commune and I've bought another camper van, which I've named Gunnar II. You remember my lovely old camper van Gunnar?'

I nodded feebly, vaguely recalling some kind of rust-bucket death trap Louisa used to career about in after she left her husband when she found he was being rather too free with his free-love principles, until her father sent it to the scrapyard and bought her a people carrier, in the interests of his grandchildren's safety.

'Well, I'm travelling around the country in Gunnar II, doing poetry readings and raising consciousness against oppression. I'm in a unique position to speak on oppression, having experienced it from both sexes, you see.'

Marvellous. Louisa just gets more ... *Louisa* with age. The most spoiled, least oppressed person I've ever met in my life had managed to mention oppression no fewer than *three* times before she'd even got in the door.

'And the children?' I reminded her.

'Oh yes. Well, they moaned so much at the commune, I sent the three oldest ones to live with their father. Bardo and that *awful* rich American went off back to Chicago, you know, she didn't like our sustainable life in the woods, so I sent them to him so they could see first-hand what it was like to live a conventional, consumerist lifestyle, shackled by the rules of society. Unfortunately, they've been seduced by capitalism and have rejected everything I've ever taught them. Cedric was packed off to one of those American military schools because they said he was "feral". He's a free spirit, that's all. Like me! Or he was. Apparently that's been crushed out of him and he's loving school. I'm so ashamed.'

Given Cedric was previously probably on track for whatever the modern equivalent of Borstal is, 'feral' being a rather generous description of him, I thought this transformation could only be a good thing.

'And as for Coventina, there was always something wrong with that girl. She tells me she spends her weekends at the "mall" and wants to get a *job* there as soon as she's old enough.'

'She just sounds like a fifteen-year-old girl,' I suggested.

'AND she wants me to call her "Tina". I named her after an ancient river goddess, and she wants to be called Tina!' Louisa snorted. 'And Nissien, well, *he* has joined the school football team, despite being more than aware of my views on competitive sports. I'm *so* disappointed in them all, after everything I've done for them.'

'And the younger three?' I ventured, Louisa having barrelled into the hall during her rant about her children (still with no 'Happy Birthday' or 'How are you?' for me, obviously) with no sign of any children in tow.

'Where are they now? Idelisa, Boreas, Oilell, *come here!*' shrieked Louisa, hurtling back into the night in search of her errant children.

'I'm so sorry,' said Simon. 'She insisted on coming. We won't stay long, I promise.'

'Is she staying with you?'

'Yes, worst luck. I'm hoping she moves on soon.'

'Do the kids still shit on the floor?'

'Not so far. But you never know with Louisa's fiends. On the plus side, I made her drive tonight, so your booze is safe from her and I can have a drink. Where is *your* drink?'

'I was just getting one,' I said, as Hannah came out of the kitchen in search of me, cocktail in hand ready for me, like the good friend she is.

'Why are you skulking out here with Simon?' she said.

'Hello Hannah,' said Simon. 'Ellen was just saying hello to Louisa.'

Hannah went sharply into reverse – not a mean feat when you're as heavily pregnant as her.

'Louisa,' she said in dismay. 'What the actual fuck is *she* doing here? She's not brought the Wolf Pack, has she?'

'Only half of them,' soothed Simon. 'The other half saw sense and decamped to their father's as the lesser of the evils on offer. I'll remove her shortly, but the kids insisted I came tonight and Louisa insisted *she* came with me.'

'Hmm,' grumbled Hannah, 'I don't think we've enough ca-naypes for Louisa and co.'

'Don't worry,' said Simon grimly. 'She's still gluten free and vegan, and probably sees M&S as an agent of globalisation, and ca-naypes most likely are symbols of middle-class capitalist glut-tony so she won't eat them – by the way, why can't we call them "canapés" like normal people?'

'Yes,' said Hannah tartly. 'It's funny how Louisa has never had a problem with other people's expensive drink being a sign of capitalist gluttony, though, isn't it? Right, come on through. Everyone is wondering where you are, and we have *presents*!'

Louisa interrupted my lovely friends giving me tasteful middle-class presents to announce she wanted to give me *her* present, and handed me a copy of her latest book of poetry, titled simply *Cervix*. I braced myself. Louisa was the Queen of Giving with One Hand and Taking with the Other – usually literally. Last time she 'gave' me a book of her poetry she demanded I paid her for it in the same breath.

Sure enough, Louisa didn't disappoint. She announced that she'd generously decided to help me out as a fellow single parent, giving me the opportunity of simultaneously generating some extra income and spreading the word of the sisterhood and her groundbreaking *Cervix* (sounded painful) by 'gifting' me the opportunity to buy two hundred copies of *Cervix* at £1 less than she usually sold them for, to resell to all my friends and family. She'd then 'allow' us to split the resulting 'profit'.

I politely declined, suggesting that I could not possibly siphon such valuable funds from Louisa's consciousness-raising mission, but she was quite insistent. Finally Simon intervened and firmly announced it was time to go.

'But I haven't even *read* from *Cervix* yet!' protested Louisa. 'I had a special birthday performance of "The Cup of Blood" planned, about sustainable sanitary protection, just for Ellen's birthday party. Although of course at your age, Ellen, that's probably not something you need to worry about, is it? But Jane might find the message of returning your monthly offering to the Goddess by burying it outside very empowering.'

Jane retched.

'I think Boreas is eating the salmon pinwheels,' said Simon tactfully, and Louisa let out a howl of dismay and beetled off to rescue her offspring from the Snacks of Doom. Simon managed to bundle her out the door without much further ado, although the last we heard was her protesting, 'But Simon, you didn't even give me a chance to ask anyone else if they wanted to buy a copy of *Cervix*, since they won't be able to get one from Ellen. I think I should really go back and see who wants one, as I don't want anyone to miss out.'

Katie and Tim departed shortly after that, dragging their little girls Lily and Ruby with them, sleepy but protesting, so it was just Hannah and Charlie and Sam and Colin left, along with all our giant, definitely non-sleepy children. Hannah yawned.

'I should take you home to bed,' said Charlie.

'No, I'm *fine*!' said Hannah. 'It's Ellen's birthday and I'm *determined* to stay up past 9 pm.'

Jane and Sophie and Emily burst into the kitchen.

'Mum, can the girls stay over?' asked Jane.

'What about school?' I said. 'Uniform, school bags, etc?'

'Oh, they've got those with them,' said Jane airily.

'Fine,' I said, spotting a fait accompli when I saw one.

Peter slouched in a few minutes later to complain it was unfair that Jane was having a sleepover and so could Toby and Lucas stay too? Quite by coincidence, Toby and Lucas had brought their school bags and uniforms along too … Having thoughtfully organised me a surprise birthday party, the children had then thoroughly outmanoeuvred me, so I resigned myself to a night of earplugs and having to fumigate the house in the morning. Maybe one day I'd enjoy a birthday that was all about *me* and didn't involve a houseful of children. But would I even know what to do with myself in that eventuality?

'So what *was* that all about, with that woman with the book?' asked Colin faintly.

'My former sister-in-law writes terrible poetry about her unmentionables,' I explained.

Colin shuddered.

'You know, in some ways I envy Louisa,' yawned Hannah.

'Envy her?' I said incredulously. 'Why would anyone *envy* Louisa? She's appalling. And in permanent need of a bath!'

'She is,' agreed Hannah. 'But she doesn't give a shit, does she? She's completely self-centred, a monster of a human being, and through it all there's not one moment of self-doubt or mum guilt or worrying about whether she's doing the right thing. Louisa is eternally convinced that she's right, and even if she does a complete 180 she still doesn't ever think she was wrong; she just convinces herself that she's found an even *better* way. It must be wonderful to go through life with that degree of self-confidence, instead of constantly doubting and second-guessing and wondering if you're enough, if you've done enough, if you've fucked everything up.'

'Oh God,' I said, 'I see what you mean. I never thought I'd find myself saying I wanted to be more like Louisa, but in that sense – in the not-giving-a-fuck sense – you're right. I do wish I could be like that.'

We all coughed as the children came back into the kitchen again on a choking cloud of Impulse and Lynx, a homogenous mass of shiny swishy hair from the girls and improbably large feet and gangling limbs from the boys, in noisy search of yet more snacks.

'Were we ever that young?' I marvelled to Hannah, 'with metabolisms that fast?' as we looked at our daughters inhaling some disgusting-flavoured, overly sweetened popcorn, while the boys insisted it wasn't too late to cook frozen pizzas because they were STARVING!

'It does seem unbelievable, doesn't it?' said Hannah. 'So much hair. Such youthful capacity to breathe in synthetic scents without vomiting. Lucas, ONE PIZZA EACH. ONE! Emily, Christ, what are you doing now? Nutella, jam and maple syrup on ice cream? Won't you be sick? And your teeth. It will get stuck in your braces. I haven't paid all that money for you to rot your bloody teeth.'

There were too many people in too small a space. The girls were now screaming at full volume because the boys had flicked crisps at them and the boys were howling with laughter and Hannah and Sam were bellowing loudly, trying to regain some kind of parental control over the situation.

'I might nip out for a fag,' I said.

Outside, it was very quiet after the noise and chaos that had reigned indoors all night, with only the occasional chirrup from the devil birds in their coop to disturb the silence of the night.

I leant against the apple tree, lit up and slumped in contemplative silence for a moment or two. The apple tree was actually quite uncomfortable to lean against, so I decamped to the bench.

It occurred to me it was my first birthday without my dad and I felt dreadful for not realising that sooner. I wondered what he would have made of me, sitting out here on my own on my birthday, driven out of my house by hordes of feral children. I suspected he'd have told me to pull myself together, and either put my foot down and not agree to them all staying or get on with it; but either way, that there was no point in wallowing in self-pity out here. I could almost hear him saying, 'One life, Ellen. That's all you've got. No point wasting time on regrets. Change what you can and deal with what you can't. Now buck up, have another drink and make the most of what you do have, instead of crying over what you don't!' He'd have been quite right, of course. I took a few deep breaths. God, the chickens needed cleaning out …

The back door opened and Sam came out, bearing a bottle and glasses.

'Are you OK?' asked Sam.

'Yes, I'm fine,' I said firmly.

'You always say that though. I think it's what we're conditioned to say as British people. "Are you OK?" "Yes, yes, totally fine." "Only your leg's just fallen off." "What's that? No, just a flesh wound, nothing to worry about!" Maybe it's all Monty Python's fault?'

'Maybe. But I *am* fine!'

'See, you can say that till you're blue in the face, but I don't think you're as OK as you insist you are. You've had a hell of a year, darling. You're getting divorced, you've moved house and you've had what's apparently known as a "significant bereavement". The three most stressful things we're supposed to go through in life, you've done in the space of less than twelve months. Now, I know you don't like to do things by halves, but even so, that's a lot for anyone. And you hardly talk about any of it. You've barely mentioned your dad since he died, or how that makes you feel, for example. You and Simon seem to be up and down, and I don't know if the poor bloke knows if he's coming or going when it comes to you. And yes, that was a deliberate pun. Jack … what's happening there? Obviously we didn't invite him because we didn't know if you'd told the kids about him, and we could hardly ask them. We just worry about you. Is there anything you want to talk about?'

'No. I'm fine. My dad – what's the point in talking about it, it won't change anything? Simon … I'd just like us to be friends, but it's all so complicated. Jack's on call tonight. He texted about ten minutes ago to say "Happy Birthday" and sorry he hadn't been in touch sooner, he was removing several large stones from a daft Labrador's stomach. I think it has a death wish, that Lab. He said it's the same one he had in last week after eating a large fruit cake and three bars of Green and Black's finest –'

'We're supposed to be talking about you, not Labradors,' interrupted Sam, 'and anyway, all Labradors have an insatiable desire to eat anything that might kill them. There's every point in talking about your dad – it won't change anything, no, but it might make you feel better than bottling it all up. Tell me what you most miss about him?'

I sighed. To be honest, I was on more familiar ground talking about Labradors.

'I was just thinking about him there, and what he'd have had to say about me sitting out here on my own. He wouldn't want me to be wallowing in grief – he'd want me to be getting on with things – but I suppose I miss having someone who is always there for me. Unconditionally. I thought Simon was always going to be there for me, but he wasn't, but at least I knew I always had Dad, that he'd always support my decisions and believe in me, even if no one else did, and now I don't have anyone. I'm on my own. Totally. Dad said he was proud of me for divorcing Simon. Everyone else thought I was mad or overreacting or I should have tried harder. But Dad said he thought I'd been strong and had done the right thing. And now, for the rest of my life, no one will ever love me like that again. And that's scary. Scarier than losing my marriage. Scarier than anything. Except the thought of something happening to one of the children, of course. But being alone like this frightens me. I know it shouldn't. I tell myself every day that I'm a strong independent woman. I *know* I'm incredibly lucky compared with most people in the world, just by virtue of having a roof over my head and enough to eat, but it's still hard, just not having that ... safety net ... of someone to fall back on.'

'Oh Ellen,' said Sam. 'How can you think you're alone? Hannah loves you like a sister and her mum thinks of you as her own child. Colin and I would be bereft without your sarcastic take on life and rambling drunken witterings about otters. We're all here for you, whenever you need us. You just have to let us help you.'

'It's not the same, though, is it? You all have your own lives. Hannah is about to have a baby – *I'm* supposed to be supporting her, not the other way around – you and Colin have your own teenagers causing you drama, and jobs and families to deal with. You don't need me flapping around, weeping and wailing and gnashing my teeth whenever I have an existential crisis.'

'You'd hardly do that. And it might not have occurred to you, but we *want* to help you. We all do. Just remember that, next time you're feeling alone, OK? Now what about Simon? You said it was complicated, and you seem to think that everyone considers you made a mistake in leaving him. Do you *want* Simon back?'

'I don't know. Hannah's mum asked me that at Dad's funeral. She told me to close my eyes and visualise the future and see if Simon was there.'

'And was he?'

'I didn't know. Someone was. But I didn't know who.'

'Right. Well, do that again. Close your eyes and visualise the future.'

I sighed and duly did as I was told.

Sam asked, 'Is he there?'

I opened my eyes in surprise. 'No. No, he's not.'

'Well then, what's the problem?'

'Because it's messy. The sex made everything more complicated, he's being so nice most of the time now and I'm definitely getting vibes that he'd like to try again. But I don't want to go backwards, I *don't* want to go back to Simon, even though it would be so easy and it would make the children so happy. That old life didn't make *me* happy, and we're just settling into *this* life and I'm enjoying doing the things *I* want to do, without having to think about whether Simon will want to do this or eat that or go there. But maybe I didn't try hard enough before with him and maybe I should give him another chance for the sake of the children.'

'Ellen, you tried with Simon until you reached breaking point. We all watched you and *our* hearts broke for you because you wouldn't let any of us in, not even Hannah. Not even Hannah's mum. Which is why I'm trying so hard to make you let us in now, OK? This isn't about the children, this is about you. You *know* you're happier now than you've been in a long time. You were with Simon for so long that I think this has been your first chance to discover who *Ellen* is as a grown-up, as opposed to Simon-and-Ellen as a single entity, and so I think you and Simon getting back together right now would actually destroy you. Sometimes you need to put yourself first, not the kids.'

I snorted unattractively (is it actually possible to snort attractively?). 'You know that's nonsense, Sam. Mothers who don't put their children first in all things forever might as well just cut out the middleman and eat their own young, according to most of society and the *Daily Mail*. It's different for men. Apparently it's fine for them to put *their* needs first, but not for women. As with most things.'

'OK then. Look at it like this. Your children are currently self-ish, self-centred, self-obsessed teenagers –'

I started to protest that they weren't *that* bad (even though they probably were), but Sam stopped me.

'No, Ellen, they are. They *all* are. I read this thing about it – they can't help it, apparently, it's just the way their brains are wired at that age; they can't comprehend or empathise with a situation they haven't experienced. Even if they *have* experienced it, quite often they just can't understand it from someone else's point of view. That's why teenagers are monsters. But they're not bad kids, and when they come out of that teenage fog what will they see? Their mother, desperately unhappy, in a marriage she doesn't want to be in, with a man she might love but doesn't love like *that* anymore. And why is she there? Because of them. How will that make them feel, do you think?'

'Not great? I mean, we're assuming Simon even wants that. It's a bit of a leap, based on one shag, being nice to me, liking my Instagram pictures and asking me for brunch.'

'He wants that. He can't take his eyes off you when he's with you. He knows what an almighty mistake he made letting you go. But that's his problem, not yours. Back to the kids, though. They'd feel guilty, definitely, and quite possibly responsible for *you*. So while you might think that trying again with Simon is a good thing for them, it would only be good for them in the very short term. So putting yourself first now is actually putting them first long-term, because they're going to grow up and leave you, and they need to know that they can go off and do their own thing without worrying about you.'

'Oh. I hadn't thought of it like that.' A tiny part of me was smug at the thought of Simon pining for me, and an even less nice part of me couldn't help but think, 'Ha! Serves you right!'

'Shall we have one more ciggie and a last glass of wine?' suggested Sam. 'Since it's your birthday, and you've nobly put up with both Louisa *and* me lecturing you? On the subject of Louisa, Hannah is right, though. You should try to be more like her and give far fewer fucks about everything instead of worrying about everyone around you and trying to fix everything. What do you say?'

I raised my glass.

'To no fucks given!' I toasted.

'To no fucks given!' said Sam.

Suddenly a window opened above us and a furious voice boomed out, 'MOTHER! Are you *smoking* down there?'

'Err, no,' I squeaked guiltily. 'I'm, err, I'm just keeping Sam company.'

Sam made appalled 'why are you dropping me in it?' faces at me.

'DAD! You shouldn't be smoking either,' chimed in Sophie disapprovingly. 'Put it out, or I'll tell Colin.'

'I wasn't *really* smoking,' protested Sam. 'We just, um, lit them to keep the night wasps away. They're a real problem this year.'

'NIGHT wasps?' said Jane in disbelief. There was a brief silence.

'We've googled,' announced Sophie, 'and there are no such things as night wasps. We're very disappointed in you both.'

Fuck's sake. Forty-six years old and still being busted for smoking like a fifteen-year-old, only this time BY a fifteen-year-old. Fucking fuck my fucking life!

Wednesday, 19 September

Peter's birthday. My little boy is all grown up. Well, not quite, but he's certainly not my little boy anymore. In the last few weeks his voice has properly broken, so it's no longer doing the weird up and down squeaking thing that caused Jane so much amusement. It's extremely disconcerting to hear him rumbling about the house and think, 'FUCK! There's a strange man in the house, and why is he calling me "Mum"?'

Despite Peter lobbying hard to be allowed the day off school for his birthday, I had a meeting at work that I really couldn't miss, and so I cruelly and callously made him go to school. He announced as he slouched out of the car that it was very unfair and he'd decided that when he grew up he was going to work for Timpson's, the key-cutting people, because he'd seen a sign in one of their shops that said it was company policy that all employees got the day off on their birthday. I must say, this does sound a very sensible policy, and one that would definitely improve company morale. I considered suggesting it to Gabrielle in HR, but then I remembered that she doesn't hold with birthdays, what with sleeping in a coffin and having no soul. Debbie would never endorse such a policy either, as it would considerably eat into the time she gets to spend ordering cakes and faffing around getting people to sign cards, and would take away her excuse to snoop in people's files under the guise of checking when their birthdays were. I once asked Debbie her views on data protection and she just laughed.

After school I took Peter, Toby and Lucas to an all-you-can-eat pizza buffet. In the interests of being civilised, I invited Simon too, but he was in Birmingham for work and wouldn't be home till midnight. I did ask Jane if she wanted to come, but after a brief ceasefire between the festival and my birthday, she's gone full-on supernova teenage arsehole and is storming around ruining everyone else's lives while accusing them of ruining hers, so she said she'd rather stick pins in her eyes than be seen in public with her brother and me. The pizza buffet was Peter's choice. I usually refuse to take him to them, especially with friends, as I can't stand seeing the manager on the verge of tears after the boys take the 'all-you-can-eat' part *very* seriously.

I attempted to have a 'moment' with Peter when we got home, exclaiming how big my baby boy was and digging out his first pair of shoes to compare with his giant trainers now. He sort of shuffled awkwardly while I hugged him, and said, 'Um, Mum, I told the other boys I'd be online to play *Fortnite* when we got home? Can I go now?' So that went well. I had a whole speech prepared about safe sex now he was getting to 'that' age, and respecting women and everything else, but it seemed it would have to wait. In fairness, for him to have *any* actual sex he'd have to get off his computer and interact with actual people in the real world, so I suppose I haven't really got much to worry about there yet.

He slouched back downstairs half an hour later to announce that he'd left his PE kit at Simon's yet again and so would need another note off games. I'm running out of ailments with which to excuse his forgotten PE kit (at least with Jane, I can pretend it's 'Women's Problems'). Since it was his birthday, and since it was also partly my fault he had to split his possessions between two homes, I couldn't even shout at him.

He turned around to shuffle off back to his beloved Game of Death ('It's only, like, really cartoon violence, Mum,' he insists. 'No worse than *Tom and Jerry*'), then stopped and gave me a hug. 'It's quite cool, actually, you and Dad not being together, because now I get to have another birthday on Saturday and Dad said he'd take us all for a pizza buffet too and I get two lots of presents. Don't forget my note, Mum.'

Oh. I hadn't expected that. I'd expected something about it being a shame that Dad wasn't here tonight (even though it was because he was being Busy and Important, not because of the divorce). I was going to remonstrate that birthdays are not about presents and why hadn't he told me before that he was fleecing his father for pizza too, because then I could have made them all come here and given them frozen pizza and saved myself a fortune, but I was too relieved that he finally seemed to be coming to terms with Simon and me no longer being together. Thank God for that. And thank God also for mercenary children whose emotional resilience can be bought with material goods. There's much to be said for a capitalist society after all … At this rate, who knows, at some point he might even start remembering his PE kit!

Saturday, 29 September

I'd just got in from picking Peter up from the cinema when my phone rang. Oddly, it was Jane. Jane never calls me. At best she deigns to send a terse text if she has to communicate with me over the electric telephone.

'Jane! Is everything OK, sweetheart?'

'Hi Mum, I need you to come and pick me up, please,' sobbed Jane.

'Are you at the party?'

'Noooooooo!' she wailed 'Muuuuum! Harry dumped me and then he got off with Tilly, and what am I going to doooooo?'

'Oh God, Jane. Where are you?'

'At the bus station. I thought I could get the last bus home but I missed it, and it's really scary here, Mum, it's dark and cold.'

Oh Jesus Christ. My baby girl, on her own, at the dubious bus station in town, in her skimpy party dress on a Saturday night with her poor little heart broken. At least she'd had the sense to call me.

'I'm coming now, sweetheart, OK, just – is there anywhere you can go? Any cafes open, or shops where you can wait?'

'No, everything's closed. The only things open are the pubs, and there's lots of drunk people and lots of horrible men keep trying to talk to me.'

'Oh shit, baby girl! I'm on my way. I'll be with you as soon as I can, but it'll take me about twenty-five minutes to get there.'

'Please hurry up, Mum,' begged Jane.

'What's happening?' said Peter.

'Jane! She's on her own at the bus station in town, and I need to go and get her.'

'Why you?' said Peter.

'Because I'm her MOTHER!' I shrieked.

'No, Mum. I mean it'll take you ages to get there. Call Dad, call Sam. One of them can be there in five minutes instead of Jane having to wait for you.'

'Oh God, why didn't I think of that?'

'Because you never ask for help.'

'OK, OK, I know, this isn't the time for the lecture,' I gibbered, as I found Simon's number and called him. Thank God he picked up and I blurted out the situation.

'OK, I'm going now, but there's roadworks on my side of town. Call Sam as well and see if he can go too. He might get there sooner.'

'I will, I will,' I gabbled. 'And Simon, if you get there first, don't say a *word* about what's she's done. Just bring her home to me, all right? She doesn't need you lecturing her and giving her a hard time just now.'

Simon said, 'OK, if you say so. I'm on my way,' and then, once I'd rung Sam, I sat and bit my nails and stared anxiously at my phone until Simon called.

'I've got her!' he said. 'She's fine. A bit shaken, but fine. Sam got here about five minutes before me. A couple of guys were trying to chat her up but they didn't touch her. Thank God you called us, though. It's payday weekend and the town is carnage tonight, no place for a fifteen-year-old girl on her own. I'm bringing her over now.'

When they arrived, I ran out of the house, and Jane hurtled out of Simon's car and into my arms.

Simon put down his window. 'She says she just wants to talk to you and has asked me to go home,' he said. 'Text me later and let me know how she is.'

'Oh Mum,' she wailed, 'I'm sorry, I'm sorry. I was so stupid, I know, but please don't be angry with me, I was so scared. And Harry's such a bastard. How could he do that to me? I thought he *loved* me!'

'Oh Jane, darling. I'm just so glad you're OK – I was so worried about you. Thank God you're all right.'

'Aren't you mad with me?'

'I'm too relieved to be mad with you. And however angry I got with you for going off on your own like that, whatever punishment I gave you, would it really make you think about things any more than how scared you got being on your own in town like that?'

'No,' she sniffed. 'Mum, what am I going to do about Harry?'

'Umm, Jane, darling, how far did things *go* with Harry?' I asked carefully, while reflecting that Cersei Lannister's threats in *Game of Thrones* to burn down cities to protect her children were nothing, NOTHING AT ALL, to what I'd do if I got my hands on that little sod.

'Do you mean have I slept with him?' sniffed Jane.

'Well, yes.'

'No, I haven't. That was the problem. He's been going on about it for ages. He kept telling me if I loved him I'd do it, but surely if *he* loved me he wouldn't make me before I was ready, would he?'

Jesus Christ. How many problem pages in *Just Seventeen* were devoted to exactly those lines? Teenage boys simply do not change, so thank God Jane had the strength of character to stand firm.

'No, darling, if someone loves you they'll never pressure you into doing something you're uncomfortable with,' I assured her.

'Well, then tonight he said I couldn't love him if I wouldn't even do that one little thing for him, so he said I was dumped if I wouldn't, and I said I just wasn't sure yet, and then he said would I at least send him some photos –'

'Photos?' I said faintly.

'Yeah, you know, like topless ones.'

'Please tell me you didn't.'

'Of *course* I didn't,' said Jane indignantly, with a brief flash of her usual stroppy self. 'So then he said I obviously didn't care about him and that it was over, and then two minutes later he was snogging Tilly. But I *do* love him, Mum, I really do! What am I going to do? How am I going to face everyone at school?'

I refrained from trying to make light of Jane's woes and telling her that of course she didn't love him – that at fifteen you had no concept of what real love is and when you did find it you'd realise how different it was from those teenage infatuations – because I remembered myself how unhelpful it was to be told that my feelings were silly and didn't really matter.

'I know this is awful now, sweetheart,' I said, hugging her, 'but I promise it will pass. It might not feel like it, but it will. And I don't doubt you loved him, but I think maybe you loved a version of him that wasn't the real him. Now you know what he's really like, you don't love the person Harry actually is, only the ideal-ised Harry, who never really existed.'

Jane sniffed hard again. 'Maybe you're right,' she admitted. HA! Jane said I was right! Damn, why wasn't I recording this conversation for posterity?

'After all,' she went on, wiping her eyes bravely, 'I don't want to love someone who can be so horrible. I want someone who respects me for more than my tits! Tilly is welcome to him.'

'That's my girl,' I said encouragingly. 'I'm proud of you. Shall we have some ice cream?'

'No, Mother,' said Jane. 'We're not in some mother–daughter American sitcom.' That was more like the Jane I knew and loved and feared.

'But being a teenager is so hard, Mum. I just wish I was grown up and it was all easier.'

I contemplated telling her that it didn't get easier when you were a grown-up – if anything it got harder – but I didn't want to crush her hopes, so I just gave her a hug instead.

'Mum, I do love you,' she whispered.

'I love you too, sweetheart.'

'Mum?'

'Yes, darling.'

'Is that what happened with you and Dad? You loved an imaginary person, not who he really was?'

'No, sweetheart. I loved him very much, but we were very young when we met and I suppose we just grew into different people who weren't so meant for each other as we were when we first got married. Relationships are difficult, Jane. They aren't black and white.'

'Oh, I know!' said Jane grandly. I made a mental note to brace myself for Jane in future to be an expert on all things relationship on the strength of her first break-up.

'Mum, did you ever do anything stupid like I did tonight?' she asked suddenly.

'Darling, I did more stupid and dangerous things than I even want to think about.'

'What did your mum do?'

'I don't think she ever knew. I never would have told her or called her for help.'

'Why not?'

'Because she'd have been angry and told me it was all my fault. I always just sorted things out for myself, because the alternative wasn't worth contemplating.'

'But you're not like her – and you're not a mum like her. Why not?'

'Well, I suppose because I made a conscious decision not to be like her. To try to be a different mum, a better mum. All we can do is attempt to break the cycles and not repeat the mistakes our parents made. You'll probably do the same too if you ever have children. I was lucky, though. I did have an example of what sort of mum I wanted to be, in Hannah's mum, Mrs P.'

'Mrs P is lovely,' agreed Jane. 'I'm glad you try to be like her, not Granny.'

After all the drama, when Jane had finally gone to bed and I was letting the dogs out for a last pee, Peter came into the kitchen and pulled a milk carton out of the fridge.

'See, Mum,' he said, after taking a long guzzle straight out the carton, 'sometimes when you actually ask for help it turns out for the best.'

'Yes, I know,' I said. 'I will try, I really will.'

'You think we don't see what's going on with you, but we do, you know. You don't help us when you don't let people help you.'

'I'm sure the life lessons should be from me to you, not the other way round,' I said.

'It's the internet generation, Mum. We know everything,' said Peter cheerfully.

'You don't know enough to use a glass for your milk,' I pointed out.

'I'm saving on washing up. For the environment,' he protested.

'Well, make sure you brush your teeth again after that milk,' I said. 'It's a myth that you don't have to brush your teeth if you've been drinking milk.'

'I *know*, Mum,' said Peter patiently. 'Milk's acidic, it erodes your teeth.'

'No it's not. Everyone knows milk is alkaline – that's why it helps with heartburn.'

'Nope. It's acidic. Not very, but still acidic. Trust me. Like I said, internet generation. We know everything.'

After he'd gone, I googled the pH of milk. It's acidic. Maybe these children really *do* know everything.

Sunday, 30 September

Jane spent most of the day moping around the house in a black polo neck, looking pale and tragic. Several times I caught her scribbling furtively in a notebook, which, combined with the polo neck, led me to suspect that she was trying her hand at writing poetry. I could only hope it was better than her father's and her aunt's attempts. She also announced dramatically over breakfast that she was Swearing Off Men forever.

Later that afternoon, though, she burst into the kitchen with an anguished wail.

'Muuuuuuum!' she howled.

'What? What is it?' I shrieked in panic, as the dogs started barking madly, just in case we were being broken into.

'I was trying to block Harry on Instagram, and instead I tapped on his stories and watched them. Oh God, and now he'll think I'm stalking him, when I was trying to be all ice queen and pretend he didn't exist and that I didn't even *care*, and now WHAT AM I GOING TO DO?'

'What do you *mean*?' I said in confusion.

'Stories. STORIES, MUM!'

I continued to look blank. 'When there's a little red circle around their profile picture, they've put up a story but they only last for twenty-four hours. It's a bit like Snapchat,' she offered helpfully.

'I know what stories are,' I said indignantly, 'but what's the big deal?'

'Because people can see who has looked at their stories, and you'd only look at someone's stories if you were, like, really good friends or going out or, like, you really *liked* them or if you were stalking them or something.'

Oh dear. I'd been completely unaware of this Instagram etiquette. As if the horrors of those 'Does he like me?/Doesn't he like me?' days weren't bad enough, how much worse to be negotiating all that with the added complications of social media thrown in for good measure. Who knew that one accidental click on a boy's photo and your life would be over? Though the Stories thing now has me slightly worried that Nigel Slater thinks I *like* him like him, when really I just want his house. And his dinners. And his garden. Not that I'm really his type, anyway.

I was also very relieved that Simon had never mastered Instagram to the extent of putting up stories, back when I wasn't averse to a bijou stalk of the 'gram myself …

'So what am I going to DO, Mum?' Jane demanded.

'*I* don't know! Can you delete it?'

'Well, *no*, Mother, that's sort of the point. Oh God, this is soooo mortifying,' she groaned. 'Oh my God, he's messaged me. Telling me to stop stalking him, I bet. Maybe I shouldn't even open it. Oh God, I need to know what he's said.'

Jane read the message and then looked up. 'Mum, he says he's really sorry, and he was a twat and he was totally out of order and will I give him another chance? What should I do?'

'What do you want to do?'

Jane thought, then typed rapidly. 'There!' she said with satisfaction.

'Soooo, what did you say?' I ventured.

'I told him to fuck off, that we were over and that I was blocking him and deleting his number because I didn't want to hear from him and also that Tilly has herpes.'

'Does she?'

'She gets cold sores. That's herpes, isn't it?'

'I think so. Wasn't that a bit mean, though?'

'No. She didn't even know he'd dumped me and she snogged him anyway. That's not a good friend. And as for him, he hurt me, so why would I want to have anything to do with him after that?'

'Well, quite. Well done, sweetheart.'

Jane smirked. 'And also, Sophie said that after I went, Millie's neighbours called the police because the music was too loud and Luke Allison was taken home in a police car for calling them fascist pigs, and so after all that, no one even remembers that Harry dumped me, and anyway, after his last message, I dumped him back, so we're even.'

Oh, for the fickle heart of a teenager!

If Sam is right and Simon does hold out hopes for us, and I dump him back, will that make us even?

OCTOBER

Saturday, 6 October

Autumn is upon us at last. I love autumn, when the mists are mellowing and fruitful at last, even though CBeebies ruined that poem for me. The trees start to turn, the squirrels begin squirrelling (probably – we don't get squirrels in our garden because of Judgy's murderous tendencies, and if he didn't kill them the bastarding chickens probably would – chickens that I've discovered will stop laying over the winter, which would be fine if they'd ever bloody started laying in the first place. I've taken to hanging around the coop and dropping heavy hints about how maybe we won't be having *turkey* for Christmas dinner this year, but they give not a single shit – well, technically they give a lot of shits that I have to clear up), and we can all start thinking about hibernating and eating our way through to spring.

At last one can cast off the flimsy clothes of summer, the ankle-baring trousers and the floaty skirts that you constantly fear might be just slightly *too* floaty and float up and show your pants, and the shoulder-exposing tops, and we can huddle into the Sensible Boots and the Big Jumpers, under which all manner of bulges and bumps can lurk, unclung to and unexposed. And best of all, now that not an inch of flesh shall be shown until spring, I can also relax and grow my winter pelt, which is a definite bonus of being single and will probably also help with keeping warm. It might even reduce the heating bills, although that is probably just wishful thinking, as no matter the thickness of my winter pelt and the cosiness of my Big Jumpers, it will have no effect on my fucking children's habit of wandering around in a T-shirt and simply turning up the heating when they feel a draught, however much I scream at them to put some bloody clothes on and step away from the thermostat – I wonder if this is a Sign that I'm now a Proper Grown-up?

Every autumn, I somehow find myself overcome with visions of turning into some sort of wondrously wholesome apple-cheeked country sort, merrily bottling and jarring and preserving the glorious bounty of nature, even though I'm not entirely sure a) what bottling, jarring or preserving entails and b) where the extra hours in the day to do all this are supposed to come from. I think I read the *Little House on the Prairie* books too many times at an impressionable age.

Still, we do have an apple tree in the garden, and I had high hopes of at least managing a lovely day with the children picking apples, so that should I desire I could commence on my Autumnal Wholesomeness, making apple pies and apple sauce and whatever else you make with apples. Apple chutney? Is that A Thing? It sounds like it should be A Thing.

Like all my Glorious Autumn Visions, however, the children thwarted me. My apple-picking day, during which they were supposed to frolic and romp and end the day rosy-cheeked and weary from the fresh air, munching on a delicious apple they'd picked themselves while they told me how much they loved me and how they'd treasure these #happymemories forever as they were #soblessed, went exactly the same way as the other Glorious Autumn Visions I'd tried to enlist the children in over the years – i.e. a complete and utter clusterfuck.

Each time I tried to get the children to come on a delightful autumn walk with me when they were little, kicking up leaves and throwing them in the air, they'd invariably find the dog shit lurking in the leaves and kick that – on one particularly unfortunate occasion Jane managed to kick the dog shit all over Peter, ruining his new coat and causing him to attempt to smear it back over Jane while throttling her, which meant *her* new coat was also ruined, and both of them were covered in shit, as was I when I attempted to de-crap them using a packet of baby wipes, and everyone ended up crying and it was a miracle that I didn't actually divorce Simon *that* day when we got home, as upon surveying his tear-stained, shit-streaked family he asked us if we'd had a nice day out, having been too Busy and Important in his shed to accompany us.

Anyway, back to the apple picking. Obviously, it took me forever to lure the children from their fetid pits and out into the bracing fresh air. In fact, this was only achieved by changing the Wi-Fi password and, when they came hurtling out of their rooms in fury, refusing to disclose it to them until they'd come and helped with the apples.

I was, if I do say so myself, dressed *adorably* for apple picking, complete with cosy jumper, rugged corduroy and quirky boots. I was a vision straight out of a Laura Ashley catalogue, because it's important to do things *right* (I've given up channelling Felicity Kendal; I really couldn't pull off the dungarees!). Despite trying to instil the importance of this into the children over the last fifteen years they did not appear to have got the memo, and so Jane was still in her pyjamas and Peter was wearing *shorts*. Shorts did not conform to my Autumn Vision, but he was unrepentant, as was Jane, and they said they could help as they were – or they could fuck off and leave me alone.

There was much debate about the windfalls, as my precious moppets refused to touch them in case they harboured 'worms or crap', and they were even more horrified at the thought of eating them in case foxes had peed all over them or snails had done unspeakable things under them. Finally, they agreed to pick them up, if I promised they'd only be fed to the chickens. Predictably, the fucking chickens were unimpressed by the rosy apples I merrily chucked into their coop and I found myself secretly wishing I'd managed to twat at least one of them with an apple, as maybe that would have encouraged them to buck up their ideas.

Then the apples on the tree needed to be picked. After survey-ing the tree, which is quite a big one, I suggested a ladder. The children seemed surprised to learn we owned such a thing, but they ambled off to look in the shed and came back claiming there wasn't one there. I went over to the shed with them and pointed out the large, ladder-shaped LADDER hanging on the wall. The children claimed they just 'hadn't seen it', so I bit my tongue and bade them bring forth the ladder. In the process they managed to smash the shed window. I suppose I should just be grateful I haven't got a greenhouse.

The ladder finally in position, there was much debate about who should be the one to climb it. Jane said she couldn't because she was afraid of heights. 'Since when?' I demanded, at which point Jane launched into a lengthy description of how she's *always* been afraid of heights, and if I was unaware of this it was yet another sign of my lax parenting and clearly, therefore, I loved Peter better, because I'd have paid attention if *he'd* been afraid of heights and thus it wasn't fair, until I lost the will to live and agreed Jane did not have to climb the ladder. So then, of course, Peter declared that it was also unfair if *he* was expected to climb the ladder, because obviously I valued *him* less than Jane because I was willing to risk his life and limb up a ladder, but I wouldn't make Jane do it, and he'd probably have *issues* now because I had made my favouritism clear because I didn't even *care* if *Peter* fell off a ladder and died, I only cared about *Jane*, at which point I climbed the ladder myself, half hoping that in fact

I *might* fall off and have some sort of injury necessitating a long hospital stay (although ultimately making a full recovery, obviously) just so I didn't have to listen to my fucking children arguing about who I loved best, because at that particular moment the dogs were definitely my favourites.

The children shuffled around at the bottom of the tree while I hurled apples down into the waiting Amazon Prime box (I'd toyed with a trug, but Jane told me it was a 'bit extra', so I'd desisted), and bickered some more, until I'd picked all the apples within reach of the ladder and decided to clamber into the tree itself.

I was proud of my tree-climbing skills. I was good at climbing trees in my youth. Sadly, however, it seems that it's a lot harder to climb trees at forty-six than it is at six, as one has lost a certain amount of suppleness and flexibility that it turns out is quite important in tree climbing. And thus, as was inevitable, I got stuck. There's nothing dignified about a middle-aged woman stuck in an apple tree, no matter how cosy her Aran sweater or adorable her corduroy skirt. In fact, skirts are a most ill-advised garment for tree climbing, as the children informed me, when they objected that they could see my pants. Strangely enough, when clinging to a flimsy branch that threatened to give way at any moment and send me hurtling hundreds of feet through the air to the ground below (well, at least ten), my stout gusset was the least of my fucking worries.

'Shall we ring the fire brigade?' enquired Jane.

'God, no,' I squeaked. 'I don't want anyone *else* to see!'

'Well, what do you want us to do?' complained Peter. 'It's cold out here, you know.'

'That's because you're wearing bloody shorts,' I snapped. 'I don't know what you can do. *Think* of something.'

Jane looked up from her phone and said, 'Mum? I need a lift.'

'Bit difficult, sweetie,' I pointed out.

'Mum. I need a lift *now*. I've got a date with Will Anderson!'

'Wow! And you're actually *telling* me?' I marvelled.

'Why wouldn't I tell you?' she snapped. 'For God's sake, Mother, just move your foot about ten centimetres to the left and down a bit, that's it, and the other one needs to go about fifteen to the right and down a bit, and that's it. See. You're fine.'

It would have been helpful if she'd directed me like that in the first place, I reflected, but I was too delighted at actually being *told* about a date instead of having to Insta-stalk to care. *And* she'd unblocked me on Instagram, so I didn't have to use Peter's account, though I was under strict instructions not to tag her in *anything*.

'Can you drop me at Toby's when you take Jane into town?' said Peter.

'I thought we were going to make apple pies and chutneys and be Visions of Domestic Bliss tonight,' I protested.

'Yeah, well, it's just Toby's Grandpa bought him *GTA 5* and he said we could all go over and play?'

'Peter! That game isn't suitable.'

'Mum, you know I've been playing *GTA 4* for, like, *years*, don't you? Please, Mum, all my friends are going. I can stay over, so you don't need to come and get me.'

'Fine,' I said. Jane also announced she was getting the bus home (a lift into town clearly being acceptable, as long as I dropped her round the corner where No One Saw, but your mum picking you up being Deeply Uncool). So instead of fulfilling my Rustic Vision, I texted Jack, who for once wasn't on call and dealing with a greedy Labrador-based emergency, and we went out for a drink and got mildly squiffy instead. I only just made it in the door before Jane, who'd actually managed to get the bus home for once, and was so starry-eyed and in luuuurve that she didn't even ask why I was rather flushed and the dogs were looking at me so reproachfully …

Wednesday, 17 October

Tonight I had to go to Jane's Parents' Night (or rather Parent's Night, as Simon was off on one of his many Busy and Important Work Trips). As Simon has never actually yet managed to attend a Parents' Night, going alone wasn't a big deal for me. In fact, I was quite agog to see what Jane's teachers had to say about her, as she'd remained resolutely deaf to my increasingly anguished insistence that this is a Very Important Year for her and that GCSEs really do matter, and maybe she could think about doing some studying instead of Snapchatting Sophie or fucking off to yet another party that she expects to be picked up from at 2 am.

All these pleas still elicit the same response of 'Chill, Mum!' and 'It'll be fine!' (I don't know where she gets that from), so although on the one hand part of me was obviously hoping that her teachers were *finally* going to tell me that Jane was a genius child of quite startling ability and she might as well forget such mundanities as GCSEs and go straight for her PhD in astrophysics (at least, I only hope this in secret; Jessica is quite open about her outrage that no one has yet spotted *just* how gifted and talented Persephone and Gulliver are and rewarded them accordingly), on the other hand part of me was also hoping that her teachers would make dire predictions about Jane ploughing everything if she didn't knuckle down *immediately* and spend the next six months closeted in her bedroom working her arse off.

Parents' Night at Big School is a bit of a bear pit. The positive bit is that you're no longer made to sit on a tiny chair with your knees wedged underneath your chin while the teacher smugly looms over you from their proper-sized seat and reflects that witnessing your humiliation in the miniature chair is small consolation for enduring your child's rancid farts and inane questions over the course of an entire school year. The negative bit is that you have to see eleventy fucking billion teachers, in a large hall, and need to fight for access to them with all the other parents, who decided years ago to just ignore the carefully planned appointment times and turn trying to see Mr Butler the maths teacher into something akin to a gladiatorial competition.

You're only supposed to have five minutes with each teacher, but I always but *always* seem to get stuck behind the class fire-starter's mummy, and as a consequence have to wait for twenty minutes while the unfortunate teacher attempts to explain exactly *why* Little Johnny isn't allowed to light the Bunsen burners anymore and how they'd really be quite grateful if he could refrain from trying to sell glue to his classmates during English. Alternatively, I get stuck behind the class swot's mummy, and spend even bloody longer waiting while Libby's mummy boasts to the teacher about how Gifted and Talented her daughter is and demands new ways to stretch Libby even further, because she's Just So Bright, as the teacher tries desperately to get a word in edgeways to point out that while Libby is far from *stupid*, she's also really *quite average*.

Now we've all finally escaped the playground, Parents' Night is at least a good place to catch up with everyone you don't really see anymore. Hannah had cunningly played the pregnant card and waddled to the front of every queue, pleading imminent labour for the queue-jumping, and had been in and out within an hour – she was very smug about this, but as she said, at least I get to go home and have a big fuck-off glass of wine afterwards, and she'd rather have that than all the queue-skipping in the world. Poor Hannah. She's so over this whole being pregnant thing. I can't say I blame her, as at the best of times the last few weeks really drag by, with only the prospect of some or other part of you being ripped open to get this succubus out to look forward to.

I bumped into Perfect Lucy Atkinson's Perfect Mummy (apparently *she* had ended the Speed Dating Night by getting off with the geography teacher – 'Thank God Lucy takes history,' she shuddered), and had a nice chat with her during the excruciatingly long wait for the maths teacher. Well, a 'nice chat' is probably not quite right for the topics we covered, given she kicked off by asking if I'd had my post-break-up shag with Simon yet. When I admitted I had, she revealed this is more common than I'd at first thought – apparently loads of people do it, for a variety of reasons. 'As long as you weren't hoping it would entice him back,' she said. I was vehement in my denial.

'It's quite a good form of revenge,' said Lucy's Mummy wisely. 'I did google whether one could buy some form of STD on the internet to infect yourself with first – nothing really awful, something that doesn't really affect women and could easily be cured with antibiotics but covers his cock with pustulant and painful weeping sores that a) he'd find very uncomfortable and b) he'd have to explain to Fiona. It turns out such things can't be bought on the internet – probably the only things you *can't* get! I just took some selfies of us together in bed in my new flat when he was asleep that I saved to send to Fiona at some point when the bastard is annoying me. That'll teach him! What did you do for revenge?'

I hadn't really done anything for revenge, unless you count annoying Simon because I had a shed and he didn't. I didn't even *want* revenge, not anymore. I just wanted to get on with my life. I told Lucy's Mummy this and she tutted.

'God, Ellen, you're not even *trying*,' she complained. 'Of course there has to be revenge.'

Luckily at that point, Olivia Jessop's mum finally finished and it was my turn to see the maths teacher, but I struggled to concentrate on what he was saying, due to wondering if trying to give her ex the clap in a fit of revenge meant Lucy's Perfect

Mummy wasn't so Perfect, or whether her sheer level of dedication to vengeance made her even *more* Perfect?

Sam joined me in the queue to see Mrs Jennings, the French teacher, and given I'd been standing there for twenty minutes as Libby's mum was giving Mrs Jennings a blow-by-blow account of their summer holiday in a French gîte in the Loire, while protesting in outraged tones at Mrs Jennings's unreasonable refusal to say whether or not she could predict an A* for Libby at A level ('Yes, I *know* this is their GCSE year, but surely you must be able to give me *some* idea. She has *got* a tutor, but should I get another one? Recommend me one! What do you mean, you can't really do that?'), I was very glad to see him. There's no greater love than standing in a queue for what feels like forever, only to be told that Jane would really be quite good at French if she just stopped buggering about and participated more in class, which was pretty much what all her teachers had said so far.

Sam nudged me.

'How long has she been?'

'Twenty minutes.'

'Fuck me. What's there to talk about for twenty minutes?'

'They went to the Loire – not to a touristy part, *obviously*; to a proper, authentic *French* part – but she took umbrage because Mrs Jennings wasn't personally familiar with all of the properly authentic French towns they visited (she listed them, by the way. Every single one. And she offered to show her photos), and so she began to doubt Mrs Jennings's credentials as a French teacher and thus whether or not she's really qualified to predict that Libby will be lucky to get a B, because they went to the motherfucking *Loire*, don't you know. And now she's moved on to tutors, like she asks every teacher about. I was stuck behind her at biology as well. Thankfully I only have Spanish to go, but she'll beat me to it, and no doubt they've also been to Barcelona, knowing my luck …'

'Ha!' said Sam. 'I've done Spanish and I still have maths to go, so I've dodged her. You've not done very well at this, have you?'

'Have you been to English?'

'No.'

'Ha, right back atcha then, because Luke Allison's mum has just joined the queue, so you'll be stuck behind her arguing that Luke scrawling "Fuck the Police" on the very expensive interactive whiteboard in indelible marker is just him exercising his right to free expression.'

'Bollocks,' said Sam. 'How are you, anyway?'

'I'm … better. Thanks for the other night with Jane, by the way.'

'Anytime. I mean that. Are you sure you're OK?'

'Yes … except Perfect Lucy Atkinson's Perfect Mummy says I'm letting the side down by not exacting some awful retribution on Simon for leaving me. Do you think I should put itching powder in his pants or something?'

'No. I think Perfect Lucy Atkinson's Perfect Mummy probably has a lot of issues she has to work through due to the nature of how her husband left her and who he left her for. Your lack of desire for reprisals is probably quite healthy. Although they do say the best revenge is to live a happy life …'

'Well, I'm certainly trying to do that, but not to spite him. It's for me.'

'Then I think you're doing fine, sweetheart.'

'Do you? Good! Argh, quick, look, she's getting up … she's getting up … fuck no, Holly Ellis's mum is trying to make a break for my slot. No you don't, bitch, I am IN THERE. Oh wait, no, she's sitting back down again. Oh fuck! I just rolled my eyes like a sulky teen and Mrs Jennings saw me.'

Jane looked up from giggling with Sophie over their phones and said, 'Oh God, Mum, WHY are you so embarrassing?'

Sam sniggered. 'Ha ha! *I* haven't embarrassed Sophie once tonight.'

'That's not true, Dad. You made a terrible dad joke in front of Mr Matthews and he only laughed because he doesn't get out much and Parents' Night is the most social interaction with adults he gets in a year,' objected Sophie.

'She's UP! I'm going in. Come on, Jane,' and I barged Holly's mum, the cheeky queue-jumping fucker, out the way, and threw myself down in Libby's mum's barely vacated seat. It was still very warm. Which was unpleasant.

When we were finally finished (I was wrong, Libby had been to Seville not Barcelona) and were all shuffling out, drained of the will to live, ears ringing with the mediocre achievements of our offspring and their teachers' hopeful suggestions that maybe they could just 'apply' themselves a bit more, Sam caught up with me.

'Just remember. If you need to talk anytime, you know where I am. Where we both are, OK?'

'Thank you.'

I felt I'd earned the very welcome glass of wine I sank into when I got home. Judgy looked at me reprovingly and reminded me that *he* had never made me go to a Parents' Night, and had I stuck to dogs like a sensible person I'd never have had to endure such events. He had a point.

Sunday, 21 October

Simon has been being increasingly nice to me and even remarked on how well I'd handled the whole Jane/Harry thing, though he was appalled to hear she had another boyfriend already, even when I pointed out that at least she'd *told* us about this one. The other day he brought me a bunch of flowers when he came to pick the kids up – said he'd just thought they were pretty and I might like them. I genuinely can't remember the last time Simon brought me flowers, but it seemed pretty clear that I should really say or do something in case he was getting the wrong idea about us.

I agreed to his oft-repeated suggestion of brunch on the basis that if a meal was going to be ruined by an unfortunate scene, it might as well be a bit of a rubbish one, and also the Bloody Marys might make it more bearable. Nonetheless, I still very much hoped that Sam was wrong, and that we'd just have a nice brunch and there would be no need for awkward conversations. And if there were any – well, I'd just have to put on my Big Girl Pants and deal with them.

We started off with some polite small talk, then turned to the subject of Louisa, who had finally departed with the Wolf Pack. Simon complained that she'd broken his blender before she left.

'What, the Kitchenaid blender?' I said.

'Yes. Those things are expensive.'

'Have you ever used it, since you moved in?'

'Well, no, but that's not really the point, is it?'

'It is a bit. She's probably done you a favour, breaking it. There's a reason I let you have it when we split up …'

'What?'

'Mmmm. Do you remember that Christmas that she came to stay, just after she spawned the last hell beast? When she was still with that hippy twat Bardo?'

'Yes?'

'Well, I came downstairs one morning and found her making a … special smoothie in it.'

'A special smoothie?'

'I'm sure I told you about this at the time. Yes, she was making a smoothie containing, among other things, Bardo's jizz.'

'Jizz. As in … jizz jizz? As in … semen jizz?'

'As in semen jizz.'

Simon retched.

'So obviously, despite scrubbing it out with bleach, I couldn't quite bring myself to ever use it again. Nor did it seem fair to give it to a charity shop, given what had been in it … but on the other hand it *was* expensive, so just throwing it out seemed wasteful as well, so I stuck it in a cupboard and bought a cheap replacement. And then when we split up, I kindly let you have it. Like the good wife that I am!' I chortled with glee.

'But the children could have used it,' said Simon in horror. '*I* could have used it!'

'I know. I was quite amused by the idea of you using it. I doubted the children would have bothered with it, as it would have involved using ingredients rather than instant gratification.'

'Why would you think that was funny?'

'It wasn't just funny. It also seemed like a small revenge on you.'

'Did I really deserve that, though?'

'Yes,' I said, sniggering.

'I thought we were getting somewhere, that you were starting to forgive me. And now I find out you've been hoping I'll somehow end up drinking my ex-brother-in-law's festering semen. That's really not nice.'

'Sorry! Anyway, I've told you now.'

'I suppose. Anyway, I've got something for you.'

He reached under the table and pulled out a sheaf of papers.

'For you,' he beamed, sliding them across the table.

'What are they?' I asked suspiciously.

'Open them and see.'

I opened the papers and found the plans for the kitchen extension we once talked about what seemed like a million years ago.

'Oh,' I said.

'Do you like them? I know I should have talked to you about what you wanted, but I wanted it to be a surprise. I think I remembered everything you said you'd ever want in your dream kitchen.'

'Simon, I don't know what to say,' (apart from 'Yes, this *is* a lovely Grand Gesture, but it would have been nice to be consulted on what I wanted,' but obviously I didn't say that).

'Say you like them.'

'But Simon, this is *your* dream kitchen, not mine. Look at it, it's a glass box. I've never been into that minimalism look, I like clutter and vintage and Cath Kidston, even though apparently it's a bit naff now. Apart from anything else, I have two dogs. Can you imagine the nose prints?'

'I just wanted to do something nice for you,' he said. 'I just want to make you happy. Because if I can make you happy, maybe we have a chance of a fresh start?'

'Oh,' I said. 'Simon, I can't go back. You said yourself, we can't change the past, we can only change the future.'

'I know. But I'm talking about the future.'

'No, I can't. I'm sorry. I'm moving on, Simon. You're part of the past, and I don't think it would actually help either of us to try to bring that back again. We've been there, we've done that. I'll always love you as the father of my children and I hope as a friend, but there's too much water under the bridge.'

'So you "love" me, but you don't love me like "that"?' said Simon bitterly.

'Like you once said to me,' I said sadly.

'Yes, but I was wrong. I was confused. I know what I want now. I want *you*!'

'And I know what I want too, and it's not you. I'm sorry … We both were at fault. I pushed you away, and I should have tried to talk to you instead of shouting. You? Well, let's not even go there.

But I think that time is past and we need to move forward. Separately.'

'Oh,' said Simon, 'so that's it? What about that night we had?'

'That was a mistake.'

'It didn't feel like a mistake to me. You seemed to enjoy it.'

'Well, yes, I did, but I want more than that. I don't want to just go back to how we were.'

'But we wouldn't. That's the point. Things would be different. *I'm* different!'

'And so am I. That's rather the point. We're not the kids who met over twenty-five years ago and we're not the people who tore each other into shreds a year ago, but that's all the more reason not to go back there. You hurt me, very badly, and I don't think I can ever feel the same way about you again, however hard I try. And these plans – I know you meant well, I know you were trying to help, but you're still trying to make me want what *you* want, not listening to what *I* want, so things aren't really that different. So even if we *did* go back, we wouldn't be happy. *I* wouldn't be happy, and I'm sorry if this sounds selfish but I think I deserve to be happy.'

Simon looked at the table for a long time. He swallowed very hard. 'You do deserve to be happy. I owe you that at least. I just wish I was the one who made you happy. Ellen, I'm sorry. For everything.'

'So am I, Simon. For everything.' I stood up. 'Look, you should keep these.'

I pushed the plans back towards him.

'No, they're yours,' he said. 'You might suddenly change your mind and see the light and go minimalist. Stranger things have happened. Anyway, they're not much use to anyone else, are they? If I took them back that would just be petty. But Ellen?' he caught my hand and kissed my palm. 'I just, I need you to know – I'll never love anyone else like you, OK?'

'I doubt I will either,' I said sadly. 'I wish things could be different. I'll see you next week anyway. Bye now,' and I walked out without looking back.

I didn't feel like I'd got even. I just felt sad, but also like a line had finally been drawn under our marriage.

NOVEMBER

Friday, 2 November

I got home from work to find both children and both dogs waiting for me in the sitting room, looking very solemn.

'We've been talking,' announced Jane.

'About you,' added Peter.

'Well, obviously about her. Why else would she be in here?'

'I'm just not letting you do all the talking. We're taking it in turns.'

'What have I done now?' I interrupted, wanting to get the lecture over with, so I could actually go and do something constructive, like the laundry mountain threatening to engulf the landing and avalanche down the stairs.

'Nothing. That's the point,' said Jane.

'We want you to be happy,' intoned Peter in sepulchral tones.

'You don't sound like it,' I said.

'I'm using my *serious* voice,' said Peter indignantly. 'So you take me *seriously*!'

'OK, darling, sorry.'

'So, we want you to be happy,' said Peter, again in his undertaker's voice.

'We just want to say that we know you're seeing someone and we're OK with it,' said Jane, thankfully in a normal voice.

'How do you know?' I said in a panic.

'Sophie heard Colin and Sam talking about it,' she said. 'And we know things haven't been easy for you, and if he makes you happy, then we're fine with it. You don't have to sneak around with him, and you could even ask him over sometime. I realise now that relationships sometimes just end and people move on. Like Will and me. I moved on from Harry. It's only fair we let you do the same.'

'Only don't get pregnant,' said Peter. 'Like, really, don't get pregnant. And you know, it would be best if you just didn't have sex at all, but if you do, use proper precautions, not one up the bum, no harm done.'

'Peter!' I said, appalled. 'Where did you learn such a revolting phrase?'

'It's everywhere,' said Peter in surprise. 'You even get birthday cards with it on. How have you never heard it before?'

'I've definitely never heard it before, and what's more, I never want to hear it again.'

'Whatever. Oh, and talking of not hearing things, no noisy sex either. We don't want to hear that.'

'Peter,' said Jane faintly. 'I think you're getting a bit ahead of things here. Can we not discuss Mum's sex life, please?'

'Yes,' I said. 'I quite agree, Jane.'

Saturday, 24 November

Having been given the official thumbs-up by the children to get on with my life, I've now found myself in a very nice country house hotel with Jack, facing the terrifying prospect of doing Actual Sex with him. The sex thing is obviously why we're here, though – for all Jack suggested it as a 'mini break' and a 'nice weekend away', we both know that we're only here to make the beast with two backs on neutral territory, where there's no chance of children returning unexpectedly or judgemental dogs doing their best to put a stop to the proceedings. It's slightly awkward.

The hotel is lovely, though, proper olde worlde, beams and roaring fires and rusticness abounds (an actual hotel, with People in it, instead of a cottage, as Simon would no doubt have insisted on – even when he consented to hotels they had to be futuristic and sleek and gadget-filled, whereas Jack had actually *listened* to what I wanted). I can't help, however, looking surreptitiously at the other guests and wondering who else is here for a dirty weekend. We unpacked and had a bracing walk by the river (holding hands), then we had a couple of drinks in the bar and Jack suggested I might like to have a bath before dinner 'to relax', by which I hope he meant 'to put me in the mood' rather than 'because you're a bit whiffy'. So it was that I found myself standing starkers in the bathroom, looking at myself in the mirror, and hoping Jack wouldn't be too repulsed. My tits could be better, but then again they could also be worse for a forty-six-year-old with two kids. My stomach … well, there *are* stretch marks, yes, and it's neither taut nor very toned, but at least it doesn't flop right down over my pubes.

I froze. My pubes. I'd carefully shaved my pits and legs for this outing, but I realised with horror that it had been so long since there had been a hint of romance or the need to make a real effort Down There (unlike shaving your legs, which you have to do in the summer anyway), that I'd *completely* forgotten to tackle my now extremely luxuriant lady garden. In fact, such was the condition of said lady garden, that I feared it needed attention from a set of pruning shears and a strimmer. A petrol-driven one, actually, as the small and handy razor I'd brought with me wasn't going to make the slightest dent in the foliage. At the very least, I needed something to hack it all back with before I could start on a more finessed tidy-up. Scissors. Scissors would be good. I'd already inspected all the hotel freebies, including the sewing kit, and alas it was one of the stingy ones that only contained a few needles and some thread – and no scissors. Aha! I had a brain wave. I had a small penknife on my keyring and there were scissors on there. I wrapped a towel around me and dashed back into the bedroom, much to Jack's surprise.

'Just getting something!' I trilled, diving into my handbag. 'Won't be long!'

It turns out that a small Swiss Army Knife is quite unequal to the task of trimming a minge that has reached the epic proportions of the forest surrounding Sleeping Beauty's castle, but nonetheless, I persevered. The worst trimmed back, I went in with the razor. Fuck, I was lopsided. OK, even up a bit on the other side. Nope, too much off that side now, tidy up the other side. Before I knew it, not only was my penknife clogged with my own pubes, but I'd gone from overgrown thicket to a somewhat scorched-earth look. My fanny was bald. FML! For one thing, it was definitely draughty like that. For another, Jack would now clearly think this was normal for me and expect me to keep it up.

All through dinner I struggled to concentrate on my food or Jack's conversation on account of the icy wind whistling up my skirt and even through my stout gusset to chill my poor denuded bits, and also the anticipation of Having to Do Actual Sex with someone new after all this time. My vague answers to his chat must've concerned Jack, because he leaned over and took my hand.

'We don't have to do this tonight?' he suggested. 'If you're nervous?'

Well, no, we DID have to do it tonight, before the stubble started growing back in, which I was already dreading, as last time I managed to do this (you'd think I'd have learnt, really, wouldn't you?), it itched like bloody murder afterwards, and I certainly didn't want him to think I had crabs!

'No, no!' I laughed merrily. 'Let's do it! As Victoria Wood said. Mind you, she also said, "Beat me on the bottom with a *Woman's Weekly*", although I'm more of a *Take a Break* girl myself. Come on. Might as well get it over with!'

'The romance,' murmured Jack.

I did start to feel a bit sick on the way back to the room. What was I *doing*? Why was I doing this? If I wanted sex, maybe I should have stuck with Simon, who at least knew which buttons to push, so to speak. What if Jack's foreplay didn't live up to his snogging and it just felt like he was trying to use my nipples to tune me into Radio 4? I reminded myself to be brave, that it was just a shag and what was the worst that could happen? I tried muttering my new mantra of 'no fucks given' to myself, but it somehow didn't really seem appropriate under the circumstances. I took some deep breaths. If Jack was repulsed by my nudity, then that was his problem, not mine. Maybe he'd have a weird willy anyway, and *I'd* be the one to be repulsed by him. At the very least, I reminded myself, Jack wasn't an eighteen-year-old Adonis (obviously – it would be very wrong of me to go to bed with someone of that age), and he wasn't going to be perfect either.

Upstairs I continued to babble nervously, pointing out 'interesting features' of the room and remarking on the soft furnishings. I was about to embark on my famous soliloquy about otters and their opposable thumbs, when Jack shut me up by kissing me firmly. He paused to gaze deep into my eyes and remark, 'I take it from your recent comments that talking dirty is probably not your forte?'

'Well, no!' I admitted. 'I never know what to say. "Oooh, what a lovely willy! Shag me senseless with your splendid cock!" That sort of thing?'

'I think,' said Jack, 'that it might be best for everyone if you could stop talking for just a mo'.

He had a point. Proceedings were conducted in silence until he managed to get my knickers off (matching my bra – it was a special occasion, and I *do* have standards) and he said, 'Oh! I never had you pegged as being so … tidy … down there.'

'It's not usually!' I gabbled. 'It kept going lopsided, and I kept trying to even it up, and then there was nothing left to even up and so, well there it is!'

'I see,' said Jack. 'So … you're not really into that? Because to be perfectly honest, neither am I. It's all a bit … unnatural.'

'Oh God,' I wailed. 'I was just trying to make it look less unkempt, and now I've totally put you off. As if my saggy tits and my stretch marks aren't enough, my bald fanny is the nail in the coffin and you can probably see the scars from where it was sewn together, and OH GOD, I KNEW this was a bad idea and I'm destined to never have sex again!'

'Ellen,' said Jack. 'Really, I'm not into S&M, but you're starting to make me think there's something to be said for a gag. Your tits are great, though I'm not sure if I'm even allowed to say that anymore, I hadn't even noticed your stretch marks and I'm not going to look for scars. I'm just not into the porn star look, that's all, but if that's how *you* like it, that's up to you. But as far as I'm concerned, I couldn't care less about your bikini line.'

'Oh. So, do you still want to, you know?'

'You know?'

'DO IT!'

'Do you mean sex? Well, obviously! I have a gorgeous woman here naked, even if some people might think her attempts at pillow talk are expressly designed to put me off, but nonetheless, yes, I still very much want to "do it", as you put it.'

So we did. And it was very nice. And no attempts were made to pick up the BBC.

Afterwards, Jack said, 'Will it be itchy, when it grows back?'

'Hideously.'

'So why …?'

'I didn't want you to think I was some sort of hairy beast.'

'You know they call it a pussy for a reason – bald cats aren't overly popular either.'

'Is that really why it's called a pussy?'

'I've no idea. I made it up.'

'Oh. It seems plausible, though. Maybe I should ask the Urban Dictionary. Then again, maybe not. I still haven't recovered from looking up teabagging, which I thought referred to overly agitating your teabag in your mug.'

'It really doesn't.'

'I know that now. But I'm somewhat scarred for life.'

'If I promise no teabagging, would you like to, you know, again?'

'I could be persuaded … not about the teabagging, though. I'll never be persuaded into that. Also, I'd be tempted to bite if you ever tried it.'

Jack shuddered. 'Well, my darling, it's just as well I've no intention of ever trying teabagging then, isn't it? Though once again, your dirty talk isn't entirely conducive to the mood.'

'I just don't see why anyone *wouldn't* bite if someone did that, that's all. *More* magazine used to tell us to do something called "humming on his plums", which sounded equally vile.'

'And did you?'

'God, no. Apart from anything else, I'm tone deaf. It would have been debatable which was the more unpleasant: my humming or my attempts not to bite his balls.'

'Shut up now, please. I'm begging you!'

'OK.'

'!'

'!'

DECEMBER

Saturday, 1 December

Finally, the festive season is permitted to begin. After the nonsense of Christmas puddings in the shops since September, and people starting to post photos of their Christmas trees in November, it is, at last, the start of Christmas. Jane marked the occasion by announcing she was going to a Christmas party and then staying over at Millie's (I made the fatal mistake of asking *which* Millie, which earned me an eye roll and a contemptuous hair flick, despite the fact there are six Millies or Millys in her year that she's friends with, and possibly several more that I don't know about, but apparently I was supposed to telepathically know which one she was staying with – Millie Robinson, she finally told me, after much pestering on my part and huffing on hers). Peter marked the occasion by going to see a very non-festive and quite violent-looking sci-fi film at the cinema.

Saturday, 8 December

We had Hannah's baby shower today, as it suddenly occurred to us a couple of weeks ago that we were running out of time before she dropped. We decided to make it more of a Hannah shower than a baby shower, since Charlie had already bought the entire

contents of the John Lewis baby department *and* Mothercare, so
we thought we'd just get lovely things for Hannah instead. Sam
volunteered to host it, which I agreed to with glee, as it meant
not having to clean my own house, we invited everyone we knew
that Hannah didn't actively hate, including Jack, since the children had decreed I could be seen in public with him, with strict
instructions that any gifts were *not* to be baby-related, we
eschewed pink and blue cupcakes in favour of posh ca-naypes
from M&S, and reluctantly decided that perhaps we should not
serve potent and delicious cocktails because that might push
poor Hannah over the edge as she was so near, yet so far from
enjoying a lovely little drinky herself. Colin made mocktails
instead, which were very nice, if not quite the same.

Charlie was in on the plan, of course, and lured a grumbling
and disgruntled Hannah to Sam and Colin's house, at which point
we flung open the door and shouted, 'SURPRISE!' and Hannah
gasped, 'Jesus CHRIST, are you TRYING to make me piss myself?'
which to be honest wasn't quite the reaction we'd anticipated.

She cheered up immensely, though, at the realisation that
there were lots of presents for *her*, rather than for the baby. I
always think it's much more civilised to give the presents to the
woman who has incubated the spawn for nine months and then
pushed it out of her fanny or been sliced open to have it hoiked
out of the sunroof, and who after all that then has to wait on the
tiny dictator hand and foot while it lies there, bellowing demands
for food at all hours of the night and day and merrily shitting
itself. I mean, really, what has a baby ever done to deserve
presents? Mothers – they're the ones who deserve presents! I
may have ranted that a little at the party.

'And dads?' put in Sam. 'Don't we deserve presents?'

'Sam,' said Hannah. 'If the day ever comes when you happen
to shit out an 8lb pineapple, I'll buy you a present to mark the
occasion. Until that time, it's all about the mothers, thank you

very much. Unless your genitals are permanently scarred by the baby-extraction process, there will be no presents for you …'

'Hmph,' said Sam in disgust. 'Doesn't that rather undermine the important role of fathers, dismissing us like that?'

'Fuck off!' said Hannah. 'It's not about the importance of whose role, it's about having a lovely fucking present to take your mind off the fact that you have to sit on a rubber ring and take a gravy jug to the loo to pour water over your fanny when you piss because your vagina has just BEEN SHREDDED!'

'OK, OK,' said Sam shuddering. 'I didn't realise it was a *competition*.'

'It's not,' said Hannah darkly. 'There *is* no competition, not until it's standard NHS practice to be allowed to take a cheese grater to your partner's penis while you're in labour. *Then* and only *then* will men be allowed to complain about how hard it is being the father of a newborn, when they too are hobbling around trying to keep a screaming tomato-faced shit machine alive while hoping that their insides don't fall out of their ravaged bits!'

'I like that idea,' I said. Charlie had turned pale, however, so I decided to change the subject.

'So, Charlie, are you getting Hannah a push present?' I enquired brightly.

'A what now?' said Charlie.

'A push present. It seems to be a new thing, from America I think. One of their better exports, if you ask me. You're supposed to buy the mother of your child something shiny and expensive on account of the aforementioned ravaging of their lady bits.'

'What, like a new telly?' said Charlie, looking perturbed.

'*No*, Charlie,' I said patiently. 'Like diamonds.'

'Diamonds!' spluttered Charlie, 'But birth is a perfectly natural process. Women have been doing it for millions of years. Since when are we supposed to buy them *diamonds* for it?'

'Since about 2011, I think.'

'Did Simon buy you diamonds?'

'No, he gave me a handful of change and told me to get myself a Twix from the vending machine to cheer myself up. Just one of the many reasons why we're no longer married.'

'Yes, but diamonds,' moaned Charlie.

'Well, look at it this way,' I comforted him. 'On the plus side, Hannah isn't a nubile twenty-three-year-old popsy with twenty potential child-bearing years ahead of her, all requiring push presents.'

'Wow, thanks, Ellen. I don't feel ancient and decrepit *at all* now,' complained Hannah.

'You know what I mean,' I said. 'This is almost certainly Hannah's last baby –'

'There's no "almost certainly" about it,' snapped Hannah. 'This IS my last baby, even if I have to give Charlie a DIY snip with that bastarding cheese grater. Argh!' she groaned, and clutched her stomach.

'Oh God, are you in labour?'

'No. Heartburn. HEARTBURN! PASS THE GAVISCON, QUICK!'

Hannah necked half a bottle of Gaviscon in much the same way as we'd once downed Mad Dog 20/20. 'Oooh, that's better.'

'See what she's going through, Charlie?' I said. 'The least you can do is get Hannah some lovely diamonds to mark the occasion. And to take her mind off the cheese grater.'

'OK, fine,' said Charlie.

'White gold, please, darling,' said Hannah sweetly. 'Not yellow, if you wouldn't mind. Also, can I just say how very touched I am at you all abstaining for me? But really it's fine. These "mocktails" are great, yet I bet they'd be a damn sight better with a slug of vodka, so do go ahead. I have one week to go and then I'm *done*, and since my lovely presents included two bottles of champagne, three bottles of gin, a bottle of elderflower liqueur and a bottle of tequila, I'll be quite sorted, post-birth!'

'Oh thank goodness,' everyone sighed, as Colin dived for the vodka bottle and topped everyone up.

Jack arrived at that point and kissed me in front of everyone as Hannah cooed 'Oh, it's SO romantic! Do you remember when we were like that?' until Jack said, 'SO sorry I'm late, darling. That FUCKING Labrador again.'

'What did it eat this time?'

'A vat of French onion soup and a box of mince pies. One of which gave it explosive diarrhoea,' which rather ruined my smugly romantic moment. I'm starting to wonder if the Lab's owners are actively trying to bump it off, the amount of poisonous food they seem to leave lying around for it to eat …

Sunday, 9 December

Well, it seems we might have tipped Hannah over the edge with our Hannah shower after all – I woke up this morning to a text from Charlie announcing, 'Edward Charles Jonathan Carrhill was born at 3.32 am, 8lb 4oz, mother and baby doing well' and one from Hannah that simply read, 'Had it. Boy. Had forgotten how vile it is. Bring me cake and booze and a gravy jug.'

In the event, by the time I'd woken up and got these texts, Hannah was demanding to be discharged and go home, so my mercy dash with cake, booze and gravy jugs was unnecessary, and instead we'll go round next week for the official Baby Viewing.

Tuesday, 11 December

We all popped round after I finished work to visit Hannah and the baby – Peter was suddenly struck by a terrible thought as we pulled up outside and whispered, 'Mum, she won't have her *boobs* out, will she?'

'No, Peter,' I assured him. 'You won't be able to see anything, don't worry.'

'Oh good.' He breathed a sigh of relief. 'I mean, I don't want to be rude, but it's Hannah. It would be weird to see her boobs.'

I reminded Peter that breastfeeding is perfectly natural and breasts are not just for sex, etc, etc, and both children begged me to shut up and stop talking about sex and breasts because it was just mega embarrassing and gross, and so we went in to View the New Arrival.

Baby Edward was quite nice for a new baby, in that he had a bit of hair, so didn't look like a squashed miniature Winston Churchill, like a lot of newborns, but he still pretty much just looked like a baby. Apart from my own, all babies really look the same to me, in varying degrees of ugliness. Although nature cleverly manages to do that thing where you're convinced that your own babies are supremely gorgeous and much nicer than everybody else's hideous creatures, thus enabling you to make sure you've got the right one, because all the others are vile. When I look back at the photos of my precious moppets as babies though, I'd be hard pushed to pick my own out of a line-up, because really, they just looked like babies.

'Do you want to hold him?' asked Hannah.

'Not terribly,' I said politely. 'I'm always scared of dropping other people's babies. I was quite scared of dropping my own, but everyone knows it's much worse if you break someone else's children.'

'What about you, Jane?' said Hannah.

'Um, well, I dunno,' mumbled Jane. 'I might drop him too.'

'Nonsense, you'll be fine,' said Hannah briskly, plonking Edward into Jane's somewhat unwilling arms.

Jane clutched Edward gingerly, as she peered at him and attempted to make cooing noises. She sounded rather like she was being strangled.

'Oh God, oh no, someone take it!' she suddenly shrieked. 'It puked on me, and oh Jesus, I think it's crapping! Noooooo! Take it!'

Hannah grabbed Edward before Jane flung him to the floor and handed her a muslin to wipe the puke off.

'So, what do you think of babies, Jane?' she said brightly.

Jane shuddered. 'I'm not keen.'

'Ha!' said Hannah. 'Well, they're easy enough to avoid, if you take precautions.'

Peter opened his mouth to trot out his favourite phrase about preventing unplanned pregnancy and I snapped, 'Don't you DARE, Peter!'

Jane and Emily retreated upstairs, and Peter and Lucas slouched off to play on the Xbox.

'There!' said Hannah with satisfaction. 'You're welcome! Edward's little eruption has just ensured that Jane will not be shagging any unsuitable boys, or indeed any suitable ones, without being on the Pill, possibly having a coil fitted, and making them wear at least three condoms as well. I'm thinking of hiring him out to the parents of teenagers. I'll get Peter to change a nappy later, if you want. I know the boys are a bit young, but no harm in putting the fear of God in them either about what happens after unprotected sex. Edward is a public service, really, and at least we won't have to worry about being grannies anytime soon.'

I had to concede that Hannah had a very good point there. I warmed somewhat towards Baby Edward, though not quite enough to hold him myself just yet.

Thursday, 13 December

The children sat me down to talk to me again tonight – I think they've figured out that it scares me when they work together and thus they're more likely to get what they want. What they wanted tonight was to talk about Simon.

'I've been thinking, it won't be very nice for Dad, will it, all by himself on Christmas Day?' sighed Jane.

'And it won't be very nice for us, either, worrying about him on his own. What if he falls and hits his head and no one finds him for days, and by then the body has started to decompose and he has to be identified from his dental records,' added Peter, who does seem to have a remarkable knack for focusing on the worst possible scenario.

'And you *always* over-cater at Christmas, Mum. Food wastage is a terrible thing and is destroying the planet for future generations,' put in Jane.

'OK, why don't you both stop with the guilt trips and cut to the chase,' I said. 'Is this worry about your father's potential fatal accidents and my singlehanded destroying of the polar ice caps with my extra pigs in blankets a roundabout way of saying you'd like me to ask him over for Christmas Dinner?'

'Well, that would be nice, now that you mention it,' said Jane, trying to look innocent.

'What a good idea! Why didn't we think of that?' said Peter, doing his best 'I'm completely astonished by this and knew nothing about it' face that he usually reserves for when I find an empty milk carton put back in the fridge.

'Fine,' I said.

I texted Simon and issued an invitation, adding the caveats that he was to bring decent wine and he wasn't allowed to complain about anything or muse out loud that he was just wondering when dinner would be when it was only two hours late, and he was not to unfavourably compare my stuffing to his mother's and he was not to object to the Five Second Rule if I dropped something on the floor and served it anyway, and when I had my Annual Christmas Meltdown he was NOT to roll his eyes, tell me it was just a big roast dinner and what was all the fuss about or mention the words 'hysterical' or 'drama queen', he was simply to ply me with wine until I calmed down, and make sure the potatoes didn't burn while I wept feverishly that it was all TOO MUCH and I COULDN'T DO IT!

Simon said he thought he could do all that, although he nearly had his invitation rescinded straight away when he sent his acceptance with a link to an article about how the Five Second Rule isn't actually A Thing, which is clearly bollocks, as everyone knows that the Five Second Rule is TOTALLY A Thing.

Monday, 24 December

I did it. I finally bloody did it! After FIFTEEN YEARS of trying to have a magical Christmas Eve with my children, where I listened to *Carols from King's* on the radio while peeling potatoes, before we all snuggled up on the sofa and watched *It's a Wonderful Life* together, before they toddled off to bed all sleepy and tousled and adorable, and I tiptoed upstairs with their stockings and watched them sleeping and thought how much I loved them, I FINALLY achieved a Christmas Eve that didn't consist of me running round like a blue-arsed fly, trying to prepare an enormous Christmas Dinner for vast numbers of ungrateful family while fretting about whether we had enough tin foil, without a second to sit down or relax before finally falling into bed half cut at 3.30 am after wrapping eleventy fucking billion presents and nearly waking the kids up when I lurched into their rooms, staggering both from exhaustion and the best part of a bottle of Baileys I'd consumed while wrapping.

Of course, it wasn't entirely the Magical Experience I'd always hoped for. The children objected vociferously to listening to *Carols from King's*, Peter arguing that it was against his human rights as an atheist to be made to listen to religious radio programmes (he still hasn't forgiven me for when he was in primary school and discovered that he could opt out of the Christmas and Easter church services if he was an atheist, but I refused to give him a letter for this, as then I'd have had to go and pick him up early, bad mother that I am).

No one could agree on any music, Jane declaring Peter's music awful and Peter declaring Jane's music stupid and me declaring both their music just some sort of hideous *noise* and they both informed me that *my* music was beyond lame, so we peeled potatoes in silence, broken only by the cherubs occasionally complaining about how unfair it was that I STILL didn't trust them to help decorate the tree and insisted on doing it myself – an argument that has been rumbling on for the entire week. I don't care if they call me a Tree Nazi, though. It is MY tree and I want it done RIGHT!

I was so delirious with festive joy at ACTUALLY FINALLY AT LAST getting to sit down on Christmas Eve and watch *It's a Wonderful Life* that I foolishly succumbed to Peter's badgerings that he's fourteen now and so why *couldn't* he have a beer? One small bottle of beer resulted in a spectacular amount of belching and foolish giggling from Peter – I'm not sure if he was actually pissed or just winding me up, but it was very bloody annoying either way.

Jane, who had talked me into letting her have a large Bacardi and Coke, seems rendered even more sarcastic by booze, and so was scathing about *It's a Wonderful Life*, declaring it boring and corny. Peter belched agreement, and I lost the plot and screamed it was a fabulous film about hope and the human condition and the effect even our smallest actions can have on those around us, and if they wouldn't shut the fuck up they could just piss off somewhere else. So they did, and Judgy and I watched the film alone, as I sobbed my way down a bottle of (festive) red wine.

Despite neither of the children having believed in Santa Claus for approximately ten years, they were still quite insistent that the mince pie and whisky for Santa (the whisky was originally Simon's idea, rather than a glass of milk) and the carrot for Rudolph were left out. Although we also had to leave their stockings out for Santa, I was also told in no uncertain terms that I was to leave them downstairs and not put them in their rooms, as it was 'creepy' and 'weird' to come tiptoeing in while they were asleep. I argued that they could not insist on their traditions and deny me mine, but they threatened to put chairs against their doors unless I agreed.

The precious moppets were finally dispatched to bed, grumbling that it was too early, and I got on with wrapping the bits and pieces for their stockings, as all they really wanted was money, and Amazon and iTunes vouchers. Peter's stocking presents consisted of things I'd seen that I thought were very cool and that he'd love, but in reality he would almost certainly never look at again, and Jane's were mostly make-up that was more expensive than mine. As the tree looked rather bare without many presents under it, I'd got presents for Judgy and Barry and the bastarding chickens and wrapped them up too.

And there we were. I was done. Done. At 11.59 pm! I briefly tried to tell myself that I *missed* being sweaty and furious and over-worked and put-upon, that it wasn't Christmas without

Sellotape in your hair at 3 am, but actually it was jolly nice. I downed Santa's whisky, took a bite of the mince pie and broke off a bit of the carrot to give to Barry to make it look like Rudolph had had a chomp. Judgy, outraged that Barry was getting something that he was not, promptly insisted that he had some carrot too, only to immediately remember that he hates carrot and so registered his protest by chewing it up into tiny pieces and spitting them over as wide a radius as he could manage.

'Thanks, Judgy,' I said. 'Merry Christmas to you too!'

Tuesday, 25 December – Christmas Day

Again, for the first time in fifteen years, I wasn't awoken by someone trying to prise my eyelids open while screaming 'PRESENTS! PRESENTS NOW!' in my ear. Jane has been a little more laid back about Christmas for the last couple of years, but even last year Peter was still delirious with excitement on Christmas morning. This year, however, they were both still out cold when I woke up at the delightfully civilised hour of 9.30 am. In fact, even Judgy was still snoring, head on the pillow beside me, dog breath panting in my face, despite the number of times he's been told he's supposed to sleep at the end of the bed. Barry, luckily, given his enormous size, had sneaked off to join Jane when I went to bed, though he came skulking through as I went to let Judgy out.

I had a bath, then got dressed in the sort of outfit that glossy magazines recommend for Christmas morning – clingy jeans, cashmere sweater and nice boots, which made a change from not having time to get out of my pyjamas until I realised people were arriving in half an hour. I even did my make-up. Then I lit the fire, took my nice boots off and put my wellies on to take the dogs for a walk. I'd rather envisaged the children being up by then and joining me for a merry caper across the fields, but my forays into their rooms had met variously with a 'Laters' and a 'Bugger off, Mother', which wasn't very festive of them.

By the time I got back the children were up and sprawling messily across the sitting room, quite ruining the tasteful Christmas tableau I'd created with the tree, the stockings and the blazing fire.

'*There* you are,' grumbled Peter. 'You've been ages. Why were you so long?'

'You were the ones who wouldn't get up,' I protested.

'Whatever. Can we open our presents?' demanded Jane.

They professed themselves politely delighted with my offerings. Peter was restrained from demonstrating that he could eat a whole Chocolate Orange in one bite and they both started demolishing their selection boxes while I gave the dogs their presents.

Judgy, a veteran of many Christmas presents, shredded the paper and was thrilled to find a new squeaky toy inside, which he immediately 'killed' by ripping the squeaker out and tearing it apart so it no longer squeaked.

Poor Barry, who had never had a Christmas present, was still puzzling how to get the paper off with some help from Jane when Judgy, his own present thoroughly deaded, came bustling over, snatched Barry's present off him, opened it and 'killed' it for him, while Jane yelled at him and Barry cowered, unsure of the protocol. Once Barry's toy was also in several pieces, Judgy sauntered off with a self-satisfied 'You're welcome' look.

'That bloody dog of yours is getting *worse*, Mother!' said Jane. 'Poor Barry. He stole his Christmas present!'

'Well, Barry doesn't really know what a Christmas present is,' I tried to console her.

'Of course he does,' insisted Jane. 'Would you say Judgy doesn't understand what Christmas presents are?'

'Well, no,' I conceded.

'Right then. Don't imply that Barry is less intelligent than Judgy. Come on, Barry, come upstairs and I'll give you your other present from me, away from Judgy.'

Jane was locked away with Barry, and Peter plugged into his iPad with his new headphones on, so it was left to Judgy and me to take the chickens their presents. Oxo, Paxo and Bisto were unimpressed with their new chicken swing and treat dispenser, and looked at me with their customary disdain.

I'd been super-duper awesomely clever, since it was just going to be the three of us for Christmas dinner, and ordered everything ready prepared from M&S. Even when the children added Simon to the mix, when I looked at what I'd actually ordered there was more than enough to go around, so, leaving the surly chickens to spit on their lovely swing in disgust, all I had to do was remove some cellophane and pop everything in the oven.

I was just surveying the fridge, so bountifully stocked with the wares of Mr Marks and Spencer, and checking that it was all still there and no one had started on the Important Cheese, when the children shuffled into the kitchen.

'Mum,' said Peter. 'Want to watch *Love Actually* with us?'

'A Christmas film? You're volunteering to watch a Christmas film with me?'

'Well, we figured you'd probably try to make us watch one anyway, so we thought this way we got to choose. At least *Love Actually* is in colour,' said Jane.

'Yes, of course, darlings,' I said. 'That would be lovely. Shall we have snacks?'

'And Buck's Fizz?' suggested Jane hopefully.

'Why not?

We all curled up under a blanket on the sofa, the fire was roaring, and we grazed our way through a box of After Eights, a tub of Twiglets and a packet of those cheesy footballs you only get at Christmas. Both children rested their heads on my shoulder at one point or another, and it was actually Magical. Jane even shed a small tear at the end, although that might have been either the effects of the Buck's Fizz, despite my trying not to make it too strong, or the fart Barry let off after too many cheesy footballs.

Simon arrived while the final credits were rolling. He grumbled somewhat because I hadn't even started making the dinner (and in truth wasn't really looking forward to it, as I felt a bit sick after all the After Eights).

I was in the process of giving him a stern 'Don't You Dare Ruin Christmas, You Bastard' look when Jane said, 'Chill, Dad, there's loads of food. You're not going to starve.'

'Yeah, Dad,' said Peter. 'Here, have a cheesy football. Oh, there's none left. Well, anyway, there's lots to eat. Dinner will ready in a bit. Just be nice to Mum, OK.'

In fairness, Simon stopped grumbling and instead said, 'I tell you what, then. If we're not eating yet, I noticed that nice pub in the village was open today – why don't we walk down there and have a drink while dinner's cooking?'

'But what about the kids?' I said, the thought of going OUT to the PUB on CHRISTMAS DAY being both a very attractive idea *and* something I simply could not compute.

'Well, they can come too. What about it, kids?' said Simon.

'Can I have a cider in the pub?' asked Jane.

'No, you're not old enough, they'll lose their licence.'

'Then I might just stay here.'

'I might stay here too,' said Peter.

'Just you and me then,' said Simon.

'Right. Peter, Jane. We'll only be about an hour. Keep an eye on dinner, and don't burn it and ruin your mother's Festive Vision,' ordered Simon.

'We might be more invested in her stupid Festive Vision if she'd actually let us hang a single decoration on the sodding tree,' grumbled Jane.

'Just do it,' said Simon. 'You never know, this might be the first year we get your mother through Christmas without her Epic Annual Meltdown.'

'It won't feel like it's really Christmas, though, if Mum doesn't burst into tears, accuse no one of caring about her and lock herself in the garage with a bottle of Baileys,' protested Peter.

'Nonetheless,' said Simon, 'I for one would be very glad to have one Christmas without your mother hurling a mince pie at me, so do as you're told while I take her out for a drink.'

In the pub I felt slightly judged by the lady behind the bar for turning up with yet another man, as I'd had a drink in there on Saturday night with Jack, before his daughter arrived to spend Christmas with him, and I'd been in a week ago with Colin. I started to worry that perhaps she thought I was some sort of slapper, possibly an escort. I resolved that next year there were going to be no earth-changing dramas, and so as part of my new policy of Letting People In and Not Trying to Do Everything Myself I was definitely going to make more of an effort to integrate into village life, even though I no longer needed a sexy farmer to fall in love with me over the bonnet of his tractor. Once I was welcomed into the bosom of the village, then surely I could find some subtle way of saying 'I'm not a total slut, I'm only shagging one of those blokes, and one is my ex-husband and the other is just a friend, actually.' Maybe I'd find some quaint and charming chicken whisperer, who'd get to the bottom of the bastarding chickens' issues, while uttering bucolic words of wisdom and ancient proverbs? Unless, of course, they refused to welcome me to their bosom on account of my loose morals and stoned me instead.

'What on earth are you thinking about?' said Simon. 'You look very peculiar.'

'Nothing,' I said quickly. 'Nothing at all. This is nice, isn't it? Merry Christmas!'

'Merry Christmas! I did sort of suggest it because I wanted to talk to you away from the kids –'

'Oh? Sounds ominous. But it's bloody *Christmas*, Simon. Don't ruin it with whatever it is you're going to say.'

'They told me you were seeing someone. The kids, I mean. Jack, they said he was called.'

'Um, yes, well, yes, I am.'

'I just … I just wanted to say, you know, "all the best" with it. I was a bit, I dunno, when they first told me, but as long as he makes you happy, I just want what's good for you.'

'Well, thank you!' I said. I'd not expected that. In fact, I'd hoped not to have to tell Simon about Jack for a while longer in case he threw a hissy fit, but he seemed to have decided to be an adult. The thing about not being married to Simon anymore is I think I like him a lot better than I did when we were married. He still has his moments, of course, but he doesn't seem to be quite as much of an arsehole these days.

'So, is it serious, you and him?'

'Oh, I don't know. Early days, isn't it? I haven't farted in front of him yet.'

'Is that still your yardstick for the seriousness of a relationship?'

'It seems as good as any,' I said.

'I remember the first time you farted in front of me.'

'Do you?'

'I'll never forget it. You made my eyes water. I could feel them stinging.'

'That's not true!'

'It is! Anyway, I know you're moving on with your life, and I'm trying to as well, but I'd like it if we could be friends. Proper friends, not just exes who only see each other because of the kids and are polite. Good enough friends to fart in front of each other. Unless you've been eating cabbage. Cabbage has a terrible effect on your digestion.'

'I'd like that too,' I said.

'Well then – cheers! To friendship!'

'To friendship! Cabbage doesn't make me fart that much.'

'Ellen, I once googled gas masks after you'd had cabbage.'

'That is just rude.'

After that rather grown-up conversation (apart from the fart chat) and very civilised drinky, we got back to find that although the children had not burnt the dinner, they had failed to keep the kitchen door closed and Judgy had opened the fridge door and eaten all the Important Christmas Cheese. He was looking a little green around the gills and rather bloated when his crime was discovered, and as I wailed for the lost Important Cheese, he retched and puked a large fondue all over my nice Christmas boots.

'Oh you BLOODY DOG!' I shouted. Barry smirked and made it clear he'd had no part in the cheese theft, as Judgy was hurled outside until he felt better and I spent half an hour mopping up cheesy dog vomit and resigning myself to the fact that the smell was probably never EVER going to come out my boots.

'But LOOK, Mum,' said Jane when she came back in from the garden where she'd been sent to watch over a still somewhat queasy-looking Judgy to make sure there was no more sick before he was allowed in the house again.

She opened her hand, and there lay a lovely, still warm, brown speckled egg!

'No,' I breathed.

'YES!' said Jane. 'Oxo laid it! I heard her squawking about something, and went over to see what she was doing and there it was. Our first egg!'

'It's a Christmas miracle!' I said.

The rest of Christmas Day passed without too much incident, apart from a heated game of Pictionary where Peter's every guess was to shout 'IS IT A PENIS?' and then collapse in a heap of giggles until it was discovered he'd been at the Baileys, and I finally made it through a Christmas Day without a meltdown or throwing anything at Simon, which is also a Christmas Miracle, and definitely a huge improvement on last Christmas when we were in the hideous dying throes of our marriage but still living in the same house and so I'd happily have thrown knives at him at the slightest provocation.

There was a small unfortunate moment when Jane took Simon outside to show him the chickens' presents and he enquired why I had bought my chickens a sex swing. On the plus side, Oxo was actually swinging on it and gave me quite a kindly look. Perhaps the swing was the breakthrough and now they'll love me. And chat …

Monday, 31 December – New Year's Eve

Since I really felt like I was #nailingit and #winningatlife and was now some sort of #QueenOfTheFestiveVisions, two days ago I decided that it would be a really, really good idea to have a spontaneous New Year's Eve Party. 'Why not?' I reasoned. 'What, after all, is the worst that can happen?'

Obviously, the worst that can happen is the same thing that happens every time I decide to have a party. I spend hours making sure I've selected the exact right photo for the Facebook Event. Then I go through my list of Facebook 'friends' and make rash decisions like, 'Well, they're not *that* bad, why not ask them? It's not like I *hate* them. They're sometimes irksome, but basically good people.' Then, in a flush of hostess with the mostessness,

I press 'add to event' on a variety of people that I've had no interaction with for years on end, except for when I decide to have a party. And then, as the acceptances start to flood in, I remember that I dislike most people and feel a huge surge of resentment towards all these awful people who've been so rude as to accept the invitation I sent them to a party, thus forcing me to actually *have* a party, and why would they do that to me?

The good thing about all the divorces at our age, though, is that they halve the number of people you actually have to ask – for example, I asked Perfect Lucy Atkinson's Perfect Mummy (Gemma – I must try to call her Gemma, though she will always be Lucy's Perfect Mummy to me), but now I didn't have to invite Lucy's Daddy as well, nor Fiona Montague and her husband because I felt obliged to because I'd asked the Atkinsons – that would be very awkward apart from anything else.

Colin and Sam had spent Christmas skiing and were just back, looking disgustingly tanned, but I forgave them, because it was so nice to see them, and also they brought me duty-free fags, which I had to hide from the children before they had an intervention.

I did invite the rather uptight-looking lady from the cottage down the road, as part of my new campaign to not be judged as the Village Jezebel and thus be able to find a charming chicken whisperer, although that one egg had made all the difference to my feelings towards the chickens. Her name was Margaret, and although she was rather sniffy that I didn't have any sherry and she'd have to make do with gin, once she had a couple of stiff G&Ts down her neck, she proved a most excellent and scurrilous source of local gossip. It turns out that there's some competition for the position of Village Jezebel, and I wasn't even close to being in the running, which was something of a relief, but does mean I might never be able to look the man in the butcher's in the eye again. I can certainly never ask him for sausages!

I decided it was as good an opportunity as any for Simon and Jack to meet, and so they both came along and managed to be polite, although with a *certain* amount of alpha male posturing at each other. Indeed, they were so busy trying to show off that I didn't have to worry about refilling anyone's drinks or keeping the fire going, with both of them jostling for position to be the Better Man.

I was feeling very smug about how civilised and grown up we were all being, until Simon asked Jack if he'd seen the new Jeremy Clarkson show, and Jack had, and they started talking about that. How rude! Jack is *mine*. Simon shouldn't think he can *actually* have him as a friend – they're only meant to affect a surface veneer of courtesy, not bond over Jeremy bloody Clarkson taunting poor little Richard Hammond. If they're going to bond over some giant petrolheads on the TV, they could at least have the decency to do it over my beloved Edd China. I suppose it was childish to feel a bit left out by how well they were getting on, but my nose was decidedly out of joint.

Hannah and Charlie came with all the kids, Edward was put to sleep in his Moses basket upstairs, though how he slept through the shrieks and screeches of the mass of teenagers in the children's rooms was a miracle. We all pretended not to notice that the older ones had filched a bottle of vodka to share, and the younger ones had made off with several cans of beer.

As midnight approached, I sneaked out for my last cigarette of the year. My last cigarette ever, I reminded myself, as obviously I'd be giving up smoking in the New Year. And drinking, as I'd be subsisting entirely on kale and good intentions. Probably.

I looked at the stars, and thought about the year that had just passed and everything that had happened. I'd spent most of the year feeling very alone, but somehow I was ending it surrounded by people, many of whom I was actually quite fond of.

I started making a list of the year's achievements:

I'd lost a husband, but it seemed I'd gained a friend instead.

Lost a father, but learned to let go of the past.

Lost my en suite bathroom, and gained three mildly
terrifying chickens and a divinely soppy giant wolf dog,
who, thank God, seemed to have finally finished
growing.

Lost my babies, and gained a pair of smart-mouthed, foul-
mouthed, possibly borderline alcoholic teenagers, who
nonetheless never failed to surprise me with their
kindness and maturity when it was called for.

And I'd gained a Jack. I still didn't know what the fuck I
was supposed to call him. We still haven't found a
definitive word for a boyfriend, when you're too old for
a boyfriend – he's not a lover, we're too British, he's not a
partner, we're not that serious, but he's more than just a
shag too. He's just Jack.

Almost bang on cue, Jack came out of the house. 'There you are!'
he said. 'I've been looking for you. What are you doing skulking
out here?'

'Thinking.'

'About what?'

'That although this has been the shittiest year of my life in
many ways, on balance I think the good things have outweighed
the bad.'

'And am I one of the good things?'

'You are.'

'Good. Then I'm going to kiss you now, before we go in for the
bells, because if I kiss you in there, I think your ex-husband
might actually manage to kill me just with a look!'

'I thought you two were getting on like a house on fire.'

'I was being polite. He wouldn't stop talking about Jeremy Clarkson and I could hardly say, "Sorry, I'm bored," could I?'

'But you –'

'Just stop talking till I kiss you.'

Once Jack had finished, and I'd reapplied my lipstick, we went back in, just as the countdown began.

'HAPPY NEW YEAR!!' bellowed everyone.

I was overcome with emotion, and then I had a very good idea. It was possible that I was a little drunker than I'd realised.

I banged on my glass with a handy knife, somehow managing not to break it.

'I just want to say a few words,' I yelled. 'I just want to say, I love you all. I love you all very much! And this year, this year's going to be a fantastic year, for all of us. Hannah's not knocked up anymore. I think I know what really matters and what doesn't now. I'm not going to spend any more time worrying about things that I can't change, I'm just going to chuck it in the fuck-it bucket. I have my dogs, my children and my friends.'

'Thanks, Mum,' shouted Peter. 'Nice to see we're second in your list of priorities. At least we're ahead of the chickens.'

'It wasn't in order!' I protested. 'But yes, I have the chickens too. Even the bastarding chickens might cheer up now they've got a sex swing. Maybe I'll get them a rooster so they can make proper use of it. But this year – this is going to be the best year yet, because I love you all, and that is the only thing that really matters. And I'm old enough that I don't give a fuck about anything, but young enough that I still have my own teeth and don't wet myself every time I sneeze. This is going to be OUR YEAR! Did I say that I love you all? HERE'S TO NO FUCKS GIVEN!'

A slightly stunned silence greeted my impassioned words, and then a voice spoke. 'Oh my GOD, *Mother*!' snarled Jane. 'Why are you *always* so embarrassing!'

ACKNOWLEDGEMENTS

Once again, this book has been a big team effort, and there are so many people who deserve enormous thanks for their help. First and foremost are the wonderful team at HarperCollins – it's such a privilege to work with such lovely people. In particular, a huge thank you to my fabulous editor Katya Shipster, for her endless patience. Massive thanks also to Rosie Margesson, who deserves a special acknowledgement not only for being a great publicist, but also for putting up with me wittering endlessly at her about dogs and ponies on long train journeys around the country, while I did my very best to thwart her efforts to stop me getting lost/missing trains/accidently stealing phones from innocent bystanders. And a very big thank you to Jasmine Gordon, who is not only brilliant at marketing, but is also very understanding when I insist on sending her emails full of photos of my new puppy with the cunning caption 'Very Urgent and Important Book Stuff – Open Immediately'. Thanks to Jenny Hutton for all her excellent editorial advice, when I couldn't see the wood for the trees, and for making me dial down the exclamation marks! Thanks also to Ed Faulkner, Julie MacBrayne, Oli Malcolm and Kate Elton, and thank you very much to Oscar for

all his help and suggestions. And thank you so much to Sarah
Hammond for coordinating us all and keeping everything on
track. The glorious cover design is the brilliant work of Claire
Ward and Tom Gauld, who do such a wonderful job of creating
the perfect cover every time, so thanks a million. And the hugest
of huge thank yous to Tom Dunstan and his amazing sales team,
because it doesn't matter how good a book is, if the sales team
don't get it out there on the shelves, no one is going to read it! A
big thank you is also due to Marie Goldie and all the staff at
HarperCollins in Glasgow, in the office and the warehouse, who
all work so hard to get the actual books out to customers and
shops.

My lovely agent, Paul Baker at Headway Talent, is not only a
marvellous agent, but is also extremely long suffering, so thank
you once again for putting up with me!

To Claire Scott, who gave me the push to start all this off, and
Grace Cheetham, for taking a chance on me, you both have my
eternal thanks!

And then there are my friends, who get me through the self-
doubt, the desire to smash my head repeatedly against the laptop
and the sudden realisation that I cannot spell for toffee. You keep
me going with wine, laughter, bad puns, brilliant chat, dubious
dancing, awesome cake and excellent soup. To all The Sisterhood,
a million thanks, but especially Alison, Eileen, Katrina, Liz,
Lynn, Mairi and Tanya. Special thanks to Tanya for all the cake!
And thank you so much to Linda and Graham for always being
there, for the soup, and for everything else. And thank you to the
Dahlings, past and present, you know who you are, but especially thanks to Kate C, for singlehandedly buying most of the
copies of the previous books!

Finally, my family. Thank you once again to my husband – for
the Manhattans, for putting up with my dogs, including the
demonic puppy, for believing I could do this even when I didn't,

and for wiping Solitaire off my laptop for me to stop me procrastinating. And my darling children – thank you for being funny, sarcastic, putting up with my demands about 'What The Youth Say/Do' and for not being Peter and Jane …

Now you know
Why Mummy Doesn't Give A ****...

Discover how her precious moppets
led her to drink and swear!

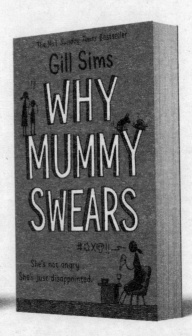